# INTO THE HELLS

## Axe Druid Book Three

## CHRISTOPHER JOHNS

MOUNTAINDALE
PRESS

# CONTENTS

# DEDICATION

This one is dedicated to my dear friend and roommate who's always had his voice, but recently found a way to express it again.

Welcome back to the fold, brother. I look forward to seeing what you can do.

# ACKNOWLEDGMENTS

I would like to give a shoutout to the model for Bokaj, Jake Earley. Friend, gamer, and amazing musician. Thank you for being you and for writing the amazing song that you and Cory did. Into the Hells was amazing and I honestly never thought that the adventures these characters went on would touch anything but people's imaginations. You gave these words and this book a tune I never could have dreamed of.

Please, check out lostpasteverest on Instagram and the song, "Into the Hells", to be featured on their upcoming album "Wizard Oil".

Next, I would like to thank an amazing artist whose vision was able to craft a symbol that I hope you all like as much as I did. Britni, you lovely nerd, your vision is as superb as the skill behind your artwork and I couldn't be happier to have been able to trust my thoughts to you.

If you like the symbol for the Axe Druid series, please check out nerdsthewordprints for amazing artwork and mind-blowing skill.

And finally, a word to those of you who have made it this far:

Thank you. You're a badass in your own right, and I'm proud to share these adventures with you all.

Welcome back to Brindolla.

# THE STORY SO FAR

Hey! Zeke here, and if you're reading this—you probably know that my friends and I have been through some shit.

We were brought to this crazy world called Brindolla—this entire world with video game style rules and laws—by Radiance and her fellow gods. Why? Well, to fight a big, bad galactic conqueror called War—why else?

They told us that if we can help stop him here, the vain bastard won't turn his sights on the next world—you guessed it —Earth. All we had to do was kill the minions and Generals to keep them from creating too much havoc so the gods can focus on keeping him out.

Before I go too much deeper into this rabbit hole with you in tow, I'd better reintroduce you all, right?

Yohsuke, my brother from the Marine Corps and someone I trust with my life. James, another of Yoh's Marine Corps buddies that we gamed with together regularly. He's a good dude. My roommate Muu, crazy, smart—never the two together—and insanely sarcastic at times. Our friend Jaken, lovable guy with a surfer-like mentality at times, new dad, and probably one of the nicest people you could ever hope to meet. Bokaj and Balmur, two of my friends from when I worked at a gym, both of whom are huge gamers. Bokaj is the thin one with a love of music because of his band life. Balmur is kind of quiet, but when you get to know him, he's hilarious. Also, Balmur is kind of stuck in the Hells right now.

We're working on that, I promise.

We all took up the challenge and have been through, well, some shit. Like I said—I said that, right?

I'm rambling. Sorry.

We've fought a Bone Dragon, killed some weird creatures, beat some beasts, and mangled a few monsters along the way. We'd even managed to kill one of War's Generals—Rowan, real asshole—then our friend Balmur was sent to the Hells by some kind of spell.

Since we figured out where he was, we've been working on getting stronger and trying to find a way to get there.

While we were doing that, we helped out the Primordial Fire Elemental by me taking in a flame wolf. Got some better gear. Fought and almost got our asses handed to us by a would-be world killer, a Greater Fiend possessed by one of War's minions.

Okay, we did get our asses kicked. Satisfied? The only reason we came out alive was that Maebe, the Unseelie Queen of Winter and Darkness and my girlfriend, helped us. She's super powerful. Beautiful. Deadly. Seriously—she fed a guy his heart, then froze him alive. Yes, alive—I know, right?

After that, we rescued some kids from being eaten by a fake god called Lothir. Big serpent. Big attitude. She ate kids, man. What were we supposed to do? Leave the little folks there to be a midnight snake and shake run? Yeah. No—not happening. Big experience. Yeah, we killed her too.

I picked up a subclass—Primal Warrior. It's a good time. Muu, my roommate and one of my closest civilian friends, received some much needed training from a nice green Dragon.

Now that we have her assistance and some more information, we're headed off to find the black Dragon!

We also know where we need to go to bust our way into the Hells and get our friend back. And there's another General possibly hiding among the denizens there. So, there's that.

Wish us luck, yeah? Or—you know—read along?

# CHAPTER ONE

"So, let's beat feet, man!" Bokaj growled anxiously.

I stood there surrounded by my friends in the village we recently liberated from a Greater Fiend called Decay, who had been possessed and infected the jungle with a plague-like sickness causing things to grow mushrooms. It was trippy. Since eradicating him, we used the place as our base of operations while we cleansed the area.

Muu, a Dragon Beast-kin—Dragon-kin—with green scales covering his body and the matching-colored metallic scale mail he wore, stood closest to me on my right. His royal purple eyes were focused on me, and his facial features, partially obscured by the horned helm, were much finer around his snout, eyes, and mouth. The slightly pointed protrusions that hung from his face to mirror a goatee shook the same as his slightly dreadlocked hair did. He looked concerned, yet still managed to smile, somehow. His small but sharp teeth shone in the moonlight that filtered through the jungle around us.

His clawed hands motioned toward the group of children we had rescued. "We need to make sure we can take care of them first."

I nodded. "That's fair. I'll go talk to Maebe. You guys sort out our next step."

Maebe had gone home to the Fae Realm to check up on her people and some disconcerting news that she hadn't shared yet.

"That is our next step, man." Yohsuke grunted. "The kids come first. So if she's planning to come back any time soon, she will need to let us know, or you'll have to go get her or something because we're taking these guys to Sunrise Village."

I nodded. Yohsuke walked over and put a gray-skinned hand on my shoulder. His sickly-yellow eyes stared at me from under his black and red embroidered cloak.

"You good, bro?" Some of his pure-white hair poked out of the opening to the hood, the long hair staying surprisingly out of his way all the time.

"Yeah, just a lot going on and seeing the little man like that reminded me of a bad time when I was a kid." I tried to smile but shivered involuntarily. "A terrible horror movie I watched as a kid involving one of the little bastards on a bloody rampage looking for his gold."

My Kitsune mouth attempted another smile. "I'll be good. Just lemme go talk to Maebe, and I'll get us to Sunrise. Shouldn't take too long at all."

I walked away from the others and went to the other side of the village—close enough to be heard if any sort of danger came to find us but far enough for a modicum of privacy.

Once I was alone, I cast Shadow Speak. I felt the pull from my mana and watched as the deeper shadows began to rise and coalesce into a familiar form.

"Hello, Zekiel Erebos," the figure greeted playfully formal.

"Queen Maebe." I bowed low, wiggling my hips and wagging my tails playfully as I did so. "Empress of the Shadows and Ice."

"Oh, you do know how to flatter. Tell me, what new stupid thing did you do while I have been home for all of a few hours?"

I smiled. She knew me too well by now, even with the time dilation. "Oh, you know—killed a wanna-be goddess. Forcefully liberated a people who, well, let's be honest, didn't want to be liberated. Saved some kids." I saw her shade stiffen. "There was much yelling of the stupid word 'pie'."

Y'all know what a safe word is, right? Thought so. Mine is butterscotch. What's yours? Sorry, tangent. The reason I bring that up is because Maebe asked me to come up with a sort of safe word for when I planned to do something stupid and likely ridiculously dangerous. Pie was that word.

She relaxed again. "And I take it you were victorious?"

I put my arms up and flexed my muscles in reply. My body, while covered in beautiful raven-black fur, is a giant muscle. Don't get me wrong, I lift at home, but I would have to lift *crazy* heavy and eat *so* much better than I did to be even remotely close to as strong or well muscled as I am here. Broad shoulders, narrow waist, and five *gloriously fluffy* tails. Mmm, I do love my tails.

Stop judging me—you should know this by now. Come on, there's more happening.

Maebe giggled. Her shoulders shook from it. While the majority of the detail was gone from the shadows, I could still see her outline. She was shorter than me, around five-foot-four with a curvaceous figure, long hair, and long, pointed ears that shot straight out from the sides of her head at almost right angles. They were angled back a bit though, and the various earrings dangling from them were super cute. The amount of metal she had in her ears would make most punk rockers want to genuflect.

"Good, my pet." She stepped forward, closing the distance between us. "It has been days there for you. Is all else alright? It has been a few hours here for me, and already you have put yourself in great danger. What will you do now?"

"The guys are fine. The kids too. But we need to get them away from here. We're going to take them to Sunrise. After that, we'll be going to try and get James the blessing of a black Dragon. I guess it's the 'nicest one?' Something for us to do that could give us enough strength to be ready for the Hells and getting Balmur back."

She looked left for a moment and said something I couldn't understand, then she addressed me, "According to Winterheart, there are no 'nice' black Dragons. They are monsters. Little better than beasts."

Winterheart was Maebe's... uncle? The ancient white Dragon has a lot of love for the queen and was very intelligent.

"Of course," I grunted sardonically, "but, yes—we will be taking the children to Sunrise Village first. How much longer do you think you will be?"

"I do not know," she answered sadly. "The new king of the Seelie has put things into motion that my people must be prepared for. I am issuing orders and making decrees as swiftly as I am able, but if they call me while I am away—I will need to return hastily. And I do not know that it will be wise to travel the realms with so little time to rest."

Nodding, I added, "Your duty is to your people. Just like mine is to the people of this realm and my home. I understand completely. It still sucks, but I understand."

"Things are moving swiftly, especially with Winterheart here, as well as my most trusted advisor. They aren't quite where I need them to be for my return, but things should remain well in hand until I am truly needed again," Maebe explained. When I looked at her questioningly, she sighed. "My mother."

"Oh," my eyebrows shot up, "how is she?"

"She is well," Her voice was suddenly much more reserved and royal sounding. "She is curious of many things that I will discuss with you when I am with you once more. It should only be a few more days in your time on the Prime realm. I will contact you as soon as I am able and on that side of the veil."

"Thank you, and please—be safe." I smiled at her and

began to step forward to touch her but stopped short. It hadn't worked the first time—why would it now?

"You as well." She hesitated for a moment longer, watching me. Then the shadows dissipated and fled back to their origins.

I returned to the group. Jaken, a tall, purple-skinned man with a thin but highly muscled build hidden under plate mail armor of a blue hue, was the only person in the party who spoke Fae-Orc and was speaking to the oldest of the children. He, the oldest, was a pain in my ass, Set. The boy wore a simple loincloth, same as the other kids, and was trim with a good bit of muscle for a kid. He was a good fighter with a bow, but it hadn't been enough.

He was the first of the local Fae-Orcs that I had met and accidentally interrupted his trial. It was a weird situation that had gotten him kicked out of his home and left him and his siblings struggling. It had been his leader's fault, but I felt responsible.

Jaken shook his long black hair that had been pulled back into a ponytail and rubbed his mustache and goatee. His hazel eyes considered the children. Then he looked my way.

"Everything cool?" His normally relaxed, surfer-like voice held a small note of worry in it.

"She's going to be a few more days." I looked at the others. "We ready to roll?"

They nodded, and I noticed Muu off to the side with Ampharia, the green Dragon in her Dragon-kin form. Her scales were a deeper green than his, and her head remained the same as her true form. The shape of her horns reminded me of tree limbs or antlers.

She reached out and pulled him against her and rubbed the side of her head against his chin. Muu stilled, then hugged her back, saying something I couldn't pick up. After a second, she turned and waved goodbye to us and ran into the tree line behind him.

"What was that all about man?" Bokaj said from my left.

I turned to find the Snow Elf Ranger grinning broadly

under the unruly and long, side-swept black hair covering some of his face. The sides were clean-shaven, and his pointed ears made the stark contrast between his skin, a pale blue, and the hair a little easier. His blue eyes held mirth and merriment that was characteristic of him, and we all knew the teasing would be coming soon. His lithe build was clothed in a white shirt that looked almost like a hoodie made of leather with a matching pair of breeches and boots.

"She just wanted me to know that she would miss me. That's all." Muu looked away from us bashfully.

"Uh huh," Bokaj grunted conspiratorially. Tmont, Bokaj's black panther companion with slightly faded stripes and tufts of fur on her ears rubbed herself against her master and watched the rest of us.

"Come on, man. There are children here! Have some class," Jaken half-heartedly reprimanded Bokaj before turning on Muu. "You join the mile high club or what?"

"Oh my god, you guys are insufferable." Muu sighed resolutely and just dealt with the playful ribbing.

"Agreed." I chuckled. "Let's go. How many have we got again? Me, Jaken, Bokaj, Muu, Yohsuke, the four kids. Hey, where's James?"

"I'm over here!" a voice called from the building we had been using as a shelter. All of the other buildings were destroyed during our fight with Decay. Luckily, that one hadn't been because beds were nicer than sleeping on the ground.

James sauntered over toward us. His Elvish body was tan with smatterings of black scales scattered in patches all over his body except just beneath his chest, and his stomach was bare too. He wore gray sandals and black padded breeches like my own.

He sported some pretty cool tattoos on some of the less scaled portions of his skin—not ones I would have picked, mind you—that added to his strength and defense. One was a set of pointed horns on his stomach that reminded me of a rhinoceros's horns. Or a Belgar, as I'm certain that's what they were meant to look like. The next were spirals of blue that began on the inside of his elbow and wrapped down his forearms into his palms, as well as a pair of thick, black swirls on his pectoral muscles and gold and black wings on his back.

The dude was shredded, and as our monk, he had to be. He hit a lot of shit. Martial arts was on point too.

With him in the headcount, that made ten. I looked down at Tmont and sighed. Eleven. I could carry eleven creatures with me with Teleport. Well within my limits, by one. Ha, one. I shook my head and opened my status screen. I had made it to level 29. So, time to place my available stat points and grow a bit.

*Name: Zekiel Erebos*
*Race: Kitsune (Celestial)*
*Level: 29*
*Strength: 50*
*Dexterity: 40*
*Constitution: 35*
*Intelligence: 60*
*Wisdom: 36*
*Charisma: 17*
*Unspent Attribute Points: 20*

Pretty decent stats, if I do say so myself. Still, always room to improve oneself. I decided to add ten points to intelligence, five to constitution, four to wisdom, and one to charisma.

This made my sheet look like so.

*Name: Zekiel Erebos*
*Race: Kitsune (Celestial)*
*Level: 29*
*Strength: 50*
*Dexterity: 40*
*Constitution: 40*
*Intelligence: 70*

*Wisdom: 40*
*Charisma: 18*
*Unspent Attribute Points: 0*

My body felt a little more at ease and healthier than normal, and I could feel my mana reserves deepen as a full 100 MP was added in.

I rolled my shoulders and grinned. Now I'd be able to Teleport *much* farther and with a lot more creatures.

I took a look at Coal's stats as well. The fight with Lothir had brought him up to Level 13. Two of his natural points went into strength and dexterity, meaning each got a point without me spending anything because he had used those stats the most in the last fights he was in. That left me six points to use, so I added one each to strength and dexterity, two to intelligence, and one each to wisdom and charisma. Which left his stats looking good.

*Name: Coal*
*Race: Flame Wolf*
*Strength: 20*
*Dexterity: 20*
*Constitution: 14*
*Intelligence: 5*
*Wisdom: 4*
*Charisma:8*
*Unspent Attribute Points: 0*

"Let's get this show on the road then, ladies." The others smiled back as I spoke and took each other's hands. No point telling the kids what would be happening because they would be harder to corral and keep safe. Better they experience it first-hand and get used to the idea than waste time.

Jaken grabbed one of the little Fae-Orc children's hands. Their skins were slightly green and their features a perfect blend of Elf and Orc. The other children took each other's hands nervously, not knowing what was going on, but it was Set who began to balk.

Tmont herded him into the circle, and I grabbed him. The others shifted grip, and I cast the spell with Sunrise Village in mind. The earth fell from beneath our feet, and it felt as though we were being pulled through an ice cold tunnel that was much too tight to go through. Then the sensation stopped, and we plopped back on to the ground in the center of the village.

One or two of the kids may or may not have begun tearing up, sniffling, and looking about in both awe and horror. Set vomited profusely, all over the ground. Luckily, I had moved and avoided the worst of it.

Sunrise Village was a small village nestled in the bosom of a large forest south of the Lightning Mountains. Secluded but not unfriendly, the people here knew us and our mission—and they had volunteered to host us.

The square hadn't changed one bit. If it weren't for the fact that it was the middle of the night, people would be haggling for items and better prices. Humans, different kinds of Beast-kin, like bear, wolf, and cat, and even a few Dwarves would be milling about the place as children ran around playing with each other. Not to mention bears who owed fealty to Queen Kyra, the bear queen of this portion of the world, who wandered through often. A few people were in the place, either talking or walking somewhere.

A couple of them waved at us.

"Let's take the kids to the—well, that's new," Jaken began then stopped.

I followed his gaze and noted the large fence that had been erected since the last time we had been to the village. Before, there had been no barrier between the village and the world, the tree line of the forest being plainly visible.

"How much you wanna bet that this was Zhavron's work?" Muu asked in a hushed tone.

Zhavron was an Orc mercenary who we had brought with us on a trip to the north from a town called Lindyburg. He was a stubborn, old bastard, but he was one hell of a fighter and had trained not only Muu but as many of us as would have him on how to fight and kick ass. He was a cool dude when he wasn't going full drill instructor on you.

"I'll take that action," Bokaj grunted. "I'm pretty sure I know who it could've been if it wasn't him."

"Five gold?" Muu offered. The two shook hands without really tearing their eyes away.

"Take them to the tavern," James grunted. "Willem will know what to do with them."

We walked away from the square toward Sir Willem Dillon's tavern. It had no name, but it was the only tavern in the village, so it was centrally located. When we arrived, we noted that there was a new addition to the building.

Before the building had been a simple, one-story structure made of split logs and simple wooden planks. A red door led into the main area, and toward the rear of the building, there were rooms that we had used while staying in the village at times.

Now, that structure had been added on to. There was an entirely new floor with a building built above the place, but there was another building attached to that with a fence about twelve-feet-tall around the side and rear of it. The new addition was made of the same materials, but it looked slightly better crafted.

We had been gone for a few weeks, so this kind of building, all of these changes in general, were wild. We had suggested the fence, but I didn't know for certain that they would start so soon.

"Don't say it," I growled at Muu.

He looked a little sad that he didn't get to point all the new things out, but he walked forward into the tavern anyway. He pushed the door open, and a flood of noise reached out to us and pulled further along. It was good to be back.

Inside, villagers were drinking and calling to each other boisterously. The bartender, a muscular, older human with long, gray hair and a graying, reddish beard, served drinks behind the bar.

He turned his scarred visage our way and a genuine grin of welcome split his face. "Welcome back, boys!"

Some of the other patrons cheered, scaring the children a little. When Willem saw the kids, he immediately shouted, "Quiet, you lot! There are children here now."

He tossed his rag down and immediately tugged his apron over his head. He laid it on the counter as he came through the small opening in the bar area and walked toward us.

"You will explain this, I trust." His face a stoic mask as he looked over us, then turned his sights on the children.

Jaken stepped forward and began to go through the story, a modified one, about how we had found the boys about to be sacrificed and Set had been tossed out on his ass for no reason at all for failing an impossible task.

After a moment of listening, Willem waved the explanation aside.

"I shall hear the full of it in the morning. It looks to be, so far, that you were in the right of things." He motioned to the boys and began to speak to them directly, "Are you hungry?" The one boy who could speak common nodded and translated to the others for us. "Come then, let's find you some food. I may not be the best cook, but it will suffice."

"The hell am I supposed to do then, man?" Yohsuke pretended to be hurt. "Tell you what, for the crime of even remotely thinking you would cook in my presence, take the kids to a room and let a real chef do his thing. How about that?"

Willem smiled at my friend. "Deal. You saved them again."

He ushered the children toward the hallway where our rooms were, and I called out to him, "Hey! They can take my room!"

"Thanks!" echoed back down the hallway, and I watched as both Willem and Yohsuke disappeared with the children.

"May as well grab a seat." Jaken shrugged and motioned to an empty table.

We grabbed seats, and after a while of light drinking, some food provided by our awesome chef, and a bit of terse conversation, everyone decided to turn in. The kids were safe, and the party was safe. We could learn more in the morning.

I walked outside, shifted into my owl form, and took flight. No need to tell the others while we were here. I didn't want them to worry about me. I flew for a while, just gazing at the forest beneath me. The owl's instincts, a perk from being the Primal Warrior, were silent this time, as if they knew what could be on my mind.

Of all the emotions and sensations I could be feeling in this world of magic, adventure, and awesome sights, I was sad and lonely. I missed Kayda. I missed my son. I missed home. That last bit I was surprised about and more than a little angry over.

I had hated my world. People there, while a lot of them were good, let a lot of the bad ones get away with things that made the things I had seen here look pleasant. I was quite literally living every gamer's dream by being here, and I missed home? What was wrong with me?

I landed on the roof of the new building over top of the tavern and shifted from owl to fox then into my panther form. See, the way my shapeshifting works is that it's basically instantaneous, and as a Kitsune, my forms, except the elemental ones, last until I want to shift back. Metagaming? A little. More than a little. But I can only go from a natural form. For me, those are fox-man, fox, and human, to another form. So, in this case, it goes from shapeshifted form, to natural, and into another shapeshifted form.

With me? Cool. 'Cause I'm tired.

I had slept in panther form once before now, and any night predators would leave me alone. Should leave me alone. I hadn't heard of anything other than kidnappers who had been operating around here at night, and all of those assholes were dead. I took up my bed for the night in the center of the roof so as not to scare anyone, then gazed at the stars for a moment.

How beautiful and odd these constellations seemed. How

foreign, yet comforting that somewhere out there, my son and loved ones were still safe because I was here fighting for them. Because all of us were here fighting for them.

I laid my head on my paws and yawned deeply before I shut my eyes and let slumber take me.

# CHAPTER TWO

I woke up after a while to the sound of someone barking orders as the halfway-risen sun struck my fur delightfully. Despite the rude wake-up call, I stretched languorously on the roof before rising and moving around. I padded to the side of the structure and dropped on to the original tavern roof.

As I did so, I was greeted by the sight of six men in light leather armor going through sword drills run by Zhavron.

The massive Orc, older with scars all over his visible body, called from the front of the formation, "Stab, horizontal, vertical, diagonal—no, Daggert, the other way, lad—parry, guard."

He tapped hands and feet as he walked through the sword-swinging men. His bald head had a red bandana around it that was a little damp, and his chipped tusks flashed in the daylight. His back and chest were bare for once, and I noted a great deal more scars. One was large enough that it took up a good deal of the center of his back. I was high enough up that no one saw me right away, and I could watch undisturbed—so I laid down and watched a while.

Another thing I noticed was that he was considerably gentler with these men than he had been with us. With us, he had been like a drill instructor in the third phase at Parris Island. They were knowledgeable and approachable, but they didn't fuck around, and when they gave an order, they expected you to obey.

Zhavron had been Muu's trainer, and he had even offered some of us his wisdom as he had traveled with us. It had been highly enlightening, not to mention the fact that once you got past his surly demeanor, he was a genuinely kickass dude.

"I expect each of you to practice your strokes—not those damned chops you call strokes Daggert—two hundred times today. And daily for the rest of the week. Hold each other accountable. Remember—a squad is only as strong as what?"

"Its weakest link, sir!" the six men responded in unison. They sheathed their weapons swiftly and stood waiting.

"Daggert, if you would?" Zhavron waved to the man in front.

"Atten-*tion!*" The man called, and the men snapped into a position of attention I was very familiar with. Heels together with the toes flared out at a thirty-degree angle and their fists at their sides with their thumbs on the seams of the breeches.

"Present *arms!*" Daggert called. The men crossed their right arms at a ninety-degree angle before them and put the top of their fist and thumb against their heart. "Good morning, sir!"

Zhavron returned the gesture in the same manner, brought his fist down to his side sharply, and ordered, "Dismissed!"

The men cut their salutes smartly before taking a single step back, making an about face and leaving quickly.

"Had you just planned to watch, Master Erebos?" Zhavron called to me where I watched, purring in delight.

I lazily plopped to the ground and shifted back into my fox-man form.

"Hello, Zhavron." I smiled at the mercenary turned military man. "Quite the little army you're working with here."

"They are far from the regiments I oversaw when I was leading mercenary companies," Zhavron sighed, "but as a guard? They will be the best. Better even than the capital guard of Zephyth. I take it you found good fortune in the south if you have returned here so soon?"

"We found some, and we made some enemies," I alluded.

"As is the way of these things." He turned and flashed his teeth at me.

"Ain't that the truth." The sun still shone down as he threw a tunic over his head. "Those all the men you've got, Zhavron?"

"No, only half. My lieutenant has the others, and honestly, I feel bad for them. Brutal taskmaster that one. Almost puts me to shame."

I stared at him in shock. Zhav was a hardass, and it took a good deal of respect to liken anyone to a drill instructor. How harsh could this other person be?

"Come, let's break our fast and hear about your travels. We can trade tales." Zhavron clapped me on the back and shoved me playfully toward the door.

We walked into the back of the tavern to find the rest of the party sitting around a couple of tables. The children had their own table with piles of good food in front of them—eggs, bacon, toast, pancakes, and some fruit just piled on plates. Zhavron greeted the others and grabbed a plate full of food, and I did the same.

Yohsuke popped out of the kitchen wiping his hands on a towel with a confused look on his face. "The fuck are y'all waiting for? Eat!"

We dug in and began the joyful process of clearing our plates. The eggs were perfect, and the bacon was crisp and savory. Mmm.

"Now, tell me about what has happened," Willem ordered.

We all took turns explaining things. We laughed, we cried, I'm pretty sure someone farted—it was a great time.

"And then we came here," Jaken finished.

Muu added, "To be continued—duh duh duuuuuhn!"

A couple of us laughed at the addition, but Willem and Zhavron seemed confused. So we let it go.

"I see." The older Paladin stood, then began to pace. "Two

would-be distractions for our gods, and you've commendably ended them both. Thank you."

"And you lot are thinking to do… what now?" Zhavron asked before shoving more eggs into his gullet.

"We're gonna go see a black Dragon on a small island off the coast northwest of the jungles and then after that, to see the high elves up north," Jaken supplied.

Willem looked like he wanted to comment but just sighed and shook his head as he sipped his tea.

"Wish you all luck on that endeavor." Zhavron stood and patted his belly with a nod to Yohsuke. "That sounds foolish and deadly, dealing with any kind of Dragon. But a black Dragon? One of the smartest and vilest kind? Right up your alley."

"Woah, your turn big, green, and angry." Muu stood up. "You have to have some news for us, right? Like, whose idea was it to build the fence?"

"The guard wall?" He raised an eyebrow. "That would have been one the village had but was implemented by my lieutenant, then expounded upon. 'A place isn't really defensible if it's open to all.'"

"Sound word," I grunted. "You did say you would swap stories. Spill it, old man," I added that last bit playfully, and he gave me a withering look.

With a sigh, he began, "The journey here was uneventful. I came here with thirteen strong arms, mostly men I trusted and the others had shining recommendations from people I trusted. As we were passing close to the mountain range, we were set upon by trolls and a band of marauders who fancied themselves more than enough to slaughter us. They died. All of them. But not before two of my people fell. The third defected—which I found odd, but I couldn't blame him—in the middle of the night a day or so later. The other ten are here now."

He lifted his mug and took a large gulp of his water before belching unceremoniously and continuing, "Upon our arrival here, we were met with a squadron of bears, but they let us pass after I let them catch Jaken's scent. Once Sir Dillon heard our tale and what we had come to do, we began working immediately. The construction of the fence was overseen by my right hand, and the barracks—the building next to and above us now —was overseen by the mercenary who had taken up carpentry and building when he was a lad from his da'. We have the ten who came with me working in eight-hour rotations of watch on two entrances, and the other three guards roam the interior perimeter of the walls. The bears are a godsend; they watch the forest and outer perimeter. The mayor's wife and some of the other Bear-kin translate for us if needed."

"The walls are currently being reinforced with thick logs, and a pathway along the top is in the works as well," Willem interjected. "We are working on transporting stone from the mountains so that we can have a less flimsy partition between the people and the outside, but it's not going too swiftly. The logistics of it aren't fully hashed out, but there are talks of talks. You understand how these things can be, eh?"

"Couldn't stay away from the action, huh?" I ribbed the older Paladin a little. He gave me a sly smile in return. "That's great guys. So what about the people you were training then, Zhavron? They cool?"

"They will make an excellent guard, as I told you earlier." He nodded. "My lieutenant is currently training the others in unit tactics, subject control, and close quarters battle. They should be getting back here any minute."

As if on cue, the door opened, admitting twelve men and women who looked dirtied, bruised, and much worse for wear than the tall and muscular figure behind them.

And that figure was Vrawn. Her green skin glistened slightly with sweat, her fiery orange mohawk tied into a braid that left the sides of her head clear and clean shaven. Her thick and corded muscles shook bare in a tight-fitting, sleeveless blouse the color of cream tucked into brown breeches and soft looking black boots. She took up most of the doorway, but despite her large frame and muscles, her waist was thin for her bulk, and she still boasted a very feminine build. Her blue eyes swept the room, taking in all the patrons. She saw my friends and smiled, her pillowy lips parting to flash her dainty tusks.

Before she spoke to any of us, she turned to her people. "Eat, do not overfill yourself. If any of you vomit again during morning training, I will be very disappointed. Dismissed."

"Ma'am!" they barked in unison with smart salutes. She returned it and turned toward us. The cold, ordering tone gone from her voice, replaced by warmth.

"Hello, all of you." Her feminine and breathy voice carried to us. She stepped in, her surprisingly light footfalls leading her to us. "I had not known you would be here so soon. Is Zeke well?"

I smiled softly. "Yes," she looked my way in confusion, "I'm doing as well as can be done, Vrawn. How are you?"

I looked at Zhavron, and I swear I saw the mischief in the old buzzard's eyes. He had purposely hidden the fact that she was here. Oh, I'd get mine.

"Zeke, you are not as I have remembered." A look of concern passed over her features. "Are you truly well?"

"Yes, this is one of my natural forms as a Kitsune. I have several. This, a fox, and a human. You saw my human form because I didn't want to have anyone trying to take my tails." I wagged all five of them to the right and made sure she could see them.

"That was a good idea." She nodded, smiling wider. "I would love to hear more of your travels. Do you have time?"

I looked to the others who all had wolfish grins well in place. Especially Bokaj, for some reason.

"We're just going to see a Dragon—no big deal." James waved offhandedly. "We need to restock on food, make sure we're golden from a potion standpoint, and then see to the village. He's got plenty of time, Vrawn."

"Thank you, James, was it?" When he gave her a broad, toothy grin, she clenched her fist as if to grab something. "I appreciate your candor. It really is so nice to see all of you again."

"See to the village?" Bokaj grunted in question, suddenly worried. "We got shit to do. We can't slow down now, man."

"We aren't slowing down. We're getting ready," Jaken explained. "It's a fucking black Dragon. We can't just go in half-cocked, or did you like getting your ass kicked in that cultist village?"

He slapped the table with a hand and bared his teeth at Vrawn. "We'll be leaving as soon as we can then!"

*You lot do know that I'm going to tell her about Maebe, right?* I sent them with our telepathy earrings while Vrawn went to a table at the other side of the room.

They all nodded vigorously, and I shook my head in defeat. Bunch of assholes. I piled a bunch of different foods, fruits, and vegetables on to a plate before walking toward Vrawn.

I put the plate in front of her before sitting off to the side of her position.

"Thank you." She picked up a fork and began to eat slowly before pausing. "Please, do not wait for me to finish. Tell me of your tales."

"I can do that." Talking to her was easy, even though the first time we had met, she had been working in a bathhouse. Long story short, she was a lady of the night for the bathhouse I had gone to called the Steam Palace.

No, not a vampire. Just willing to sleep with people for coin. Which I'm cool with, as long as she and anyone in that profession are completely willing participants. It just wasn't for me. Then and now. She respected that, but when I tipped her a decent amount of gold, it had put me in her good graces.

I started from where we left the hospitality of her friend Giledt's place, the Marching Mercenary. It took her a plate and a half of food for me to finish things. She didn't interrupt, she didn't move other than to look at me, eat her food, drink water, and blink.

"So, then we took the kids and brought them here." I

motioned to where the four boys sat at their table, looking like they were about to pass into a food coma. "Now, we're on our way to talk to a black Dragon to see about blessing James. And that's everything. But how did you come to be here?"

"Well, business wasn't the best for me in the city, and Giledt had heard from Captain Zhavron that he was looking for strong-armed and upright mercenaries to take to a village on your groups' behalf as a guard. I had known much from my time as a child in the ways of combat, so I offered my services with a glowing recommendation from Giledt and Remy. Remy and the ladies were sad to see me go—I protected them while I was there, but my sister offered to take over for me so they will be fine."

"Your sister is taking over as a... courtesan?" I offered lamely.

She smiled at the attempt. "We like to work—when people will have us—and she is much stronger than I. Better suited for enforcing the laws of the bathhouse, as she was a guard herself for some time in the capital. She's retired now, though. It will be nice for her to relax there."

"Well, I'm very happy for her."

"As am I." She closed her eyes and stretched until the line of her body was clearly visible to me. "And this Maebe. You called her your 'girl-friend'. Is this a similar term to lover?"

"It is." I nodded.

"And she knows of me?" Her fiery eyebrows raised slightly.

"She does, and she wasn't upset with you." I splayed my hands toward her.

"And she wasn't upset with you?" Her face was unreadable.

"No. Maebe and I were only friends, so we weren't in a relationship at that point in time," I answered honestly, then added quickly, "and I didn't know that we would be—not even in my wildest dreams—when I met you. I'm sorry."

She laughed. "You do not need to apologize, Zeke. I understand. My affections for you are real, and I do not feel that they are unwarranted. You are thoughtful, kind, considerate, and strong."

I didn't know what to do with myself or the forward compliments. I had never been good at taking compliments. Not knowing what to do with my suddenly-bashful ass, I looked away and acted as if I were trying to find something to drink.

"I like you." She shrugged. "I have since I first met you and you were thoughtful enough not to judge me based on my profession. Also, I am not afraid of a Fae Queen. If anything, I would gather she wouldn't care what or who you did."

"That may be true, and she did seem confused as to why I didn't take the, uh… service you offered." I blushed furiously despite my comfort in her presence. A knowing smile flowed over her features, and she looked away herself.

She was so nice to be around—soft-spoken, intelligent, quick-witted, and thoughtful. Why was I suddenly so self-conscious? It was like being a kid again. Shit!

"Then she is as most royals I have ever heard of." She laid a large hand over mine comfortingly. "They do not care if someone strays, as long as they are strong enough to do what needs to be done."

"That's a very weird thought." I frowned.

I mean, as a concept, it made sense. There were base urges and needs that people had that sometimes clouded judgment, but those lapses in judgment often led to darker things than what was being thought of here—things that were deplorable and vile.

Besides, those needs weren't distracting to me. Not really. I was here for a purpose. Anything else just kind of happened.

"While it might be to us, it isn't for them," she explained. "What is most important is that their power is secure and that they and their chosen remain in power, but that is not for us to decide or speculate on. I would like to meet her."

"Uh, okay. If she's around sometime soon, I'll let her know," I said haltingly. This was a very odd sequence of events for me. The thought of just *never* mentioning it to Mae crossed my mind, and I found that deeply appealing. If she asked, I'd tell her. But until then? Mum's the word.

"She is not here with you?" I shook my head, so she smiled even wider. "Then that means I have you to myself." Her eyes had taken on a different shine that I hadn't seen in anyone's gaze before.

*Uh, guys?* I projected to my friends. *I need an adult!*

"Hey, Zeke!" Muu called, and I almost sighed in relief. I looked over, gratitude on my face; I noticed the evil look on his face as he stood by the door. The others were gone already. "You enjoy your time with Vrawn, buddy—we'll take care of the shopping and whatnot. Vrawn, you take care of him. He needs a stern hand at times and adult supervision."

I blinked in disbelief, then looked back to Vrawn to see her beaming at my friends and their retreating figures. "That was so thoughtful of them. Come. I want to show you the walls and see if there's anything you can think to do as well."

I knew in my heart of hearts that she wasn't so naive as to not know that something was off, but I don't think she cared. It was sweet, but it made me wonder how smitten with me she truly was.

I groaned inwardly, vowing then and there that I would find some way to get back at those bastards. It wasn't that I was uncomfortable with the woman. Not really. It was just that I didn't want to hurt her feelings and that she didn't seem to be fazed by the fact that I was dating a Fae Queen who could wipe this village from the map with ease.

She touched my shoulder and shook me from my thoughts gently. I gave her a reassuring grin and stood to follow.

As I walked by, Zhavron called out from his seat, "Take the day, lieutenant! I will handle your instruction for the rest of today."

The trainees still eating groaned, and Zhavron's howling laughter chased us out of the tavern and into the sunlight.

Vrawn led me to the side of the tavern. Then we kept going through the houses and buildings until we got to the wall. It stood an easy sixteen feet tall, made of roughly hewn wood that looked to be hastily made. It was sturdy—don't get me wrong—but it was far from some of the better defenses I had seen since arriving here. There was a good amount of space between the wall and the buildings inside—at least twenty feet of dead space that would be a battleground if anyone made it over.

I tapped the wall with my foot, and it didn't move, but that didn't necessarily mean it wouldn't fall over if it was hit hard enough. Looking both directions, I noted that there were support logs, easily as thick as my waist leaning against the fence every fifteen feet or so.

"And there are plans to bring in stone to build a true fortification?" I asked Vrawn as I looked over the handiwork.

"There are talks of plans," she corrected. "The logistics needed elude the masons, and the amount of time it would take is reprehensible."

"What about an enchantment?" I wondered aloud.

"We do not have anyone with that ability in the village that I am aware of." She shrugged. Her blue eyes wandered the top of the fence line slowly. "I worry. The mayor and Sir Dillon informed Zhavron and I of what had happened. This wall was a quick thing. A work of haste, and while it will hold, it will not hold long. I have plans for it, but there is much to be desired."

"Well, you have me." I smiled. "I've never done something like this though, so I need to see how to do it."

"You are going to try and enchant this wall?" she asked breathlessly, a look of wonder on her face.

"I'm going to go find someone who might be able to show me how." I smiled as I cast Teleport, and Vrawn disappeared from my sight.

# CHAPTER THREE

It took no time at all to get into Djurn Forge after arriving at the entrance. The Ironnose guards let me through with no issues. I power walked to my destination as I tried desperately to justify what I had just done to myself.

*They hate Orcs here, man,* I explained to myself. *Her coming along would have made a relatively quick trip to the Dwarves almost an act of treason. Better that she possibly be a little miffed with you than potentially dead, right?*

Yeah. That would work for now. I think.

The Light Hand Clan. I arrived at the gated compound—the buildings made of a strange looking metal—and the gates swung open. I had been here so many times. All the memories of fun times I had been mentally abused by the crazy Dwarf who led the Dwarves in this compound.

I'm teasing; she was just nuts, but it was to be expected since she had spent years carefully cultivating a crazy persona to protect herself by earning people's ire.

Feeling so at home, I walked into the main building, a squat affair with one door on this side and marched myself to Shellica's room.

I heard discussion on the other side, then knocked rather than opening the door and bursting in.

"Enter!" Shellica's cultured voice shouted from the other side of the door.

I walked into her spartan-looking workroom and bedroom to find her standing with the only other Dwarf in the clan that I knew aside from Granite, Natholdi, and Fainnir—Vilmas.

Both Dwarves, thinner than the rest of their race, eyed me in surprise. Shellica, the older Dwarf with gray hair, bright green eyes with deep smile lines around them, grinned manically.

"Well, there's a face I didn't expect today." She stepped toward me and pulled me into a hug. "Why are you here, lad? You should have told me you were coming. I would've prepared some items for you to enchant!"

"Sunrise Village has a wall issue," I began. "I was wondering if there was a way to enchant the wall without having to spend an ungodly amount of time on it, or would it be more practical to have them get the masons needed to build a true wall of stone and then enchant that?"

Shellica seemed to smile impossibly wide before returning her attention to Vilmas. "Just what you needed, lass."

Vilmas looked confused, then horrified. "No!"

"*Yes!*" Shellica hissed in triumph.

Vilmas, her white hair hung over her face in disarray, looked defeated. This was the first time I had spent so much time around her that I was able to see more of her now than when we had first met a while back when she had acted as a messenger for the clan head. Her eyes were a golden hazel with long and thick eyelashes that most women had to apply a good deal of makeup for. Her round cheeks were cute and rosy in color. The rest of her figure was well muscled for a member of the Light Hand Clan, but she was still thinner than that of most Dwarves.

She stood there, wringing her hands nervously as Shellica flitted about her room gathering things.

"But, Lady Shellica, please—I don't want to go out of the compound," the younger Dwarf tried to reason. "Let alone to somewhere I don't know anyone."

Shellica stopped and forced the poor woman to look her in the eyes with an iron grip on her quivering jaw. "Vilmas. I did not ask what you wanted. I said that it was what you needed. Do you know why you are stuck at the cusp of grandmaster?"

Vilmas shook her head, and Shellica sighed knowingly. "It's because you fear the unknown, lass. You are too afraid to branch out. To try new things. Sure, with an item, there's almost no one better than you, even me."

The older Dwarf looked to me then, and I understood what I thought she was wanting.

"You know, I'll be there." I looked at her imploringly. "This village has come under attack, had their children stolen, because they dared help us. I need to do what I can to protect them. I don't want to screw this up, and I need the best. I think that's you. Will you help them? Please?"

Vilmas heaved a great sigh and looked as though she might flee before asking—her voice barely a whisper, "Are there other Dwarves?"

I nodded once. "There are a few. One of them, Rowland, is a good friend of mine. Real nice guy. A smith. *The* smith. I'm not sure what clan he's with, but I don't think he's ever been here. "

She looked from me to Shellica then back.

"Okay. I'll help you for a little while."

"Excellent!" Shellica clapped, her smile radiant more than crazy, and she reached out to grab my arm in a death grip. "Go and get a bag together while I torture Zeke here."

Vilmas fled from the room as I muttered a string of curses under my breath at the pain. Seconds later, there was a loud *bang* and a string of curses from a male Dwarf, so vehemently creative I couldn't help but be impressed. Until the last one.

I poked my head out the door and bellowed, "Hey! You retract that fucking statement!"

There was a pause, and then the deeper, likely male Dwarven voice growled, "I retract that statement about your children."

"Those are her fuckin' kids, man!" I bellowed in reproach.

The cursing stopped, and I heard footfalls moving away.

"Thank you, lad." Shellica chuckled and sat on her bed. I gave her a thumb up, and she looked at me critically. "What I said was true. She needs to expand her ability, but I don't want the girl in harm's way."

"I will be right there learning what I can from her and helping, and the lieutenant of the Village Guard has a special interest in keeping us both safe, so she will be fine."

"Special interest?" She waggled her eyebrows exaggeratedly, then calmed. "Good. See that she has the things she needs. And that she's taken care of, for me."

*Quest Alert!*

*Sunrise for Vilmas – Shellica Light Hand has ordered that you take care of Vilmas while she works on the wall surrounding the village at your request.*

*Reward: Furthered training.*

*There is no refusing this request.*

*Damn, man,* I thought to myself as I dismissed the notification.

"Yeah, she'll be taken care of." She nodded and began to gather some more things. "You going somewhere?"

"I've petitioned the royals of the high elves to come and learn how to make their damned weaponry." She grinned again, and it looked like some of the years she had on her melted away. "They've agreed to see if I 'have what it takes' to keep up with their artisans. HA!"

I couldn't help but fear for the poor bastards. And they had invited her in of their own free will. Like inviting a vampire in. I shuddered.

"Well, I hope that goes well for you. Do you have a way to communicate with anyone while you're gone?"

She reached into her pocket and pulled out two small

figures that looked like birds. No, ravens. I reached out and touched the one closest to me and yelped as a burning sensation took my fingertips.

"Silver," I hissed before I could stop myself.

My lycanthropy, you know that word. I know you do. Don't give me that look… Fine. It means my Werewolf nature, the curse I had, made silver highly painful to me. I had been "gifted" this monster by Pastela, a former Alpha Werewolf who had wanted to try and take over the Fae Realm.

"They are messengers," she admonished me with a glance. "They carry my voice and the voice of the person who holds the other for communication purposes. Highly advanced. At least master level."

"Well, I won't be trying it right away, no worries there." I cast Heal on myself, and the pain numbed a little.

"Well, good. So that you know, I will be leaving it with someone who matters." She eyed me with a mischievous glint to her gaze before adding, "Not you."

I snorted. "As if I wanted that fuckin' thing. Besides, having you yell at me from where you are now is bad enough when I'm here. Anywhere in this *realm*? You really are nuts, lady."

She snorted at my response, dismissively waving a hand at me, then returned to her task.

I watched silently as she packed some clothing, a few knick-knacks, and some items I questioned the very existence of. If they did what I thought they might, it looked like she expected a fight. I didn't say anything, but I was a little worried for her.

The high elves weren't exactly the nicest people. Sure, I had met a few, but the ones I had met had been recent enough for me to still think of them as dicks.

She finished, then looked to me with a sack in hand that was *much* larger on the inside than it was from the outside. Dimensional pouch of some kind most likely. Cool as hell. If she hadn't been so busy, I'd have grilled her about making one, but I let it slide. Maybe I could convince Vilmas to show me?

"Get out, lad," Shellica ordered gruffly. I had to laugh; the little thing ordering me around like that would make any man's ego rage. I didn't want to fight her, though.

I stepped out into the sterile hallway, the door clattered shut, and the clunks of several locks reached my ears. My head tilted left on its own, and I looked down to see the Dwarf counting as the tumblers caught.

Once she was satisfied, she waved for me to follow her, and I obeyed. After a couple of minutes, we stood in front of a closed door.

"Vilmas!" Shellica knocked loudly.

The younger Dwarf opened the door. Her face was red; her eyes were splotchy and red as well.

"You're packed, I trust?" Shellica's voice was measured and full to the brim with warning.

"Yes, ma'am." Vilmas held out a pack the same size as Shellica's, and the older Dwarf nodded in satisfaction.

"Good, lass. Don't keep the villagers waiting for their protections. Be safe, learn something of yourself, and for the Mountain's sake, Vilmas, *stop crying!*"

"Okay," the mousy Dwarf replied as she swatted the tears from her cheeks.

I sure had my work cut out for me here.

"Let's go then Vilmas." I tried to be reassuring, but she just seemed to get down on herself.

Shellica left us at the entrance to the compound, claiming that she was going to be going another direction to save some time on her trip to the northern lands of the high elves.

Once Vilmas and I were alone, things grew drastically quieter, and I suddenly needed to fill the void with conversation. Yay, social anxiety.

"So, uh—Vilmas," she looked my way a little, "do we need anything for the enchanting? Any components or anything like that? I'll cover the cost, of course."

She stopped moving and turned toward me with her eyes closed. "What is the wall made of? Wood?"

"That's correct." I added, "The planks are thick cut,

roughly hewn and workable. Roughly sixteen feet high, and there are support logs around every fifteen feet or so."

Vilmas began mumbling to herself, and her fingers began waggling in the air as if she were doing complex equations. After a moment of this, her feet began to move on their own. After a while of walking in tense silence, we came to a vendor at a stall with a large smelter behind him.

His scarred and burnt visage was intimidating, if I was honest. I didn't know whether it was the crazy look on his face or the fact that half of his beard was singed away.

"What can ah do ye fer?" he grumbled.

"I require twenty-five ingots of the purest mithral you have, please." There was a slight quaver to her voice, but other than that, Vilmas was fine.

"That'll be," the Dwarf counted on his hands, "six hundred and seventy-five gold."

I began to reach into my funds when I saw Vilmas actually crack a smile and laugh. A bellowing laugh. Almost like a bray.

When she was done, she wiped a tear from her cheek. "Oh, that was a wonderful joke, good sir. I think we will take our business to someone who doesn't mean to swindle us."

The enchanter began to turn to go when the vendor's good hand shot out and grasped her arm roughly. I stepped forward without thought and lifted him, with one swift motion, by his apron and shirt until his feet dangled uselessly beneath him.

"You ever touch someone in my presence again, and I'll even up those burn marks." My voice had taken on a menacing tone.

"Put him down, Master Zekiel," Vilmas ordered gently. Turning back to the Dwarf, she said, "You would do well to heed his words. He is a chosen and adopted member of Clan Mugfist, a close friend to Granite Light Hand, and apprentice to Shellica Light Hand."

"So?" the Dwarf grunted after I set him down. He shook out his apron and shirt a bit.

"So? That means he's by all rights a Dwarf. He can fight, and he's also a powerful and talented Mage."

I cast Aspect of the Ursolon to enlarge my form until I towered even further over the Dwarf. My muscles thickened, and my features broadened a little.

"Not to mention, I *know* that pure mithral ingots are not that expensive by far." She crossed her arms before her. "Maybe we should go to the king and report a violation in our stringent trade laws?"

The other Dwarf growled uselessly before conceding, "Three hundred gold and I never see you again."

"Two hundred and I don't call the Ironnoses to see what goods you have hidden there." Vilmas cocked her head to the side. "Gnome."

The Dwarf gasped, and then I saw it. The illusion spell that was hiding the gnome was fading before my eyes. Why had it eluded my True Sight for so long? How?

"Two hundred and you go away forever!" the gnome whispered harshly. He hurriedly counted out twenty-five ingots of uniform height, width, color, and purity on to his stall counter. Vilmas began to inspect it as I forked over the two hundred gold and was about to walk off before Vilmas reached over and took twenty-five gold back.

"The quality is not what I need, but it will suffice." Vilmas's dismissive tone made the gnome rage silently as we put the items into my inventory and walked away.

"Vilmas, what the hell?!" I whispered. "That felt like robbery! Where did that come from?"

"Lady Shellica taught me from a young age to always spot the fakes among us and to exploit their lies to great effect. The gnome has been here for weeks exploiting what few visitors we have here in Djurn Forge and knows so little of our culture or us as a people that he failed to know that I would see through his deceptions. That he thought we *actually* have a king was laughable."

"You don't?" I asked, suddenly aware once more that I was

an idiot.

"No." She smiled sweetly, then blushed. "We have a council of the Clans that makes decisions for the city. They oversee commerce, diplomacy, and all other matter of issues so that the common Dwarf can focus on their Way."

That was pretty cool to hear. I could see a drunken but dignified council of the stout folk talking politics and taxes while tossing axes at a target to see who was best. I liked this fantasy.

We spent the rest of the slow walk to get outside of the city in amiable silence. Once we were outside the rune walls to Djurn Forge, I touched Vilmas on the shoulder and cast Teleport to get us back to Sunrise Village's square.

By now, I was starting to become accustomed to the sensation of traveling great distances in the span of a heartbeat. Really should remember to warn people about that though.

Vilmas—was not. The poor Dwarf landed with me and immediately fell to her knees and tossed up everything in her stomach. Her horrid retching and the wet sound of vomit littering the grass almost made the gorge rise up in my throat.

I turned away and began trying to breathe in through my mouth so that I wouldn't scent the disgusting ground paint.

"You have returned," I heard Vrawn's drawn and careful tone behind me. "Sir Dillon told me that you arrived here last time you teleported back."

I felt her arms wrap around my shoulders, and while it was a new sensation, it irked me for some reason. Maybe a sudden closeness from someone I didn't know well enough? Maybe it was her forwardness at seemingly all times?

I took a breath, held it, then relaxed a little as I let it out. I turned to find her face a careful mask of emotionless bearing. Either it didn't bother her that I had up and cut out, or she was furious and her bearing was fucking insane.

See, bearing is the way you carry yourself and what you let people see of you from your face and mannerisms. A lot of people in the military have good control of their bearing and tend to hide their emotions behind a mask of blank faces and dispassionate observation. They seem detached or uncaring at times. To have good bearing means to have good control. So whatever Vrawn was feeling at that moment, I had no clue because she didn't want me to know.

"Lieutenant Vrawn, this is Vilmas of the Light Hand Clan. A master enchanter on the cusp of attaining the grandmaster rank in her craft. Vilmas, this is lieutenant Vrawn of the Sunrise Guard. Vrawn, Vilmas is under my care, so I would like you to help me keep her safe."

"I can do that." The weight of Vrawn's limbs left me, and she walked around the vomit to help Vilmas to her feet.

Vilmas took one look at Vrawn, squinting in the bright light, and I instantly remembered that Dwarves and Orcs didn't like each other normally. Dwarves usually hated Orcs outright. I should have fucking remembered this from my earlier justifications.

*Pull your shit together, Zeke!* I growled at myself. I would watch for now, but I had to be ready to step in if shit got heavy.

But I was surprised to see the Dwarven woman take the lieutenant's offered hand and stand shakily to her feet.

"You're so big." Vrawn, probably used to hearing that assertion, cast her eyes downward—hurt. Vilmas put her hand on the Orc's bicep, then pulled her down closer to look at her face. "It's so bright here; it hurts my eyes."

As the larger woman knelt down to get closer, Vilmas' eyes shot open wider, and she exclaimed, "You're an *Orc!* Are all Orcs so beautiful?"

I watched in stunned silence as Vrawn's cheeks glowed a deep red. "I do not know many of my kind. I was adopted, but I thank you. I am Vrawn. Would you like to be my friend?"

Vilmas looked as though she was about to explode in excitement. "I've never had a friend before! I would love to be your friend!" She looked at me and splayed her hands in a questioning gesture. "What do friends even do?"

I couldn't help the belting laughter that threatened to choke me on the way out. All that escaped was an "oh god" and chortled, choking sobs of laughter.

After I calmed down, the girls didn't look like they would string me up and do terrible things to me for laughing at them. So, I figured I was alright.

"Vrawn, will you take me to the wall so that I can take a look at it?" Vilmas held her hand out to the taller woman.

"I would be more than happy to." Vrawn took the proffered hand, and they walked toward the wall around the village.

Vilmas looked over the structure before her, then began to touch it with her hands and inspect it with a monocle that she held to her right eye.

"The wood is crude, but it will do, as it seems to be sturdy." She took a fist and rapped her knuckles against the wood. "I will need to speak with the smith. We will need to acquire nails and have the supplies we bought taken care of so that we can begin engraving them and pouring mana into them."

I nodded, understanding the task that was to come, "Well, then let's get you to Rowland's place and start this process. The sooner this is done, the sooner we will be able to rest easier."

The walk to Rowland's wasn't all that bad, except for the fact that Vilmas had lost that odd round of sureness that she had with Vrawn. She was more than a little jumpy, and the Orc with her had to hold her close at times. But neither seemed to really mind the other. I thought of that as a blessing.

We came to the smithy moments later; the light hit the wooden building lighting the dark wood and highlighting the beauty of the wood. A stone section of the wall around the forge portion itself attached to the fenced in yard where he kept wood and other materials. It was all the same as it had been.

I love Rowland, the dwarven blacksmith who ran the forge in Sunrise, and I loved to mess with him. We were basically family by now.

I kicked in the door with a huge grin on my face, only to find Jaken and Rowland in conversation.

"There's the bastard!" Rowland roared and rounded the counter coming straight at me. "Come here."

Rowland, his stout body, covered in thick muscle that would make any bodybuilder quiver, stalked toward me. His black eyebrows were furrowed, and his beady black eyes glinted in the muted light of the room. His fists were packed tight, and when I looked to Jaken to see if he knew what the hell was wrong—the stout man slugged me in the stomach.

It wasn't the hardest I had been hit, by any means, but I was confused as to the treatment. "Rowland, what the fuck?"

"Yer out there doin' gods know what, and ye don' come an see yer pal Rowland?" The Dwarf pulled me into a headlock. "Ye don' share a drink with the man whose life ye helped save afore ye went ta risk yer neck? Maybe I oughta beat manners into ye lad?"

I growled, and we tussled playfully. His grip on my neck and head lost when I shifted into my fox form and then back once my head was out of his grip. We traded good-natured blows for a second before we clasped hands and shook.

"What can I do fer ye, Zeke? Jaken an' I were just discussin' some further things he needed to work on." Rowland turned and noted the two with me. First he addressed Vrawn, "Lieutenant. I hope the weapons ye requisitioned from me are provin' useful?"

"They are, Master Rowland." Vrawn's head dipped in acknowledgment. "I would ask that we have weights welded on to our training weapons soon so that the guards can train a little harder. If you have the time?"

"Yer a monster." He chuckled evilly. "I'll be more than happy ta help ye. Bring 'em in when ye need 'em. I'll do me best."

Rowland's gaze fell to Vilmas, and he swallowed once deeply before speaking, "Welcome to me shop."

"Thank you. I heard your name is Rowland?" Vilmas began timidly. "The hammer falls."

"And rises again," Rowland finished a greeting that Dwarves

usually spoke to each other on a first meeting. It let them know that they were aware of the toil their god went to while crafting each of them and that they were equal along the way.

"Zeke says that you are a talented smith. I will have need of your skills for a project to assist in protecting the village from further attacks. Are you well versed in smithing with mithral?"

"I can hammer basic things if needed. I know the theory for hammering the metal, but it'll be me first time," Rowland admitted. "But if it be for the village, I'll be at yer aid."

"Basic is all that will be needed." She motioned for me to do something, and I figured it was lay out the mithral, which I did.

Every ingot after the first two made Rowland's black beard dip lower as his mouth fell further and further open.

"I need for you to hammer three inch by three inch squares of the metal that need to be at least an eighth of an inch thick." She eyed the smith as he kept staring at the metal. "Rowland?" She waved her hand in between him and the ingots.

"Three by three and a eighth, aye. That's within me skills." He blinked a few times. "Jaken, lad, I take it ye learned a lot more in Djurn Forge yerself?"

"I can forge mithral." Jaken's shoulders squared proudly. "Give me a piece to go off of, and I'll be able to mimic it."

"How quick ye need it?" Rowland began to hand off the ingots to Jaken who ferried them into the back.

"I need as many as you can make out of that as quickly as you can," Vilmas replied.

"Very well. It's nearly noon now. Have Yohsuke or Muu bring the two of us lunch and dinner. We'll have ye what we can by mid-morning tomorrow." Rowland rubbed his chin for a second, then looked to Jaken. "Get me splitter out. I'll make the one, then split others while ye make what ye can. Then we can work together."

Jaken disappeared into the back, and Rowland turned back to us.

"Thank you. Any nails that you might have or that the

village may have access to would be appreciated," the enchanter informed Rowland.

"Do they need to be a specific kind?" I asked Vilmas.

"They need to be able to hold the plaques in place—other than being able to do that? No specifications."

"Let me get some of your scrap iron ore or some ingots from you Rowland—I'll take care of the nails," I offered.

Rowland handed me thirteen ingots of iron that probably weighed a good three pounds each. I took them and turned to the ladies.

"What now, boss?" I asked Vilmas.

"We prepare." She looked around. "We will need a place that I can work, preferably somewhere I can be alone?"

"The tavern should work." I thought for a moment. "Though I'm not sure if there will be room, but we can always ask Willem and see if he can recommend a place."

It took us a few minutes to get to the tavern, and luckily, the chef's quarters had been vacated so that the chef could move in with his new blushing bride, so Yoh had taken his. This left Yohsuke's old room up for grabs.

"This will do." Vilmas sat on the bed and sighed. "We will need those nails in order to secure the plaques, but we will need to purify them before we use them. That way, your mana will not interfere with my own. I will teach you how to do that, but we will do so in the morning before we begin the enchanting. For now, I need to have some time alone to think about the engraving I want to use, then the list of effects. We should also see if there are any components out there that we could use to aid us. Raw ore would be fantastic."

*I'll keep that in mind,* I thought to myself. Could I possibly find some in the mountains?

"You'll be safe here, and I'll work on making those a little later on tonight." I thought for a moment, then added, "I'll be going to the mountains north of us to see about collecting some ore. Rowland has to get his from somewhere, and there used to be a rare bird who lived there. Has to be something special about the place other than just being attractive to lightning."

I'd ask Rowland, but I didn't want to ruin his focus on the task ahead, and I wanted to try out some of my own abilities.

"When do we leave?" Vrawn looked at me expectantly.

"I take it you aren't letting me out of your sight?" I sighed, half expecting this.

"No." She smiled resolutely. "I told you that I would spend time with you. Unless you do not want to? I would gather from your sudden disappearance to a Dwarven settlement made you leave me behind, and I understand why you might, but leaving without a single word makes me think my company is a burden for now."

*Where is this level of emotional terrorism coming from?* I wondered as I watched her cross the room to stand by the door.

You know what? I had earned this. I was going to make it right, and rather than risk her puking from teleporting, I'd offer a different mode of travel. Time to make up for it, Zeke.

"If you're going to come with me and we want any hope of getting this done quickly, I'll need you to get into my collar," I explained. She looked at me in confusion, and I heard Vilmas wander over to us. "It takes one willing creature into it and puts them in a sort of stasis until I let them out."

"And you promise to let me out?" Her eyes narrowed at me.

"I will. I promise." She thought for a moment before offering me her hand gingerly.

She touched the pitch-black gem in the setting, and I willed her into the item. Her large form began to dissipate into a cloud of smoke that filtered into the gem slowly at first but then fully a second later.

"That's an impressive bit of enchanting. I assume lady Shellica did that?" Vilmas asked. I nodded. "I hope I can do the same at some point. Good luck out there."

Well, there went the whole dimensional bag idea. Damn it. And I had really been hoping to pick her brain about that.

I nodded and walked out into the hallway. The tavern was

beginning to fill with people looking for an evening meal, so I dodged some folks on the way outside. Once I was out, I shifted and took flight. My owl form rose into the clouds on thermals that seemed to not care about the trees, and I was quickly on my way to the mountains.

The travel time in flight was much faster than running on the ground, so by the time I made it to the mountain, the sun hung low in the sky. Once I landed, I shifted into my fox-man form before letting Vrawn out of my collar.

Smoke filtered from the gem in the collar and solidified into a mystified looking Orc woman.

"That was a very odd sensation," she informed me a little breathlessly.

"I get that sometimes," I replied with a little cheek. "I'm going to be gone for a little bit, unfortunately. I need to go into the ground in order to see if there is any ore here that we can use."

I saw her shoulders fall a bit, and I moved to get her attention. "I promise, as soon as I get a minute, I will come and spend some time with you. This is likely going to be a process. Please, be patient with me."

That last, to me, felt more like it had more meaning than I had meant, but it seemed to work.

"I will wait for you here," she said with a sigh.

I nodded once and assumed my earth elemental form. I felt the necessary mana drain, and my body shifted into a being that looked like a large-ish golem made of diamond, my legs were roughly the same size, hell—I was roughly the same size. I just looked like a giant man-diamond.

"Shiny and very odd." Vrawn's hand smoothed over my shoulder. I looked at her, and her gaze went through me. Odd. Oh well, time to work.

I stepped away and began to trudge forward and wade into the ground as if it were water. Once I was fully immersed, I felt everything around me. Every bit of earth within, I don't know, hundreds of feet? This kind of awareness was mind blowing. I could tell where the trees were, where Vrawn stood, and the depth of the mountain in front of me.

It was massive.

The sheer depth of it was enormous, and it just felt *dense*. I pressed myself against the stone beneath the ground and tried to make my way through. I felt a little give, and there was an immediate pressure back that kept me out. I narrowed my sensory vision and focused on the mountain. How would I even try and find this ore? What did it feel like? What did it look like?

*Tiny Druid, you would have yourself in this kind of predicament. The mountain is beyond mortal understanding. Even with your flesh-made-diamond, you are not strong enough to become one with the immensity that is the stone. The bones of the world. The spine that holds the earth beneath your feet together and gives it shape. Allow me to show you a glimpse so that you are made aware.*

The world around me crushed inward, the pressure most likely necessary to make the diamonds I was made from. The shearing, grating presence of the tectonic plates crashing above me and around me. When I thought all was lost, the pressure was gone.

*It is not wise to tempt the mountains, tiny Druid. You are well, and I still like you a great deal. Allow me to show you then, what the presence of the precious metals you seek looks like to those who are like me.*

The world shifted, and the sense of connection and oneness I felt with the earth opened wide. It felt like I was looking at the night sky. The smatterings of golden and silver-hued dust off to the far north of my current position took my breath away. The clumps and clusters of the little stars looked like they were galaxies against a backdrop of the blackened earth. There were small bits of gray, green, yellow, and even a little blue one further out from me toward the western portion of the mountain.

*Thank you, Primordial Earth Elemental. I appreciate your favor and your wisdom.* I tried to sound as grateful as I truly was. It's not every day someone opens your mind to new experiences.

*You are welcome. Be wary on your travels, and remember—even the smallest pebble can bring a mountain down on something larger. Goodbye for now, tiny Druid.*

The presence of the Primordial faded from me, and I surged out of the ground, rocketing into the air toward the nearest speck of light. The green faded for a moment, but as soon as I touched the mountain again, it was visible once more.

I made it about halfway up the mountain to my destination just before I felt my elemental form beginning to fade. I quickly shot a set of five earthen spears into the stone and perched myself on top of them just in time to stop my fall.

I heard Vrawn call from below, "Are you alright?"

"Yeah!" I hollered back. "Be right down!"

I looked down; the trees had become a large shape of green below me. Once I had an idea of where I needed to be, I leaped from the side of the mountain, shifted into the owl, and coasted back down to Vrawn.

"That was rather quick," she observed. She had a small pack in her hands that she was rifling through as she sat on the ground. "Come and join me for a snack?"

I smiled at the thought of food and sat across from her. I pulled out an iron ingot and began to think of ways I could shape it. I could just enchant it with fire and then try and shape it.

No, the heat would still fuck up my hands. What did I have spell-wise that I could use to make things with?

Okay, I wanted to help, but I hadn't really thought it fully though until just now. We needed this shit done.

What if... What if I used... That was it!

I used Stone Weapon to make a shield with hundreds of thin, hollow spikes facing away from the guard portion. Then I sat it on my knees before pulling out the iron ingots and sitting them next to me on the ground. I brought one into my hands and began to channel flame aspected mana into my hands around it until the molten metal began to drip down into one of the holes. I took my time, ensuring that the metal didn't drip elsewhere. It would be shitty to waste any of the resources at my disposal.

After about ten minutes of constant heating, there were dozens of holes filled from the first ingot. My mana was recharging well, but I did myself a favor and cast Aspect of the Owl. My wisdom rose by ten, and my perception of the world around me was much deeper.

I spent another twenty minutes making minor adjustments to my work so that it was just about as efficient as I could think to do it. Once I was finished with my fourth ingot, I cast Winter Blade and used the icy weapon to cool the heated iron carefully. I was cautious with it, hoping that the superheating and super-cooling wouldn't fuck me and ruin the nails.

I noticed one beginning to grow a little brittle on the right-hand side of the shield. I brought the weapon into my hands and began to superheat it with my flame aspected mana, and the water dripped into the lip of the shield cooling the metal. This was a good turn out, so I decided to let the items cool for the minute that the weapon would stay corporeal out of my hands.

"Once that shield disappears, will you gather the nails for me? I'm going to try to go up and see if I can't get to the ore that's beneath the stone." Vrawn looked at me intently, tossed me an apple, and patted the ground. "All I need is a little bit of it, and then I am freed up. I'm trying to work as fast as I can. I promise."

"Eat that first; then I will gather the nails." I couldn't believe I had forgotten to actually eat. Her knowing look said it all. She knew I might. How was it that she seemed to just *get* me. My scatterbrained, sometimes idiotic ideas and willingness to jump to people's aid without so much of a thought for myself, and here she was reminding me to eat.

I was going to have to make this up to her.

"You got it." I sat down and bit into the fruit. It was just as juicy as it would have been at home. "So, you had some family? What was your childhood like?"

"I was taken in by an army general who found me as a child. She raised me, her own daughter, and another unfortunate youth. She was truly good to me. That's why I mesh well with Zhavron and the recruits. I lived this life at one time, but it was too much for me. I was too soft for army life. Not harsh enough."

"I can understand that." I nodded as I munched on my apple. "I was in a unit of my own for a while. Nothing big. I was trained to fight if needed. Nothing like you had to do, I'm sure. And you're okay doing this now?"

"I am." She looked wistfully at the mountain in front of us. "I grew up in a place similar to here. We would train in the summers near a mountain range like this. When I moved to the city, I could only admire from a distance. Being so close now? I think I will be doing a fair bit of climbing and hiking on my days off."

I chuckled. "I had friends like that. I never understood the need to hike and be outside like that, but to each their own."

"You did not like the outdoors as a child?" Her head tilted to the left, her hair wobbling to the left as well.

"Where I'm from, it's not as beautiful as it is here. It's not safe, or well, it wasn't safe for a child. Now? As strong as I am, I could easily defend myself," I said truthfully, but I avoided the biggest truth. I finished my apple, dug into the ground, and buried the core. I patted the ground and packed it before casting Regrowth.

I felt the magic seep into the earth, and the core took root. Ever since my last meeting with Mother Nature, I had felt closer to the earth. To nature in general. It was kind of nice.

"A tree will grow here, and it will grow apples too," I said lamely after I noticed her eyeing me.

I stood and motioned to the nails laying on the ground. "I'll be back in about five minutes."

I shifted before she could say anything and flew to my perch on the side of the mountain. I was far enough from the tree line and her that I didn't need to worry about any debris hitting her.

Not unless a landslide happened, but something told me that the stone would hold.

I assumed my earth elemental form and flexed my shoulders before I began beating my fists against the sides of the mountain. I threw myself into it, my arms pumping like I was swinging sledgehammers fired out of shotguns. It was slow progress at first, the green dots I saw growing ever so slightly. I took a second, splayed my fingers out on my left hand, and dragged it down before me then punched with my right.

The clawed strike dug in, and the punch knocked the openings a little wider. This was going to take a while. I took the five minutes to get as far as I could, then rested for a second before I jumped down and repeated the process of making nails once more. Vrawn was quiet and observant. She looked at me with interest and got close enough to see everything I was doing in greater detail.

I cooled these ones the same way, then hopped back up to the mountain to chip away. The green dusting turning more and more into a bush, then into a tree of green. I could see it just below the surface after this run, and when I dropped back down to Vrawn this time, she spoke.

"I think the way you did it with the ingots last time was better. Some of the first batches of nails were a little brittle and snapped. The mold you made works well, though. It was a very clever design. May I offer a little more though?"

I had to admit, I was intrigued. "Please?"

She indicated a spot on the ground that I dug out, roughly the size of the shield and just deeper than the molds.

"Now, fill it with water, and then cool both the bottom and tops," She brought out a nail for me to inspect. The pointed portion was still hot to the touch. "This way, you will cool both evenly."

I melted two Winter Blades into the makeshift cooling trough before I turned my attention to the ingots and molding. It seemed to be going a lot smoother this time, and I had run out of ingots so what I had left would have to do. I cooled the top as I did the bottom with the help of the water trough and kept a hand on the shield so they would cool properly.

"I think that will work much better, Vrawn—thank you." She ducked her head once in acknowledgment, and I smiled. "Let me guess, you aren't all that used to praise?"

"I am not." She shrugged. "'When you know well what you are doing, in the heat of battle, the care of a weapon or a generous moment—thanks is not required. Only knowing that what you have done is just, needed, or right. That knowledge is the reward. That is what mother used to say to us. I have not known how to take a compliment or praise since then."

I laughed, and she seemed stung. I held a hand out and lifted her chin. "I wasn't laughing at you, I promise. I was laughing because I had kind of the same mentality when I was growing up. The people who raised me, my aunt and uncle, were some of the coolest people. They'd give you the shirts off their backs and a boot apiece if they had it. And they'd do it with a smile. They always taught me that taking care of others, being a generous soul, wasn't just to make others like you or to show what you had—but that it made you feel better for having done it.

"They taught me that through actions, never words, and to be honest, I saw it in everything they did. Always there to help a friend. Always giving even when they didn't have it, or couldn't afford it. They helped make me into the man that I am today. I have no idea where I would be without them having supported me and taught me everything they did."

Her lips were parted slightly, and I noticed how close we were. I dropped my hand and looked anywhere but her expectant gaze. My cheeks burned thoroughly.

"I... uh... I should go do the digging thing." I glanced at her, and her eyes sparkled in the fading light of day. "I'll be back soon."

"I will be here," she replied with a knowing look that made my cheeks burn hotter.

I all but sprinted from the spot and took to the air once

more in owl form. I risked a glance down at the woman watching me and damn near collided with the spikes I had used as a foothold.

*You moon-struck fool!* the owl instincts screeched at me mentally. *Pay more attention to your surroundings, or you'll kill yourself.*

*Wimp,* I growled back and alighted on my perch. I shifted back out of my owl form, then tried looking at the stone to see if I could spy what I was trying to dig to. I saw something dark but, other than that, nothing that I could try and pull out by hand here.

I took my earth elemental form and began clawing my way around the ore. I wasn't focusing on completely clearing it of dirt—just freeing it from its home.

I dug faster than I thought that I could. It could have been that now there was some space between the vein of ore and the stone itself, or it could have been my embarrassment at having been so close to Vrawn.

Not that being that close to a woman like her would normally be a bad thing—but fuck, man. I resolved to stay faithful, and the second Maebe is gone, I have her breathing down my neck?

I took my frustrations at myself out on the stone and relieved another foot of the metal within. I felt the form beginning to wane as fast as the sun on the horizon. It was time to cut through this shit and get back. I brought my clawed fingers against the metal, and it took me scraping well after my elemental form reverted. It was taking so long, and I didn't dare use any of my real weapons to sever it.

I cast Stone Weapon and made a battle pick—a larger, deadlier version of a pickaxe that a miner would use and began to hammer away with the sharpened pick portion. The hole I was in was too small for me to use my aspects, so it was the old fashioned way that had to do. It was a little easier, but the stone began to give way after a few swings, and I had to switch sides.

It took having to summon another two picks in the same manner, but I got through it. It was heavy, ungodly so, but I was able to toss it into my inventory before I leaped down from the side of the mountain, shapeshifting mid-fall and flying the rest of the way down.

I landed in front of Vrawn and smiled. "I think I've got what we need. I don't know what it is, but I got it. You ready to go back?"

"Do we need to go immediately?" she asked softly. "I would like to see the stars, if at all possible."

A simple request, and with me having finished the nails so soon, I did have the time. Plus, the stars out here were gorgeous. What was the harm in a couple of friends enjoying a scenic view?

Yeah, yeah. I know. A lot could happen. But maybe this could be how I let her down gently, you know? Let her know what's up? That I'm not comfortable with doing this without Maebe knowing. Or without me even knowing what I wanted? Yeah. We could look at the stars.

But that's *it*. I am a classy broad, damn it. She hadn't even hinted at treating me like a real lady.

"Okay, sure," I thought for a second, then added, "but not here. I know a place. Let me carry you in the collar again."

She smiled and reached out, funneling into the collar again. I sighed, then shifted into my owl form once more and flitted into the air. I rose up until the plateaus of the mountainous ridge beneath me were visible—high above the trees, the view unspoiled.

I landed and willed Vrawn out of the item around my throat. As she solidified, she glanced at me, then at the stars above us.

Her mouth worked in silence for a moment, seemingly speechless.

I smiled despite my earlier reservations. Bringing someone here would have been a nice thing to do if they enjoyed seeing stars. I found myself wondering how Maebe would like the view.

She was Celestial herself—would the stars reflect along her

skin, the way that they did my fur? I looked down at my black fur, the white specks that represented the stars in the heavens all over the sky above. They gathered in spans and galaxies that I didn't recognize but were still captivating. I raised my gaze to see a star twinkling in the distance, eons having likely passed before the light ever graced these skies. Then it went dark. In the loss, I noted that the lights of the stars around it began to shine brighter in its absence.

How like us had that been? Losing Balmur, having to get stronger so that we could get him out of the Hells.

I found myself wondering if we failed here and War won out, how many of these stars would fade as the one had? How many of them would cease to exist, and it would be because we couldn't hold the line and beat them?

"You are such a striking figure in the silvered paint of the moon, Master Zeke," Vrawn's voice posed, breaking me from my internal dialogue. I looked over, and she was seated against a rocky shelf that had grass growing beneath it. "It is quite inspiring."

"Oh?" My left eyebrow raised in response. "How do you mean?"

"Fur black as night, and eyes of steely blue,
The face of a fox and a heart that is true.
Mind well your steps depraved evildoers, minions of War,
For he who hunts you will ride and search from shore to shore.
Embodiment of darkness, closed off always and cloaked in gray,
Stars pulse to life at the edge of his sword, deals with demons hold over him no sway.
Flee the darkness, weakest foes, minions of War,
For his justice is swift, you are never safe—no help you can implore.
Beard of dark flame, stout and strong,
Axes flash swiftly and sure, seeking what is wrong.
Mind well the shadows, defilers, minions of War,

For it is he who strikes when least expected, and you'll breathe
no more.
Servant of light and mixed blood with love bore,
His sword and shield will aid, his faith will restore.
Move swiftly, sinners, minions of War,
For he is retribution coming, there is nowhere left to hide
anymore.
Children of Dragons, black and green,
One who is one, and the other on wings unseen.
Do not close your eyes, cowards, minions of War,
For they will ensure together, that settled is the score.
Frigid and cold, nothing can escape his eye,
Cunning and dashing, his many arrows fly.
Accept your fate, the hunted, minions of War,
For his is the bow that will bring the end,
until thoughts of minions are no longer fore."

My fur stood on end as she finished the last stanza of the
poem. "Where did that come from?"

She blinked and shook her head with a small shrug. "Sometimes I have been known to spontaneously burst into poetry
when inspired."

"Vrawn, there were things that you couldn't have known in
there, things that described my entire party." I took a step
toward her. "How did you know about the beard of dark
flame?"

"I don't know. These things come to me, and I just speak
them. If I don't, they begin taking over my mind until I do."

"This has happened before?" I pressed.

"Yes, many times." She looked away suddenly, and I saw a
glimmer against her cheek in the moonlight.

"Fuck," I whispered before I came to kneel beside her. "Hey,
I didn't mean to press you so hard. It's just that—I don't know
—the fact that those things were said out loud. It kind of
freaked me out a little. I'm not mad."

Her bottom lip quivered a bit. "It wasn't you. It was a

memory of the last time this happened." She took a steadying breath and began anew, "It was four years ago, while I was still with the army. I was a sergeant in my elder brother, Kelvorn's command. Before a battle, a bit of inspiration struck, and in it...in it, Kelvorn fell, but the battle was won."

Something clicked for me then. "You have prophetic moments related to you and others through poetry."

"What makes you think that?" There was a look of slight panic on her face.

"The 'inspiration' comes from somewhere else, and what you say happens." She began wringing her hands together nervously. "And I take it that it wasn't actually that you were too soft to be in the army that you are no longer there. They probably thought that since you had foretold it—you would know how to prevent it."

Tears fell from her eyes now, her attempt to remain stoic gone. The façade shattered.

"They put me with him," she sobbed. "They put me with his guard that day to ensure that I could keep him alive. I watched this giant of a human with a dire bear pelt charge my brothers and sisters-in-arms and defeat them soundly, and when he came to Kelvorn, the two of them fought. Kelvorn won, but a soldier with a bow from the opposing army shot him in the heart as they were fleeing."

It took her a moment to collect herself as the memory seemed to sweep over her, flooding the memories back into her mind.

"Their army was destroyed utterly—the soldiers under Kelvorn's banner and command were worked into a frenzy over their beloved commander's demise.

"They couldn't forgive me for not knowing how he would die." Her voice was going a little hoarse, so I sat beside her and pulled her against my chest. I hated it when people cried around me, man. It was the worst. And what she was reliving... fuck.

"I held him, as the light drained from his eyes—I looked

him in the eyes, and he told me that it wasn't my fault." A wracking shudder took her body as more tears dropped like a waterfall from her eyes. "I lost my brother and all my friends that day. Mother barely talks to me, and the only person I had left was my sister."

I held her there, sobbing into my chest and shoulder, and just listened. I didn't say anything at first—the pain she was feeling in that moment would have made any kind of comfort I tried to offer seem placating. So I just held her and lightly stroked her head with my fingertips until she began to calm down.

When her breathing had evened from the hiccups that come with heavy weeping, I squeezed her gently.

"You know, you have more friends now," I offered aloud. "You have Giledt, who damn near started a fight with me over your honor. You have me, and you know that I'm not going to treat you differently because of this. And now, you have Vilmas. And she's a recluse. Hell, it even seems like Rowland respects you."

"He's a nice person," she sniffled. "He has great taste in alcohol."

I laughed, the merriment shaking my body and her head a little. "Yeah, the man has some crazy taste in booze. Just be careful of his homemade stuff. It'll knock you on your ass."

"I could use some of that right now." She sighed. When she lifted her head from my body, I could see that her cheeks and eyes were puffy from crying.

"Me too." I looked into her hazel eyes, the gold sparkling in the moonlit evening and smiled. "You gonna be okay?"

She nodded and threw her left arm around my shoulder to pull me close against her in a hug. She whispered, "Thank you," against my neck. I returned her hug in kind.

Sometimes, you gotta hug it out.

She lessened her grip around my shoulders, and I relieved mine and went to let go before she pulled my chin toward her face and pressed her lips awkwardly against my muzzle in a gentle, heartfelt kiss.

I started and stiffened instantly. Her cheeks were a little more red than from the crying, and she looked at me uncertainly.

"I'm grateful for your affections," I started. "I really am. I just don't think I can return them right now, at least not in the way that you want."

She looked at the ground for a moment, then back at me with a smile. "Thank you for being honest with me."

"Of course." I felt a small tug on my heartstrings. "It's not like I don't find you attractive. I do. Wildly so—I mean, you're beautiful. It's just that, I'm very new to this kind of situation, and I'm not sure what is needed. It's not fair to you, it's not fair to Maebe, and it isn't fair to me. You know?"

"I do." She seemed crestfallen, her shoulders slumping slightly, but she lifted her chin and smiled softly at me. "I hope I get to meet this woman someday."

"She will," I heard Maebe's voice from the shadows. I looked behind Vrawn and saw her shadowy form separate from the inky black of the sky. "I had come to tell you that my time-line has been bumped up. I will return in another hour or so my time, so it will likely be tomorrow for you."

"Awesome!" I took a quick second to mentally kick myself. "Uh, you do know that—"

"You did not initiate this, I know. We will speak again when I come." Her figure came closer to me, hips swaying seductively even as a shade of herself. "Until we meet again, Zeke."

The shadows passed through me and dissipated coolly against my fur.

"Who were you speaking with?" Vrawn asked with evident confusion on her face. Her features seemed to have regained a little composure, but she also looked like she was ready to scrap. Her arms and shoulders were tense, and her eyes darted through the area.

"Queen Maebe." My brows furrowed as I tried to think of

the meaning behind her words. "She says she will be here tomorrow and that you will meet her. Let's go home."

"Okay." Vrawn frowned and stood with my help. I took a deep breath, about to teleport us home when I caught the scent of something dead. It was a strong scent.

"You smell that?" I looked to the Orcish woman, and she frowned, her nose wrinkling a little as she scented the air. It was funny, and I smiled, but her answer made my stomach drop. "I do—and it's close."

We turned toward the wind and began moving closer to the scent. The plateau we were on currently had several paths that led to lower levels and climbable portions of ground to other secluded spots. What caught our attention was on one such slope there was a corpse, just lying there.

"That's odd," Vrawn mumbled as she crouched and moved a little in front of me. She took a stone and flung it accurately, hitting the shoulder with it. Nothing happened. "Suppose someone was attacked up here? No one has been reported missing."

I was about to respond when a low, feral growl caught my attention above. Vrawn shoved me aside. "Look out!"

A severely malnourished mountain lion with half of the face chewed off crashed into the ground between the lieutenant and me, scrambling for purchase on some of the loose stone. Three more corpses began to file up the pathway from below; the one on the ground reached out faster than I thought possible and snatched at Vrawn's leg.

She suddenly had a knife in her hand and slid it between the bone and sinew, expertly severing it so that the hand let go, then looked to me. "Behind you!"

I didn't bother with a weapon at that moment but cast Aspect of the Ursolon and whipped my now-larger hand into the creature's face. Its momentum carried it through my attack, but the connection turned it just enough that the mountain lion sailed into one of the undead behind me.

I turned to see Vrawn pull a naked longsword from her

inventory and begin a dance of weapons that looked severely intimidating.

She parried their clumsy attacks with the dagger in her left hand and sliced off arms and legs with the sword easily.

The mountain lion had untangled itself from the fallen undead and padded quietly behind Vrawn. I growled low in my throat and rushed forward to grab it by the scruff of the neck. I lifted mightily, and as I did, a flash of metal severed the head of the dead beast from its shoulders then moved on the others.

*Hot damn, she's great!* I thought to myself as I watched her move. I was too far from the others to send for help, and it seemed like we had this.

The corpse on the ground started to try and grab her again, but I stomped on its head with a satisfying crunch. I finally let myself free. Vrawn sliced and moved around two of the dead, the swiftly rotting corpses of the fallen leaving little evidence of their existence behind save for a dusty residue and no experience. I made a knife with my right hand, pressing my fingers together, and stabbed it straight. My clawed hand speared right through its throat, the spine severed, and it fell limp against my hand.

I pulled my hand back, and it fell, decomposing as I turned to see Vrawn lash out with her sword and dagger between both of her foes. The sword cut cleanly through the gaping mouth of the undead on her right, and the dagger severed the spinal cord and dropped the dead fucker.

"That was a good bit of exercise for the evening, yes?" Vrawn's dainty tusks flashed in the moonlight as she put her weapons close to her sides, not away but resting her arms.

I reached out and touched her shoulder, casting Teleport a second later.

# CHAPTER FOUR

*We have undead out roaming the forest,* I called to the others through our earrings.

*What?!* Jaken growled half asleep.

Muu came awake long enough to say, *Shhhh.*

*Get. Up!* Yohsuke bellowed. *Explain, Zeke.*

I filled them in on what happened, the basic bits and not all the emotional bits.

*Tavern in five,* James grunted tiredly.

The others were gathered around a table inside the tavern when Vrawn and I arrived.

"So we have an undead issue?" Jaken looked the two of us over. We were largely uninjured; I had some scratches but was at full health.

"It was one small party and a mountain lion," Vrawn stated. "I don't think that it is an issue so much as it is a cause for concern. This wall needs to be finished. Sooner rather than later."

"I agree," I grumbled, my thoughts taking me back a little ways to our first real quest here in Brindolla. "You know, it could be the fort."

"We killed the lich though, man." Bokaj shook his head in disbelief.

"We did." Jaken nodded.

"But we didn't break his phylactery." I sighed, then sighed again at some of the vacant looks I received. "It's an item that a lich binds their soul to, and they can use it to come back. So long as the item is safe, so are they."

"So what're we lookin' for a doll or something?" James yawned loudly after asking.

"I don't know, but it will likely either be well hidden or on the lich's person," Yohsuke intervened. "I think I remember a game that had a couple liches in it. Finding those things was a bitch."

"That all there was?" Muu blinked at us sleepily. "Cause unless we're going there tomorrow, I'm going to bed."

"We're going as soon as our business here is concluded," Yohsuke beat me to the punch. "It wouldn't hurt to investigate, but like Vrawn said, the wall comes first. Get some rest, and let's kick some ass."

"Maebe's going to be here soon as well, possibly tomorrow at the latest, so we have that to look forward to as well," I advised the others, and they smiled. It would be good for her to be back.

Vrawn tapped the table as we were getting ready to move on about our business of sleep and rest. "Please, do not mention this to the villagers. I am going to tell the guard, then Captain Zhavron, but the village would panic if they knew. Tell who you believe may need to know, but until the wall is set, wait."

"You got it, and thanks for tonight. You're a hell of a fighter." I smiled at her, relaxed and genuine. It was the truth.

She blushed as she left but nodded her thanks to us and fled to spread the word.

The rest of the night passed without incident, though I slept restlessly. Breakfast was interesting, for sure. Though they knew how things had ended, my friends still wanted to give me shit about having Vrawn alone with me for so long .

The assholes had smarmy looks on their faces all through the meal, even after I said that nothing happened. Oh, I'd get my vengeance; their time would come. Rest assured.

They'd never see it coming. It'll be like, so surprising. We'll just be hanging out and then BAM!

A platinum Dragon nukes the area and everyone dies. The end.

Nah, it wouldn't be that disastrous—but it would be *mightily* inconvenient.

I walked back to Vilmas's new room still chewing a mouthful of bacon and carrying a mug of some kind of local nut and berry tea the chef's wife swore by. I hadn't tried it yet, but it did smell decidedly earthy, so I'd let it cool a little. I also carried a plate of food for the enchanter. I didn't know what she liked, but I got her a little of everything. I'd take orders if needed.

I knocked on the door lightly, and the small woman peeked out the doorway. She didn't look like she had gotten any sleep; her eyes were red, and she had tiny little bags under them.

"Is it morning already?" she asked before stifling a yawn.

I passed her the plate of food and walked in after she opened the door a little wider. I found Vrawn sleeping awkwardly on the bed with her feet hanging off the end. She snored softly, her mouth hanging open just enough to show her teeth and tusks. I saw a shimmer on the side of her jaw closest to us and noted that it was drool. Oh, this was like all the anime... I clearly never watched.

Stop judging me, damnit.

"Was she why you look like you've been awake all night?" I asked with concern. I know that Vilmas was new to the whole friend thing, and her previous lifestyle of solitude may have meant she was uncomfortable having someone sleep in the same room, let alone the same bed.

"Vrawn? No!" she whispered as she eyed the Orc. "She stayed up with me to make sure I was okay after she returned from your midnight stroll. Seemed that she didn't want to be alone either. She lasted well into the morning while I was working on the designs and notes, but she passed out eventually. It's like living with my eight brothers and sisters all over. I missed it—but I need my space to perfect my craft. Sacrifices, eh?"

I won't lie. The number of siblings she had was impressive. Nine kids? Damn. That's a clan of their own, alright.

"So it took that long to come up with a suitable design and notes on the intent needed to make this wall a viable defense?"

"I'm a bit of a perfectionist." Vilmas blushed a little. "Never did like to go into a job with little information. Remember—it never hurts to do a little research on the active and passive effects you want to enchant into an item."

I saluted with my now empty hand. I took a sip of the mug in my other hand and damned near died. It tasted amazing. The bitter, earthy base set the tone for the drink with a slightly peanut-like bouquet, but the berries offered a slight, sweet high-light to the drink that gave it a perky note. The best part of all that?

I no longer felt groggy. I felt alert and aware.

"Vilmas, drink some of this," I offered her the cup, and she looked at it oddly.

"I don't like to drink after people," she began. I gave her a hard stare, and she took it. "If I get sick, I wi—"

"Drink it!" I barked the order a little louder than I meant.

I heard a creak and groan from the bed, and Vrawn was suddenly standing in front of me with a wickedly curved blade at my throat. Her eyes weren't focused, but her normally serene and friendly demeanor was gone. The only thing I felt from her at that moment was a sense of bloodlust and murderous intent.

My first instinct was to let the beast howling inside me out, the red ring of my vision signaling the beginnings of my trans-formation into my lycanthrope hybrid form, but every fiber of my being seemed to understand better than I did at that moment that if I made a minute mistake, some kind of hostile motion, she would cut me. So I stood frozen like an angry deer in the headlights.

"Vrawn, it's Zeke," Vilmas's mousy voice squealed from behind the Orc warrior. "It's just Zeke!"

Vrawn blinked a few times then looked at me in confusion. "What time is it?"

"It's a couple hours after sunup," I offered, my body still frozen. "Can you take the knife away from my throat?"

"Hmm?" She looked at her hand and grunted. "Oh. Yes."

"This is *amazing!*" Vilmas gushed under her breath. "Vrawn! Vrawn—try this."

Vrawn sniffed the concoction and shrugged before taking a sip. Her eyebrows shot up, and she ended up finishing the rest of the drink.

"That was delicious. Where did you get it?" She asked after licking her lips in delight. "Is there more?"

"The chef's wife, and I hope so." I smiled. "Let me go see before we get started. You two stay here. I'll be right back."

I took the mug from Vrawn and smiled reassuringly at Vilmas who still looked a little worried.

Once I was clear of the room, I heard Vilmas begin speaking to Vrawn, "You know, I'm not too familiar with this whole 'friendship' thing, but I don't know if putting a blade to someone else's throat is a very friendly thing…"

Her voice faded, and I came back to myself with a hand around my throat, checking for injuries. There were none, thankfully, but if she had wanted to kill me, I'd have been hard pressed. I needed to work on my reflexes to see if I could not throw myself into those kinds of dissatisfying positions ever again. Having already seen her fight, I wasn't comforting myself.

I stepped into the kitchens, a lovely, warm room in the tavern with pots and pans scrubbed thoroughly and hung to dry by the stove. The cook, a portly man with red cheeks, a bulbous nose, and traditional chef garb covering his body, hummed his way around the room as if on a cloud. It was surprising that Yohsuke wasn't here, but I had a mission.

"Hey, bud!" I called to the man; he turned and smiled.

"Ah, Master Zekiel!" His accent was almost as comically and insultingly French as I'd ever heard in my life. Not that there's anything wrong with the French. Just that it seems like a lot of awesome chefs are French.

Okay, I was jealous.

"What can I do for you, my friend!" He bustled toward me. "Ma chère, Vrawn! Welcome, hungry?"

I looked behind me to see Vrawn standing there sheepishly. Her large looming figure taking up the doorway. "I was coming to see about some food?"

"Chef's food is good. Glad Yohsuke learned from you! I was actually here about that tea." He looked confused, so I elaborated, "You know, the one that your wife made?"

He was busy piling food on to a platter for Vrawn when he seemed to get what I was saying. He pressed the platter into her hands with a smile and patted on her shoulder before hurrying toward the stove.

"Ah!" He removed the pot from the stove and moved toward the back door with a sad sigh. "I told her the people here were particular about their drinks. I should have dumped it and served proper tea myself, eh? The poor woman—"

"If you dump that anywhere other than a cup, I will throw you out of this kitchen," I growled. He stopped, clearly taken aback. "It's amazing! It's delicious, and it helps get rid of fatigue. Have you tried it? Is there more where that came from?"

He offered the pot to me with an uncertain smile. "I have not tried it. I am very particular about my tea, but she insisted I at least offer it."

"Get more," I ordered in as friendly a way as I could. I found a mug and poured the man a sip myself before offering it to him. "Try this."

He gave it a good sniff. "Eh, smells alright."

"It really is wonderful," Vrawn offered quietly.

He smiled at her before upending the mug into his mouth and swished the liquid like he was cleaning his teeth.

His eyes closed, and he made a noise low in his throat before swallowing the drink. He blinked slowly, and his cheeks seemed to glow a deeper red than before.

"That was…magnificent," he whispered. "I shall order more. It will become a staple in my kitchen."

I thanked him for the pot and poured four cups—two for me and one each for the ladies. I put the drinks on a small tray and headed back toward Vilmas's room.

Vrawn stood waiting in the hallway. "I'm sorry for attacking you like that, then being so nonchalant about it. I know that you are a warrior, a protector, and that having someone do those things around you probably made you upset."

"Turnabout is fair play." The guilt of yesterday was playing havoc on my heart and mind. "I shouldn't have just up and taken off like that. I did everything I could to justify it to myself, and it sounded good at the moment, but it was really just me being awkward and stupid. I'm sorry, Vrawn. You know, you and I have a lot in common, but we're so vastly different as well. You're so honest and forthcoming and such a great fighter. It's awesome. You've been nothing if not honest with me, and if I'm being honest with you, I don't know how to be able to do the same without feeling like a dirtbag."

"Because of your Queen, I understand, and I find your loyalty a discerning quality." Her features seemed sad, slightly, a small pout on her full lips. "But I don't fault you for it. It has been so long since I have felt so strongly for someone that I don't know how to be subtle about it. Then again, I am an Orc —we are not known for our subtlety."

That last bit made me laugh, and that brought a chuckle to her throat as well. I looked up at her. "Can you forgive me for being an insensitive asshole?"

Her nod was kind, and she asked in return, "Can you forgive me for attacking you? You're sure you aren't mad?"

"Mad?! That was incredible!" I gushed, almost spilling the tea. "And you had done it while protecting Vilmas. I made a promise to her clan head that she would be safe here, and I have to admit that knowing you have her back too puts me at ease."

"I am happy to know that I can help you both." She led me toward the room, and before we entered together, she stopped me. "She does not know of last night, with the undead. I didn't want to worry her."

I nodded, and we walked in.

Vilmas grabbed her cup eagerly, and they both drank furtively, glancing over their cups at me. Both women looked like they felt better. I set the tray on a clear portion of the bed and looked back at them.

"So, what's the plan for this wall?" I clapped my hands together before lifting my own cup to my lips in my palms. I took a deep drink from it, the warm cup heating my palms nicely, the delicious warmth radiating throughout my body so soothing. For a moment, I just basked in the feeling the drink elicited in me. I sighed contentedly.

"Yes, I finished the intent—translated into common for you—as well as the design I have in mind. You'll be able to mimic it once I show it to you." She pulled out a sheet of parchment with a scrawling script printed on it. "Before all that, though, I need to clear the nails of your mana. Do you have them?"

I looked at Vrawn, who pulled a bucket out of her inventory and sat it before Vilmas.

"Why do you have a bucket?" My brow furrowed at the Orc woman.

"Sometimes my recruits seem to think that waking up for morning training is optional." Her tusks flashed as she bared her teeth. "It is not, and cold water is a great motivator."

I shrugged. Solid answer. Don't know what else I could have possibly expected.

Vilmas looked a few of them over, then nodded to herself. "They will do. They are a slight bit brittle, but they will work. Here, this will help."

She closed her eyes and rubbed a thumb over the side of the bucket in front of her, and a few engraved lines remained where her thumb had been. I watched a single nail appear on it, followed by a line circling it with a kind of shining portion in the center. She added her mana to the engraving, and there was a muted pop and flash.

When I looked back at the bucket of nails, each nail was shining like it had been polished, and none of them looked bad at all.

"Now, none of them will be brittle, and we can use them without worry," Vilmas explained. Once she saw my curious glance, she offered more information, "The nail itself was the focus of the enchantment, so I put it there, in the middle. I wanted the nails inside the bucket to be perfect, so, I put the shining star. Then I only want the effect to work on the nails that were contained in the bucket, so I encircled it. With my intent focused the same as with the engraving, I added my mana—and here we are."

That sounded incredibly… simple. I could probably do that. She seemed to read my expression because she was nodding at me enthusiastically.

"Okay." I waved at them. "Now, I'm assuming that we have to cleanse them of your mana too?" A thought struck me, and I looked at her. "If we take your mana away, will they revert?"

"That is an *excellent* question!" She picked up a nail and tossed it to me. "See how when we lift it from the bucket, it stays the same? This is because the change that was made was a permanent one. It changes an aspect of the item that was used in the bucket." I looked confused because I was, and she tried a different tact. "Think about it like meat. You have a skillet over a flame, right? It gets hot until you take it from the fire—the heat. However, if you add something like, say, bacon, to the skillet. The skillet transfers the heat and cooks the bacon. If you take the bacon out of the skillet, it's still cooked."

I thought I had it, so I held a hand up to halt her explanation. "So, in this case, the fire was your mana—and the enchantment—and the bucket was the skillet with the nails acting as bacon? The mana enacted a change on the bucket that permanently altered the state of the bac—nails—is that, right? And the change, once done, is irreversible?"

"Lady Shellica had the right of it, lad—you do catch on quick." She smiled at me proudly.

I heard a deep gurgle and looked over to see Vrawn blushing deeply with a hand over her stomach. She cast her gaze toward the door. "All this talk of bacon has made me hungry."

Vilmas and I chuckled as the warrior left the room to hunt down more food. She had a good deal of muscle to feed; it wasn't anything to be ashamed of, but watching her green cheeks darken as she blushed had been a highlight of the morning.

"So, if you can enact that kind of change with so simple of an enchantment, would it be possible to do the same with a person? Say, for instance, that I wanted to give a permanent point to someone's strength? I could do that—right?"

Vilmas frowned in thought before responding, "Theoretically speaking? Yes. You could, but the amount of mana it would take to make that kind of change on the person would be immense, much more than an average grandmaster would have. For people to give you mana while doing it would be hard as well. That's why if one finds such items, they are usually objects imparted by the divine."

My hopes fell a little, but learning this way was a nice break from the normal way Shellica taught me—which was like doing something with a gun to my head.

Vilmas reached into her inventory and pulled out an item that looked like a window screen, the little slits attached to a thick wooden frame. She set a clean, white sheet on the ground beneath it, then dumped a handful of nails into the thing and began to shake it.

As I watched this, a snowfall of green powder began to sprinkle down on to the sheet. Once they looked to be clear, she set them off in a drawer in the desk. Then repeated the process.

At some point early in the process, Vrawn had returned, then had grown bored enough to leave us alone once more to go for a short run. I swore I would protect her friend, and she left us with a smile.

The pile of powder was interesting. It was a light coating of glittery green at first, but as she added more nails to the sifter, the pile began to grow. It took a little over an hour to get through half the nails; then we had to dump the powder into a bag that Vilmas produced with sigils sewn into it. Once we did finish completely, she dumped the rest of the powder into the bag.

"I take it that's my mana?" I inquired with a gesture to the bag.

"It is!" She closed it and pulled the drawstring tight. "You can use it as a component to add to your enchanting projects in the future. What level is your enchanting skill now?"

"Level 34," I answered simply.

"Good, about mid-craftsman level. You'll be able to start using it to augment the depth of your enchantments and add more mana to them at adept. From there, your efficiency to use it increases again at master level."

"That's dope!" I could see that she didn't understand the word, so I just smiled and snapped my fingers as I remembered something important. "Speaking of components."

I reached into my inventory and heaved out the large chunk of green ore. I plopped it on to the bed, and Vilmas was on top of it instantly.

"Where did you find *this?!*" She hissed at me.

"In the lightning mountains. Why?"

"I've never seen it before!" She rounded on me. "We have to take this to Granda and see what it is."

"Now?" I groaned.

"No, right now—we experiment." She pulled out a heavy

chisel and hammer and began chipping the earth from the large chunk of ore.

When it was clean—well, as clean as it would be—she took the chisel and tapped off a piece the size of my thumb.

"Call Rowland with your spell and have him come to us," Vilmas ordered. I looked at her for a second, and she added, "I know you've spoken to Lady Shellica with it before because I was there a couple times and she explained it. Now do it!"

I focused on my friend Rowland before I cast Mental Message, "Hey, Rowland, it's Zeke. Can you come to the tavern real fast? I need your help."

"I'll be there in two gulps of a Dwarf's mug, lad!" the Dwarf shouted back.

I shook my head; normally the conversations took place mentally, quietly. It was like using my telepathy earring, but that had been loud as fuck.

"He's coming," I informed Vilmas.

Vrawn walked in a moment later, with a towel in her hand as she dried her head. She had changed clothes. Now she wore a pair of green trousers with a black, sleeveless top and no boots.

"Sorry, I took longer getting washed up after my morning run than I expected." She glanced over my shoulder. "That was what you were working on last night?"

"Yeah, and there's a pretty big vein of it in the mountain where I had been digging." I walked over to it and felt it. It was surprisingly warm to the touch.

I heard a roaring shout and wood splintering toward the front of the building. Vrawn flinched and sprinted toward the front.

"Vilmas, stay here!" I barked and slammed her door shut on my way out. I sprinted down the hall and brought my great axe with the invisible blade and hammer, Magus Bane, into my hands.

I ran into chaos. The door to the tavern was splintered, and chunks hung from the hinges. Chairs were upturned, a table was upended in the middle of the room, and in the center of a group of confused and scared patrons stood Rowland with a large hammer in his hands, casting his eyes wildly about and shouting.

"Where's he?" He spat. "Where's the trouble? Zeke! Lad! Where be ye?"

"I'm over here, buddy," I answered him as calmly as I could. My adrenaline had spiked, and it would take a minute to calm myself. "What's going on?"

"Ye said ye needed help in me mind, lad!" He was still looking for an enemy. "Ye never done tha' afore. So ah came a haulin' with me hammer fer a fight!"

"Shit," I grumbled. I walked toward him after I put my axe away. "I didn't need help from a fight, man. I found some ore that we didn't recognize, and we wanted your help with it."

Rowland stood there, ashamed of his actions and clearly abashed. He looked toward the counter area where Willem stood, calmly cleaning a plate.

"I'm so sorry, Willy." He sat his hammer down on its head and crossed his hands over it. "Ye know I be more than happy to pay me recompense."

"I know you are, and I know you're good for it." The Paladin came out from behind the counter, marched over to stand next to the smith, and put a comforting hand on his shoulder.

His voice was much quieter now, but I just caught what was said, "You haven't been quite the same since you were attacked, my friend. Are you alright?"

"O' course I am, lad." Rowland shrugged off Willem's hand and looked up at the taller man. "Am fine. Just a little confused. Call me lass—she'll have yer door fixed right proper afore closing tonight."

"I will. Go help Zeke." Willem began to approach the patrons as Rowland took up his hammer and began to follow me toward Vilmas's room.

Vrawn fell in behind him as we walked passed her, then into Vilmas's room we went.

"Well, what can I do fer ye? Good Mountain—what is *THAT*?!" Rowland rushed over to the large clump of green ore.

"I found it in the Lightning Mountains. Can you tell us what it is?" I walked over and sat on the bed, the rush from the prospect of fighting having passed and the adrenaline sapping a little of my will to stand around.

"I've not seen the like before, lad. I do knows that in certain climes, metals will turn green if exposed to something like the seas or high amounts of salt in the air. This? This metal is new to me."

He began to tap it with a smaller hammer he produced from his inventory. He would tap, listen, tap, listen, tap again, and listen as he moved around the piece.

"Has a good sound to it, rings true. A light metal. If ye get me to it, I can get ye a good read on what kind of properties it has."

"This will be more than enough for our purposes I think— if you want enough to make an ingot, please go ahead." Vilmas nodded at it.

I noticed it a little the last time Rowland had been near her, but now it was apparent. He looked at her, and his pupils dilated, he licked his lips, and he began to nod. But even though there was a new metal in the room, a smith's dream and nightmare—his eyes were only for Vilmas.

I cleared my throat loud enough to get his attention before speaking, "I'll help you get a chunk of it if you like, Rowland. Do you have a large file I could borrow? We need to get this bad boy turned into powder."

He blinked up at me a few times and nodded. "Aye, lad. I have one. Help me, like ye said, and I'll fetch it for ye."

Getting a good sized chunk off the ore wasn't hard. This piece was about double the size of my fist, long and wide. Rowland put the item into his inventory before bowing awkwardly at his waist to Vilmas, turning and walking out of the room swiftly.

"I'm gonna go and get that file," I smiled at the others, "as well as however many of the plaques that are finished. I'll be back shortly."

"Take your time." Vilmas smiled serenely.

"And do make sure that he is okay," Vrawn requested. "I would hate for the guard to have to become involved."

I nodded once before I exited the room and left the tavern to find the Dwarf.

I sent a call to the others over our earrings. *Everything is okay. It was Rowland, and he's not doing well, mentally, I think. Willem pointed it out. I'm gonna check on him and speak to you guys later.*

*Be safe, man,* Jaken responded. The others were silent, but it was okay. He would pass the word on or not. What was done was done. We needed to see what was going on.

It was about halfway to his smithy before I found him. He was panting a bit and leaning against the side of a home. As I came up on him from behind, he whipped around and swung his large hammer at me with a savage shout.

I ducked the blow and smacked the smaller man across the face with a light open palm. "Rowland! It's me!"

His mouth twisted in a frown of recognition. "What'd ye strike me for, lad?"

"You swung that big-ass hammer of yours at me," I growled, then stopped. His reactions, mannerisms, and even how he looked—I'd seen it before when I had been in the Marine Corps.

I could see it now; his eyes had shadows beneath them. He looked tired—yeah I know he was up all night working, but this looked different. His beady, black eyes darted about behind me distrustfully, and he had a death grip on his hammer.

"It started when we brought you back, didn't it?" I asked softly.

"What did?" He looked confused and irritated.

"Watching your back constantly. Having trouble sleeping.

The mood swings that you can't explain. Anxiety, maybe?" He stared at me hard. Then he turned and stalked away.

"It's okay to be afraid, Rowland!" I called after him. He stopped. "It's okay to not know what waits in the shadows. Those guys jumped you. Like cowards. In a fair fight—you'd have taken them."

He turned and marched toward me with a tear in his eye. "And what would ye know o' bein' afeared o' the dark? O' seein' the dancin' flames o' the forge ye once loved mean little. Needin' to beat and shape metal ta keep the nightmares at bay when ye cannae sleep? What would ye know, lad?"

His beard was a little damp as he asked the last question. I knelt down in front of him and looked him straight in the eyes. I looked as if I was looking through him and told him.

"When I was home, I would constantly have dreams about my friends and family being tortured in front of me as I watched, helplessly chained to a wall," I sighed and looked at the ground, the memories claiming me a little. "I had a shitty life at times, and I was—still am—my worst critic. I beat myself to a pulp when I can't help the people around me because I can't help myself. Because I feel sad, and I can't figure out why. So I throw myself into everything I can to just stay out of my own head."

"I know a little of what you're going through, man. I have friends, some of the best people I know—great warriors, great artists—consumed by what you feel now. They deal with it every day, just like you." I reached out and touched his chest lightly. "And just like you, they have strong hearts, but they still hurt. They don't all have friends and family who made sure the bastards who hurt them are dead."

He frowned. "Me cousin Craglim never related the tale to me. Before ye leave, could ye tell me? The lads and ye?"

I looked him in the eyes and nodded. "I'm going to do you one better. Some people dealing with what you are have pets, dogs usually, who help them cope with the things they're feeling and help them work through it."

"I don't have time to train a dog, lad." Rowland waved dismissively.

"Let me see what I can do, okay?" He looked at me skeptically. "If you don't like it after a couple days, no hard feelings, and I'll even see if Vilmas would like to have dinner with you?"

"Deal!" Rowland held out his hand, and I shook it.

"Give me an hour or so, and I'll be back to the smithy to see what's what, okay?"

He grumbled and got on his way. I shifted into my owl form and took off for the forest.

After about five minutes of breakneck flight, I set down in a small glade before shifting back and sitting on the ground in the center.

In Druidic, I prayed out loud to Mother Nature.

"Mother, I hope you have a moment to spare. I wondered if you have any creatures in the area who would be willing to befriend a Dwarf in need. He suffers from something that eats at his mind, and he needs a friend to love him and comfort him. Someone smart. Lovable. Who doesn't mind the heat of a forge? Someone he can trust and befriend."

I heard the trees shifting in the breeze. Birdsong and the flutter of wings in the air above me and out around me made me open my eyes. The trees here were beautiful. Their bark was untouched, despite the fresh deer or elk tracks.

I heard a rustle behind me, the faintest sound I had heard since arriving here, and cast Nature's Voice for the first time today—just in case.

A small, vulpine figure limped out of the bushes behind me; her fur was a deep red, deeper still around her injured left hind leg. I reached out slowly and cast Regrowth on the fox kit.

"Hello, little one," I whispered softly. "What happened?"

"Snake," it whined. "It attacked my nest while mother was gone. My sister... she didn't make it."

My anger flared, and I scooped the little creature into my arms.

*I know that you oversee all nature, but damn Mother, that was cruel,* I growled inside my head.

*I give, I take. All my children must eat, and not all make it away from a predator. I gave her my blessing. Her mother was taken by a mountain lion a day or so ago. She is an orphan now. Take her to this friend of yours and explain the situation.*

The response—while biting—was true. I still couldn't help being a little pissed about it though. As I sat with her, I explained where I would be taking her.

"Will there be food?" she asked shyly.

"There will, and my friend Rowland will help take great care of you." I thought a moment about how best to put this and opted for honestly. "But he needs caring for too. See, he needs someone smart and lovable like you to help him. Some people hurt him really badly, and while he's not injured anymore, his mind still hurts. And his heart."

"His heart hurts?" Her large ears perked up. "I've never heard of someone's heart hurting. Does he need a friend?"

"He does need a friend." I smiled, her innocence was adorable. "What's your name?"

"My name is Min." Her little face fell. "It's what mother and sister would call me."

"Does it remind you of them? If it hurts, we can call you something else." I patted her head. "If you're ready, I'll put you into my collar, and I'll take you to meet Rowland."

"You won't eat me?" she asked nervously.

"No, baby, I won't eat you. I swear it to all the gods and Mother Nature." Her eyes widened at me for mentioning her deity.

She looked uncertain but tapped the stone with her nose, and I willed her into the collar. A short while later, I was landing in front of the smithy. The sun was high in the sky by now, meaning noon had arrived.

I walked into the forge in my fox-man form and called for the smith. Jaken walked out, his face covered in soot, and his clothes were filthy.

Rowland waddled out of the forge area behind him. "Yer in

luck, lad—we just finished the last of the plaques. Got a hunnerd and twenty-five."

"Awesome, you guys!" I shook both of their hands. "Rowland, I need you to clean your hands, then come back in here. I have a friend I'd like you to meet."

To his credit, Rowland seemed to be in a better mood, so he just did as I asked. He tossed his apron aside on to the counter, then went out back to a trough of water to wash his hands.

I turned to Jaken who looked at me curiously. "He has PTSD man, bad. You noticed it yet?"

"I had been wondering why he smacked me with a hammer last night when I came back in from taking a leak." He rubbed his head at the memory. "There are other things I've noticed, sure, but I thought he was just getting cagey with wanting to work after not being able to. Makes sense now. Who's the friend you mentioned?"

"I found a fox kit who lost her family to natural causes, and she wouldn't have been okay on her own." I eyed around the corner.

Rowland had dunked his whole head into the trough and came back out sputtering. He raised an arm and took a whiff of it before grunting and looking away.

"Looks like he's taking a hobo bath," I grunted at Jaken.

"Does that a lot—I don't think he's gone home since the attack, man." He walked around me and stood there, watching his trainer. "The place was a complete mess when we first came back. Took a whole hour to get it somewhat back to rights."

I looked at him oddly, and he sighed. "Before I could close my eyes and know where every single tool was by touch alone. It was that perfect. At first, I thought it was just because he was trying to get back into the swing of things and didn't want to worry us. I left it alone because he asked me to. Now? I'm not so sure I should have."

My eyebrows raised. Shit.

"Alright, lad. I even changed me shirt. Who am I meetin'?"

"Close your eyes," I ordered with a grin. I loved giving

surprises.

"Oh, fer the Mountain's sake, lad." He grimaced and followed my order.

I called Min out of my collar and pointed to Rowland, her large eyes taking him in before I gently spoke, Nature's Voice still in effect, "This is him."

She looked at him curiously and began to snuff close to him. I crossed the couple feet between us and pulled Rowland's hand up and out so that Min could step on to it.

The Dwarf's eyes shot open at the touch, and he looked at her in confusion, then at me in outrage.

"Ye kitnapped a wee baby?" He pulled her protectively toward his burly chest.

"I'll explain." I raised my hands to fend off his accusations.

I told them both the story about what I had done, what had happened to her mother and sister, and Rowland had taken to petting her gently the entire time.

"So she's like me own daughter then? Got ye no ma, no kin o' yer own?" He held her up to his face, and Min yipped at him. "Well, I cannae very well leave ye out there on yer own, can I now? Ye said her name was Min?"

The little fox kit whined sadly at the sound of her name.

"It was what her family called her," I explained. "It kinda makes her a little sad to be reminded of the loss."

"Well, there be no shame in loss, little lassie." Rowland stroked her head for a moment longer in thought. "I wouldn't want ye to lose yer heritage, but I don't want ye sad, neither. How about I call ye Mini? Cause yer such a wee thing?"

The kit seemed to think about it for a second, then butted her head against Rowland's cheek.

"I like it. He smells funny," she observed as she shoved her nose into his beard.

"If you don't need me, Rowland, I can take those plaques off your hands and head back to the inn." A mischievous grin came over my face. "I'll go ahead and put that good word in for you too, but you'll need a proper bath before the date."

"Take care of him, lad." The Dwarf motioned to Jaken. "I'm off to get Mini something to eat. Poor thing's skin and bones. Gotta get her fed right up, we do."

He set the fox on the ground, and the kit looked to me; then with a flick of her tail, she rushed after Rowland for food.

"I've got them all in my inventory, so I can just go back to the inn with you." Jaken took his apron off and hung it on a nail just inside the doorway to the forge. "Come on."

"The file, we'll need that too," I let him know. "Rowland already agreed to let me borrow it."

Jaken popped back into the forge area and grabbed a file the size of a sword with a hilt almost like one.

After that, it was a quick walk to the tavern, but on the way, Jaken told me what the others were up to.

Muu was resupplying and using his time here to train his skinning and leatherworking. He was trying to work through his lack of knowledge and wanted to be left to it, so I didn't have a chance to tell him about the Bear-kin armorers. Damn. They'd love him.

James had been researching several different islands that the Dragon could be on with little luck so far.

Bokaj was trying to write songs because he had heard that it was possible to use the music to buff the party. That was wild as fuck to me.

Yohsuke was in charge of all the food, duh.

Jaken had been balls deep in helping us with the metalworking.

"Any word from Maebe yet, man?" he asked curiously.

"Not yet, but it should be later tonight." We walked into the tavern.

The broken door had been removed, and I assumed that Rowland's daughter, Sarah, had come to take measurements already. The girls were in the room giggling about something when Jaken and I walked in.

Vilmas was instantly shy, and Vrawn stood to greet Jaken and I both.

Once he had unloaded his cargo, Jaken mentioned some-thing about visiting his former class trainer Willem for some one on one time.

"So, we have a hundred twenty-five of these," I informed the enchanter as she made sure that the plaques were to her specifications.

"And how many planks are there in the fence?" Vilmas asked. I groaned at the thought of having to count, but Vrawn actually had the answer.

"Two thousand eight hundred seventy-five planks," Vrawn answered matter of factly.

"So, that means that we can put a plaque every… twenty-three planks?" She began to clear a space on the floor for a large sheet she had with symbols carved into it. It looked so perfectly done it could have been carved by the gods.

*Damn, man,* I lamented to myself. *Everything she does is fucking perfect! I really need to up my game with my own enchanting.*

"What's that?" I asked as I stared at it. It was a square with a circle in the middle and five lines leading from the center to smaller circles with runes carved around them.

"It's a copycat sheet. It allows an enchanter with enough mana to replicate a single enchantment to items of the exact same quality. It's meant to be used for bulk enchantments," Vilmas explained. "We will use this to finish this job much faster than normal. Luckily, I have a large mana pool."

She took a plaque into her hands and closed her eyes before running her hand over the front of it. As she finished, there was a simple design left behind that reminded me of a coat of arms. It was a ridged shield with three points at the top that rounded down to a slight point at the bottom. Behind it were a crossed crooked staff and a longsword.

"This is the design," she stated, then looked at me and asked, "Can you duplicate it?"

I took the image in for a moment longer, then duplicated the image with my mana for her to see. By now, my control was much better, and the small corrections she made took almost no effort.

I used the floating image like a brand and began to stamp each plaque with it until we were finished. The whole process was finished in about twenty minutes as we stopped every few to check the design.

We went through the same purifying process with these as we had the nails, but the powder yield for the plaques was minuscule in comparison. The quick press of mana left less residual mana behind. Even with there being less residual mana, they were still being done one at a time for around thirty seconds each just to be safe.

"While you're doing this, I'm going to go ahead and go back to the mountain and see about getting some more of that ore. I'll be back as soon as I get the goods." Before anyone could tell me otherwise, I teleported to my spot at the mountain. Better to get there sooner.

While I was enjoying myself with digging for once—I had never really been a fan as a younger man or even as a kid—I felt slightly closer to the mountain.

It wasn't as intimidating as it was before. Granted—I still hate enclosed spaces to an ungodly degree, but this wasn't all that bad. I could ask what it was from the Primordial earth elemental, sure, but that didn't give me permission to bother them at every given opportunity. I'd muddle through it properly.

In the twenty minutes I had been there digging, I had unearthed a foot of the mystery metal. It was during my second cycle of digging that I felt something extremely off.

A shift in the world around me brought me out of the hole in the side of the mountain. In the shaded portion of the tree line, shadows fled from their homes to a central point where they deepened until they were black as pitch and began swirling like a whirlpool. The pool raised from one side and stood completely vertical before light began shining through and a figure stepped out.

I couldn't drop my form fast enough. I was so happy to see

her, so relieved that she was here again. "Mae!" My voice echoed louder than I had meant.

The woman looked up at me and smiled. I took my owl form and flew down to land in front of her, shifted into my human form, and picked her up in my joy.

"Hello, Zeke," the queen whispered against my neck. Her arms around my shoulders felt like being home again. "How have you been?"

"I've been okay, though we have a lot to catch you up on." I looked into her sparkling deep green eyes and ducked my head down to kiss her.

Her pillowy lips met mine in a tame kiss. I stroked her multi-colored, highlighted hair behind her left ear and set her down.

"You had some things you wanted to talk to me about as well?" She nodded, patting her travel clothes—a simple set of dark breeches, thigh-high leather boots, and a red blouse with sharp-looking sleeves.

"We can discuss that later," she replied softly. She looked around. "I had not expected to find you in the mountains. What are you doing?"

"I found a strange, green metal, and I wanted to collect some more to see if we can figure out what it does." I pointed up to the spot I had been digging. "How did you find me this time? Have you learned how to travel somewhere specifically?"

"I have, and I can explain that later as well—tell me more of this metal." She began to walk toward the hole; the line of her body seemed a little more rigid. Formal.

"It's green, and I have no clue—hey, is everything okay?" I asked, stopping as I asked my question.

Maebe turned and looked at me—really looked at me—and then looked away.

"I do not know," she replied, and I could hear a sadness in her voice that made me want to comfort her, "but we can discuss it later. There is much to be done in order to have your party at full strength."

She began to levitate off the ground, then up the side of the mountain toward my spot. I flew up myself at a distance. It was clear there was a lot on her mind at the moment, and I didn't want to upset her.

I stayed at the back of the small cave and heard her say inside, "This is Fairy Iron."

"Fairy Iron?" I smirked. "Isn't that a little bit of a misnomer? Aren't fairies and Fae crazy allergic to iron?"

"We are, but this metal is called that because of the Little Folk who use it to make powerful weaponry. There are some among the Little Folk, fairies as most call them here, who would rival even the Dwarves of this realm as far as craftsmanship is concerned."

"Does it take anything special to work it?" I wondered aloud. She looked askance of me, and I continued, "I gave a little to Rowland, the smith here, and he's going to try to discover what the properties of it are. Try to work it. If there are special considerations to be taken into account for him to be able to work it, then he needs to know."

"I think so long as he does not use iron tools or use an unenchanted flame, he should be fine." She mulled over something for a moment before continuing, "Then again, I am no smith."

"And if he does use those things?"

She thought on it for a moment. "If I recall correctly, the metal will not heat properly without enchanted flame, and then working the Fae metal with iron will likely make it brittle and weak."

*Oh, okay, cool,* I thought to myself. *My friend isn't in danger.*

I sighed, then looked at Maebe. Her cultured tone, regal stance, and aloofness had returned. I wanted to ask her what was wrong again, but I didn't want to push her before she was ready to talk.

"Okay, then once I take what I have exposed here to him, I'll take you to the village, and we can explore it together. I don't think Vilmas, the enchanter I brought from Djurn Forge, will need me for the enchanting process, so it's more what I want to learn from her. Though I do want to see how she enchants multiple items at a time."

I eyed the metal and sighed. "It took a while last time to get through the full thing."

Maebe turned and addressed me softly, "You promise to take me to this 'Sunrise' and show me about?"

"I give you my solemn oath and swear also on my affection for you, that once this is taken care of, I will personally take you through Sunrise Village with pride." As soon as I finished the oath, I bowed at my waist. I felt a familiar weight settle over my chest.

**WARNING!**

**You have given your word to a denizen of the Fae Realm. While you are not within the realm, the beings of that plane of existence carry with them a true power to hold others to their oaths. If you break your word, the consequences could be dire.**

For the first time since she had arrived here, I saw a genuine look of excitement and mirth pass over her face. "Thank you."

She reached out with her hand, clenched her fist, and slammed it down on the chunk of ore near the rocky wall. With a resounding *crack* and a slight shake, the ore dropped on to the ground.

"There, what needs doing next concerning this material?" She looked to me sweetly and for a moment—a fluttering of my heartbeat—I felt fear at the immense power she held, among other things.

Just something about a lady who can beat the hell out of anyone gets the mind working. I'll shut up now.

I hefted the ore into my inventory and took Maebe's hand gently in mine. "We take it to Rowland, and I warn him to leave it alone until I can enchant his forge and other things to see what he can do. After that?" She watched my face stoically. "Nothing else matters but my completing my oath to you. I can't wait for you to meet the people who took—and continue to take—such great care of us. I think they'll like you. Keep in mind though, these are simple folk. They're isolated here. They don't know much about royalty, let alone royalty from the Fae realm."

"This will not be an issue," she said calmly. "While I am here, I am simply here for you and my other champions. They owe me no allegiance, but if they are open to me, and treat me well—

I may offer them my favor."

Her reference to me was odd but oh well. We would see later how it was going to turn out.

"Then let's go." I cast Teleport and brought us into the square.

It was afternoon; the children were romping and playing in the streets and alleys. Merchants hawked wares and folks milled about discussing events and happenings. One couple who had been walking, clearly enamored with each other, almost walked into us. The man had bumped into me—I had barely noticed it—and had made some comment to watch where I was going.

I paid him no mind. Maebe, on the other hand, was eying me considerably.

"You are not going to assert yourself?" she asked in confusion.

"What use is there to it? I don't need these people to fear me —I like them. If he wants to take a love-struck walk with his lady friend, let him. Better that he walk into me than you. If it had been you, I would've said something."

She seemed to consider that for a moment; then I offered her my arm. "Shall we take a walk together, my Queen?"

She smiled and took my arm, and despite the open stares of curious villagers, I showed her the village on the way to Rowland's forge. I showed her Sarah's carpentry building that was down the road. She seemed completely taken by the place. And the children—she loved the children.

"They let them run wild here? They do not have someone watching them?" She was confused, bordering on truly worried for them. "Children are precious gifts. Are they so numerous here as to be treated so frivolously?"

"They are a gift, I should know. But no. There are forces in place here—the bears in the trees surrounding the place on patrol, the guards on the walls and in the village itself. There are more being trained as we speak. And now, they have us. And I hope you?"

"Yes," she growled, surprising me.

"You like children?" I questioned her, stopping where I was.

"Yes. They are rare for the Fae. We are so long-lived, the monarchs being strong enough to be almost immortal, that it seems to tamper with our ability to procreate. Elves and other Fae who have children are often given many gifts to help raise the child, and in villages within the Fae realm, children are raised by the community so that all may share the love of the child. With nobility, they are trained to adopt the station of their lineage from birth."

"So they don't get to have the kind of childhood a normal Fae would." I squeezed her hand gently. "You didn't get to either."

"I did not." She sighed, and her back straightened noticeably. "I am Queen. I was groomed from the womb to take the throne from my mother and lead my people. The training I received made me strong enough to stop the Seelie from encroaching further into my lands and freed my people from the curse that the Wild Hunt had been. They hunted my people freely, and the cold was not enough to stop them. I stepped up and prevailed where my mother could not.

"I do not resent the life I had, but I find myself jealous of the lives of other children. They grew up outside the politicking and machinations of the courts. They were free of the tedious classes. The lessons. The brutality of the combat tutoring. All of them necessary. All of them for the good of my people."

"So that could be part of why you like being here so much," I observed. She quirked her head at me, unsure. "Here, you don't have any responsibilities except for what you choose. You choose to take on some here and there, like with the village, but other than your emissaries working for you," I shrugged noncommittally, "you help us if you want or can—and you are awesome at it—but we allow you to explore and do things that you should have done. Rather, that you would have done, if you weren't royalty."

"That is likely why," she looked me in the eyes, "and with that thought, I want you to know that you are not something I just use to escape. You allow it, and I do enjoy my time with you —but I take this relationship seriously in my own way. You know this?"

"It hadn't really crossed my mind until now, but thank you for being up front with me." I tried to look understanding, but the thought was there now. Oh well. "So how protective of these children will you be?"

"If anyone harms a hair on any child's head in a malicious way while I am here, they will know no end to their suffering, and death will be the only mercy available to them in this realm and any other," she whispered vehemently as she watched the children playing. "With you and the Gods as my witness, these children are under my protection. I am their Auntie Maebe, and they are beloved by me."

A small human child around three or four heard this from where she had been playing in the dirt outside a small, well-made home and tottered over to the Elven woman with a smile. Her round cheeks were rosy-colored, and her golden downy hair was tied back in a loose ponytail. Her spirited-looking, gray eyes sparkled in the light, truly filled to the brim with joy and play.

"Hiya!" She waved a muddy hand at Maebe, who knelt down to be closer to her. "My name is Lena. Are you my auntie?"

"I am if you would like me to be, sweet child." Maebe's smile in that one moment was enough to further melt my heart. "Lena, what do you like to do?"

"I like the dirt!" She produced her hands for Maebe to get a good look at. "And I like to eat pies. And run. And play. And play tag." She rattled on more things that she enjoyed that Maebe seemed to take to heart. "Where are you from?"

Maebe thought a moment, then replied, "I am from far away, a place called the Fae Realm. It is a hard place, and children are something my kind are not blessed with the same way that your parents are. They are so blessed to have you, sweet child. Do you know that?"

"Ma says I was a blessing, and pa says I'm his little treasure." She puffed her chest out proudly, and I smiled at her confidence.

"They are absolutely correct." Maebe nodded her head; the light glittered off of her many earrings, and Lena's attention went to her ears instantly.

"You have so many shinies!" the little girl observed in wonder. She reached out, then pulled her hand back and asked, "Can I *please* touch your ears? Ma says we gots to ask people proper before we go touchin' things that isn't our's."

The queen laughed at the girl's suddenly stern tone at the repeated rule her mother had given her.

"Yes, you may touch them." Maebe tilted her head down so that

Lena could reach out and gently touch her left ear. She poked one of the earrings, giggling after the metal clanked into the next closest one lightly.

"Your ears are so long!" She reached back and touched her own ears, rounded and small. "I wish I had big ears. And your hair's so pretty too! I love all the colors."

"Your ears are perfect, sweet child." Maebe reached out her own hand and stopped just short. "May I touch your ears, Lena?"

The little girl giggled and pulled Maebe's hand toward her ear. Maebe tickled them gently, and Lena shrieked in delight. The queen gasped softly, pulling her hand back and looking over the child for injuries.

"She's alright, ma'am," a gruff sounding, bass voice intoned from behind us. I turned to see a man who reminded me of Lena instantly grinning behind us. "Isn't that right, my little treasure?"

"Pa!" The girl ran between us and leaped into her father's arms.

The burly man, six-foot-something with a damned-near perfect lumberjack build, gave his daughter a peck on the forehead.

"Name's Shawn, this here is Lena, and my wife, Summer, is behind you." He looked at me for a moment before grunting, "You look mighty familiar, mister. Do I know you?"

I flinched. I'd forgotten to shift back. I took my fox-man form, and the man smiled wide before coming over and shaking my hand. "I thought so, Mr. Zeke!"

I politely shook his hand back and let go. "My, that's a smart little girl you have there."

"She sure is," Shawn agreed readily, "and we owe her safety to you and your friends. Summer and I can't thank you enough for what you all did. That was brave—stupid—but mighty brave."

Lena, who had gasped and then squealed to be let down as soon as I'd shifted, was groping in futility from her father's arms for my tails. I laughed and turned so that she could feel the fur of it against her hand.

"They's real, pa!" she gasped in wonder.

Shawn patted her head. "That they are, you remember him now? He was one of the ones who brought you and your friends home to us safe and sound. What do you wanna say to him now?" He set her on the ground and prodded her toward me.

I sat down in front of her next to where Maebe stood and waited.

"Thank you, sir," she said bashfully.

"I'm happy to help you in any way that I can—and your friends." She smiled happily at me. I pointed to Maebe. "She's also here for you, and she's really strong too, so you'll be extra safe."

I leaned in next to her so that only she could hear me, hopefully, and whispered, "But I'll tell you what, she's only got one friend, and that's me."

Lena looked at her in shock. "She only gots one friend?" I nodded once. "Well, that's no good. Can I be your friend?"

Maebe looked at me, then at her smiling mother and father. Summer had come out from the house to join her husband, her strong features, tall build—only a little shorter than Shawn's—lent her a more intimidating demeanor. Her flowing, red hair and freckled visage were pretty, and if I looked hard enough, I could see that Lena had her eyes.

The two adults nodded their assent, and Maebe knelt down once more. "I would be honored to count you as my friend, if you will have me. I will honor you and treat you well."

"Well, that's what friends are for, silly!" Lena giggled. She skipped over to Maebe and pulled her into a fierce hug that the Fae Queen returned gently.

Summer, her voice gentle but firm, "Come on inside now, Lena. Supper should be finishing up soon."

"I gotta go clean up now, but I'll see you again soon, okay? We can play together!"

"How would you like to join us for supper, Zeke, ma'am?" Shawn stepped over and looked from his wife to us. "Isn't much, but Summer is a fine cook, and we'd be proud to have you."

I looked to Maebe who seemed at a loss for words. "I think we may have to come back another time, but thank you. All of you. We still have a lot to see and do here before we head on."

"Well, thank you again for all you've done." Shawn shook my hand and then patted his daughters head. "Thank you as well, ma'am."

"Of course," Maebe regained her composure a bit, "and I am honored, but first—a gift." Maebe reached into the shadows and pulled out a ring of dark metal that I recognized as Ebon Steel.

"Zeke, if you would enchant this for me?" She handed the item to me, and I looked at her with eyebrows raised. "I want it to be an alarm ring that lets me know if she is in danger. Can you do that?"

I blinked in surprise. After a moment, I replied, "I have no idea, but I can try. I might need a piece of your hair, though."

"Done." She pulled a red strand from its place on her head and held it out to me.

Okay, so how would I do this? How could I tie a warning to Maebe from the ring? How could I ensure they were linked? I started to reach for it when a bit of inspiration hit me.

"Lena, I need you to help Maebe for a moment. Can you do that?"

The little girl looked mystified but nodded. Her parents wandered closer to us so they could see what I was doing.

"Maebe, you hold one end of the hair, and Lena, you hold the other. When I tell you, I want you to drop it on to the ring for me, okay?" The two of them nodded.

I engraved the ring with a small bell with the intent that if Lena was ever in danger, hurt, or needed Maebe, the Fae Queen would hear the alarm and come to her.

I funneled my mana into the item with that intent in mind, and as soon as I felt the draw on my reserves slowing down, I grunted, "Now," and felt a line of something small hit my hand just before disappearing.

I stopped pushing mana into the enchantment and looked over my work. In total, it had taken 300 MP, but I wasn't sure how it would work if she was in the Fae Realm.

**Ring of Fae Alarm**

**Calls to Maebe, the Unseelie Queen, Darkness over the Snow and Ruler of the Shadows in the bearer's time of need. If in her absence the bearer calls, the nearest creature of Fae blood who owes the Unseelie court fealty will come to the bearer's aid in the Queen's stead.**

**Ring crafted by Thogan Swiftaxe and enchanted by Craftsman Enchanter Zekiel Erebos.**

"Oh, man," I grunted.

I passed the item to Maebe, who smiled. "It's perfect. Thank you, my love." She froze, and I felt my cheeks burning.

The parents smiled, and Maebe handed it to Lena. She looked at it. "It won't fit! My fingers are little-tiny."

"Try it," I urged her gently. "It's a magic ring, and magic rings can shrink to fit little-tiny hands. It will grow with you too."

She looked at me skeptically and slid it over the middle finger of her right hand. Sure enough, the ring shrank until it fit comfortably around her little finger. She made a sound of awe, and her father reached out and touched the item.

He looked to Maebe. "The Darkness over the Snow?"

"I am." She lifted her head. "I have sworn an oath that the children of this village are under my protection. I am Zekiel's friend and the queen who conscripted the party he is with as champions. I am no threat to any of you unless you are a threat to the children."

"I believe you. No monster would look at a child with such purity and innocence as you did. And do. And Lena isn't friends with monsters, right?" her mother called to the child, who shook her head vehemently.

"Just bears!" She giggled as her father roared and chased her teasingly around us into the house.

"She's a good girl, and you seem like a good person," Summer said as she walked by. "Thank you for being kind to her and for wanting to look out for her wellbeing. You both, as well as the others, are welcome to come for dinner at any time."

We both nodded and watched as all three of them entered the home. I noticed that it was nicer than some of the other homes in the village.

I looked at Maebe. She was still, and it looked like she was in deep thought.

"We can talk later," I offered softly. "I have my word to keep, and we have one stop to make. It's just down the way here."

"Lead on," she answered as she continued to eye the home but offered her arm to me.

I took it and led her to Rowland's, about a ten-minute stroll down the way. The door was locked, so I left it alone. I explained that I would take a moment to speak to him by spell.

"Do it now so that he doesn't ruin the ore." I nodded to her after she spoke.

I cast Mental Message, "Rowland, it's Zeke. I hope that Mini is well. Maebe told me that the ore is Fairy Iron, and it needs magic flame and non-iron tools to work it in order to make it. There's a lot of the ore, so I can make you an enchanted forge. Just let me know, and I can get it done tomorrow or so."

"Loud and clear, lad," he responded after a second. "The lit'le fox be fine, an' tomorrow works fer me. I took a day fer meself—let me know if ye be needin' me."

I smiled at the thought of him and the fox kit kicked back in a recliner with a fire going and a mug of ale. I couldn't help the chuckle that escaped my mouth.

"He's aware of it now, and you'll get to meet him tomorrow if you would like," I explained to Maebe.

"I would like that. Where is it that you stay?" she asked as she looked around. It was late enough that the children had left the streets and alleyways to go in for dinner.

"Let's go to the tavern, and we can get some dinner too." We walked to the tavern, and on the way, I pointed out a few places to her that were familiar to me.

The crowd was light tonight, and I saw that my friends weren't there, but Willem was.

"Zeke!" he called out and pointed to a table in the back. "Your spot is there, and the chef has decided that you and your lovely lady friend have been hungry long enough. He's going to bring your food out here in just a few minutes. Would you care for anything to drink? I have tea, wine, mulled wine, ale, beer, mead, and any number of liquors."

"Uh," I sputtered a moment and walked to the table. "Tea

would be fine for me. Thanks. Maebe?"

"Queen Maebe?" Willem asked with eyebrows raised. "We are honored to have royalty here among us simple folk. If there is ought to be had here that I may offer you, do not hesitate to ask."

He bowed until Maebe bid him rise. "Thank you, Paladin. I have heard much of you from Jaken. You are a tactful man and keen. It is an honor to dine here with you as my host. I am at a disadvantage, for I have nothing to gift you with for your hospitality."

"You're a friend of Zeke's, and he cares for you—that much is plain as day to me." He looked me in the eyes as he said the next part, "Treat him well, and my hospitality will be unending."

"I thank you, then." She bowed her head once. "Let us dispense with the formalities and treat me as if I were any of Zeke's friends. It would hearten me greatly to know that I am being treated as an acquaintance."

"It may seem early, but someday—I hope it will be friend." Willem smiled and nodded to us both. "Well then, Zeke, Maebe. Your dinners will arrive shortly."

He left us and came back to deposit two cups of tea and a pitcher filled with the deep brown liquid before moving away again.

I leaned closer to Maebe. "They're never this way, and I have no idea what's going on, but I think the rest of the group is behind this somehow. I am so, so sorry, Mae."

She giggled at me for a second, then reached beneath the table and took my hand in hers. "It's fine. This is what people do when they like each other, yes?"

I grinned. "Usually. But my friends are assholes. Like me. And we can be evil to each other sometimes."

She smiled at me, and it made my skin crawl for a second. "I can be evil too. If they are attempting to play—we will have our fun."

"Oh, I don't deserve you." I groaned and kissed her

shoulder affectionately.

"That will also be a matter of discussion," she stated playfully.

Dinner was served by the chef himself, his name eluding me with his rosy complexion a little defeated by the large tray of food, but he seemed proud of his work.

"Here we have a selection of venison and poultry marinated in butter, onion, garlic, and a tangy sauce of Master Yoh's creation. There is a pairing of smashed potatoes and steamed vegetables. The process was a little odd, but who knew that steaming vegetables unlocked a whole new pallet of flavors!"

With a flourish and a bow, he stepped back so that we could take the first bite under his watchful gaze. The steamed veggies were great, and honestly, I had missed them. The "smashed" potatoes had been treated with milk, butter, and a little bit of garlic for flavor. The venison was cooked damned near like a steak—chewy but not too chewy. It was really good.

Oh my *gods, the chicken.* It had been marinated in sauce alright. Barbecue sauce. And grilled over an open flame and turned until it was almost melting in your mouth. Now, I'm not typically one for BBQ, not really. The scent of it gives me a headache at times. But this? Oh, I savored this. The chef walked away damn-near floating from the praises I sang to him.

I taught Maebe how to properly enjoy the subtle flavors of the potatoes and the chicken. Cut a bite of chicken off, don't pick it up—that's important! We're coming back for him, that's okay. I had her take a fork full of potatoes, then spear the chicken. She took a bite, and I could hear chewing; for once—I was unbothered by the sound.

The meal was exquisite, and the pairing with the tea couldn't have been more a sign of someone watching out for us. It was like being back home. It made me a little sad over my full stomach and lethargic thoughts.

"That was absolutely sumptuous." Maebe sighed in delight. "I don't think I could eat any more. And if they poisoned that, I would die happy."

I saw motion from the kitchens and knew instantly what was going on. It hadn't been my friends who were doing this.

It was Vrawn carrying a tray of desserts on a platter in decidedly French maid-like outfit. Who the fu…

She sat the tray on the table and handed two of the items to us. It was a rather flaky-looking pie that smelled of honey, hazelnut, and berries.

"Bear pie, a new concoction of the house." There was one last piece plated on the platter, and Maebe seemed to get the idea before I did. "Named after all the things that bears like to eat that are sweet."

"Please, do not stand on ceremony—join us." She motioned to a chair opposite the two of us. Vrawn curtsied and sat down.

"Thank you, Queen Maebe, is it?" Vrawn didn't meet her gaze but still looked her in the face.

"Indeed, and I take it that you are Vrawn?"

"I am," Vrawn answered. She motioned to the pie. "Please, enjoy the pie. It really is better warm."

The silence was deafening. My pulse throbbed in my throat, and I couldn't tell you why. I hadn't done anything—at least, not that I knew of—wrong. I wished I could just teleport out of the room, but they knew where I lived—sort of. So escape was a slight inconvenience for this at best.

But still, I tried, "It seems you both have some things to discuss. I'll give you both some time to discuss it."

I went to stand, but both ordered, "Sit."

I sat. I wasn't going to make it out of this alive, and fuck, it was going to be so awkward or incredibly fun.

"So, you are who he chose to deny?" Maebe asked curiously. "I cannot see why. You are a handsome woman. Strong. Capable. Experienced?"

"I was, but it was clear that he felt for someone else, someone hopelessly above his station despite how powerful he is," Vrawn countered. "I felt it my duty to show him that someone more his speed would be better suited. While a tryst with you would be fun, it would inevitably end, no?"

It was like watching a tennis match with this kind of back and forth.

"And you know so well the duties and costs of reign?" Maebe's eyebrows rose.

"I spent enough time in her Majesty's guard that I saw the lovers she took cast aside—those who truly loved her—for a marriage of political convenience. I did not wish that for Zeke." She thought for a moment but continued, "Nor did I ever try to tell him he shouldn't be involved with you. Just that he should be aware that there may come a point where your duties would force you to choose."

Maebe looked as if she had been struck.

"It seems that point has come, then," Vrawn looked hurt as well, "and in the end, the choice to be made will always favor the kingdom."

"That's not fair, Vrawn," I growled. This banter was pointless. I knew all of this. "I knew she was responsible for her people, and if I got in the way of that—I was prepared for the eventuality of her having to just be my friend again."

Both women stared at me, my breathing taking on a more ragged pace as I fought my outrage before they could halt the momentum of my reasoning. "And yeah, it would hurt like hell, but I'm not just going to abandon her or my feelings for her to save myself some heartache. Who does that help? Would you want to share yourself with me, knowing I pined for someone else?"

Vrawn looked away, and I couldn't help adding, "Because I don't think that would be fair to you. Or me. Or Maebe. So, whatever conversation needs to happen, whether it's pride on your part, hope on hers, lust, love—what the fuck ever—leave my choice out of it. I made my decision. What the two of you choose to do is on you."

I looked up, and the rest of the place was doing that thing where they pretended not to look but they were really intent on what was being said.

"Yo, Willem, my room empty or what?" I shouted, and the Paladin flinched.

"The boys were taken in by the guard earlier today. The sheets have been changed, and the room swept."

"Awesome." I looked at the two women at the table.

Vrawn and Maebe both looked either too stung by my words or deep in thought to care that I was angry. "I'm going to my room. It was lovely to have dinner with you, Mae, and it was nice having dessert with you both. Sort yourselves out."

On my way past the kitchens, the chef poked his head out of the doorway. "And the food was acceptable?"

"To die for, man," I grunted. "I'll wax poetic about it tomorrow. I'm pissed off at the moment and don't want to take it out on you."

I turned down the hallway and marched to my room. I opened my door, looked inside, then closed it behind me. I let Coal out; the poor little guy not being able to stretch much with so many people around and the potential for people to get hurt touching him.

I laid back on the bed after petting the flame wolf affectionately for a few minutes. This whole day had been weird, and I wasn't used to this whole people fighting over me either. Never happened at home. Oh well. There'd be heartache for sure. But honestly, it was about our mission here.

The sooner this wall business was over, the sooner I'd be out of here and back out there fighting for my brothers.

I sat in my room for a bit, my thoughts swirling painfully. I didn't want to be alone right now. Not really. Instead of turning my thoughts inward, I called Coal over to me. The flame wolf whined happily and wagged his tail. I pulled some pocket jerky out for him, and he wagged his tail harder.

"Hey, buddy." He snatched my offering up gleefully then bumped his head against my hand. "Wanna listen for a bit?"

So, there I sat in the dark, just talking to my other familiar until I was tired enough to nod off.

# CHAPTER FIVE

I felt a hand on my shoulder and woke with a start. I looked up to find Maebe sitting on the bed with Coal at her feet, wagging his tail.

"Hey," I greeted her groggily. I must have passed out.

"Hello." Her simple greeting felt flat.

"I take it you're ready to have that talk?"

"No, it's less a talk and more telling you what has come to pass in my time away and hoping you will understand." She looked at me. Her deep green eyes were troubled. "Will you listen?"

"Of course." I tried to smile at her comfortingly, but I was uncertain.

She took a steadying breath, then began her tale.

"When I arrived, the palace was in upheaval over a concerning decree by the new Seelie ruler—his name is Kaligor. Don't worry— his power is nubile still, and he will not know we are using his name here until he is a little stronger or we say it multiple times. His decree was that he would be routing out the spies near his lands and setting the Wild Hunt free to truly dispose of those who displease him.

"We had to bolster our defenses and offer shelter to those in our lands who might need it, easily managed and taken care of, but the people were frightened. After they were taken care of, my mother wanted to speak with me. She had reservations about my dalliances in the Prime realm, but she respects that as queen, I choose to do what I will."

"So, then she has to be okay with it," I offered.

"Yes, but some of the things she stated made me wonder— why am I doing this?" She looked at me, her cheeks lightening a little. "And it was for the reason that I slipped earlier. It's because I don't know how I feel about you. I've had trysts. I've had lovers. But they never treated me the way you do—not by choice and never without an ulterior motive."

I offered her my hand, and she took it in both of hers before continuing, "I've never felt this way before, and my mother knew this. She thought it would make me weak. Unsure. If anything, I was more ruthless in my dealings with the Seelie than before just so I could hurry back to you."

Another steadying breath. "I sent you a shadow so that I could just see you, and then I heard everything you said, how you felt. And I was hurt when she kissed you. Angry. Not because she had dared and not at you but because it didn't seem like she was respecting your wishes."

"I can see that being frustrating." I squeezed her hand comfortingly.

"And that made me so angry, and that's when I began to question these feelings." I could see a ghost of the rage pass over her face fleetingly. She sighed and spoke again, "Where they came from, I don't know. I'm not sure what they are or what they mean."

"Do you want to explore them?" I proposed. "I'm willing to explore these feelings if you are."

Her face turned toward me, haloed in the light of the moon and stars; her eyes were larger than normal, and they looked to be on the edge of tears.

"Do you think this could be budding love?" Her voice was soft as she watched me for some kind of sign, as if I might run.

"It could be, and I'm honored." I pulled her closer to me gently. "We can explore this, and I will help you through it. But like I said—if you want out, all you have to do is say so. This includes for your people's sake too."

"Alright," she took another breath and looked toward the door, "and what of Vrawn?"

"I don't hate her," I said carefully. "She's sweet, thoughtful, loyal, and friendly. I think if you wanted to—the two of you could be friends. She seems to have quite the rampant stubborn streak to her, though."

"Beautiful too," Maebe added after that.

"She is," I agreed, "and I'm attracted to her. I'd have to be stupid not to be. But she's not you, and unless you want to be with her yourself, I'm good just being her friend. I don't want to hurt her feelings. She's a good person, but if I have to draw the line, I will."

"That is not needed. She will be a fine addition to my guard here."

I looked at Maebe oddly. "Your guard?"

"I have claimed this village under my protection, and the Seelie King has issued an assault on those I hold dear. I will protect this place." She looked at me then. "And I cannot always be here to comfort you. If I had to choose someone, I'd say she would be a reasonable stand-in."

"I don't get a say in this, do I?" I grumped. "I'm not one for a harem, Mae. I doubt that I can keep you happy all the time, though I want to try. Multiple women? I don't know."

"You can deny her, but I will think you stupid for it," she teased. "But yes, you do have a choice. I am not so taken that I will begrudge you having someone I think is infatuated with you enough that you could trust them to care for you in my absence. I have no other lovers, and I am too new to what I feel for you to want to attempt anything more with anyone else. But it doesn't need to be a harem. You are not royalty. There is no need. I simply suggest having her be here for now. Who knows what more could happen."

I frowned. That was something I hadn't grown up hearing from anyone. Sure, there were many differing views on love, and I had been fortunate enough to see many and read about many others. But it was entirely different being there yourself.

"Let's just give this whole thing a shot, and we can work on it as we go, okay?" I kissed her forehead. "We just need to be sure that we talk to each other and that everything is open."

"I can do that. Come, let me show you how much I have missed you... my love." Maebe pressed herself against me and ran her hands over my back.

---

I woke up later in the morning than I would normally have liked, but Maebe surprisingly hadn't wanted to watch me sleep and laid with me so that she meditated as I slept. Normally, I would wake to her watching over me in a chair. This time, I had gone to sleep with her in the bed, and I woke up to find her still there.

"Good morning," she whispered against my shoulder. I flinched. It was difficult to tell when she was meditating and when she was alert.

"Hello, dear." I kissed her forehead, and she rolled to the side of the bed, flashing her bare hip and the swell of her leg.

Oh boy. I sighed. *Be a damned adult, man.*

I got up and cleaned myself with some of the water in the basin on the desk when I felt a cold chill against my body. I looked down to see shadows creeping up my body, clinging to every bit of my fur. I looked over and saw that the same was happening to Maebe, but she looked unconcerned.

"I take it that this is your doing?" I asked, fighting to keep the panic out of my voice.

"It is." She eyed me, then her teeth flashed in the morning light. "It is to cleanse you. No need to worry."

The shadows warmed significantly as they rose over me and passed over my head. Once the sensation was through, I felt cleaner for certain.

"Thank you." I smiled at her. "Think you could teach me how to do that?"

"What level are you now?" she asked. "I see—you are level 29. You should be able to do this simple of a thing. Have you received any other spells as you have leveled up?"

I shook my head. I was a little worried, actually. Sure, I was stronger thanks to my new subclass as a Primal Warrior, but my spell list hadn't grown at all.

"Then you are past the point where you can learn things without having seen someone who is stronger than you." Maebe frowned. "Is your trainer a higher level than you are?"

"She was, and what do you mean?"

"From what I understand, with many classes in the Prime realm—it takes someone showing you or taking you into their care for you to learn more naturally. Even if it is them teaching you a single skill, or spell, that gives the system a path to give you for growth. Up to level twenty or so, your path was clear. You had all of the spells available to you up until you reached that level. Now, there is not a set path for you, and you need someone to show you how you can grow—or make your own path."

"That's... possible?" I glanced at her, and she smiled. "How?"

"Well, I can only speak to my experiences. For example, my mother taught me all that I know of ice magic, but she was decidedly lacking in shadow magics. So, what she couldn't teach me, I had to spend time learning and mastering it myself. There were the basics that she could show me, of course, but after getting to where her skills had peaked, I delved further into the darkness. Made it my own."

She held her hand out, and the shadows in the room deepened visibly and slithered to her touch like a pet.

"My degree of control is somewhat influenced by my very

nature as well as what I am. I am a Celestial Fae—she who walks between the shadows of the stars. The Netherling. The perfect shadow. What I call from the void is mine to command by birthright and by mastery." The shadow shot toward me like a viper but pulled up short. "You, on the other hand—though you are now Celestial like me—have a more natural affinity to nature and her elements. Gifted by fire, loved by earth, and the other elements treat you better than any other Mage on the face of this planet and many of the other planes of existence. I could teach you simple shadow spells—but you would be better suited toward strengthening those other abilities."

I sat on the bed, my pants pulled up to mid-thigh, and just stopped to think. If this was the case, then I should try to find Dinnia and Sharo to see if I could get some more help. Or go on with my love affair with the Primordial Elementals and try to gather strength there? Fuck. I mean, I could spend the time going through my spell list with my Elemental Tinkering to add an aspect of flame to each of them. It could be useful, but it was imperfect. Sure, it could create amazing abilities, and it had before—but there was a lot to be desired.

The increased mana cost being one thing, and then there was something about mixing spells with one element that just seemed so weird to me. Like, they may not mix well.

On hope, I used Mental Message to call out for Dinnia, "Dinnia! If you're there, please respond. I need your help to grow as a Druid."

"You don't have to shout, Zeke. I'm behind you," came a muffled voice from outside my window. "Rude."

I cast Nature's Voice and called out to both her and Sharo, "I'll be out in a second. I have someone special to introduce you to!"

Maebe was smiling sweetly at me, already wearing a loosely-fitting, tan sundress that did nothing to hide her figure beneath and was waiting by the door. I finished dressing in a green shirt, brown pants, and my normal boots. I wasn't expecting a fight today, but if anything happened, I had spells I could use in a pinch. Or just mercilessly beat the crap out of anyone who tried me.

Maebe and I walked out to the tavern's dining area and found Sharo waiting with his tail twitching by a table that Dinnia sat at.

Sharo, her sleek, muscled black panther companion, munched on a plate of meat and eyed me lazily with emerald green eyes.

"Hello, Sharo." The great cat knocked back a thickly cut slice of ham and winked at me in greeting.

Dinnia, the Druid who had trained me, a lithely built Elven woman with an athletic build, stared at me with brown eyes that seemed to glow a little in the dull light of the room. Her once short, brown hair had grown a little longer since I had last seen her, touching the nape of her neck slightly.

"Dinnia." I pointed at the Elven woman, her bare feet tapping under the table. Then I motioned to the woman on my left. "Maebe. My… lover."

"The title I believe is 'girlfriend,'" Maebe corrected teasingly, "but there is much that he says that does not make sense. I believe you trained him in Druid craft?"

The Druid stood and so did Sharo. Both bowed before she spoke, "Welcome, Maebe, Queen of the Shadows and Cold."

"Be well, child." Maebe nodded at her once. "There is no need for such formality. We meet here as mutual acquaintances, not emissaries."

"Leave it to the cub you reared to find such a dangerous mate," Sharo commented dryly as he poked at Dinnia.

I laughed, and Dinnia pulled his tail rather hard. He growled at her and flicked his tail away out of reach before turning to find Maebe kneeling in front of him.

"You're a beautiful creature," she observed as she continued to look him over.

Sharo, visibly shaken, whipped his eyes toward me. "Cub… does she bite?"

"Keep calling me cub and she may," I teased back. Dinnia and I both laughed as he retreated a couple paces from her.

"What did you say to scare him?" Maebe asked me sullenly.

"He asked if you bite—I said if he kept calling me 'cub,' that you might."

Her lip quirked up for a second before she shook her head. "That's not true, Sharo?" Sharo ducked his head once. "I would not bite you. I will not hurt you. I like cats. And you remind me of a snow leopard I knew in the mountains near my castle. I did so love her."

"What excellent taste your mate has, cub." Sharo lifted his chin before he stood and padded toward Maebe to rub against her affectionately.

"So, you need to learn more about our class, then?" Dinnia asked over Sharo's obnoxious purring.

"Yes, but why were you so close?" I asked as I joined her at the table.

"Well, I do live here," She snorted at the question, "but the Mother told us that you might come seeking advancement. The way I see it now, you're a peer as much as a student. There is little more I can teach you now."

She looked at her companion in thought, then at Maebe.

"He was right, you know—it would be me who has a student bring forth such a powerful entity as a... girlfriend." She smiled sardonically. "You're already the swiftest shapeshifter I know. I would venture that your animal forms are diverse, but you may not have as many as I do. The best I could probably do for you is to teach you a spell I learned before my master passed from this world."

She held out a hand and touched my shoulder, and suddenly, through the agony that reared up in my mind, I knew where every living thing around me was as if they were a blip on a radar I didn't know I had.

**NEW ABILITY UNLOCKED!**

*Life Sense – The caster can sense anything living near them within a certain radius. Cost: 35 MP. Range:*

***30-foot radius. Duration: 1 minute. Cool Down: 30 seconds.***

"What would you use that for?" I looked over the spell description again.

"It is a utility spell. It helps me know who—or what—is around me. If you actually use it and aren't experiencing it through someone as you are now, friends will appear green, neutral entities gray, and enemies or hostile people in red."

"That's incredible. Where do you use that?" I saw her blink at me and look around.

"Everywhere." Dinnia motioned to Maebe. "That's how I knew she wasn't going to attack me. She was gray."

I nodded. "That's fair. So, nothing else then? Is it difficult to learn more spells?"

"You have plenty of them—what do you think?" She eyed me sagely. "If you had learned them on your own, do you think you could have? What if you had the knowledge you hold now? Could you then?"

Thinking on it, I wasn't sure. Sure, some of them were complicated formulae overlaid with mana usage and coupled with motions, intent, and force of will. If I thought hard enough, with a little more thought—and no small amount of luck—I might be able to replicate some of them in different ways.

"You've given me a lot to think about, Dinnia." I reached over and pulled her into a half hug. "Thank you for being here for me."

"Of course. It's my purpose, given to me by the Mother. If I learn anything else, I'll send some friends to find you." Dinnia smiled, then looked at her companion in shock. "Sharo!"

The big cat was laying on his back, batting playfully at Maebe who hovered above him with a length of rope with a knot at the end.

"Wha—what?!" He looked up and realized we were watching and sat up. He tried to look dignified but failed. "What do you want?"

"You wait until I tell Kyra and Thayron that you were playing like a kitten. They will never let you live it down." She laughed as he ducked his head. "We need to go now, Sharo—you big kitten. Tell your new friend goodbye."

Sharo grimaced at his Elven partner before he stood on his hind legs in front of Maebe, using her shoulders to support his massive bulk before gently running his teeth across her cheeks. The entire time, he rumbled like a lawnmower.

"Maebe, we can go take our walk and get breakfast if you like?" I offered, but she shook her head.

"You need to ensure that you get your lesson from Vilmas. On my way to your room, she sent Vrawn to let me know that she would be doing the initial enchanting this morning. She wanted you to observe." Maebe took my hand and motioned for me to go. "I am interested to see how this will work and to meet another of your friends."

I shrugged, happy that she was taking an interest in what I did. I took her to the chef's old room and knocked. Vrawn opened the door wide; she offered me a mug, then Maebe.

"Zeke." She smiled at me radiantly, then turned her gaze on Maebe. "My lady."

"Good morning, Vrawn." I blushed a little, partly because I knew what they had talked about last night but mainly because I had been an ass. "Hey, I'm really sorry about my outburst last night."

"It's fine." She waved the apology away. "Queen Maebe and I had a very heartfelt discussion last night, and what was said on your part was true, more so than either of us knew. I know how she feels now. She knows how I feel. Your feelings weren't taken into consideration, and for that, I truly am sorry. She has told me what she wishes—I am okay with that."

I looked to Maebe, and she simply nodded. "You know, being my replacement if I need to go home?"

"I'm probably just stupid, so I'm not entirely sure how I feel about that yet, but let's turn our sights on the enchanting. Vilmas? You ready for me?" I looked around to see the poor

Dwarf passed out with several empty mugs surrounding her on the floor. She was snoring loudly and came awake with a start.

"I'm ready, Master!" She blinked blearily at us. "Whassat?"

Vrawn handed her a large mug of steaming tea that smelled like the go-go tea from the other morning. She took a deep draft of it into her gullet and sighed. Almost as if by magic, her drowsy, groggy demeanor perked up. She looked to be fully rested and alert now.

"That tea is amazing," I muttered.

"Mmm. It is!" Maebe agreed. She sipped it again and smiled dazzlingly.

"He-hello," Vilmas greeted softly.

She was standing now, her hands clasped before her, uncertainly gazing toward Maebe.

I held a hand out to Vilmas. "There's no need to be shy, Vilmas. This is Maebe. She's important to me, my girlfriend."

"She's a queen," she squeaked. Her eyes stared intently at Maebe, growing wider as she took more in.

"I am," Maebe smiled, "and you are fine. There is no need to be fearful."

Maebe walked toward the Dwarven woman slowly. Vilmas shook her head as if trying to dislodge something.

"Vilmas… can you see me?" Maebe asked curiously.

"Of course I can see you, m'lady—you're right there in front of me."

I knew where this was going and took Maebe's right hand in an attempt to ground her.

"That's not what she means, Vilmas. Like how you knew that Dwarf in Djurn Forge was actually a gnome. You saw through his disguise and spell. You can *see* her." She still looked stumped, but I continued, "You can see the stars along her skin. You can see her true beauty through her glamour that dulls it down. You're getting the full version of her."

"And more than a few Fae find that to be an issue," I watched her flinch when Maebe brushed her fingers over her left cheek, "but Maebe isn't like those other, elder Fae, right? Honey?"

"I let Zeke live," she whispered as she continued to eye Vilmas. She blinked, then with a serene smile, stated, "I will leave you alone too. Though, please—do not tell others what you see. I want them to love me or fear me based on my own merits and not my beauty. Is this something you can do for me?"

Vilmas nodded readily enough before her mousy voice piped out, "You are really beautiful though."

"Thank you. I believe you had something you wished to teach Zeke?"

She put her special sheet on to the desk and placed one of the plaques into the center circle, then four more in the orbiting circles.

Vilmas took a soothing breath, then turned to me. "I wanted you to see this and finalize my intent with you. The enchantment I want to impart is simple. I want the wall to be sturdy as metal but also protected from magic and make entrance by anyone who isn't a villager, or with a villager, unpleasant."

"I don't know about the unpleasant part, due to the wildlife in the area and the bears." I frowned. "What if we hid everything inside the fence?"

"How do you mean?" Vilmas took out a sheet of parchment and an enchanted quill.

"Like an invisible village. The people who give some kind of biological donation to the thing, like blood, can see the fence and village for what it is." Continuing another thought, I added, "After that, we can place charms or befuddlement enchantments in the area that will turn away people who aren't attuned to them."

"That last one would be really hard to do, both financially and enchanting-wise, but if we were to attach it to the wall itself?" Vilmas tapped her thick fingers on the desk. "After the wall is established and the attuning circle is laid down, it wouldn't be too terribly hard to attach the two. A foreboding feeling? Something that caused them to go around or in the opposite direction."

"That sounds like it will take time that my friends and I don't have." I sighed.

"I'll stay and take care of it myself." The enchanter lifted her head, squared her shoulders, and looked around the room. "I know you have things you have to do. Balmur needs savin'. I'll be able to do all the rest of this today. Then the other enchantments I'll do on my own."

She pulled out a large sheet like we had used to catch my sifted mana, but this had something in it. A loose, green pile of filings.

Fairy Iron. I checked the tools she had used; neither they nor the file were iron so they were safe.

"Be careful what you use to work this metal, Vilmas." I pointed to the green metal, "It's called Fae Iron, and it will be ruined if you use normal fire to heat it or iron to work it."

The enchanter's brows raised in surprise. "Mighty kind to let me know, thank you." She scribbled a note on some paper on the desk before turning back to me. "Whatever it does for certain, I do not know, but it will help to add more strength to the wall as a component to the enchantment. I'll show you this process, and after I get them attached to the fence, you'll be free to go on."

She put her hand over the center plaque and closed her eyes. A few heartbeats later, she touched the metal beneath her hand, and a dull glow of red spread from her hand to the black lines along the paper. The red glow worked its way around each of the other items to be enchanted, and Vilmas finished the enchanting process by sprinkling the Fae Iron filings over each of them.

She took her hand away and nodded to herself. "The process takes the mana for each item, then enough to connect them. This is a well-made piece of equipment, so the cost is lower than having to do the thing over and over again on each individual one. The initial time is the five portions of mana, but now it'll be four."

She took the four on the outside away. "Now, I leave the centerpiece—the key—and replace the four enchanted plaques with blanks. This will be over in no time. If you're ever in the market for one of these, I'd suggest going to the Light Hands. We have some high quality ones that we can give you a discount on."

"I just may. But I do have a question, and I'll be brief." She waited, curiosity all over her features. "If it's possible to share an enchantment perfectly like this—would it not also be possible to amplify one with a similar technique?"

"It is!" Vilmas clapped. "Very astute! The blueprints for such an item are jealously guarded, and I think we may have one in the clan vaults, but the materials and time it would take to make one are outrageous. It would likely take nothing short of twenty grandmaster level enchanters, a grandmaster smith, and any number of other highly skilled craftsmen to even attempt making one."

"That's disappointing, but I'm happy to know that it's out there." I shrugged. "The process is interesting. Thank you for letting me see it, Vilmas. If you need anything else, let me know."

"Vrawn has already had her men putting the beginning touches on the slats in the wall that we will use as hosts to the plaques. If you would help us, we will be able to properly do this." She must have seen me pause for a moment too long because she explained a little more. "The plaques will need to be attached to the wall within seconds of each other, or the enchantment will not take properly. It could fail, and all this work would have been for naught."

"I will do this for you tonight," Maebe interrupted me. She was staring intently at the Dwarf as she spoke. "If you will allow this to be done tonight, then I can do this for you perfectly."

"That's fine, I suppose. It will give me time to find a large enough diamond to use as a focal point for the—" Vilmas stared wide-eyed at Maebe and sputtered, "Is that a diamond or ice?!"

Maebe chuckled at the other woman and passed her a gemstone easily the size of my head. I whistled out loud like a cartoon wolf. *Hello, sugar momma.*

"I gave my word that I would do what I could to protect the children of this village." She stepped over to the window and peeked outside. "That includes the other residents too, I suppose. Use that, allow me to help you, and you may consider it an act of both good faith and a gift to prove I mean you no ill, Vilmas."

"Something smaller would have worked fine, but with this, we can have more materials added over time without having to upgrade the catalyst as often!" Vilma's sat the large gem on the desk before marching right over to Maebe, stuck her hand out, and waited for Maebe patiently. The Fae Queen looked to me for guidance, then took the offered hand. They shook once, and Vilmas began to try and prepare for the rest of the day.

We were dismissed, I guess. Vrawn opted to stay and watch over the enchanter, while we went about whatever other business we had.

"Shall we see about getting food before going to see this Rowland you speak so highly of?" Maebe offered.

"Yeah, but I want to eat out today." She seemed confused by the idea, so I took her hand and tugged her out of the doorway. "As a way of showing you my appreciation for being so thoughtful."

Her eyebrows raised, green eyes shining in the light. Her tan dress flapped a little in the breeze. "I am a queen, and I am Fae. I must be prepared to sacrifice for things at times so that my subjects will prosper."

"And I can almost promise that Titania and the new Seelie monarch don't see it that way," I offered. "You didn't have to do that. That diamond was huge. Gigantic. This whole village could likely live comfortably off what that would sell for here.

That was sweet and thoughtful, and I'm treating you to one of my favorite things in the village this morning. That's final."

She narrowed her eyes at me and stepped toward me, her body barely touching mine, her eyes raising to find mine steadily.

"Say that again," she whispered.

I looked down at her, firm and resolute. "That's. Final."

I felt her nails drag down my back, rough enough that I knew I'd likely have marks, and I shivered.

"I like that." She butted her head against my chest and stepped back. "Lead on then, and I will follow."

I grinned wolfishly and pulled her toward the square, and we walked together until the scent of my favorite kabobs hit me. The meat was sweet, sandwiched between fruits like apples and pineapple, and there were little, diced potatoes fried on them.

I ordered four. Two for both of us. Maebe liked them so much that she ordered another two for both of us. Seeing her so excited about all of these new things in the Prime realm was endearing.

Sometimes, it was a little jarring knowing that this woman before me was hundreds of years old in her own realm, which meant countless centuries here, but she was still young to her people. Relatively speaking. She was so capable. Elegant. Strong. Wise and intelligent. She put her people first.

Granted—she still had some seriously bad and murderous things that she'd done in the past, but she was so much more complex than that. She acted like a young woman, her eyes so full of wonder at seeing and trying new things, bordering on naïve. Then at the flip of a switch, she was regal and imposing, her rule unquestioned. She was an enigma.

"Let's go and meet Rowland before I stop to play with all of these children," Maebe's voice sounded strained as she looked at all the children dashing about playing.

It was rough going for her, but we made it there eventually.

We walked in to the sound of hammers falling on metal. Mini was asleep on the front counter in a nest of blankets with a small contraption on her head that looked to be padded with something soft on the inside. It reminded me of a helmet.

A small breeze wafted through the shop and rustled her fur, causing her to lift her head from the bed she laid in. Her tail waved about behind her, and she stood with a stretch.

"Maebe, this is Mini. She's Rowland's friend." Maebe had stepped over to the fox in quick strides while I introduced her.

The fox, spooked by the fast-approaching woman, ran into the back of the shop where the forge was.

The hammering stopped, and Rowland's voice rang out, "Wha's got ye scared, li'l lass?"

He poked his head around the corner of the door and eyed us.

"Zeke!" he bellowed happily. He looked much better than he had before as he hefted Mini into his brawny arms. "And ye brought a friend?"

"I brought Maebe. She's my girlfriend, but yes—I brought her to introduce to you. And I came to get your forge fixed up." I smiled proudly at him before asking, "What's up with the contraption on Mini's head?"

"Awful nice of ye, lad." Rowland looked to Maebe, giving her a friendly grin. Mini eyed her nervously outside her hiding place in the Dwarf's beard. "He's a good lad, m'lady. Take good care of him. An' tha' be a noise dampener. Me hammerin' gets her real skittish, an' I be needin' her ta be able ta nap while I be workin'."

"I mean to try, and a pleasure to meet you, Rowland." Mae stepped forward and held her hand out for the Dwarf to shake. Which he did. Mini was tantalizingly close, but Maebe didn't try to touch her again.

"That fox was a right fix there, lad—thank ye. She's quick as a whip and lovin' to boot." He waved for us to follow him into the back. "I knew ye'd be over today, and I had a bit of inspiration. I made meself a new forge, finally. Been meaning to get it together, but I haven' had the mind for it. 'Til now. It be bigger and better than me old one."

When we came in to see it, the back door was open so that the room was well lit for Rowland's work. The old forge, a simple, raised pit with coal and other things on a brazier had a flickering flame heating it, a bellows attached to the bottom to stoke the flames.

The new structure was larger. Rather than a simple bowl-shaped brazier, it was longer and wider—rectangular shaped—and lidded. The roof to the structure was held up by three-inch rods of dark steel every foot or so for five feet. There were slats on the roof element that looked like they would slide down over the gaps.

"Ye like it, lad? Long, for swords, axes, and other larger items—for when I finally reach grandmaster." Rowland motioned from the bottom to the top. "The sides get covered, helps reflect and keep the heat in when these metal latches are dropped. There's a foot bellows that I can jump on to raise the heat if needed. There also be soft lids, hard, *hard* leather jackets that go on the ends to help keep it to temperatures I need."

"That's awesome, man!" I whistled in appreciation. "How long did it take?"

"Well, I had the parts and the know-how already. I just had to do it. Took about two, three hours? Mini helped me when I saw me shadow and went out o' sorts." Mini had since moved to his side and nipped at his pocket.

Rowland fished out a strip of bacon and tossed it to her gently. The little kit fell on it ravenously.

"Okay, so then I will enchant it for you. It'll burn hotter and longer. The metal will be protected from heat, and the flames themselves will imbue magical properties. If I can." I had a thought for a moment and looked at Rowland. "If I were to have you chalk a glyph that you understand for cooler and hotter, would that help you control the temperature of the flame?"

"Aye, but it needs to be even throughout. Whatever else ye throw in, I'll learn to work with. Thank ye, lad. Yer too generous." Rowland clapped me on the back and took some burnt coal that had turned white and began to draw at one side of the front portion of the new forge.

By the time he was finished, there was a small flame at one end—the left side—and a blaze on the other with a straight horizontal line between the two. I brought my mana out of my finger and matched the drawing perfectly, then made a connecting line to each side that dipped down below it to connect with a large circle about six inches in diameter. After that, I put a flame in the center of a shield, inside the circle to protect from heat, but to keep it contained as well.

I called the mana back in, then thought better of this whole thing. An engraving that complicated was bound to be too difficult for me to do alone. So I split the enchantment. The bottom would provide the heat protection and contain the flames. The top, I engraved with... fuck. What kind of symbol could I engrave for magic?

"Hey, Maebe?" I looked at her where she leaned down, admiring my previous work. "What is a good symbol for magic?"

She thought for a moment, then shrugged. "I am uncertain. I could give you a symbol for Fae magics, but I do not think it would apply here."

As I thought, I felt a stirring within the core of my being. It was Coal. The flame wolf closed his eyes and focused, before sending me an image of a flaming crown. A simple image, but the idea behind it was power over magical flame. *All* magical flame.

It was the symbol of the Primordial Flame Elemental.

I shrugged and used my mana to impart the flaming crown on to the lid on the inside. There was no flame inside now, so I wasn't worried.

*Help.* The thought came out of nowhere, and I realized that it was the flame wolf inside me trying to speak to me. He paced around the den that he held as his home inside me and kept thinking that same thought to me.

I blinked and spent the menial 50 MP to summon him to

the Prime realm. Mini started, but it seemed that the normally playful Coal had eyes only for the forge.

On the outside of the crown, I made certain to engrave symbols that I took as a blessing, waves of light coming from it like a child's drawing of the sun. It was as creative as I would get this far out of my depth. I was going to have to try and find books for symbols or things to assist me in my engravings.

I heard a thump and noted that Coal was now inside the enclosed space with me. He looked me square in the eyes and thought, *Help.*

"Okay, buddy." I reached over and patted his head affectionately. "You can help, but I need you not to roast me, so we need to make sure that if you're going to breathe flame on it— you do it small, okay? Intense heat but pinpoint accuracy. Got it?"

*Help.*

*Wolf has a one-track mind,* I thought to myself.

I closed my eyes, corralled my intent, and focused my will. I used my Elemental Tinkering to give my mana the flame aspect and began to feed it into the engraving. Giving normal mana to it while Coal fed fire to it may not mesh well. So I used the fire mana. It seemed the best course of action.

"Now, Coal," I whispered.

I didn't have my eyes open so that I wouldn't be blinded accidentally. Even with my eyes closed, the impression of a deep orange flame crossed my eyes, inches from me, and the inside of the heat was suffocating.

It was almost to the point where I felt my will wavering. I wanted to be out of that damned heat. I gritted my teeth and collected myself. I wasn't going to bitch out now. After a long few minutes of funneling the mana into the engraving, we stopped; I had spent 650 MP.

Coal was panting and didn't look so hot anymore. His fur had gone a little darker black than I would've liked. I cast Filgus' Flame Blade and gave it to him, like a bone. The wolf gobbled it up and looked a little healthier. I admired my handiwork.

The crown now had a red and orange sheen to it and looked as if it truly were ablaze. I took a deep breath and sighed. There. That was done.

The enchantment for the lower half went well too, and with it, the cost was 457 MP. The two would hold, so far as I could see. There was no way for me to check the enchantment until the flames were introduced. I found a large lump of coal that Rowland had. The fuel for this thing alone to burn as hot as it needed to was going to be immense. He would likely need to stop forging to keep the flames fed. That was unsatisfactory.

"Love, do you have a ruby I could buy from you?" Maebe held her hand into the shadows and pulled her hand out with a ruby the size of my palm.

"I will give you a steep discount, *or* you can share a portion of the Dragon's hoard with me when we find it." She grinned at me, and I knew then and there that I was going to have a hell of a time with this woman.

"A share of the hoard is fine—thank you." I dismissed the notification about entering into deals with the Fae and took the offered ruby. I pulled out a large sack and grabbed a handful of the contents. I used my mana to engrave a flaming lemniscate—infinity symbol for those of you who don't like big words—then began to charge it with my mana. Halfway to the mana limit of the item, I began sprinkling my powdered mana. It took the whole handful, greedily absorbing it and only filled a little. I grabbed another handful. And another. I fed more of my mana into it, this time with the flame aspect, and it began to heat in my hand.

*Throw!* I heard Coal bark savagely and tossed the gem into the forge.

"GET DOWN!" I roared as a wave of pressure and flame hit us, knocking everyone from their feet.

Rowland had scooped Mini into his arm and tossed her out of the forge where I lost her in the light.

Coal leaped in front of Rowland, and I shielded myself as best as I could.

Maebe's quick thinking saved her from being thrown through a wall; a thick blanket of shadows rose behind her and stopped her.

*She'll be okay,* I thought. The rush of relief going through my heart and body was immense—even as I was flung high into the air by a second gout of searing fire. Heat ate at me, and I fell unconscious.

———

I woke up to Maebe standing next to me and Vilmas sobbing. I tried to sit up, but Vrawn put a hand on my chest.

"Don't move," she spoke softly.

Since I wasn't allowed to move, I took inventory of my body. I was burnt—badly. I was sore, and hurt all over.

"Where is he?" I heard Jaken's voice somewhere off to my right.

"Hey, how's Rowland?" I rasped at Vrawn.

"He's here, Master Jaken," she called before floating back into view. "He is alright, bruised and beside himself that you got hurt, but Coal took the brunt of the blast for him."

"I am fine as well—you stupid, idiotic fool," Maebe spat vehemently.

She leaned over me, and I saw worry in her gaze. "What were you thinking? How could you risk yourself like that?"

"Get out!" I heard Jaken bellow. Vrawn fled, and I heard other boots scattering behind them. Maebe stayed where she was, tears gathering in her eyes.

"Maebe. Maebe! You need to move so we can start healing him. If we don't now, the damage will be worse!" Jaken tried to reason with her.

I saw Willem come into view as well, and Maebe blinked, a single tear falling on to my cheek.

I wanted desperately to reach out and let her know I was

sorry, that I hadn't meant to do something so stupid. I thought I had it under control. I tried to reach up with my right hand and couldn't.

I felt a rent tear the air and radiant light. "Yes, summoner?"

"Help us heal my friend—please!" There was an edge of panic to Jaken's voice, and then there was a searing pain in my chest.

"AAhhhrgh! *Fuck! Me!*" I screamed. Tears sprang to my eyes as the wrathful pain flashed through my body in waves that robbed me of all sense of time and reason.

I was gone.

———

Sometime later, I woke up drenched in sweat, panting, and trying to remember the dreams that I had been having. I sat up.

The only person in the room with me was Vilmas, bathed in the light of a candle.

"Why?" she whispered.

"Why what?" My throat felt dry, but it wasn't the worst.

"Why'd ye do it?" She looked up at me, her eyes puffy and swollen from crying. "Why'd ye try and enchant an item so far above yer realm o' understandin'?"

I had never heard her speak this way before, and now I *knew* I had fucked up.

"I thought I had it under control," I muttered. "I knew that if I tried to do all that I needed to at the same time, it would overwhelm my mana reserves, so I split the work up. Top, bottom, and then the fuel issue."

"Why did ye no' come to me then, lad?" she shrieked. "I'm responsible for ye! I was to be trainin' ye! ME! And ye went off and enchanted somethin' so far outside yer realm that ye... ye almost killed Rowland. If it weren't for tha' strong containment enchantment ye did, lad—you could've taken *half the village* with that explosion."

My heart dropped into the pit of my stomach. I couldn't

believe that. It had only been a ruby. Barely larger than my palm. How could it have caused that much damage?

"Ye used the mana powder." She stood and stalked toward me. "Ye used *handfuls* of it, much too far before ye were ready, and then ye shoveled in still more mana, fire aspected mana into a *flame type gem*. Zeke, tha' were a powerful bomb ye made withou' knowin'. Ye'll ne'er do tha' again."

"No, I wo—" I began, but she slapped me so hard across the face that it turned my head to the right.

My gaze fell to my arm, and she whispered her forcefulness bringing back her usual cadence and speech, "No. You will never do that again because now you have a reminder of what it could do to you and those around you."

My forearm from just below the crease of my elbow was gone. Hand and all. Tears came to my eyes at the realization of what I had done. In my hubris—my foolishness—I had thought myself better than the other enchanters before me and had overstepped. I had looked into the void of my own lack of knowledge and thrown my arm in digging for results. And something had bitten me.

# CHAPTER SIX

I stayed inside my room at the tavern while the others helped Vilmas enchant the wall. I was too numb and angry at myself to go through the notifications that blinked at me in the lower right corner of my vision. I just laid there—alone with my self-loathing and rage.

I tried to cast Regrowth, but all it did was make the appendage itch a little. The scabs that still leaked a minute amount of blood here and there didn't even heal. They just stayed.

I did my best not to think about anything and went to sleep shortly after. Coal was out and about. I could feel him. He felt stronger now. Much stronger. I closed my eyes and wept. I had fucked up. I had fucked up so badly, and now, our mission was in jeopardy.

Going to get Balmur was at risk now. Going to beat the other minions? Fuck. Don't even get me started on the damned Generals.

None of my friends came to me that night. For the first time in a while. I was truly alone.

Darkness claimed me just before exhaustion, and I fell into a fitful slumber inlaid with nightmares of laughing demons.

I felt a burning like a brand on my chest, a crushing pressure, cold, and then something wet. I scrabbled to get the blankets away from me to see what the hell was going on.

The four symbols of my gifts with the Primordial Elementals had migrated from my hand to my chest around the white-inked pentagram tattooed over my heart. They each had taken a place corresponding to a tip in the pentagram, but outside the circle, as it had been before—the top point of the star was gone. It belonged to Storm Caller who resided in my inventory.

The flame symbol that had been on my right hand had shifted from a normal-looking flame to an image of the flaming crown, a deep red on top and blue at the bottom near the top right tip.

*Little flame, you thought yourself much hotter than you were and have suffered for it. You now know that all that burns bright too quickly fades in time. Do not fade away. Do not burn out. Carry your torch farther and see that you learn to burn more efficiently. Thank you for the monument. Now —burn brighter with my flame.*

The wall of white diamond tattoo that had surrounded the flame previously had turned into a mountain of platinum diamond on the top left tip.

*Do not allow this loss to crush you, tiny Druid,* a rumble of stone and pressure inside my mind spoke softly. *I have felt the loss of much of my blood in the mountain near you. Someone digs swiftly for what they think they need—and I give it to them readily. Regain yourself, and feel the calming of the stone as my blessing.*

The wind tattoo that had been on my left hand as a small swirl of blue was now a tornado of deep green at the bottom right tip of the pentagram.

*You still will never tame me, Druid—but I see that the gusts of your work have begun to affect the lands. You have fought alongside the children of the sky and blown away your enemies, tamed Lightning and the Storm and call them friend. I delight in seeing where the winds of change take you and your friends. I gift you my breath that you might last longer than a fleeting breeze.*

And finally, the green river that had surrounded the wind tattoo now resided at the bottom left tip as a tsunami wave in bright blue that looked as though it would drench your hand if you touched it.

*Hail, Druid of the elements. The Mother's Primal Warrior. He who filled a lake once and saved a bunch of trees after. You still fear me, and that fear will be addressed soon—but I sense respect. I sense potential. You have caused a fire to burn bright but kept it contained. I will cool your skin and heal your wounds, but there is only so much water to fill such a broken vase. Know succor, droplet—and know I will call upon you soon.*

I hissed as cold water that smelled heavily of salt ravaged my wounded arm, making me stand. The scabs peeled painfully away, and a yellowed, brackish ooze seeped from the flesh beneath and coated the floor beneath my feet. I instantly felt a little better even though the salt in the water stung like a moth-erfucker.

Eventually, the pain subsided and all that remained was flesh around the nub—that seemed insensitive, so need to find a better name for it—seemingly whole, though scarred. I sat back down to contemplate what I had just learned and what had happened.

Monument? Call on me soon? Who was digging out metal in the mountains? And fuck, was that wind Primordial a dick or what?

What would I do?

"Hey!" I heard a voice growl from the outside of the door. Yohsuke kicked it in and charged right for me. "Smells like shit in here, fucking gross. You done being a lumpy, sad sack of shit or what?"

"Fuck you, man," I spat back. "I was just about to come out there and see what was going on."

"You lying asshole." He punched me in the shoulder; it didn't hurt. "You lost an arm—so what?! Balmur is in the Hells, and I fucking *died*, remember?"

"Yeah, I do! You gonna get out of my face so I can get myself sorted the fuck out or not?"

Yohsuke grumbled something, and I shot out of the bed at him. "You wanna call me a pussy to my face?"

I lifted him with my one good arm by his shirt and cloak and pinned him against the wall.

"And what're you gonna do about it?" He shot me a shit-eating grin and looked right at my cocked right arm. "Give me a good thump?"

It took me a second to get what he was saying, but when I did—I didn't know whether to be pissed off or to laugh, so I let him down and laughed. We both laughed until it hurt. We laughed until I was in tears.

"Don't you ever do something so asinine and shitty again, fuckstick. Or I'll kill you myself. You feel me?"

I looked at him and pulled him into a fierce hug. "Yeah, yeah—tough guy."

"Man, you better get your Luke Skywalker ass away from me. Fuckin' scally-wop lookin' ass." He grunted and tried to push me away, but I was much too strong to budge.

"Speaking of, maybe we can get a prosthetic?" I began to think on it a little while longer, but I figured it would be a good idea to check my notifications.

***CONGRATULATIONS!***
***Enchanting level up!***
***Level 40 enchanting reached!***
***Welcome to the Adept ranks of enchanting!***
***LEVEL UP!***
***ALERT!***
***You have created an artifact worth having. This is a secret best kept, and you should be aware that there are those who would see it fall into their hands and don't care how much blood is spilled. Watch your back and that forge, Traveler.***

Holy. Fucking. Shit.

First, I allocated my points. Two to strength and dexterity.

One to wisdom. Maybe that would help me be a little less apt to making idiotic mistakes?

Probably not—but I gotta try, right?

I also saw that Coal was level 11 now. Three natural points —one for each level—had gone to charisma, intelligence, and wisdom. So the other nine, I could play with. After some thought, I put three apiece in strength, constitution, and dexterity.

I cast Mental Message and called to Maebe, "Mae? Where are you?"

It took her a minute to answer, but she did, and she didn't sound happy. "I am making preparations for something I hope will help rectify your mistake. Do. Not. Do. *Anything.*"

That last word had been a hissed order, and I blinked in surprise. Fair enough.

I wandered out into the tavern's dining area in search of food and found Rowland, Mini, Vilmas, and Vrawn sitting at a table. Coal thumped his tail against the ground as I entered the room, and he sauntered over to walk around me.

Rowland sat Mini on the floor and lunged at me. He was on top of me so fast it was like being taken out by a race car.

"Oh, lad," he crushed me in his grip even though he laid on top of me, "thank the Mountain ye only lost the arm. Ye saved me life again, damn ye! Ye gave me the best forge, and ye still managed to protect me and me girls. I cannae thank ye enough, Ze– Oof!"

Vrawn had pulled Rowland off of me and tossed him— gently—away. She reached down gruffly and hauled me to my feet, then higher until I was eye-level with her.

"If you ever risk yourself or Lady Maebe like that again—I won't be responsible for what I do to you. Okay?" I could only nod mutely at her sudden rage. She had seemed so concerned when I had woken up that first time.

Satisfied, she pulled me into a bear hug then kissed me roughly on the muzzle before dropping me to my feet. I took it. I wasn't in any shape to fight.

Nor did I have any right to fight. I'd take my lumps. I'd earned them.

Vilmas called, "Come and eat, Zeke. You've been asleep in that room a day and a half. Wait, how are you healed like that already? None of us could get that infection out."

"The Water Primordial. She wants me as healthy as I can be. I guess she'll be calling on me sometime soon." I came over to the table and sat down.

Vrawn sat a plate of eggs, toast, and that lovely tea in front of me. I sipped the tea slowly. It helped me recover a little more of what truly little sanity I had left.

I picked up the fork and carefully began to eat with it. It wasn't as efficient as with my right hand, but my time training in the Marine Corps to be able to work with things as well with my left hand helped immensely. I wasn't at square one, but I wasn't too far from it to be where I needed, either.

"I recovered yer rings for ye as well, lad." Rowland laid two rings on the table—my Ring of Inferno and Ring of Storing. "They had just been blown away by the blast. Cleaned em for ye."

"Thank you, Rowland. I appreciate that, man." I took them, and Vrawn put them on to my left hand for me.

My Elemental Bracelet was full to the brim of what looked like fire magic. If that was the case—I would have taken even more damage from that blast. Fuck.

No time to dwell, man. Move on. Grow.

"Where is everyone?" I asked between bites.

"Queen Maebe has gone to collect ore and her people to come and protect the village, as well as to help with a project," Vrawn explained. "She advised me that she will return as soon as she can."

Yohsuke popped out of the kitchen. "Muu is still out with Sam, hunting and learning to skin shit. Jaken is pissed off that he couldn't do more about your arm, so Sir Dillon is out trying to track him down with James helping. Bokaj is doing his whole music thing. Being a puto. You're here. Being a puto."

"Right on." I shrugged. "I'm level 30 now, you?"

"I hit thirty-two days ago, fool." He smiled. "I got to forty in cooking, and now I'm learning shit faster than ever. My intelligence is sixty-seven. What's yours at?"

"Seventy, but my other stats except for charisma are all pretty even except for strength. Which is why you can't move me when you hit me." He just shrugged and played it off.

A thought occurred to me, and I stood frozen for a moment before walking into the center of the room. I shapeshifted to my panther form, and sure enough, my right forepaw was missing.

The others watched me sadly, and I shifted back. "Worth a shot."

The door swung open, and Maebe strode in followed by two figures. Before I could get a chance to take a good look at them, she nodded to Rowland.

"Rowland, we have need of your forge and your assistance." Rowland took to his feet swiftly. Mini leaped up on to the chair, then on to the Dwarf's shoulder. "If you would be so kind as to assist Thogan, champion of my realm and a talented smith, as well as Xiphyre. Xiphyre is a talented enchanter and an expert in the magical metals. I feel you would benefit from their presence.

"Lieutenant Vrawn, some of my personal guard are outside, as well as a dozen of the newest recruits from the realm—vetted and vouched for by trusted advisors and truth seekers. Train them well and have them secure the premises of the smithy until such time as it is not in use. No one is to be around that place unless we know them. No one is to die, but being detained is not out of the question. Protect the children. Am I understood?"

Her orders were absolute, as she stared coldly about. It left little to the imagination that someone who failed would be... remorseful for quite some time. Or dead.

Vrawn saluted Queen Maebe, and the other two figures stepped into the light around her. One of them I was very familiar with.

"Thogan Swiftaxe, you ugly sonofabitch!" I strode forward to pull the Dwarf into a bear hug.

His features were hidden under heavy plate armor that was pitch black in places and icy-blue in others. A helmet hid his face too, but this close, I could see his rock-like skin, covered in pebbles and stone.

"How are ye, lad? I heard ye had a run in with a forge that got ye good?" his deep, bass voice rumbled at me. He saw my right arm and clapped my shoulder. "I'll see that little me and little Xi here get ye back to fighting shape. Don't ye fret."

The other figure was a pixie, about a foot and a half tall with violently green hair spiked in a mohawk of sorts, pointed ears that jutted from the back of his head, and angular features that seemed well in place for how stick-like the rest of his body was. He wore a pair of green and brown breeches and a matching shirt with no boots.

"You're the only one I allow to call me that other than her majesty, Thoooogan." The little man's voice was surprisingly light and lyrical for someone who looked like he could smoke a pack an hour, wash it down with bourbon, and scream songs for days on end. "Master Rowland? We have much to do and less time to do it in. Let us away."

As Rowland and Mini came toward the group, I worried about Thogan's tendency toward other Dwarves.

See, he had been the only Dwarf in Maebe's palace. And especially the only one of his particular type. For centuries. So he was a little homesick for his family.

Thogan clapped Rowland on the shoulder as he attempted to cross the room. "Your beard looks like it has red in it, lad. That a fox, or were ye dropped in the forge on purpose?"

"Yer armor looks like it was made by an expert at piling shit together." Rowland grinned at the other Dwarf before offering a hand. "The hammer falls, brother."

"And rises again," I could hear the emotion in Thogan's voice as he replied, but he only clasped hands with the other smith for a second. "There be work needs doin'. We can get to know each other as true Dwarves do—over the heat of the forge and with the heartbeat of our craft. Come, lad."

I heard Xiphyre mutter, "Bloody Dwarves and their secret handshakes," as they left the tavern.

Vrawn joined them in their exodus from the room, and I was left standing there next to Maebe, who looked as led by her fury as her role as queen.

"You're well?" she asked me softly.

"I am." I reached out toward her with my... not hand and pulled it back. She stepped toward me and pulled me close to her.

"I was so worried for you," she whispered against my neck. "You scared me so badly. I thought I would lose you."

"I'm sorry, Mae." I kissed her forehead. "I won't overstep my knowledge again, and I'll make damned sure if I ever do something like that again, I have someone better than me with me to help. Or I do it where I'm the only one caught in the blast."

An iron-like grip found my bad arm, and I looked down to see Maebe grasping it and glaring at me. "You will do no such thing."

She looked over to Vilmas. "You are capable of making long-distance means of communication work, correct?"

"I am, and I've already begun looking for the components and materials needed to make the necessary items. I also took into account his lycanthropy and am seeing that they are made without silver."

Maebe raised her chin and eyebrows in appreciation, her version at least. "Excellent work, Vilmas. I will pay you handsomely for them. If you need something specifically—speak to Xiphyre. He will likely be able to assist you."

"I will, m'lady."

"Vilmas, you are not to address me as such. I would prefer you think me a friend, though I may issue orders at times," Maebe said matter-of-factly.

"I'm going to try, but it seems odd." Maebe cocked her

head, so Vilmas continued, "You're a queen. You could kill me with a wave of your hand. I'm not sure a lowly enchanter such as me would be worthy of your friendship."

Maebe looked at me for help, and I stepped in, "You don't have to be a worthy friend—you only need be a *chosen* friend. Maebe could destroy this whole village at a whim, but she doesn't because the people she chose to befriend are here. So, if you don't think you can be her friend, that's okay, but you needn't worry about qualifications to be one. Does that make sense?"

Vilmas seemed to take it to heart and nodded. "I think so. I'll think on it some more."

Maebe nodded once before turning to me. "Is there anything you wish to do?"

"I need to find Jaken." I sighed.

The door to the front of the tavern burst open, and Bokaj sprinted in, panting. "Jaken… fort ruins… lich."

"Fuck," I growled. "Yoh!"

Yohsuke burst out of the door from the kitchen with his Astral Adaptor at the ready, his cloak and battle gear on.

I pulled my padded armor from my inventory and sprinted into my room with Maebe hot on my heels. She helped me get myself dressed, then assisted me with my boots, and I walked out of the room ready to go.

I wasn't sure how I was going to do this, but my friend needed me.

"Let's roll to Rowland's and nab a weapon you can one hand for this, so you aren't at a disadvantage," Yohsuke grunted as we got ready.

I looked to Maebe and saw her reaching into her inventory once again. "No. I'll make do. I need to make sure that I'm okay to fight without your constant aid. You've done enough, Mae. Stay and protect the children."

She snapped her fist out and grasped a handful of my shirt before pulling me close to her so that she could look me in the eye.

"You *will* return to me," she stated.

"I like you, too." I kissed her forehead affectionately and smiled reassuringly. I looked at my brother. "Let's go."

I didn't want to give her a kiss on the lips before I left because that could seem too final. No. I'd be coming back to claim her lips once more when I was finished with this business.

"I already sent word to Muu to meet us at the forge," Bokaj stated as we took off at a jog.

We reached Rowland's place a moment later, and I barged through several light-skinned elves who looked confused to see us but didn't stop us, likely knowing who we were because of Maebe.

"Rowland!" I shouted. "I'm taking an axe!"

"AYE!" his voice roared from the other room, and the hammering resumed. The whole place was hot enough that it was truly uncomfortable inside the building.

I selected a simple one-handed axe from the wall rack, engraved it with a diamond, sat it on the counter, and enchanted it for durability and sharpness.

***Diamond Axe***

***+5 to attacks, +12 to sharpness and durability.***

***Axe forged by Master Smith Rowland and enchanted by Adept Enchanter Zekiel Erebos.***

It wasn't my normal fare, but it would hold, and if anything, I could sling spells still.

I walked outside to find Yoh, Bokaj, and Muu standing ready. They all tapped my shoulder, and I shouted, "Coal! Come."

The flame wolf slunk from the shadows of the forge and sat on my foot. I cast Teleport, and seconds later, we stood outside the ruins. Aside from the almost-overwhelming stench of rot and decay, it was as I remembered it.

It was a decrepit wall with piles of loose stone here and there leaving openings all over. A castle ruin, one of the rear walls looked to have fallen in some time ago, and foliage, vines, and other plant life grew throughout it where there were strength and soil enough to lift them up. Then I began to notice the decay—the rot along the plants and the black, brackish liquid that seeped from open gashes in them.

*Bokaj, explain, quickly as you can,* I ordered the Ranger silently through our earrings.

*Jaken got mad, stormed off into the forest. James followed. I saw them go in. Then they were gone.* He shoved me toward the wall. *Let's move on. Who knows what's gone on. Or what is going on.*

"Bet anything that it's poison," I grumbled quietly. There was much too much of it to purify it within reason, even if Bokaj and I could both do it. The pile closest to the entrance to the inner yard we had used before was clear enough, so we chanced it.

"No response from either of them on the earrings," Muu advised with a low tone. "How are we going in?"

I looked for any sign of enemies and wasn't surprised to find nothing. I wondered if I would be able to fly if I took my owl form?

I decided that it would be a viable option and shapeshifted. I landed on the ground, wobbling and more than a little relieved that I would be able to fly—maybe? I looked over the feathers on my right wing; they were rough-hewn and shorter than before.

*It will be very difficult to hunt like this,* the owl's instincts griped. *We may be able to glide if one of them throws you.*

I shifted back, irritated. "Muu, throw me up. Straight up."

I shifted back to my owl form, and Muu picked me up near my legs and threw me straight into the sky like he might his spear. I was about eighty feet into the air when I spread my wings and began to try and navigate the drafts.

From the sky, I noted more than a dozen heaps of bone and decaying waste in the front courtyard that we had originally used to gain entry into the fort itself. Other than that there was nothing to—

*Bank left!* the owl screeched. I did as it told me to, raising my maimed right wing to bank left, and I felt something brush past me. I saw a raven in my peripheral vision, and it dove low, the top of its head gone and eaten in by something. Maggots pulsed inside it, and even as an owl, the sight made my stomach churn.

*More! It's a murder of them! Dive, Druid—NOW!*

I tucked my wings and plummeted on the spot, then spread my wings slightly to cut the wind and steer myself back toward my friends. I didn't know what the hell was following me, but I wasn't stupid enough to look back now.

Once I was a dozen feet away from my friends, I shifted, low to the ground and forward shoulder rolled a couple times before I released a Fireball at the swarm of crows behind me. Our element of surprise was most assuredly ruined if the lich hadn't known we were here already.

A good half of the birds had been singed enough to fall to the ground, and the other half scattered to the sides of the blast and regrouped far up above. Once they were in formation again, they dove as one like a spear thrown at a target.

"I got this," I growled. I used my Charge Spell ability for five seconds, doubling the cost and damage of one of my newer spells—Lightning Storm.

I threw my hand and nub out before me, and a sixty-foot diameter cylindrical blast of pure lightning roared into existence sixty feet above us and carried on for one hundred twenty feet. Raven upon raven turned to dust and ash in the resulting elemental fury and blew away in a light breeze.

"Zeke… did you just do a kameha—" Muu began to ask in a shocked tone, but I interrupted him.

"No, that's silly. That was a charged Lightning Storm. I have enough mana to charge it for five seconds, so that was what happens when you do that." I bared my teeth at him in a savage grin. "Increased destruction. Let's move cautiously—my mana will be fully recovered in less than a minute, so we can move on now, but our presence is likely known."

We moved toward the wall as stealthily as we could, but the rubble had grown treacherous since we had come here last. Avoiding the ivy leakage was difficult too but not impossible.

After a few minutes of indecision, Bokaj spotted the best route over and helped guide us into the area.

There was no ivy inside, but there was a horde of dead animals. Voles, mice, rats, snakes, and other critters littered the ground. None of them moved as we passed through. I used Life Sense and found that all of the creatures in here were dead and truly gone. I wondered if I would be able to sense the undead if they came at me; I would have to test it to make sure.

We made our way to the courtyard cautiously, and the piles of rot and decay were there for a reason. The place looked torn apart. The door was blasted from its hinges, and the corpses of whatever these things were had burn marks and gashes all over them. Broken and splintered bones littered the ground, and their rusted and pockmarked equipment was sundered and split in places.

"Fuck, this was definitely James and Jaken's work." Yohsuke observed one of the rougher looking corpses. "These burn marks are from James using his weapons, and the larger gashes are from Jaken's great sword." He pointed at some blood on the ground—not much, but it was fresher. "He's not using his shield."

"No, he's not, and he's been captured by the lich." We heard James's voice but couldn't see him.

"Up top," Bokaj whispered. "That's not James."

We looked, and sure enough, it wasn't James. It was the lich. His green, ghostly skin seemed more normal now, more like he had when he had been a dude sleeping in a bed. His long, brown hair was done up in a ponytail behind his head and a newly clean shaved face. He looked to be in his early thirties with a well-chiseled jawline and thick eyebrows.

"Hello, all of you who assisted in freeing me from that wretched curse!" His voice was cultured and deep. "I shall thank you the same way that I did that Paladin, but first! A game. Your other friend is somewhere inside this small castle. Find him before my minions do, and you might win a prize—

your Paladin. If you don't, you'll stand no chance of defeating me."

"What's to stop you from having your minions waiting inside to ambush us?" Muu called.

"They are too busy working to find him. By the way—time is running out, for your friend and that village that you call home." His head tilted back, and his nostrils flared. With a sigh, he opened his eyes and looked at us. "All those fresh souls to feed on, to sacrifice and play with. How delightful."

"Fuck him. Let's go," I barked, sprinting headlong into the open doorway and casting Aspect of the Ursolon just in case.

True to Muu's prediction, shambling dead were waiting for us, but what we weren't counting on was them being so easily dispatched. It took us a minute to blast through the line of twenty or so creatures who fell after one or two smacks of my axe and the others' weapons of choice. Coal trailed behind me, clawing or burning the ones who fell to a rogue attack but didn't stop moving. Tmont worked with him, the panther knocking the stragglers down for him to finish off.

Inside, the layout was changed. Before, where things had been decrepit and run down, they were now cleaner. All trace of time, wear, and decay were gone. If I didn't think it was magic, I would've thought all of it a lie. The walls were well-maintained stone, cut perfectly. The carpets were thick and a crimson deep—enough that it could have been spun blood.

The major difference was that the stairway was gone, now. So we had to find a different way to get everyone to the top floor.

"When you released me, my powers returned and with it, the well of souls beneath this place," the lich's voice projected all around us. "Welcome to my humble abode. May want to hurry—my hounds have found your friend's scent."

An idea struck me. "Anyone have anything of James's? Anything at all?"

Bokaj and Yohsuke shrugged and looked to Muu who

looked embarrassed but pulled a pair of undergarments from his laundry bag.

"I lost a bet, and the loser had to do the winner's laundry." He looked anywhere but at us.

"I am not smelling that," I grumbled. "Coal? Can you track James using that?"

Muu tossed the article of clothing on to the floor in front of the flame wolf. Coal stepped forward and took a few deep inhalations and Tmont even stepped over to assist. Though Coal sneezed, and Tmont didn't want to get to close to it.

Coal blinked as he scented the air deeply, then started to nose the ground. *Find.*

"I think Coal has him," Tmont hissed at the garment on the ground as I spoke. "Thanks for trying, furball."

Muu collected the item; then we were on our way with Coal in the lead. We turned down a hallway, into a small door that we thought was a closet but looked like it led to a cellar of some sort. The entry room was nondescript; it really looked like it could have been a broom closet. But the back wall was hollow, and when Yohsuke closed the door, the back wall slid down to reveal a set of stairs that led down. I heard a howl from down below and snarling.

"Me first, Yohsuke, Bokaj, then Zeke," Muu ordered, to our confusion. "You guys wanna take your own damage or you want me to off-tank like I'm supposed to?"

We switched, and he motioned for Coal to lead the way. We hurtled down the stairs as quickly as we dared. Bokaj found a few murder holes along the walls, but after stopping to inspect them, we found them unmanned.

We reached the bottom to find the dark cellar full of shelves stacked with bottles of some sort. They were filled that I could see, and the bottles themselves were a deep green like some beer bottles I knew from home. Ghostly light shimmered from floating lights that seemed to wander about in specific areas, casting eerie shadows along the walls and rows of shelves and bottles.

Roaming some of the aisles between shelves were savage-looking dogs the size of ponies.

*That's no good,* I growled to the others telepathically, but none of them seemed to notice. Not this bullshit again.

I tapped Bokaj to get his attention, and when he turned, I tapped my earring lightly and mouthed, *You hear me?*

*Nope. Probably blocked like in the jungle,* he mouthed back exaggeratedly.

The dogs looked like wolfhounds. Large slabs of muscle moved as they paced and hunted for a scent. They didn't look very strong, nor did they seem very well put together, their rotting flesh shifting and sloughing off at times. I counted at least seven of them though, and numbers without a dedicated healer could be a huge factor in an ass whooping.

I saw Muu turn to look at Bokaj; he motioned as if he were firing an arrow and pointed to the right. Then he motioned to himself and his short spear and motioned left. He pointed to me and Yohsuke into the center.

He pointed to Bokaj, then himself, turned, and held up three fingers and a thumb up. Then three. Two fingers. One.

I watched, almost in awe, as four arrows shot into the wolf to our right, then Muu hiked his spear straight through the wolf in a center aisle off to our left that almost speared it to the wall.

Yohsuke and I quietly fell on the wolf in the center and hacked it to pieces with it only having time to get out a small whimper.

We went through the same tactics with the other wolves, and then finally, found what we were looking for in the rafters in the corner of the room. James—eyes closed and completely motionless—high above us. While Coal burned the corpses of the wolves and watched the door, we tried to get to James.

Climbing up the side of a shelf, Yohsuke was able to swing himself up into the rafters and tapped him. The monk came to alertness in a flurry of curses and motion.

"Hey, relax—it's us, man," Yohsuke grunted at him, deftly ducking under a fist. "Quit tryin' to hit me, you bastard."

James blinked a couple times, then sagged in relief as he realized it was us.

"What happened, James?" I asked from below as they maneuvered down from the hiding place.

"After Willem and Jaken did everything they could for you with that angel's help, Jaken was pissed off." James rubbed his face and stretched. "He took off toward the ruins, and I followed him to just make sure he was cool. When we got here, though, he started to act really weird. Intense. We found a bunch of undead. Rather than wait, Jaken went all uber-Paladin and started tearing into them with his greatsword. He looked like he was going to get fucked up, so I joined in. We fought our way to the courtyard, and after taking out some of the duke's guards, the lich ambushed us. That lich we fought before is the duke; this lich and that one are one and the same."

Bokaj piped up next, "I had T' follow along just in case. She saw that they had been attacked by the lich and rushed back to me, and then we are current to now."

James bumped Bokaj on the fist appreciatively and continued, "After he attacked, he took us somewhere, and I was able to escape. His damn dogs have been hunting for me for more than a day since. I found this little cubby and was finally able to get some rest."

"More than a day?" Bokaj was shaking his head. "It's only been a couple hours at most, man."

"Like I said, this is his realm. Everything is new. Everything is different. And he's so much more powerful than before. Astronomically so—I wouldn't put a minor time dilation outside his realm of influence."

So, that would put him as un-*fucking*-believably strong. This was going to suck.

"So we're going to need to bring the full group down on this asshole and big time. Holy spells—whatever we got—the whole shebang," Yohsuke muttered to us. "There's no telling what the hell is out there, so we need to be careful."

James eyed me for a moment, staring pointedly at my missing appendage. "You gonna be okay? Can you keep up?"

I nodded as the others watched me carefully. "I should be okay. I can still cast and whatnot. I'll manage."

What James had said explained a lot, but why had Jaken been so pissed off? I lowered my gaze to a bottle that had rolled on to the floor in Yohsuke's scramble up the side of the shelf and examined the interior. It looked liquid, so I opened it and heard a moan as a spirit filtered from it. I tried to put the little brown stopper back in, but it was too late, and the spirit was gone.

"Hey, Zeke—what was that?" Bokaj asked nervously.

"I don't know, a spirit?"

Yohsuke took a bottle into his hands after I spoke, and a diabolical grin split his face. "These are souls. Remember the threat to the villagers? 'All those fresh souls to feed on.' This is what he meant. What if he stores these tortured souls and feeds from them?"

"That could be the case. Maybe if we free them, he will be weakened?" Muu suggested with his arms crossed.

"Worth a shot," James shrugged.

I took a couple steps back from the shelf on my immediate right. It was free standing in the center and didn't look to be secured to the ground in any way. I recast Aspect of the Ursolon and rushed forward, tipping the shelf into the others opposite where I stood. I crashed over with it and tipped the next. The cellar itself wasn't the smallest room, but the sound was deafening as the clatter of wood on wood and smashing bottles surrounded us.

"Think this is the only one?!" Muu hollered over the din.

Yohsuke shook his head, and I agreed with him. There would be other places.

As we made our way out of the cellar, I turned to cast a charged Fireball at the mess to ensure that the bottles were all truly smashed. I spent 200 MP as it careened toward the bottom of the stairs while we made a hasty retreat up the stairwell. The burst of flame shook the walls around me, but the place held as I thought it would.

Once we were back up the stairs, we quickly filed out into the hallway. This hall was empty so far as we could see.

"Anyone else getting vertigo looking into the distance of these halls?" James asked, and it surprised me.

I was seeing things just fine. Sure, it looked long, but that was just a distance thing. There was no logical way for the hall to be this big in a small castle like this. Guess that means space dilation as well. Damn it.

The others were staring at me now, and I smiled nervously. "Looks like I'm the only one unaffected."

"Zeke's in lead then." Bokaj waved me forward, and we began to move down the hallway to our right.

I found several empty doorways with rooms inside that held little more significance seemingly than a servant's room. The further we moved, the more and more spartan they became until we came to a room with a single rocking chair in it. There was blood everywhere. The room stank so deeply of iron and violence that it was all I could do to keep looking. Behind the chair was a circle of dark bricks a couple feet tall that creeped me the fuck out.

"What do you see, man?" Yoh asked behind me, and I jumped.

After I slowed my breathing enough to speak more than curse words that would salt the earth and burn the village down, I related the scene.

"Sacrificial room?" James shrugged. "They kill someone, put the body in the well?"

"Or they pull someone in the room, and there's something that comes out of the well at you." I groaned. This was starting to look like a straight-up horror movie. The only thing missing was a fucking clown.

I *hate* clowns.

*We have to go in there, don't we?* I whined to myself. *Of course we do, man—that's the business end of the damn monster nest here.*

"You know what?" I shook my head and backed up. "If we're going in there, I need an ace up my sleeve. Give me a couple minutes."

"Gotta work up your courage?" Muu asked quietly. I raised my eyes to see him genuinely scared as well. "Me too. Take your time."

I sat down on the opposite side of the hall, looking into the terrifying portal to hell for inspiration. Holy magic. I didn't have anything. The closest thing I had? Purify. How could I make that work for me?

I had to forge my own path, make my own way, and I would be doing that however I could with some of the new spells and abilities at my disposal.

"I'm going to use my abilities to try and make some new spells," I told the others quietly. They eyed me wearily, Bokaj shifting down the hall a little in response.

"Not gonna blow yourself up," Yohsuke stated more than asked. He stood where he had been resolute.

"Nope. Not gonna blow myself up."

Elemental Tinkering and a little love from Fire. Fire always fucked up the dead. Or undead. Or anything in between. Fuck that scary-ass room.

I focused on the Purify spell, what it did, the intent behind it; then I began to try and add fire to it using the tinkering ability. The extra blessing from the Primordial Flame had better help with this, or I'd be up shit creek. Paddle or not—that room would need a motorboat.

I envisioned Purify as a rubber ball, then began to wrap flame around it like rubber bands. I focused on what I wanted the spell to do and was rewarded with a notification after spending 674 MP trying to craft something—anything.

***Phoenix Burst – Caster summons a ball of purifying radiant flame that explodes on contact causing damage and destructive purification in a 50-foot radius. Cost: 250 MP. Range: 200 feet. Cooldown: None.***

That was amazing! But that wasn't going to be good enough

for what was likely going to be coming. And with that? I had two shots; then I'd be out of mana until it recovered. Sure, every five seconds I'd be back up by 56 MP, and that's a good amount. That meant I'd be topped off a little over a minute, but in combat, a minute can feel like a lifetime. With one paw and who knows what kind of situations and environments we could be fighting in, I might not be at my best in my Ursolon form.

No, I'd need something to smack the shit out of people with.

Repeating the process with Filgus' Flame Blade. I threw the mental image of the weapon into the flames of my intent like a forge and treated Purify like the fuel for that flame. I fashioned my will into a hammer and beat a new spell into life.

*Falfyre – Forged with unbending will and heated by the Heart Flame, this holy blade will cut through almost anything. Answerable to the caster's will wholly. Cost: 235 MP. Duration: Until dismissed. Cooldown: 5 minutes.*

I was so going to have to play with this some other time. Having these two new spells in my tool bag went a long way toward making me feel better.

"Looks like you're done and no one died yet," James teased nervously. "You good?"

"Yeah, bud. Before we do this, what do you guys see when you look in there?" I looked at the others as they glanced inside the room.

"A chair and an empty room," Muu answered nervously.

"But it's wrong." I looked at James as he shivered and waited for him to clarify. "It feels... grimy. Like if we go in there, we'll be somehow less than if we just stay out here."

"Cold," Yohsuke grunted. The rest of us looked at him, and he just stared at the room and repeated, "Cold."

"Alright, time to get to it then." I pointed at Muu. "Time to tank. Yoh, James, on me. Bokaj, you enter just after me while Coal and T' cover our asses. Let's see what's so interesting in there."

James and Yoh seemed to fall back on their training in times of high stress, like me. It was how we reacted to most things outside our wheelhouse as Marines. The others didn't have that training and ability to fall back on, so we took lead here.

Bokaj nodded and listened because he trusted me to know my shit, and Muu trusted me period because we were family. My orders, given in slight stress and a need to get the job done, had been obeyed swiftly. I just hoped this wasn't something that screwed us over.

Muu entered first, and as soon as he did, the temperature in the room dropped, his breath becoming visible in the small bursts of mist.

"Go!" I spat, and we hustled inside.

Spectral light appeared where the blood was, and I knew the others could see it because they all gasped. James threw up violently against a wall, and Yoh cursed so loudly that it almost mixed with the otherworldly wail resonating from the well.

Rather than letting whatever the hell was coming get to us, I cast Phoenix Burst, tossed it over the lip of the structure, and bolted to the side of the room near my friends. I shoved James to the wall, Bokaj and the animals ducked outside the room, Yohsuke bolted to my side, and I jerked Muu in front of us.

His brain finally engaged, and he raised his shield with a shout. Finally, there was a deafening detonation. We all braced for impact, the silence and surprising stillness lulling us into a false sense of security. Then a stone shifted somewhere below.

And the floor dropped out from beneath us.

# CHAPTER SEVEN

The fall, thankfully, wasn't all that long. Just enough that landing on the rubble did about 50 HP worth of damage. A decent chunk in the grand scheme of things, but I could heal us all quickly with Mass Regrowth. Everyone else could heal themselves relatively quickly with items though, but rather than letting them, I just cast Regrowth on myself and the others swiftly. Mass was more expensive mana-wise, and their injuries minor.

It looked like we were in a small cavern with a larger opening south of where we were grouped. Whatever had been coming for us had either gotten the hell out of dodge or was destroyed. Bricks and muddy mortar littered the ground around us, and there was so much blood. The dirt was slick with it, and I had no doubts these clothes and this gear would need to be deep cleaned.

The air was frigid down here, but there wouldn't be any escaping it unless we wanted to ignore going deeper into the depths and trying to destroy what we could. I looked up, the eerie light from the blood on the walls and floor of the room above giving us a little light to see by. Bokaj poked his head over the edge of the well mouth.

"You guys dead?" he called.

"Yeah," Muu called back sarcastically. "My tombstone has to say something like, 'Here lies Muu Ankiman—his spear was short, but it got the job done. 'Til it didn't.'"

"You got it, man." Bokaj laughed, his voice sounded relieved. "Something cool down there?"

"Big cave mouth, come on down, man." I waved to him.

I heard him mutter something to Tmont, and the panther yowled angrily. "You're a cat! You'll land on your feet!"

I snorted and pulled the small handaxe into my left hand, felt for Coal, and called him back into my body, his warmth and presence filling me comfortingly. I summoned him once more. The flash of flame was bright enough to illuminate the cavern for the barest second—and I wished that it hadn't.

"Get ready for a brawl!" I roared and slashed a blackened skeleton across its chest with my hand axe.

It crumbled, but there were *hundreds* of them separating from the walls. This wasn't a cavern as much as it was a mass grave—the perfect trap for dungeon divers like us.

If it was any more of a perfect time for this, I'd never know it. I summoned Falfyre. The mana drain was instantaneous, but I felt almost as in tune with this weapon as I did my great axes.

"Coal, turn up the heat, buddy," I ordered, and the flame wolf's fur bristled and roared into a large flame that illuminated the area.

My friends were doing their best. Tmont had dropped on to a half dozen of the undead, and her paws slashed and mowed down boney person after boney person. The skeletons did little more at first than try to grapple us, their bone fingers grasping at cloth and tissue alike. Their clattering and clacking jaws were filled with yellowed and gross teeth that had gone unused for gods knew how long, reaching and chomping at us. I smacked one of their heads off and watched another take its place.

I saw a blur of black next to Coal; James was damned near

flying through enemies, and Yohsuke's Astral Blade flashed in a wave of death that felled anything it touched. He shot a few Astral bolts here and there, but it seemed like he was aiming for creatures that threatened to overrun Muu.

Muu stood with his back to us, swinging the counter balance portion of his spear like a club, "There's too many of them!"

Bokaj was trying to use his arrows, but the piercing weapons had little effect. I thought I saw him put his bow away, but I had to keep fending the boney bastards away myself.

Falfyre was beautiful in the light of Coal's flames. The platinum blade was three and a half feet long from the base to tip, and the hilt was a foot long itself. Each swing brought a different lighting effect, casting the golden flames along the cutting edge in shimmering beauty. Runes carved in the flat of the blade were inlaid in varying colors that I took to be the varying degrees of heat it could reach. The lowest was white, then purple, blue, orange, yellow, and finally red.

As soon as I cut through the first couple skeletons, I abandoned all reason. The weapon was killing them as soon as it even came close to them. I avoided getting too close to my friends—just to be safe—until I began to hear a sound that I had assumed I would never hear unless I was home.

Rock. Sweet, glorious, throat stomping, face melting, delicious chords from a riff so tasty I felt my mouth begin to water rang out around us.

*"Those skeletons, they ain't so bad—not when there's an ass whoopin' to be had! So take your sword and swing it fast, make your mark and KICK SOME ASS!"*

My blood, already pumping from the fight, began to boil and race through my veins in a wave of fury that I didn't think possible. I cast Aspect of the Ursolon and began to wade into the skeletons around me with a gleeful roar.

I lost count of how many skeletons fell around me, but the music playing in my ears saw to it that I just didn't give a shit. I swung and kicked and even clotheslined a few of the undead with my nub in my rush to kill them. I wanted—*needed*—them to die as brutally as possible. I held my nub up at the far north wall and released Phoenix Burst.

The soundless cries of the dead sweetened by the shattering of bones and the purifying fire they fed urged me on. I cast it again to the east away from my friends, then waded into the group of skeletons that had surrounded the group of them. They slashed and stabbed while Muu pummeled the skulls with his counterbalance.

Eventually, the skeletons were all decimated. All of us fell to the ground, exhausted. I leaned over, my breath coming in great, heaving gasps that made me vomit twice. My head pounded fiercely.

I assumed that it was Bokaj who had played the song, and sure enough, he was standing at the ledge to the cavern above us strumming a soft melody on his guitar. It looked just like one of the ones he had at home. I wasn't much of a musician, so I didn't know the name, but it had damn sure been useful.

"Good," *huff*, "shit, man." I collapsed on to my side next to the others and just rested. My mana was closing in on full recovery, and I hadn't taken much damage during that fight. I was simply a wrecking ball of hate and rage with a shiny sword.

"The fuck is that sword, man? That one of the spells you made?" Yohsuke pointed to Falfyre.

It took me a minute to catch my breath enough to speak correctly, but when I did, I answered, "It is, and it's called Falfyre. I made it using my tinkering ability with my flame blade as the base and Purify to augment it. I sure as fuck wasn't expecting this though."

"That's fucking awesome!" Yohsuke whispered as he leaned closer to the spell weapon. "It's still hot."

I shoved it into the ground, the dirt parting for it with a musky stench of burning iron. True enough, the somehow-still-slick blood boiled and began to evaporate around it. Rather than dismissing the sword, I left it. Who knew how much time we would have between now and the next fight.

"Inventory, how are you guys doing?" I grunted to the

others. I was fine, my natural healing bringing me to full health rather quickly.

"Little bumped and bruised, but okay," Muu admitted. "I used that ring you made me a couple times in that fight. My mana is recharging slowly."

"I get that you were out there kicking ass and all, I don't know what the hell all that was," James grunted looking pointedly at Bokaj, "but you're the best healer we have right now. You gotta pay attention to us in a fight, man."

I watched Bokaj drop from the lip of the floor. He landed and, even with his high dexterity, slipped and fell on his ass.

"Ow." He stood and rubbed his ass. "That was kind of my fault. While I was training for buffs, I figured out that if I tailor the song to who I'm buffing, it's stronger. When Zeke pulled out that sword, and it was working really well, I figured he was our best bet at making them dead again. My bad, guys."

Aside from a good sixty damage, the worst of it was to his pride it seemed, Muu was the first to offer him a hand up.

"You keep falling like that, sweetheart, and maybe, next time I'll catch you." The Dragon-kin waggled his eyebrows provocatively.

"What's with the tunnel?" James asked as he stepped a little closer to it. "I don't know what's down there, but it could be a way out."

"We can recon it and see if it's a viable way to get the fuck out." Yohsuke stepped next to him. "Be cautious, stealth-like steps. Lights on. We can't afford another ambush like that.

The tunnel we went down was clear, easy to follow, and most importantly—clean. There was no blood or viscera here to be seen. The ground was bone dry, and nothing seemed to be out of the norm. Seeing was easy enough thanks to Coal's constant glow, Falfyre's dull radiant light, and our combined night vision.

After twenty minutes of constant, cautious travel forward at a moderate downgrade, we found a large, twenty-foot wide fissure in the ground that led far below us, and the roof to the cave was outside sight range as well. Across the fissure was a crudely-made bridge of bones strung together and secured by thick cut leather. I didn't think much of it until I saw a lump that looked suspiciously like—

"Is that an ear?" I asked the others softly before pointing to my find.

"Elven," James murmured.

Out of nowhere, flames burst to life on the other side of the crevasse.

"It's been soooo long since I had visitors," a voice cooed. "Leaves me here for so long to hunt and feed on bats and other undesirable things, tending the well for centuries while he sleeps."

"Fuck me…" Muu grumbled.

A bent over figure hobbled into view. Their form was grotesque, twisted beyond all belief. Lights flared above us, illuminating the whole area. The roof to the place was high up above, and there was a thick-looking liquid in the crevasse, but they didn't stop walking closer to the bridge.

They were isolated on the other side of the bridge. The creature looked worse in the glowing light. Her green skin, marred with boils, scars, pustules, and gore shifted with movement.

"That's a hag of some kind," James spat. "Expect more magic and some terrible shit. She's probably the only thing here. Hags hate other living creatures, but she said something about the lich, so she may be serving him or a slave."

"You speak as though I cannot hear you," she said sweetly. Her voice didn't match her features as she spoke and kept hobbling toward the bridge to get to our side of the moat-like barrier.

"Stay there," Yohsuke barked at her harshly.

**Hag level 43.**

"No, no," she cooed again. "You want me to come over, don't you?"

This cloying scent reached toward us, and I found myself

feeling more relaxed. The others were slack-jawed and looked dazed as well, but the creature was still ugly as sin, her thin, scarred face with a large bulbous nose protruding like an elephant's trunk. The worst thing was that she was much, much closer. Almost completely across the bridge.

Rather than instantly crossing to meet her, I let her keep coming. Coal was growling at my side, leaning against me. I let my left arm droop with my sword and stood there, hoping I looked sufficiently dazed. I wanted to lure her closer so I could kill her swiftly.

"Poor Lagran has been so, so lonely all these years." She was close enough that she reached out and stroked Yoh's chin almost tenderly. "So lonely. So hungry. I think I will skin the lizard first, then make a stew of his bones while I keep the others for company. Then the fox after that. His tails will make a fine scar– OOF!"

*Damn it!* I growled in my mind. *There goes my surprise. I can save this.*

An arrow pierced her cheek the same time Coal lunged forward and shoved her away from me. As she backpedaled to regain her balance, I burst forward and kicked her as hard as I could. She flew across the fissure, hit the edge of it, and shrieked as she fell into whatever was below us with a splash.

The others came out of the stupor and blinked.

"What happened?" Muu asked groggily.

"She rolled you guys, but somehow Zeke and I resisted it," Bokaj spoke up.

"I could see the real her," I admitted as I picked up Falfyre. "Truesight."

The sound of liquid beneath us began to grow louder and louder until there was a blood-red wave coming over the side. Black orbs floated to the side facing us, and the same huge nose and thin features came with them.

"You cannot drown me, new scarf." The hag cackled.

"Scatter!" Muu shouted over his shoulder as he took his position as tank.

The others were moving instantly. In my hurry, I stupidly dropped my sword as a hand of blood came crashing down where I had been.

"Ahhh!" the hag screeched. Where she had touched the blade, the blood had turned solid, like a scab or a clot.

The sword itself was unsullied by the blood and lay still on the ground. I would need to go get it as soon as I could. That would help a lot.

As I watched for the next attack, the sword lifted into the air and shot toward me hilt first. I snatched it out of the air in wonder and was instantly reminded of the last line of the spell description—it answers to the caster's will wholly. I tossed it into the air and willed it to stay there. It did. There was a small drain on my mana, 1 MP per second, but this was amazing!

I focused on keeping it in front of me like a shield and began to charge Phoenix Burst. The double mana cost of 500 MP would suck, but the damage would be worth it, I hoped.

I sent the sword out to distract her with my friends running interference by firing arrows and spells as best they could. James was firing Ki blasts where he could, and Muu was trying to spear her face by launching his weapon at her. The mana cost rose by a point every ten or fifteen feet per second, but it was worth it at sixty feet and 3 MP a second. I could hold it for at least a minute, and that was way more time than needed.

*Sending a charged spell at her, mind your heads!* I growled to the others through our earrings, then remembered that they couldn't hear me that way. Fuck a warning, she could hear it too.

I felt the first pulse of energy in my palm signaling the double of the spell and released it at the base of her body. Time seemed to move to a crawl as the projectile careened toward her.

I saw a flash of light above her head from one of the others, and she shrunk down away from it with a cry of pain. I worried that she would sink too far, but Yohsuke shot a spell toward her right flank that made her pull her midsection tight together. I cried aloud in victory as time returned to normal and the spell hit; the detonation was a golden implosion of light that burned, then burst from the center in a red supernova that cut the bloody hag in half.

Her blood-curdling shriek almost deafened me, then she— her actual body—plummeted to the ground near the lip of the crevasse and landed with a sickening crack.

"Fire damage hurts her the worst!" James shouted. His fists burst into flame, using his elemental fists if I recalled, and he leaped the distance between them.

I sent Falfyre forward with a flex of my will and stabbed it toward her head. It almost took her out, but she was just able to move it out of the way in time. Coal worried at her legs as she tried to kick him away. As I walked toward her, I noted the cut and burn mark that it left behind on her disgusting face.

She held her hand up, and a lance of blood leaped from the crevasse and shot into James's body. His health dropped by half, and he stopped punching and kicking the downed hag and began to struggle visibly with himself.

He gritted his teeth, started to sit back away from her, and slowly reach for Coal with one hand and his own throat with his other.

An arrow struck her in the jugular while she motioned for another of the bloody spears to come to her aid. The spear, already arcing toward me, dropped limply to the ground and splattered the earth in crimson. She growled and spat, but no sound left her throat. So, there was that question answered.

If a muting arrow hits a spellcaster who uses non-verbal spells—can anyone hear her scream?

No. But the look of impotent outrage as I snatched Falfyre into my only hand and stuck the blade through her throat, cutting her head off, was pretty damn mean. Actually—it was a permanent grimace of hatred I don't think I'd forget for some time without booze.

Once we finished looking over James, we began to cast our

gazes elsewhere. There didn't seem to be any more enemies around.

"Let's go see what's on the other side of this bridge." Yohsuke started the trek across the bridge. It held him easily, but we all went one at a time just in case.

The other side was fifty feet by fifty feet but a more rounded area. There was a tent made of leather. I would only think of it as leather and not what it probably was, but I sure as hell wasn't going near there.

Muu had no problems outright, then seemed to notice something that made him jump away from the structure in fright.

"There's a face!" He shrieked. He stabbed at it with his spear, and the tearing that came about, as a result, seemed to relieve him.

Eventually, we found a stone that had runes carved on to it that looked slick in the low light. I picked it up carefully, and my hand came away drenched in blood.

"Damn it," I gagged. The spot I touched seemed to grow slick once more. We left it and searched some more.

There was a hole in the ground that we found in the exact same shape and size as the stone. I grabbed an old, frayed cloth I found in my inventory and grabbed the stone to take back to the impression.

"I'm pretty sure she was here guarding something important," I muttered to the others. They seemed to agree, and I grimaced. "I already lost a hand being stupid. Wanna see what's in there?"

I looked at the others, and James made to go before Bokaj smacked him.

"Hey!" He gave his arm a half-hearted rub. "I was only kidding. Put the stone in, man."

"Yeah." Muu sighed. "Could be treasure. Could be more souls. It could even be back up. Either way, we need to open that up so that we can be sure and not have an even more fucked up situation at our backs."

I blinked at him; the others blinked at him. They looked at me and nodded before Yohsuke put a hand on my shoulder, "Well, looks like we open the damned thing. We're right here with you."

I looked at the others and put the stone into the depression. There was a dull glow, then a ring of sickly-green light burst from it with symbols radiating from the center like chains. All five of us backed up as far as we could to get away from that light. Every foot for twelve feet, the chains clanked against a new line of a circle.

Once the circle of glyphs and lines stopped growing from each other, they rotated first left, then right and then began to ebb into the portion before it toward the center stone. As they went, the circles stripped away the stone beneath them and left a pool of brackish liquid that stank of... I have no idea how to describe the stench.

If I had to try and relate it, I'd say it was the scent of despair, broken dreams, and uncle Jeff's gym socks after leg day. It was putrid.

I heard retching to my left and right. That made me dry heave, but I held my shit together. I was a Druid. A Primal Warrior. I wouldn't lose my shit over this.

I puked—shut up already. You come smell this shit and not throw your cookies all over the damned ground.

Once the rock beneath them had been taken away, the liquid began roiling as if alive—the moans and groans of tortured souls buffeting us as if they were crying out in our faces.

It was heart-wrenching. I hated it. It made me want to jump from the side of this rock in the center of the earth. I reached out and beckoned for the others to back off.

"Get on the other side of the bridge. Bokaj, as soon as you see the ball of fire pass you, cast purify on it. Okay?" He nodded and put a hand out. "Guard your eyes, boys."

I charged Phoenix Burst again, and as the flaming ball of golden fire sped past him, Bokaj purified it; it grew larger, seemingly stronger for the added holy aspect. The spell landed in the center of the pool, and the same thing as last time happened. The whole thing evaporated, and I felt a chill rend my body.

I fell to my knees as a sourceless voice of rage and anguish shouted in pain. Then the voice changed.

"You think you can stop me? Soon I will take your precious friend from you, and there will be nothing you or anyone else can do! You had better hurry." The lich's voice was hoarse and furious. With a cackle, he added, "His mind is already falling apart!"

I looked at the others and grimaced. "Think he was mad?"

The others nodded together, but Yoh offered me a hand up. "I think that was a large source of power for him. We need to get to Jaken."

We all looked toward the exit to the cavern and smiled. It was a straight shot back to the hole. I looked at my friends, and the race was on. It was difficult sprinting with the sword in hand, but that's how I did it. No sense in wasting the mana to make it float or dismiss it.

Thanks to our high dexterity and no need for caution, we made it in a quarter of the time it had taken to reach the hag's den.

Once we reached the end of the tunnel, Muu laid on his back and gave each of us a lift up with his feet. Like playing a game with a toddler, but this one would hurt if you smacked into the side of the wall or cave. I brought T' up in my collar and summoned Coal the same as I had earlier.

Once we were all up top, Muu leaped up himself. He made it look easy.

"Hey man, what's your strength at now?" I asked him curiously. He hadn't seemed to struggle with being our boost up, and each of us had made the transition relatively easily.

"Oh, my strength is at eighty-five, bud." He flashed a huge, reptilian grin at me. "Figured since we'll be fighting a Dragon sometime soon, it would be a good idea to be able to hit things harder. Ya know?"

I whistled at that. That was thirty-three points higher than mine. Fuck, man.

"Yeah, I hear you. Let's get out of here then." We exited the room and came face to face with a group of maids and butlers —five of each—sweeping the halls and dusting as we went to leave the room.

We looked at them, their outfits pristine black and white; they looked alive. Several of them looked like they were malnourished, sure, but they seemed alive.

They saw us, curtsied and bowed before beginning to move on.

"Excuse us," Bokaj tried to get their attention, but they kept moving. "Well, I guess I'll just go fuck myself."

We stepped on to the red carpeting and immediately the butlers and maids turned with a shriek. Their once-pink skin turned gray and drawn. Their teeth elongated, and their mouths opened so long they could have eaten my entire foot. Clawed hands flashed in the light of the hall, and the fight was on.

"These vampires or something?" Muu yelled. "I sense vampires!"

"They're undead! Kill them!" Bokaj ordered and began firing arrows into the crowd of monsters.

A couple of them staggered, but without silver or some kind of holy spells, we would be hard pressed. The vampire help moved so fast it was difficult to keep up. It was almost all I could do to keep the damned things away. A few minutes of fighting and I got more and more pissed off as they kept picking on me. What was left of my right arm was cut and bleeding again.

"Gather together back to back," Yohsuke barked and shot an Astral Bolt at one of the undead fuckers, and it shot back down the hall.

We grouped up and set about killing them as best we could. It took casting Aspect of the Owl on myself to be able to antici-pate their movements, but as soon as I did, I was able to call shots to my friends. Bokaj was fine, somehow. He could see and easily predict their movements, but Falfyre's flame began to make the spell even more worthwhile.

Soon enough, the help was a pile of dust and a source of irritation for me, but oh well. Can't blame them for going after the guy missing the majority of his damned arm.

The experience was negligible. Sure, it was a drop in the bucket, but it seemed like all of these creatures were lesser somehow. Like summoned creatures didn't give all that much experience in video games because it was the summoner who mattered. Even the hag had given an okay chunk of experience, somewhere close to a thousand or so. It had been difficult to pay attention with the lich bitching at us.

I cast Mass Regrowth, and we healed ourselves as we went further on down the hall to a staircase that led up. This one looked like it was used by the staff of the place, and it was easily accessible if we went up one at a time.

"You guys want to go up or explore the other side?" I asked.

"No time, we need to get Jaken." James shook his head. He was already six steps up the stairs before the rest of us made our way to them. The top floor was a myriad of bedrooms and offices that weren't guarded, nor did they hold anything of value. Not a single copper. No items. Just this warped reality.

After doing our due diligence and searching each of the rooms for potential enemies, we crossed the bridged balcony that we had seen from below into the other portion of the wing. This wing had more than a dozen suits of armor lining each side of the hall. They were black and white like the knights that we had fought the last time we had dealt with the lich.

The armor stood on raised pedestals on the edge of the carpeting a foot and a half from the wall. The only thing they could possibly have been guarding was the set of double doors at the end of the hall.

"Fuck..." I groaned. "Not these assholes again. There are so many of them!"

Muu tapped his foot before snapping his fingers and tapping on my shoulder. "You want to do a large fastball special?"

I gathered what he had planned and grinned at him. "Make it an extra large."

I shifted into my fox form and jumped into his arms. He cocked back with his right arm and grinned at me savagely. "Using the bracelet. As soon as you're close, I'll shout, and then you shift. I'm going to see what I can do about the other side of the hall too."

I nodded once and settled my body in for the flight. He launched me forward, and the wind flying around my body seemed to squeal as I broke through the calm air.

"Now!" Muu bellowed.

I shifted into my Ursolon form and crashed into the first four suits of armor and thrust the last one into the others. They managed to stay together, but they were knocked down. I shifted to fox before scampering away from the armor as fast as my three good legs would allow. A clatter to my left drew my attention. I saw the suits of armor on the opposite side of the hall drop, their helmets gone. I looked toward the end of the hallway, and Muu's spear wobbled with them pierced straight through.

"There's more!" Yohsuke warned before all hell broke loose.

Doors hidden by alcoves on each side opened, and the shambling dead came out—half-rotted corpses who hungered for the flesh of the living. They wore any number of bloody, decayed garments that barely covered them anymore.

I jumped as high as I could and shifted into my panther form, hoping the size and muscle would help me get back to my friends. A sharp pain pierced my left hind leg, and I turned to see an arrow sticking into the bone; the leg went numb, then I listed to the right, overbalanced before dropping. I fell closer to my friends but not close enough.

Suddenly, James was there, snapping his fists into faces, and he barked, "Go, fox!"

I did, and he scooped me into his arm; then we blurred toward the others. He pulled the arrow from my leg, and Bokaj cast Purify on me before I shifted back.

"Thanks," I huffed. "Step aside—I'll blast these guys away with Phoen–"

"You cast that spell and you could blow the whole place," Muu warned. "We go in the old fashioned way," he punched his left hand with his right, "like men."

I laughed at his serious demeanor and simply commented, "Sploosh."

He growled and lunged forward, punching an undead in the jaw so hard that the skin tore and the gooey bone turned into a projectile that smacked another undead in the face.

"No more punching!" Muu shouted, clearly kind of freaked out more than proud over that.

Thinking to preserve my mana a bit, I stabbed Falfyre into one of the dead where I left it, reached into my inventory with my now-free hand and pulled out Magus Bane.

"Here!" He looked my way, and I tossed it to him. "Look near the top—axe side cuts, hammer side, just hit shit!"

"Ooooh!" he cooed in delight before swinging the great axe like a scythe in front of him, mowing down the undead in a path of gore that wasn't quite the ideal situation. Some died again, but the upper portions of the still-animated dead began to grasp at his legs as he stepped through. Coal scampered behind Muu. As the Dragon-kin swung, the flame wolf stood on to his hind legs and crushed skulls here and there like a fox pouncing after something in the snow.

I began to follow along while keeping the monsters from flanking him. The others followed me, and soon, we had a working murderous congo line. Every person covered a different section of the bodies coming at us and dealt with the dead as swiftly as they were able. It was brutal work but efficient.

We took cuts, scrapes, and even a couple of nibbles here and there, but it was much better than being overrun. Arrows flew over our heads, not really getting too close. The creatures who died—again—were only downed by severing the spinal cord at the neck or severe brain damage. So those like Yohsuke, Bokaj, and James were able to rely on precision to get the job done. I carved through my enemies and finished those who fell close to me with quick stabs.

It took us ten minutes to get midway to the end of the hall, and it was hilarious watching the suits of armor. They simply stood there, unable to move in the horde of dead. Except for the one in the back with the bow who now had a clear shot at us as the dead parted!

"Bow!" I shouted and threw Falfyre at the armor archer, hoping to stop that shot.

A gauntleted hand snatched the weapon from the air and stopped the momentum completely. The armor began to take on a reddish hue, then I willed the sword to burst into flames, melting the armor and peppering everything up to twelve feet from it with shrapnel. The weapon was gone, but I could always summon it again.

But rather than wasting the time, I simply took the hand axe I had acquired from Rowland's and cast Star Blade on it. The weapon took on a dark hue like the night with multicolored stars along the cutting edge.

I turned to the others and grunted, "Either we get in that room right now, or we take care of the armored assholes."

"Get inside," James and Bokaj answered together before Bokaj finished, "there are too many of these assholes, and they just keep coming from the rooms."

Sure enough, they did. They had no qualms about stepping on their dead—deader, fuck if I knew the right term—comrades, though many of them fell on the uneven terrain.

"Let's get you to your weapon then, Muu." Yohsuke sighed.

All of us were starting to feel the effects of the continued battling, but our friend was in danger, right? We do everything we can together, and we were gonna do our damnedest to see him freed.

We got to the door, huffing and puffing from having to continually beat ass to get there. We had Bokaj paying more attention to the archer. He would fire and force one of the protectors to get in the way of the incoming shot.

Muu pulled his spear from the wall with a grunt and then gave us all a nod before opening the doorway to the room at the end of the hall.

We filed through the door into a darkened room, turned, and threw several shitty weapons that we had collected from other fights into the door handle and I melted them with my flame mana so they were stronger and welded to the door.

"Bad move, you guys," Jaken's voice echoed behind us.

The sound of air being cleaved in two erupted, and a sickening crunch greeted us. I looked over to see James pinned to the wall by a large, black greatsword as lights burst to life all around us. Except they weren't lights.

They were luminescent souls, their mouths open in silent, terror-filled shrieks. They flitted from the floor to the ceiling where they began to coil and spin with a growing flow in a circular spirit cloud above us.

"Why is that?" Bokaj spat. "And who the hell threw that? Where's the lich?"

I pulled the blade from James's chest and rapidly cast Heal and then Regrowth on him. His health shot back up from half to three-quarters full and rising. While he was healing, I looked about our surroundings for the threat.

The room was empty except for a couple things—a desk that served as a holder for books and papers that I couldn't make out from this distance. It was a mid-sized room, maybe thirty by fifty feet. Then there was a throne that looked comfortable where Jaken watched us from.

His skin was pale in the light, and his mithral armor had been traded away for a set of black plate armor and a helmet that looked like a skull cast in metal. His hair was down and over his shoulders, and the way he sat just wasn't him. It seemed off.

But I mean, if you had been held captive, you may be a little high strung or out of sorts too, right?

"So you finally deemed to come and find me?" His voice held sardonic mirth, ignoring Bokaj's questions entirely. As if the fact that we had arrived was something he had doubts about but was pleasantly surprised to see come to pass.

"Of course we did, puto," Yoh grumped. "We've been looking for you for a bit now. We were lucky to find James before those hounds did."

"I see." He leaned his head to the side like his head was falling, and it just stopped bouncing slightly, then stopping completely like some sort of clockwork puppet. "Well, I can't say that I believe you. Out there collecting all that 'experience?' I mean, we've been hunting for ways to get stronger while we 'tried' to find a way to get to the Hells for Balmur, right? While he's stuck there going through who knows what?"

"Hey, man, you know that's what we're doing!" Bokaj stepped forward angrily. "No one wants him back with us more than I do! You and I have had countless conversations about this."

Jaken's head rolled down until his chin rested almost-drunkenly on his chest before he looked back up at Bokaj.

"Talk is cheap." He lifted his hand to stare at it before waving it at us angrily. "I've been enlightened on the things that have been going on outside in the world. The army's massing against us. The Children group. The Mages. Hell, even the little city north of here is out looking for us, and all because we weren't powerful enough to protect our own—because we couldn't take what was rightfully ours! How many times has Zeke, Muu, or any of the rest of you gotten in our way for moving on? Becoming so distracted by petty things?"

I cast my eyes down. Was that true? Those things had been necessary evils, right? Something we had to do in the moment so that we could be accepted and supported. We wouldn't make it here on our own. We needed our allies. We needed each other. And seeing some of the glances my friends were throwing around… they didn't seem to feel the same.

But why now, of all times, would Jaken bring these doubts to light? That wasn't him. That wasn't like him at all.

"No more. I'm taking what I learned here, and I'm going to

get Balmur back. With or without all of you. Because I'm stronger now." He held up his fist and clenched it. The armor creaking in protest, then quieting. "So much stronger. Stronger than I've ever felt. And no one will stand in my way. Never again. This world will bow. All will bend the knee!"

As the last words left his lips, I got a good look at my friend. I saw an ethereal light around his body, and the eyes that stared back at me weren't Jaken's.

"Get the hell out of my friend, you dead asshole!" I roared and shot forward, my vision cloaked in red almost instantly.

Something took my legs out from beneath me, and I fell backward despite my forward momentum. As I flipped, I saw the black greatsword hurtle into Jaken's outstretched hand as he stood looming over me now. My righteous rage was gone, replaced by worry and doubt.

How could this have happened to my friend?

"And there are sacrifices to be made to see this through," the lich hissed from my friend's throat.

A spell clanged off his armor, getting his attention away from me for a heartbeat, long enough for me to take the hand axe in my hand and slash at the armor. There was small nick in it, but it filled back in almost instantly. Fuck.

I scrambled away from him on my hand and feet just as the sword came down where I was supposed to land. James was pulling me by my shirt, and I threw my hand axe at the lich's face to see if it would help.

"Got an idea!" Bokaj called behind us. "Muu, for the trick shot. Screwball, corner pocket!"

I looked over in time to see Muu raise his shield in time to deflect one of Bokaj's arrows into Jaken's neck. The man flinched but pulled the projectile out. The shot had taken a sizable chunk of health, but it was going up so fast, it was like he was healing. Then I saw a flash of radiant light spill around me from behind, and there was a cry of anguish.

"The souls above are healing him! That's his po—" Jaken's

voice was panicked for a moment; he was straining, in pain. Then he grimaced and spat. "Ow."

Jaken was gone, and I heard a grunt of pain and saw Bokaj flying through the air above us before landing on the other side of the throne. He hit the desk, and the whole thing toppled over. He wasn't moving; then Tmont was over him, licking his face hurriedly. Her tongue glowed a little, but it could have been the souls around us making it seem that way.

James was instantly next to the lich, punching him full on in the armor. I heard portions of it crumple and snap like tin cans, then a grunt of pain. Jaken's health dropped a bit, and this time, the recovery wasn't *as* quick. It was fast, don't get me wrong, but it didn't seem as fast as before.

I summoned Falfyre, then stood. I cut a soul to my left in half and started to move toward the lich in Jaken's body. I began to weave through a system of sword attacks that was surprisingly easy.

I'm lying. I cut the soul in half, and as soon as I stood in front of him, he started to wallop me with that damned sword he was swinging.

"You got some overcompensating issues going on there, duke?" I teased as he pushed me yet another foot back. He didn't seem to care about James or even Yohsuke who had begun to attack him from behind. For a full five seconds, I just tried to keep him intent on me. 56 MP returned, and I kicked the asshole as hard as I could.

He slid back a couple feet, then Muu was instantly on top of him, thrusting his short spear as fast as he could, forcing the lich to back away.

I thought better of my original plan when I saw our opponent's eyes slide to me and simply stabbed my sword into the ground and cast Phoenix Burst into the gathering spirits above. Then again. 21 MP left now. Time to get up close and personal.

I lumbered forward and began to channel my rage into my sword strikes. I would stab and parry while we attempted to overwhelm him. The damage was starting to add up, and his crazy regeneration was nowhere near where it had been.

We fought him down to half health before he screamed in frustration, and an unseen force picked us up, threw us against the walls like an angry child tossing away a toy, and held us there. Was I going to have to kill one of my best friends? How were we going to get him out of this one?

"You dare stand between me and my destiny?!" The lich's face came more to the fore, and Jaken looked to be in extreme anguish. Tears fell from his eyes as he bit back a cry of pain.

*No room for doubt, Zeke. Put in the work, and have faith.* I tried to center my tumultuous mind and quell my aching heart in vain. I would do my part. The others needed me to be in this moment with them. And I, them.

The lich held out a ghostly hand and tugged at the air in front of him like pulling a weight from the ground. The souls began to gather faster and faster. It had only been twenty seconds, so I was at 245 MP; five more seconds and I could fuck with him. I didn't dare let go of my only viable weapon to drink mana potions, but if those spirits healed him anymore, the weapon wouldn't be of any great help.

I willed Falfyre to go forth and harry the lich and the spirits while he was distracted. I pulled two of the newer, more potent mana potions from my inventory, pulled the corks with my teeth, spit them out, and downed them both at once. My mana replenished by one hundred points, and I instantly cast my new spell at the growing nimbus of light above us once more. As soon as the spell was cast, the souls burned with purifying light, and a great sword was shoved savagely through my stomach.

I was down to little more than a quarter of my hit points after that blow, and the pain was immense. My eyes went bleary, and everything was dull now. I used my stored spell, Heal, and recovered 100 HP. That was better.

A howl of anger came from Coal, and he bum-rushed the evil specter and began to bite at him.

*"Light the flames and burn the stars, archers arrows fly so far, but the*

*light in you will shine so true, little Paladin,"* Bokaj's voice, strained with suffering, rang out around us a slow melody on the guitar carried his words farther. I felt better and watched as my mana and health both began to restore by small amounts. *"That light so true comes not just from you, but the friends in your life and your sweet little moon. She watches from afar, you know who you are, little Paladin."*

The lich chuckled once, then began to laugh deeper as he slowly meandered over to the singing figure prone on the floor. "You think a song will save you, you inept bardling?"

It didn't matter that Coal was cutting the fuck out of his mouth trying to bite the mail and pull him away. It didn't matter that Tmont had pounced out of nowhere and tried to pull the lich away. He smacked the cat away like a fly and kept walking forward unfazed.

The lich lifted Bokaj by the front of his shirt, and the man smiled weakly. "No," he spat in the lich's face, "I think it's all a friend needed to hear."

James had managed to sneak close enough to sunder the lich's armor once more and stuck an arrow in the hole. Bokaj swung his ringed fist at the arrow, and a wave of concentrated force shoved the improvised shiv into his target.

The lich shrieked once, then fell silent as Jaken's face came back to the surface with a grimace of pure determination. We watched as he struggled to regain his body.

"Come on, man," I heard James mutter from right next to him. Jaken gnashed his teeth, and I saw the ghostly lich return. Then the inner struggle began in earnest.

"Fight that bitch back, motherfucker!" Yohsuke shouted as he stumbled to his feet. "You ain't no punk ass."

"Do it for Luna," I growled. "Your daughter needs you. *We* need you. So get your *ASS* up!"

Bokaj reached out and tapped his forehead, and Jaken fell to his knees. I walked over and cast Purify on Jaken once.

"Luna," Bokaj stated, then looked at us to get us to join him as he said it again.

"Luna," we implored together. Jaken's head fell into his hand, and he shouted mutely.

"Luna," we repeated, watching as he slammed the ground with his fist, and the floor beneath him cracked.

"Luna!" The mute from the arrow began to wear off. The ghostly moan from the lich and Jaken's cries of anguish as they battled started as a whisper.

"LUNA!" we shouted, and another wave of force shoved us away from our friend, but we had been ready this time.

I downed three mana potions in preparation and was shocked when Jaken stood slowly to his feet, the lich looking out at us in triumph.

"No child's name can best me—Luca vel Couervith—you foolish mortals!"

Bokaj and I hit him with Purify once more, and he fell to his knees again. Finally, Jaken's face came to the fore.

He took his fist, held it over the pommel of the great sword, and shouted, "*LUNA!*"

A light so painfully bright that it blinded all of us flashed into his hand, and I had to look away. Through the radiant chords, the sound of glaring, unerring, holy power rang out, and I heard something I had been waiting to hear.

"I, Jaken Warmecht, Paladin of Lady Radiance and father to the Moon, renounce you, evil spirit. I am the hammer forged in holy light so that I might smite you. Leave this vessel, and face Her judgement!"

"Nooooo!" the lich, Luca, hissed.

The light died a little, and when I could see again, my health was full and so was my mana. I felt rejuvenated, and I could see the others did too. When I looked at Jaken, the black armor was dust on the ground, and a set of pure platinum plate armor had replaced it. Wings of golden light flared from his back and wrapped protectively around him.

"Zeke," he held a hand out to me, "your holy sword, brother."

I tossed Falfyre and willed it to go to him, a dozen mana spent to get it to him.

He gripped the weapon, and the radiant fire along the cutting edges began to pulse until flames of orange and gold radiated from it.

"I call to the heavens that they may bless this hand, this unworthy tool, with their might. Let he who would see this world fall see the error of his ways and glimpse majesty in his final moments!"

Thousands of voices sang through my mind as the shadows in the room faded, and the sound of wings flapping overlapped with what Jaken was saying.

Luca looked horrified, his spectral form no longer handsome and debonair but moldy and fetid. Bone was visible, and his legs dangled limply. When the spirits refused to come as he wordlessly beckoned to them, he tried to lunge forward, his clawed hand reaching for the Paladin, and only a single flash of Falfyre was needed to cut the foul spirit in two. The wings rushed forward, and the souls that left the lich from the cut seemed to be shepherded away.

The light in the room grew dimmer and dimmer until finally, we were left in a derelict courtyard that seemed familiar. It was familiar. We were in the courtyard in the center of the old ruins. Under the night stars. So we hadn't been gone all that long. I hoped.

I had a notification stating that I had leveled up after that fight and so did Coal, putting him to level 14. About fucking time too; it had taken so long. Felt good to level up. I'd take care of that later though. Jaken was kneeling in the center of the courtyard, staring at the stars above us. His eyes were closed, and his mouth was moving.

He was bathed in a batch of moonlight, and the platinum armor he wore returned to the polished, perfect mithral he had worn before. The light faded, and I approached slowly, but James got to him first.

"Jaken, buddy—I'm sorry," James started, but the Paladin held up a hand.

"It's cool, man," he said, his normal voice and mannerisms back. "You had a chance to escape. And that's great. You did the best thing you could have. I understand."

Jaken pulled James into a tight hug and gave his face a light slap. He came over to the others and gave each a word of thanks and a hug before getting to me.

"Thank you, man," he said sadly. "I was so mad that I stormed off after I couldn't heal you. When I did, a messenger told me that a great evil was brewing in these ruins, and I thought I could take it. I was wrong. And not only could I not heal you, but you all had to come and save me from myself. I don't deserve you guys."

"Hey, man, I know that wasn't you in there," I tried to comfort him, but he shook his head.

"Yeah. It was." He looked at me sadly. "Eventually, he broke me down. Took all memory of my life away from me and fed me lies. Based on those lies, I was angry. I had almost gone to the dark side and let him in willingly. That fight was me still struggling a little. I guess I knew if I didn't fight, I'd never see my baby girl again, but you guys knew that, huh?"

We all nodded, and he sighed. "Never again. My faith is stronger than ever—in my goddess and in my friends. Let's get back to the village."

I agreed and cast Teleport as soon as all of us were touching.

We landed in the center of the village with the scent of decay everywhere around us. The inner portion was fine, but there were wounded people laying on sheets everywhere in the center of the village.

"The fuck happened here?!" Yohsuke spat as he grabbed the nearest person.

The unfamiliar woman answered, "The dead crawled through the forest and attacked us. Lady Maebe and the guard held 'em off for three days while anyone who volunteered to help did their best. They—the dead—began to fall earlier in the day, a few here and there, then finally, all of 'em." She looked about worried, the shock forcing her to repeat herself. "These is the ones what got hurt tryin', tryin' to help."

"I'm on it. You guys go see what's going on." Jaken waved us away and began to step through the place, casting healing spells as he went.

I cast Mental Message to Maebe, "Where are you, dearest?"

She responded tiredly, "I am with the children. I will meet you at the tavern."

"Tavern," I grunted. "If any of you want to help with this, I don't blame you for staying."

"I'll chill here and play some recovery music for the group." Bokaj smiled and turned to go toward the wounded behind Jaken.

"I'll be going to the kitchen to whip up some grub. I'm hungry as fuck, and I have no doubt Chef and his lady are in there cooking up a shit storm." Yohsuke jogged off.

"I think it's all done here, so I'll go do some research. " James wandered off on his own, and when I looked at Muu, he shrugged and motioned toward the inn.

We jogged there and ran into several more injured guards outside the barracks, and Maebe stepped from the shadows as we walked closer.

She walked over to me and threw her hands around my neck in a hug. "Where were you? You were gone for days."

"It was a time slip of some kind. Is everyone okay?" I couldn't help the rising panic building in my chest. She nodded once, and I sighed in relief, suddenly exhausted. "Let's go inside, and I'll explain everything."

Muu left us a second later. "I'm going to go check on everyone I know, not many, but see if there's anything I can do."

I nodded, and Maebe and I were off. We entered my room, and I told her about everything that happened. It took a little bit, and as time went on, I felt more and more tired.

"Everyone is okay?" I asked again. Why the fuck was I so tired? My friends were possibly hurt. I looked about, found my water basin, and rushed to it, dunking my head fully. It helped a little bit.

"Yes. The volunteers were injured, but the worst of the injuries weren't truly life-threatening." Maebe looked concerned, her lips in a small frown, but continued, "Vrawn, Zhavron and their guard recruits held the line amazingly. Rowland and Sam, with the help of some of Queen Kyra's bears, kept the dead from flanking us. During the daylight hours, they were significantly weaker, so the villagers had a much easier time of defending us. They would stop so we could rest some, then resume in the evening as dusk fell."

A wry grin graced my lips. "Then night fell, and you let loose havoc, right?"

"You know me well." Her triumphant smile was endearing, but she frowned. "I dared not release my full strength though. I did not wish to further worry the children."

I understood where she was coming from.

I cast Mental Message, "Hey, Rowland, you okay, buddy?"

"Busy, lad. Glad yer back. Stay 'way," he replied as he grunted. Weird.

I did the same for Sam, who answered tiredly, "Fine. Thank you for taking care of that issue and for bringing Queens Maebe and Kyra to help protect the village. We owe all of you a debt I fear we could never repay. Good night, Zeke."

*We all okay?* I asked the others.

Yohsuke grunted, *Soup's on, man. Gonna fix this and knock out. Later.*

*Doing good. Jaken and I have most of the folks here taken care of, and they're healing nicely. We'll be back in about ten to fifteen,* Bokaj answered softly.

*Researching a bit more before bed. Sleep well, man.* James yawned loudly.

Muu yawned as well. *Everyone seems taken care of, and the wall is still good. Going to bed in a minute.*

The relief I felt was immense, and now, with all the worries and doubts free from my mind, the toll of all the fighting began to wear on me. It was soul deep. I could've lost my friend. We could have died, had almost died. Fuck, man.

Maebe brought me against her and began to rock back and forth soothingly as my emotions, turmoil, and anger at myself and that evil bastard's accusations began to roll down my furred cheeks. There was no red in my vision, only cold, unending, and calculated anger at myself.

I stayed there like that until sleep took me into oblivion, and I knew no more.

———

I woke up the following morning with my head in Maebe's lap and her humming a soft tune as she stroked my fur.

"Good morning, sleepy head," she greeted warmly. "I have some good news. Enter!"

Xiphyre entered with Thogan and an exhausted-looking Rowland dragging behind.

I sat up slowly and waited for them to speak.

"For the mist's sake, just show it to him, you lumpy shit," the faerie cursed and kicked Thogan in the shoulder.

Thogan smiled at his friend, bowed his head respectfully to his queen, then looked at me before saying simply, "Here."

I caught the bundle he threw me and opened it cautiously.

**WARNING!**

***Do you wish to sacrifice one (1) level's worth of experience to this cursed object?***

***Yes/No?***

I pulled my good hand back as if I had been bitten.

"Told ye, wings—most lot wouldn't give up precious experience at his level." Thogan sighed. "Especially not to a cursed item like that."

"It isn't actually a curse, though!" Xiphyre huffed. "The Gods categorize it as such because it demands an experience and mana sacrifice to work" he flitted over to pull the item from the satchel and pointed at it, "and the experience is a one-time thing. The mana draw is a daily thing, but that's not too bad if he's got mana as high as I think he does."

The item he held up was the same size as my original hand, but it was made of the green Faerie Iron. There were joints that were trimmed with some kind of purple metal I was unfamiliar with altogether.

"You'll find that once you pay the required fee, it is quite pleasing." Xiphyre looked pointedly at Thogan, who shrugged. "This is not the first limb replacement I have done and surely won't be the last. Though this is the first time I have been approached by royalty so directly. As always, Lady Cloaked in Shadow, 'tis a pleasure."

"What does it do?" I asked with a feeling of trepidation.

Thogan and Xiphyre looked at each other, then at me, and Thogan tried to speak over the guffawing faerie.

"Tha's a hand, lad." Thogan coughed in his hand to keep from showing his mirth. "Ye wear it, an' it works like yer ol' one. 'Cept maybe better. Could catch and hold a sword by the blade with this one, I'd imagine."

"The—oh Gods, that was Prime—enchantment makes the item work as though it were your natural hand," Xiphyre slapped his knee, his hair brushing his toes as he bent in two laughing, "and it's specially enchanted to work with spells and shapeshifting. That's both parts of the reason for the mana and experience costs."

Maebe brushed her hand across my left hand and looked at me, her face coming into my vision out of the corner of my eye. "You did state that you felt weaker. Like the team had suffered for your lacking."

I sighed. I did. And to me—it had seemed true. Falfyre and Phoenix Burst were amazing spells, but I needed a hand to do a lot of things like use potions and grab things. It was crucial.

"I will not make this choice for you, Zeke," Maebe spoke softly. "It is your decision, and it will be there for you. Xiphyre owed me a great debt, and this has helped repay a portion of it."

I leaned over and butted her head with mine affectionately. She really was too good to me. My team needed me at full force for what was coming.

Time to advance the plot, eh?

"How do I attach it?"

Xiphyre grinned and shot Thogan a look that screamed victory. He hovered over to me and simply pushed the prosthetic portion of forearm over my own, and it fit almost seamlessly.

The same notification popped up, and Xiphyre nodded vigorously that I should accept it. "Does it take a level already acquired, or does it need to be a level that I haven't used yet?"

"It doesn't specify. All that matters is that it is *your* experience." That made sense, I suppose.

I accepted the experience drain, and it asked if I was certain, that if I had any unspent attribute points, they would be sacrificed along with the experience and any that had been attached to the level sacrificed would be taken away. I accepted.

A burning in my core tore a shout from my lips that I tried to stop. The notifications went fuzzy; then I noted that my level up alert was gone and I was level 30 once more. I felt dizzy and put my hand to my head, aching from the sudden drain of mana on top of the rest.

It was the green hand, and I *felt* my head through my hand. In my excitement, I turned and gently touched Maebe's face. Her look of worry changed to one of joy and wonder.

"It's warm, like you." She closed her eyes and leaned against the hand on her cheek. She turned and looked the faerie in the face. "Consider the three favors you owed now two, Xiphyre."

He lowered his head in deference and then floated back to hover next to Thogan.

"Lady Maebe," Rowland started from outside the doorway.

Then Thogan clapped him on the shoulder and sent the tired smith stumbling forward on to a knee before her.

"We are fast becoming more than acquaintances, young Dwarf." Maebe's voice suddenly took on a more formal, regal tone. "We fought together while your new smithing trainer and his friend made this fine piece of equipment in your forge. You shed blood beside me—does that mean so little to you?"

Rowland grinned despite his baggy eyes and haggard beard. "No. It meant the worl' to mark meself a protector o' me friend's lady love and queen. I'd fight at yer side and yer back any time, yer Majesty. Best ye believe'n tha'. If ye would honor me—I'll lift a mug with ye to celebrate our victories and the blood we shed."

"I would like that," Maebe said simply.

"Good," Rowland clapped his hands, "but I have a request, m'lady."

Maebe waved for the Dwarf to stand, glanced at me then back at him. "You have caught me in an exceptionally generous mood, Rowland. I will hear this request."

Rowland smiled as he stood, his black beard rising and bowed his head before continuing, "I would like for Thogan ta stay and train me in me smithin', if ye'd be willin' to let him."

The queen's smile was replaced by a look of concentration and introspection. Her face was, for once, open to be interpreted while she sorted her thoughts.

"Thogan, do you wish this as well?"

The rock-skinned Dwarf stepped forward and took a knee before his queen. "Ah've stood as yer loyal champion and protector as I did yer ma. I love ye like ye were me own niece. I would nae leave yer side forever," he glanced over to Rowland and put a hand on the other smith's forearm, "but it's been so long since I've known me kin. I wish ta preserve what I know of me culture from when the first Dwarves roamed these mountains. I wish ta pass that stone on to the next generation lest we truly be forgotten."

Maebe stood and began to pace in front of me, between the

Dwarves and I. She paced for a moment in thought before stopping in front of Thogan.

"Thogan Swiftaxe, rise." Thogan did as she bid him. "You have been found guilty of treason against the crown of Winter and Darkness." The Dwarves gasped, Xiphyre looked ready to fight, and I had to admit that even I stood up in fury. "Your punishment is banishment from my realm and my service in that realm."

Thogan's face broke. He sniffled once and looked as though he may have just lost everything he loved.

Maebe leaned down and looked him in the eyes, her face calculated and cold. "You are hereby formally banished from my realm and my service—for two years. By this realm's standards of time."

She smiled and kissed his forehead before noticing the tension in the room. "Come now—Thogan served even my mother loyally. He has spilled more blood than even I have in service to the Cold and Dark. He is as much Unseelie as I am now. This was the only way I could justify my allowing him to stay while still maintaining the safety of my people and security of the crown."

I blinked a couple times and looked down at Thogan who stood both shocked and seemingly confused.

"I, uh, thank ye, yer Majesty?" Thogan blustered a moment, then regained his composure and mastery over what had happened. "I'll use me time well."

"Thank you, m'lady." Rowland looked around happily.

"Please, leave us. There is little time and much to do before we are to travel I expect—correct, Zeke?" Maebe looked expectantly at me.

"Yeah, that's right. We gotta go do a couple things. One involves a Dragon." I smiled, and Xiphyre's eyes sparkled dangerously.

"You mean to do what to this Dragon?" He drifted closer to me on the air. "Will you fight it? Subdue it?" His eyes took on a crazed light. "Kill it?"

"We will do what we have to do—why are you touching my face?" I growled at the little man, and he seemed unperturbed as he latched on to my cheeks.

"Bring the scales here if you do manage to kill it. Or old scales. They are difficult to work with, but they can be made into armor and ingredients to potions. Oh! And their scales can be used as components for enchanting." Xiphyre's feet were kicking in the air as he fluttered away.

"I will keep that in mind," I grunted. "I don't know what's going to happen, but with all of this settled, we'll most likely leave today or tomorrow. We have to resupply, then head out."

"Then we will leave. Come then, Rowland. Lemme show ye the way of elder Dwarves!" The younger Dwarf looked ready to keel over, and Thogan just chuckled. "First, a wee nap, eh? Get to yer fox, lad. We'll pick up tonight afore we drink."

The two Dwarves scuttled out of the room, and I watched as Xiphyre simply eyed me while mouthing *scales* as he exited too.

A small pair of hands shot out and pulled me close. Maebe's hug was gentle at first, then insistent. I felt something wet touch my cheek and looked to see her crying.

"What's wrong?" I asked with concern.

"I never thought I would speak that way to Thogan." She frowned in thought, then collected herself a bit more. "He looked so hurt. I wish there had been another way, but I couldn't think of anything."

"Hey—you did what you had to, to give him what he wanted and to save face with your people. You did what you could. He still cares for you. I saw it!" I brushed her hair away from her eyes. "Hey, why don't you and I go get something to eat, then buy some new clothes for us both? I know I need to return this axe I borrowed from Rowland."

"You go and purchase your things. I will be going to check on the children and let them know I will be gone for a while." She kissed me fully on the muzzle, and I returned it gently. Then I shifted, and it was *not* so gently. We were crunching on time here, so I ended it sooner than either of us seemed to want.

I changed into a fresh pair of clothes—a brown shirt with a pair of black breeches, then decided to shift back so I wouldn't look like a total stranger to the villagers. It was time to buy more clothes. But first?

Food.

———

I had eaten, purchased some new clothes, and was having my old ones laundered as I walked back to the tavern. Rowland had been asleep, so I left the axe I had borrowed on the counter with two gold pieces for him. I even spent Coal's points for his level up. One point to both strength and dexterity, putting them to twenty-one each, and both his last point and natural point went to constitution, leaving him at a healthy sixteen and 160 HP.

The others had been chatting and wanted to leave the following day, and I couldn't blame them. Time passed swiftly today, and some of the villagers were still recovering from the fighting. Jaken had healed them—sure—but that wasn't enough to stop them from reliving the nightmares of the undead hordes that had kept attacking them for three days.

I spent the rest of the day observing from the ground or flying above the village, watching the people as they shrank with each flap of my wings. I looked down and was pleased to see the prosthetic had shifted into a perfect mirror of my old feathers except for the colors, which was really damned cool.

The thermals felt good beneath me, and I turned my thoughts toward what we had been through recently. We had so much to tell Balmur if—*when, gods dammit. It was when. We would be getting him back.*

We were almost strong enough that we could go to the Hells and hold our own. Hopefully. Going to see this Dragon was just a way for us to try and ensure that we came out of it without someone else losing an arm or leg.

I spent some more time mindlessly flying before banking and turning around.

That night, we partied. It was a proper sending away like we had before going to Maven's Rock. Rowland had Vilmas, Thogan, and Maebe trying his home-brewed mead. They loved it. Maebe ordered a barrel of it be kept on hand for her to take home if she so wished it, and Rowland gave her his word.

Vrawn was sullen but understanding that we had to leave. Eventually, everyone ended up going to their rooms or passing out on their own in the tavern's dining area in chairs, on floors, and benches. One particularly sloshed Dwarf had passed out on a table. It was a wild night.

# CHAPTER EIGHT

I smacked my lips and loosened my tongue as I came to consciousness the following morning. I was immediately greeted by a large draw on my mana pool flowing directly into my right hand. I had 2 MP left after that and the beginnings of a headache.

"That's going to suck every morning." I harrumphed and looked around me. I noted that I was on the floor, to my surprise. I sat up and looked around. I was pleasantly surprised to see that Vilmas lay sprawled out between Vrawn and Maebe on my bed.

Maebe was awake, stroking the smaller woman's hair gently, and when she saw me poke my head over the edge of the bed, she smiled at me.

Last I had remembered, Vilmas had been passed out on the table, and Vrawn had been right next to her on a bench.

I looked down, felt a hand touching my leg, and noted that Vrawn's massive hand was on my thigh. I blushed and gently took it from the limb.

"Party pooper," she grumbled groggily and then went back to snoring.

Maebe sank into a pool of shadow, then reached out from beneath the bed to touch me, making me jump. I started to speak, but she held a finger to her lips and pointed up to the two in the bed.

We snuck out of the room, and she filled me in, "They came in shortly after you had fallen asleep. They wanted to cuddle, and you simply weren't having it, so you rolled off the bed and started snoring. They laid down, and you seemed content."

"Well, thank you for letting me not be in the center of that. I have a thing about not being able to move freely, so being in a puppy pile like that without knowing beforehand would have freaked me out."

"Puppy pile?" She quirked her head in thought, then smiled. "Yes, that fits well."

*You all eating?* I called to the others.

*James, Bokaj, and Jaken are in the dining area at a table with chow,* Yohsuke responded. *Muu went to go purchase some more potions and other supplies for me. The Chef's wife, Daliah? She gave us a whole fucking supply of that tea, and she taught me how to make it.*

I grinned—that tea was the shit. We walked out to the dining area, loaded up our plates, and proceeded to wolf down the snackrifice Yoh had thrown together for us with gusto.

Muu joined us shortly after and handed me five more mana potions, enough to put me back up to ten.

"That's all they had this time." He sighed and bit into some bacon, almost moaning. "Fuck, his bacon is so good."

While he chewed noisily, making the fur on my neck stand on end, he pointed to my new arm. "They give you a fake arm?"

I grinned. "Sure did! Feel it."

He reached his bacon-grease covered hand out to me and grasped at my arm curiously. "That's dope."

I flipped him the bird with it and smacked him in his jaw as the others laughed.

"Real arm, but it required an experience sacrifice." The

others seemed confused. "A whole level's worth of it—and a mana sacrifice daily for it to stay active."

"Damn," Bokaj muttered. "That's heavy, man."

We finished our meal after that, gathered what we needed to —for me, it was my freshly-laundered clothes and the ones I had ordered for Maebe. They had been existing styles, but they were altered a little to fit her better.

We said our goodbyes to Willem, then left with a note to the people we needed to say things to on the table. There were people I wanted to say goodbye to, but then again, others that would make a hasty departure difficult altogether. Like Vrawn.

Rather than going straight to the now-abandoned cultist village, we Teleported outside of the jungle and began our trip toward the ocean north west of our position.

Now, some of you might be thinking that it would've been better for me to fly off and find the location we needed to go to as an owl, then teleport back to the others to bring them to the new place. If we hadn't had our asses handed to us for doing things on our own a few times, I'd be tempted, but we needed to be together after all of that. It was a security thing, feel me? Awesome, I thought you would.

There were no towns on the first couple days of our ride, and the city that we did see was too far out of the way to really condone going to see it. Each day, we stopped to spar and train with each other.

Jaken spent more time in silent prayer than he had before, and the others were a little more respectful in how they treated him. It made me curious, though.

On the third day of travel, the ocean was visible on the horizon. I rode Thor up next to Jaken's battle charger, a sturdy war horse wearing radiant armor that protected him.

"Hey, Jaken, those things that were said back there…" I left the question out in favor of a pregnant, hopeful silence.

He responded simply, "They were true." He seemed to think better of that response and added, "At least in some respects. I was angry over not being able to overcome the mana poison in your body to heal you properly. Then feeling useless because we keep getting fucked around while we level up to go get Balmur. I'm homesick, and I miss my baby—we don't belong here. And Luca used that to get into my head."

He sighed and let his head fall back on to his shoulders, his gaze skyward. "I've been asking the Lady for guidance since we returned, hoping she can spare a moment, but she's busy with the other Gods keeping War from coming here or sending more of his Vanguard."

"You know you can speak to us, right?" Muu rode up beside him on his Plague Wolf mount, Nolorn. "I mean, Zeke has a kid, and all of us miss Balmur. Hell, I only knew him in our world from conversations with Zeke; I can't imagine how much cooler he is here. I may not completely understand—but I'll always listen with an open mind and an open heart. So cheer up, sugar lips."

Jaken looked at Muu oddly, the reptilian man waggling his eyebrow ridges suggestively. A roar of laughter made me flinch as the Paladin smacked his knee and bent over in his charger's saddle.

"My faith is stronger than ever, and if that display in the lich's presence was anything to go off, Lady Radiance sees me as Hers still." Jaken's shoulders squared, and he looked forward. "We're going to need to find a way across that water. Hey, James, you have a clear idea of where this thing is?"

The reading monk shook his head over his book and responded, "Just a circle the size of the several islands that are there."

"Think you could turn into a whale or something, man?" Yohsuke joked.

"Probably," I shrugged, "but I'm not into that whole Jonah stuff. We need a boat, and we have our woodworker right over there!"

"You lazy bastard," Bokaj grumbled. "I don't have that much wood."

"We can get to the ocean and then just teleport to the jungle to cut a tree down for the work if needed. Then I'll help it get back to rights!" I smiled, and a thought occurred to me. "I'm a Druid. I should be able to help nurture and grow trees. Right?"

In Druidic, I turned my attentions inward and prayed, "Mother? Would I be able to grow trees? *Should* I be able to?"

A warm ray of light burst through the cloud cover, and I felt a stirring in my soul. Mother Nature's matronly voice reached out to me, and I felt it more than I heard it.

*You can, with your Regrowth spell, but you need seeds, and you do not have them. Being able to seed a tree at any time would be too close to what I do, and while I like you, you are not ready for that kind of responsibility, little one. Grow as a Primal Warrior. You will find ways to take on new aspects to grow your power and even obtain new spells, but let me do what I must. Find your way, but do not inhibit mine. I will allow you to take four trees from the edge of the jungle in order to make this boat. But you will regrow them.*

I smiled as her warmth bathed my face and responded with a sincere, "Thank you, ma'am."

I looked at the others and grinned. "We can get a boat from the jungle. Four trees—hope that's enough?"

"Plenty. I'll start trying to come up with a suitable blueprint. Might need you to chop it down though, man." Bokaj started to try and draw on a large wooden board while he was riding his large, icy-pawed polar bear. Then he decided that trying to draw while bobbing up and down was a shit idea.

By the end of that day, we came to a cliffside that led down to a long beach with tan sands.

The sounds of water crashing against the side of the cliff and the waves sloshing against the sand below were both relaxing and a source of trepidation for me.

Once we got down to the water, I noticed a sea turtle coming on to the beach from the water, his large, heavy shell just skimming along the sand, green skin glistening with salt water, but he seemed off, somehow—not entirely natural. Then I realized what it was—there was a trail of water behind him that his tail bled into.

"You're an elemental?" I asked, hoping I was doing okay by using one of the four elemental languages—Aquan.

"You're a fox?" the slow, sarcastic reply came. It blinked at me once. "Tell me when you're ready to go, and we will leave. The Primordial has blessed you with the spell Water Lung. It is a long way to swim without fins, so if you desire a boat—build it swiftly."

I relayed his message to the others, and Bokaj snorted. "Funny thing for a tortoise to say."

The sea turtle looked at him and blinked once before simply saying to me, "I hope he swims better than he thinks he tells jokes—otherwise, he will drown."

I laughed out loud at that one and simply shook my head when they asked what was said.

"And Druid?" I looked back to the turtle. "Do not use your water elemental form in the ocean here. You will lose yourself, and then you will be susceptible to the pollution."

I wasn't about to argue with my guide in one of my worst nightmares, so I just clamped my mouth shut.

After that, it sat there, staring at me, so I ignored it and looked out into the ocean.

I grew up in a land-locked state. The largest body of water I had seen as a child had been a lake. When I enlisted, I had expected to travel the world. Possibly go on ship, you know— Marines do that occasionally—but when I first saw the ocean, I was both enchanted and stricken by fear. See—I watched a lot of movies as a kid, and some of those were shark movies. You know the ones.

Duh-nuh-duh-nuh—SHARK!

Yeah, those ones. So, I had been terrified of going into it, but it didn't seem so avoidable now.

*It will not be,* the gurgling voice of the Water Primordial swam through my mind. *I have a task for you. I need you to rid this place of this Dragon as well, and I can ensure that you find it. Its influence poisons these waters, and they run dangerously close to a byway into my realm. The poison mutates creatures in the water and kills many others. I do*

*not want my children affected by this. Clear this infection, and I will*
*reward you all handsomely. Fail? And you will know what it means to*
*drown.*

**QUEST ALERT!**

**On Cleaner Tides – The Primordial Water**
**Elemental has ordered that you find the Dragon and**
**rid the area of it in whatever way you deem necessary.**

**Reward: What the Primordial deems "Handsome"**
**and a hefty monetary sum.**

**Failure: A slow, torturous death by drowning.**

**Accept? Yes/No?**

"I guess I'll accept," I grumbled. To the others, I explained,
"Lady of the Oceans wants this Dragon found and gone. A-S-
A-P. Standard awesomeness for a reward, but if we fail, she's
going to drown me."

The others started to laugh at me, but when I just stared
back blankly, they realized I was being honest.

"Then we don't fail." Jaken clapped me on the shoulder.
"Let's go."

Muu and James stayed with Yohsuke to make the camp
ready, while Jaken and I went with Bokaj to cut down the trees.

I teleported us to the jungle, and after an hour of searching,
we found trees seasoned enough to try and make a boat out of.
Bokaj pointed them out to me, and I summoned a great axe
with Stone Weapon. It took us a couple more hours from there
to cut the trunks into more manageable pieces. Jaken and I used
a saw that Bokaj produced to trim them down to blocks that
were small enough to transport out of the jungle. Bokaj cut
them into halves, then the centers into boards for easier transport. It was sloppy work at first, but he said that he would be
able to refine them when we sat up shop by the ocean.

Once we were ready to go back, I cast Regrowth on the four
stumps, muttering a word of gratitude to each for their sacrifices, and left the area.

James ended up helping Bokaj come up with the blueprint
for the base of the boat, but that was too difficult without

specialized equipment, so we ended up designing a large raft. We spent some time making minor cuts in the wood where Bokaj asked us, then left it alone. We ate, sparred a little, then went to bed. The sparring wasn't really helpful for anything other than us learning to adapt to attacks quickly. And we almost never used deadly force, though some of us slipped occasionally.

James. The asshat.

———

The following morning, after the daily draw on my mana for my prosthetic hand to be normal, I rose to go look around the water.

Maebe was off in the distance talking to a shadowy figure with Shadow Speak, and I didn't want to interrupt.

It was high time I got used to the idea of being in the same area as the fish. I took my shirt off, the breeze from the water chilling me a little, but my fur helped to mitigate the cold from it a bit.

I cast Nature's Voice and leaped into the water. I immediately hit sand and heard a soft chuckle behind me.

I turned to find Maebe watching me in a dress I had bought her. The deep green of it made her eyes sparkle so much brighter in the light blue sky that served as a backdrop. Her dark skin, sun-kissed and warm looking even though I knew she was likely cold to the touch. The cloth fell mid-calf and flowed effortlessly in the ocean breeze. I had to pull myself away from gazing at her.

"Yeah, that was hardly cool of me." I sighed to myself exasperatedly. I saw the water move, and she was there.

"It was not cool at all. There was no ice to be seen." She smiled and motioned to the water around us. "I have never seen so much water. It is exhilarating to see it all." She helped me stand and patted my rump to get the moist sand off of me a bit. "What were you planning to do?"

"I was going to go explore the waters and see if I couldn't acquire a few animal forms to help us in the future." I pointed to where the parts for the raft were. "That won't get very far without a sail or someone to pull it, and it'll need to be something strong."

"But you are uncomfortable with the water, so you will do this to prove to yourself that you can handle that fear?"

I looked at her, her green eyes unblinking and a serious look on her face. "Yeah, I suppose you could say that. You knew all that from... where?"

"I observed you while we were at the edge of the cliff." Her delicate hand caressed my cheek. "You are easier to observe when your guard is down. The water will bow to you. Or it will not. But it cannot destroy you—I won't let it."

The waters around us became noticeably colder, and the sound of ice forming rapidly reached my ears.

"I will freeze this whole ocean and claim it for you, if needed." The fierce look on her face was both endearing and terrifying.

"Thank you, dear." I hugged her for a moment, and the ice around us thawed.

"We have much to discuss when you return." I glanced down at her, and she elaborated. "The fight with the Dragon, the finding, what needs doing after that. Other things."

"Will you be coming along then?" I raised an eyebrow at her, and she nodded. "I think you'll need to wear something other than that dress for the water."

She smirked and lifted the cloth over her head. Her own small clothes clung to her body as she folded the dress and placed it into her own inventory. Then she pressed forward through the water and dove into it with little other thought. When she came out of it, she smiled and splashed at me.

I stepped closer to her and cast Water Lung.

*Water Lung – The caster and a number of creatures up to their intelligence divided by five (70 / 5 = 14) can breathe water up to 24 hours and withstand crushing*

*depths. Cost: 75 MP. Range: 35 Feet (on casting).*
*Cooldown: 30 minutes.*

So, fourteen people. That's fucking awesome. The spell took hold, and I felt like the air I was currently breathing was simply too light. There wasn't enough oxygen in it. I could breathe it, but it was harder somehow.

Fighting every instinct I had, I ducked my head into the water and trusted my magic. I breathed out as forcefully as I could, then breathed deeply under water. Air bubbles left my mouth; then a vacuum of water formed in front of my face as I inhaled water. The briny liquid coated my lungs, and I could feel the strain of not having taken a breath alleviating immediately. The thickness of the water in my lungs was odd but not too uncomfortable. Opening my eyes underwater was slightly irritating, but it was fine after a couple minutes of getting used to it.

I opened my mouth to speak to Maebe who was floating beneath the surface serenely, then closed it. Would the sound travel?

"Yes, you can speak beneath the ocean," came the sea turtle's voice from my right, "but be wary. Sound travels far under the tide."

"Thank you." My voice sounded weird, but the creature had been right. "We were going to search for larger aquatic creatures to try and see if they will let me take their forms or not."

"Try deeper waters, Druid." The turtle sighed before turning and swimming away toward the beach.

"So helpful," I grumbled mutinously.

It called over its shoulder, "I heard that," and swam off faster.

I shrugged, then took off toward the deeper waters with Maebe. The water was cold—freezing—at some points, but it got easier to bear as time went on. We didn't go too far down. Wasn't like twenty-thousand leagues under the sea kind of swimming—we just went as deep as we could. A cool thing about my new metal hand as well was that it wasn't functioning like normal metal underwater. It was almost exactly like my normal arm. Excellent.

There were small schools of fish out there, just at the edge of our vision. They looked like clouds against a black expanse with minute light smattered through. A curious eel swam by, his body writhing, but he seemed content to keep his distance no matter how much I called to him.

I was beginning to lose hope when I saw a flurry of motion lower down in the water and noted a large shadow passing beneath us.

Instantly I was wary of it and more than a little freaked out. There was no telling what kind of creatures of the deep were out here in a magical world. No way of knowing except what little water-based lore I knew. And the ones I knew were sure as *fuck* not comforting.

Multicolored fish swam toward us in a wave of fins and fear. I didn't imagine it was hard to scare fish, but it was following.

Maebe and I swam outside the swarm and watched as the hulking form of something that resembled a whale swam through the swarm of fish with its mouth open. Dozens of the smaller aquatic lives were sucked into this creature's gullet before us. It closed its mouth, and on instinct, I swam forward to try and latch on to it.

Compared to the school of fish, I was like a baby trying to swim around. Even the larger fish was able to see me coming. Luckily, Maebe seemed much more at home in the water than I did, and she beat me to him. She touched its fin, and it stiffened for a moment before relaxing. She nodded her head toward it, and I simply shrugged before completing my swim over to touch it on its dark, scaly body.

It was a deep blue or something to that effect with a lighter yellow portion on the side that looked like a stripe, but it blended much better. It could have been underwater camouflage. Maybe in certain lights, surroundings or somewhere else, it would lure prey or confuse something even larger.

That last thought made me gulp at the thought. After another moment, I felt that I had acquired the large fish's form, and we let it go. It took one last look at Maebe and decided that it wanted nothing to do with her. I looked down below us, and something there caught my eye. I had to investigate.

We both swam lower, the light of day bleeding less and less into our surroundings. My dark vision kicked in and what little light we were getting helped me to see the shapes of creatures near the floor of this section. One of whom was very curious about me.

I felt a tug on my left leg as I reached a dark band of coral at the bottom with seaweed not far away. I looked down to see a single tentacle wrapped around my leg. This tiny octopus the size of a cat had latched on to me and was slowly working the other tentacles around my leg. It didn't hurt; it kind of tickled really.

I bent and addressed it kindly, "Hello, little fellow. Can I help you?"

"Hold still while I hunt you, please," it squeaked back. "I am a great hunter of the deep, like mother, and she will be so proud to see my first kill was such a strange creature."

I laughed nervously. If this was a baby, where was mom?

A dark shadow passed over us, and I noted that it had tentacles as well. As soon as it finished passing over our position, I felt a pinch and noted a single hit point was missing from my total 400 HP. The little fucker had bitten me!

I tried to gently extricate myself from the little one as swiftly as I could before grabbing Mae and casting Teleport.

We landed with a great splash on the beach near the raft with great heaving breaths. The last thing I had seen of that deep area had been an open maw in the shape of a beak rocketing toward us with its legs fanned out around it.

I came out of my panic-induced tunnel vision to a stream of curses and a wet Bokaj. His shirtless upper body was covered in deep-sea brine, and his hair was sopping wet.

"Get. Away. From me," he growled.

He had tools in a white-knuckled grip and was baring his teeth at us. I nodded dumbly and fled to go calm down in the warmth of the sunlight on the sands by the water. But, you know—far from the water.

I wouldn't be going back in today. Not a fucking chance in hell.

I shivered despite the warmth of the bright sunlight above me and dismissed the water breathing effect so that I could breathe normally. I instantly began to hack up great lungfuls of water. Finally, with a heave that felt like I was choking on vomit, a large bubble of water ejected from my mouth with some kind of powder inside it. It popped a few feet away, and the powder dropped to the sand below. It smelled like sea salt. I felt ill all over again.

"That was an interesting reaction to the spell," Maebe offered.

She seemed to be completely fine, and that made me unreasonably angry. I let the emotion fade before I nodded and offered a small smile. "Yeah, that was really weird."

"You are unwell," she observed aloud. She looked up into the sky, which was comforting. "You feel justified in your fears."

"More than a little." I sighed. "I expected sharks. I expected larger fish. Like whales. Granted, I didn't think it would be a predatory whale, like that one, but it was a possibility. But almost being eaten by a creature of myth and legend? Fuck, man."

"It was only a giant octopus or squid. I think. I am not well versed with a large variety of sea creatures, but that was hardly a leviathan or Kraken. It for certain was not something so massive as a water Dragon." I felt her hand cover mine and squeeze gently. "You were smart enough to get away from there. You have a way out. You will be okay."

"I'll have to make sure we keep a constant Teleport on then." Blinking up at the clouds above us, I was reminded of how much better I would have felt if Kayda was around. Oh well. She was off learning to be the best she could. No worries there. She would come back stronger.

"Let's get some food and see about getting something to eat, then do a little bit of shadow magic training, yeah?" I looked over at her to see a savage grin envelope her face. "Why are you looking at me like that?"

"I had wondered if you had forgotten or if you would heed my advice to focus on your other elements." She stood and pulled her own shadow over her body like it was a second skin that fell away.

"I thought about it, and since I have one of the best shadow magic users I'm likely to ever meet at my side, I figured learning a little bit may not hurt, right? Besides, wasting the potential to learn anything from you would be stupid."

She stood there dry and then did the same for me before her lips turned up in a smile. "Dress fully and come."

She slipped the dress she had worn previously over her head, then left me to stare at her walking away as she wandered into camp in search of food. Let's just say that we all know that I am *stupid* lucky. Yeah?

# CHAPTER NINE

We had eaten the sausages in toasted buns rapidly, then moved out of range of the camp by more than three dozen yards.

Maebe cast her hand upward and mumbled a string of words that were too low for me to hear. A dome of pure shadow sprung to life around us that covered the area in darkness like night. The ground was bathed in cool shadow, but the lid of the dome was half darkness and the other, clear, night light.

The Queen of Cold and Shadow stood, bathed in the void that the stars filled. The darkness swallowing all of her features save her face. Her green eyes stared out at me with confidence.

"The first lesson is quite simple: call the shadows to you." She smiled and stepped back into the darkness, disappearing completely.

I had done something similar to this before, in willing my mana to do what the hell I wanted it to, like pulling it from my mana reserves into my fingers or into an item I was enchanting. I just had to try and turn that inward solution and vision outward.

I looked at the shadows on the floor, the ebon energy of them and called to them with my mind.

Nothing happened.

I kept at it for a solid fifteen minutes before a headache began to throb at the base of my skull near my spine. I groaned and felt a pair of arms wrap around my waist from behind. I felt the press of her body against my tails and back.

"You're trying too hard," Maebe's voice echoed toward me from where she had been before, and I looked down to see a perfect shadow copy of my lover behind me.

"How do you do that?" I started, then took a deep breath. "How do *you* control the shadows?"

"They are mine by birthright, but in order to control the depths of the void, one must bear in mind two things: their strengths and their will. A portion of my strength is my blood and my natural affinity for the darkness. My will is absolute," I saw another likeness of the queen sprout from the darkness beside me, though her voice that drifted out of the darkness where she had been, "and my degree of control comes from centuries of practice."

The shade drifted toward me and touched my face lightly. It felt so real before it spoke in Maebe's voice, "Call to the shadows."

Before trying to call anything to me, I turned my sights inward. I could use shadow magic already, and those obeyed my will. But that was all internalized, given by the Celestial gift that the queen had given me through a blood rite.

I focused on what I was now. I was a Celestial too. Shadows were as much a part of me now as they were Maebe, right? I was stronger than this. I had come to this world, and I had made so many things my bitch—the darkness was just another thing on the list.

Rather than simply exerting my will mentally, I issued a verbal command, the same I would have if I were giving orders. I *demanded* the shadows now.

"Come."

There was a strain as I exerted my will on the shadows on the other side of the dome, so I focused on the shadows on the ground beneath my feet. I forced my will into a groping hand that snatched the writhing, slippery tendrils of darkness into it and pulled. I didn't realize I had closed my eyes to focus, but when I opened them, I looked at my hand and felt a cool touch.

A small strand of shadow was in my grasp. A notification barged into my view.

### *ABILITIES UNLOCKED!*

*Shadow Control – The caster has reached into the shadows and brought them under his command. At the beginning stages, the caster will be able to perform minor tricks and spells with the darkness around them. With practice comes mastery, and with mastery —power.*

"Congratulations," Maebe purred. She stepped from the darkness in front of me; this time, it was not a copy.

The inky black behind her seemed like it didn't want to relinquish her, like a pet that hated watching their master leave for work.

"Thank you, but what do I do now?" She glided forward, her hand smoothing over the shadows in my grasp.

"You practice." We both watched as the dark tendrils slithered from my grasp. "Never-ending practice. Now, call them to you again."

And so we practiced. We spent hours going at it with little breaks. By the final hour, my concentration was shit, and my head pounded like a Dwarf was forging my brain with a sledgehammer.

It wasn't for nothing, though. I was able to make the shadows come to me rather quickly now, and even as we walked back to camp in the fading light, I had my shadow moving toward my hand before letting it fall away. It was weird and cool as fuck.

The others were already eating some of the fish that Muu had speared earlier on in the day while I was training. I know that I had eaten a lot of things since coming here, but I wasn't cool with fish. It was just too—what was that smell?

"What's that?" I asked as we came closer to the camp. The others looked up in various states of indulgence.

"My now-famous speared fish jambalaya." Yohsuke pulled his ladle from the thick, soupy food and dealt Maebe and I both a bowl. "Has diced fish and chunks of sausage in there for protein, a heap of rice cooked in a stock I made using some red beef that I let simmer in it before cooking. That's gonna be real tender tomorrow morning. Steak and eggs for breakfast. But back to the jambalaya. I used veggies and peppers I got from the village, seasoned it to taste with some thyme, garlic, and a little bit of my secret seasonings for a little o' that Cajun kick. There's no okra here in this region, but it'll have to do."

I took the spoon in the bowl, brought a bite to my lips, and had at it. The flavor was complex. There was a slight fishy musk that wasn't unpleasant thanks to the spice of the sausage and the peppers. The garlic also added a good deal to the balance of flavor. Normally, a chicken stock would be used as the base to cook the rice, but the meaty flavor of the grain fought back the seafood taste. Honestly? It was great.

"Famous indeed." I grinned at my brother, and he took a spoonful of his own food proudly.

We enjoyed our meals slowly as we planned for the following day.

Bokaj had made a good deal of headway on the raft with Muu's help, and Muu had been able to make a makeshift sail using leathers that he had tanned and sewn together. It wasn't very large, but he had tried his best—and that meant some-thing. We would leave early in the morning when the sun was rising to get the most out of the daylight hours.

After I finished my bowl, Maebe stopped me from using my water skin to clean it out with a hand on my shoulder.

"Your next lesson—order the shadows to clean it for you." She smiled at my obvious discomfort at having to will the shadows to do anything after such a long day.

But I obeyed. She was kind enough to teach me, the least I could do was what she asked.

I motioned to the darkened, elongated shadows beneath me, and they came to my hand tentatively. I focused my attention on the bowl with little left in it other than liquid and some small bits of rice and envisioned it clean after the shadows passed over it.

The shadows moved slowly over the bowl, then consumed it entirely before I ordered them to relinquish the clean item to my hand. Begrudgingly, the inky black substance slowly spat out the remaining portion of the bowl. There were chunks missing here and there where food had been. What was left was clean, though, so there was that.

"Fuck, man," I growled at the shadows, and it seemed undisturbed by my anger.

*You know what? Fuck you, shadows. Maybe we can reach an agreement.* I sighed inwardly and focused on the shadows.

"Are there other kinds of elements out there other than the four primes?" I asked Maebe after a moment in thought.

She looked taken by surprise for a moment, then shrugged before responding, "I do not know of them. Shadows are an element of their own, certainly, but I do not know of creatures who are responsible for them. Why?"

"We don't have years for me to master this, and we need every kind of advantage we can get." I stood and began to walk away from the others. "You all chill here. I need to see a man about a hammer."

"I assume this is a 'pie' moment?" Maebe stood with a look that dared me to tell her to stay behind.

"That's probably the case, but I don't know for sure." I smiled. "I'm kind of just winging it, and if you would be able to help me—I would appreciate it."

Her fingers wove through mine, and she kissed my cheek before nodding.

"Ah, fuck," Yohsuke groaned. "Get the fuck out of here and do something, you stupid, mushy bastard."

I flipped him the bird and prepared to duck the spoon he threw at me, but a small wall of shadows snatched it from in front of me and returned it to his lap as if it had never moved. I looked to Maebe, and she simply mouthed, slowly, *control, and practice.*

She and I walked a hundred yards from our camp to be sure that the others were safely out of the way so I could focus.

I closed my eyes while keeping my newly acquired ability, Shadow Control, in mind and cast Summon Celestial.

This time, rather than a rent in the air opening before us in the sky, a large, black cloud burst from the ground. It raised to about chest height before it swirled into a tornado of darkness and stopped.

The being looked like a child floating on a bed of deep shadows. The eyes glowed eerily white, like crystals, and the features seemed slightly blurred. I couldn't tell what sex they were, so I'd just have to wing it.

"Greetings, creature born of the depths, of the place between the stars and consumer of the cosmos. Being of the void." I bowed my head for a moment—waiting for some kind of response—but silence greeted me. "I called you forth seeking power over the shadows. By blood, by strength, and for the good of all creatures of the realm attached to this one."

A cold response that simultaneously sounded like it was coming from hundreds of locations and people, creatures greeted me inside my mind, sending a wild thrill of true fear into me.

*Your silver tongue means little, Kitsune. What will you exchange for this power? What have you of interest to those who care little if the stars fade or fall?*

"I offer you presence." When they didn't respond again, I continued to explain, "The other elements have realms of their own. They have Mages who use their powers. They have blessed me with their strength and their favor so that my friends and I may combat War."

*We know of this creature. He has taken many stars.*

I nodded sadly. "He has. And for that, you have suffered."

*How?*

"Without the light of life, how can darkness be anything but nothingness. Life—that spark of light—gives you depth. Purpose. Without life, what use will you serve?" Rather than waiting for the possible response, I made an offer, "Help us stop War and route him from this world and there will remain trillions of souls to ponder at what lurks and waits within you. Let me celebrate and borrow your strength so that the shadows may deepen still."

They seemed to ponder for a time before looking to Maebe.

*Hello, beloved.*

Mae bowed her head. "Darkest Night."

*What do you think of all this? Do you support this one's claim?*

"I gave him the rite." She stepped in front of me and bowed her head. "I support his claim. I support his mission. I have aided him myself through you."

The figure seemed to contemplate a moment before turning its baby-shaped head toward our camp.

*And the others? What of them?*

"I see them as friends, and they lack the affinity as far as I am aware," Mae replied.

*Seeker, a drop of your vitality.*

I held out my hand and with the nail portion of my right hand, cut the skin of my left index finger. A small drop of crimson fled from the part and dropped into the waiting shadows beneath me.

A line of black snaked from the ground around the figure and speared the droplet before diving into the small slit in my flesh. A chill so deep ran from the extremity toward my heart, Coal's burning rage keeping the darkness from reaching it before it fled toward my mind.

It moved faster than thought. By the time I had even begun to register it, the sensation had fled from me. My HP bar flashed wildly. I had 3 HP left after that. I fell to my knees and would've lost consciousness if it hadn't been for a golden nimbus of light that surrounded me and lifted my health back up to half instantly.

*We see. Call the Grey One to us and stand close.*

"Yoh!" I called, and he stepped closer, making me flinch. I hadn't known he was so close.

"What's up? Time to fight?" He had his astral blade out at the ready.

"No man, I think it wants to talk to us." I looked back to the being before us, and it floated almost inches away from us.

*Yes, you will both do nicely. There is one more among you from your memories. Who walks through our being. Where is he? I see, the Hells. We will visit him in secret then.*

"If you would, tell him that we're coming?" Yohsuke asked.

The creature nodded before it reached forward and touched us both on our heads. I saw Yohsuke crumple into a heap just before I passed out.

# CHAPTER TEN

*ABILITIES UNLOCKED!*
*Blessed by the Void – The Void has recognized you as an ally and has given you a measure of control over their newly formed element of Shadow.*
*Elemental Tinkering (Shadow) – The unavoidable darkness heeds your command unlike ever before, and new spells can be created and discovered within the proper elemental realm. Be warned that mana is consumed at a higher rate while tinkering with or discovering a new spell.*
*Shadow Friend – The void recognizes those who you ally yourself with as beloved (Maebe). So long as your relationship with that person is in good standing, the shadows will treat you as a close friend as they do for others.*

"Anyone catch the plate of that fuckin' truck that hit me, then backed up?" I groaned as I sat up.

The sky was beginning to lighten behind me, and I stared at the ocean before me as I bobbed on a hard surface. Birds called in the sky high above, and clouds dotted the horizon line. They were gray and bleak, but the sky closer to us was open and clear.

The elemental turtle swam through the water in front of us, oblivious to our activities.

"Yeah, we were out that long, man." Yoh handed me a plate of steak and eggs. "Luckily, the steaks were mostly cooked, and I could do 'em fast. Hope you like them medium."

"I like food." I wolfed down my breakfast as I looked back over the notifications, then looked around at the raft. It was a larger affair than I thought it would be. Twenty square feet with the half logs beneath us to provide buoyancy and height to keep the lapping waves away from us until we decided to go in. The makeshift sail fluttered in the wind. There were slight gaps between the pelts—likely due to Muu's low level in his craft—but it fluttered in the wind and seemed to be assisting our travel.

I thought about whether I should mention the shadows visiting Balmur in the Hells to Bokaj, but with the state he was in, he may react poorly to it. I hated to keep it from him, but it was what would be best for now.

Once I was finished eating, I called to the shadows around me as I sat on the raft. They seemed excited to come at my command, and that made me smile. I asked that they clean my plate off—without destroying it—and they did so swiftly.

"Excellently done." Maebe's hand brushed over my arm. "Did you feel any difference outright?"

"They seemed eager to please, rather than resisting me like last time." I frowned. "What did they mean when they called you 'beloved?'"

"The shadows love me." She shrugged. When I looked at her to continue, there was nothing else for her to say, so she remained silent.

I heard the turtle call back. "If you are done lazing about, Druid—we can move more swiftly if you will pull the raft."

"This fucking turtle motherfucker…" I grumbled as I stood and moved toward the water. "Anyone have some rope they can tie to me?"

"I will use a shadow tether. Rope will only harm you and inhibit your movement." Maebe coiled her hand into a fist and began to pull it from her hand like a mime. A rope of shadow coiled at her feet easily. "Go and shift."

I nodded once, then dove into the water before shifting. I assumed the fish shape, and the world and water around me took on a largely saturated view. The colors were so difficult to take in this light that I had to spend some time adjusting to it. Even then, it was annoying because my vision was split to the sides and only slightly forward.

I felt a cold sensation wrap around me just behind my fins and then disappear.

"You're all set!" I heard Yohsuke call. "Give us a second to stow the sail."

I waited until one of them called again, then took off after the blip that was the turtle in front of me. It was slow going at first, but eventually, I got used to the weight behind me and swimming using all the fins I had. I kept the turtle slightly in front and to the left of me so that I could keep him in my sights.

We followed the surly elemental for hours, taking breaks sparingly. The horizon line had little on it, barely a growing outline of an island or whatever it was that was in the distance.

That night, we slept on the raft as best as we could, taking turns on watch. Nothing really seemed to care that we were there in the waters. The elemental stilled the waters around us to keep us from floating too far off course but nothing else. Though, at one point, Muu swore he saw something orange and glowing down beneath the raft that made him wake us.

After seeing nothing down below us and casting Sense Life to ensure it was all clear, we ended up going back to sleep. I had a nightmare of a giant eye, bathed in orange, glowing light that kept me from really resting, but it was to be expected after that.

The next day went without incident—three square meals of hardtack and a lot of swimming. By that night, the island was closer in sight. I could see the outline of it growing in the haziness of the horizon line, looming in against the clouds with others in the distance beside it.

By the dawn of day three, the others were feeling restless.

"I wonder what we'll be facing," James wondered out loud after closing his book. "You have any guesses?"

"Who knows, but fighting underwater is going to be highly asinine." Yohsuke sighed. He glanced out over the water as he scrubbed the same pan he had been working on all morning. "I can't imagine underwater fighting is gonna be easy."

"It will not be," the turtle interrupted me as I began to open my mouth. "You will all have difficulty moving, even being able to breathe underwater. You must prepare yourselves. Those of you who will be fighting using ranged weapons will need to be much closer than normal for them to take any sort of effect, and if you use fire spells underwater, well—you're as dumb as you look."

"I wonder what turtle tastes like," I growled at the creature.

Have I mentioned yet how almost hilariously stupid I am when it comes to picking fights? No? Well, ta-duh!

"The water Prime wants you to make it to this island today. You will follow me now and swim for your life." It blinked at me once, then seemed to raise its mouth on the sides in a weird version of a smile, maybe a grin? "Because your life depends on it."

I grunted as I leaped over the side and shifted into my hulking fish form. It took us the majority of the day to get there, and I had to admit—the water here felt wrong. The tides seemed warmer and were scented of iron and something that smelled of raw pesticides. The murky water held more— somehow—intimidating darkness and mystery than the unfathomable depths we moved through easily before.

The umber tides, those that seemed to flow beneath the water top itself like the air flows that allowed me flight in the skies, flowed faster here. They seemed to be leading us into the waters around this grouping of islands. As we closed the distance, the water began reaching levels of taint and cloudiness so bad that I could no longer see the elemental leading us.

I clambered back on to the raft after switching forms into my fox-man form; seeing down there in that murk was going to be a huge issue.

"And this is where I leave you," the elemental advised. Before it left, it turned back. "The Dragon's lair is not a traditional one. There is a trick to getting to it."

It looked down into the depths beneath it and smiled. "Good luck."

It was gone in a small splash of water, and we were alone.

"It's down there in that bullshit, isn't it," Muu stated.

The rest of us nodded.

"Fucked up enemies?"

"Most likely," I grunted at the green-scaled Fighter.

"Big ass Dragon at the end."

"You bet." Jaken smiled.

Muu closed his eyes and tried his best to smile. "Bring it on." He jumped into the water and fought to stay afloat, losing slowly.

"Let me cast the underwater breathing spell first, you pleb!" I growled and cast the required spell. 75 MP drained from my reserves, and we all nodded to each other before plopping into the water.

Those of the group wearing armor sank quicker than the rest of us, and rather than risk losing each other, we had Maebe tether our shadows together.

We sank for what seemed like a long time, the shapes that blurred through the darkened murk leaving us on edge. We communicated through our earrings, but other than pointing out the lurking creatures—there was nothing of great import to say.

After another ten minutes of solid sinking, we found something. Rather—James did.

*The circle is tighter now. It's in front of us somewhere, north.* He began to swim forward a little.

As we began to move forward, a large darkened portion of the murk began to close on us. All of us were on edge already. High alert—if you will.

*Most likely the entran–* Out loud James finished the sentence in a shout, "WHAT THE FUCK IS THAT?!"

A gigantic shark with razor-sharp teeth and beady, black, dead-looking fish eyes lurched toward us, the mouth opening wider in an attempt to scoop us all in.

"Oh fuck that," I growled. I shifted into my giant octopus form and hauled ass toward the asshole.

But it was still huge. *Don't. Fucking. Tell me.* I chanced a glance down and saw that I was the same size as the tiny octopus that had grasped me days before.

I squirted ink in my rage and darted off—still nimble in my small size, and the inking had propelled me away.

Alright, look. The ink thing wasn't me shitting myself—it was a defense mechanism. Nature, son.

The small amount of ink did nothing to stop the gigantic fish, but it gave me room to work.

I shifted back and began to charge Lightning Storm. "Mae! Pull the others into a shield! I'm going to fry us a fish stick!"

I saw Muu yo-yo back behind me, and a large shadow moved toward me from below.

Two more seconds.

Jaws was mere feet away.

One more.

The light was beginning to leave as its teeth clamped shut.

Then I felt the held spell pulse, and a wave of electricity burst from my palms. The shark's innards were ribbons, and it opened its mouth to try and get the pain out of it, sinking lower into the water.

The others were on it in seconds, even Muu gliding through the water around him as if he were touched by Poseidon himself to drive his ice lance into the dying creature.

*We got company!* Yohsuke and Bokaj shouted.

I turned to see other shapes looming toward us. Some large,

others small but I could guarantee not one of them would be friendly. Using life sense confirmed that; all of them were not red, likely because they weren't actively hostile against me at that moment, but the dozens of large and small dots were sooo not comforting.

As we began to swim north as close as we could to the wall, I noted several misshapen and disfigured fish swimming toward the shark we had beaten down.

They had glowing, green scales or blackened ones that looked to be oozing some kind of slime behind them. Others looked to be inside out with teeth all over them.

Needless to say—I wasn't sleeping well near water. Ever.

The experience came seconds later, signifying it was finally —fully—dead. And that meant that we were back on the menu if they caught our scent. Luckily, there was enough shark chum to attract all the predators around us to the feast and possibly each other.

Another large shape loomed closer, and we were all relieved to see that it was the island.

There was a shelf there, and it traveled down further and seemed to be getting smaller and smaller.

*Likely, the bottom of the island is where we find the way to get to this thing's lair, right?* I looked at the others, and they shrugged.

"Mayhaps we follow the pollution?" Maebe suggested softly to me, and I repeated it to the others.

She pointed lower and further toward the eastern portion of the stone before us, and the cloud of murk took on a more virulent-looking deep brown.

*We touch that shit, it's going to hurt,* Muu observed.

*I have just the thing for it.* Jaken waved all of us toward him, grabbed Yohsuke's hand, then James's, and nodded for the rest of us to follow suit. *Got this as a gift for beating back the lich. Sorry I didn't bring it up sooner.*

A wave of golden light passed from him to us, and I suddenly *knew* that I was going to be okay.

**Protection from Impurity – Caster has blessed you**

*with perfect resistance to negative status effects such as poison, acid, and others. Duration: 30 minutes.*

*That's cool and all, man, but we need to work on knowing our spell inventory better than we have been,* Yohsuke grumped.

*Long cooldown of forty-five minutes, so let's get to getting,* Jaken advised. We swam as quickly as we could into the disgusting waters and were rewarded with an opening large enough for each of us to fit one at a time. Jaken led us, me behind him, and the others funneling in after us. Maebe likely headed up the rear to ensure our safety.

We were well into the cavern inside, moving as swiftly as caution would allow us when, Jaken's buff began to flash in its final seconds.

We pressed on, Bokaj and I each casting Purify on the others and ourselves to offset the multitude of status effects we were receiving. It was draining, and even with it taking about a minute or two for the disgusting effects to take hold again, we were hurting. Luckily, James seemed to be immune to the majority of it, so purify wasn't as necessary for him.

"Think it's because I'm a descendant of a black Dragon?" he asked Muu.

The Dragon-kin seemed to think about it before shrugging. "It's possible. You have some serious acid damage you can do. It would make sense that you would be highly resistant to it, like me with venoms and poison."

Which was a relief on our mana pools. Not too much, but it would help.

An opening above us signaled some kind of hope, so we took it, the watery cavern beneath us carrying the majority of the Dragon's pollution with it. All that was up in this small area was a rocky shelf barely large enough to hold us all with a high roof.

The water seemed to be easier to breathe here, if only slightly, and the debuffs finally stopped popping back up. Once my mana was back up to a reasonable level, I began to cast Purify on the others. Bokaj joining me when he could. We were so happy to be out of the detritus that we seemed to lose our damned minds

I cast Sense Life, and a large number of red blips glowed around us.

"Fuck." I tried to cast something, anything, but my mind blanked as thousands of tiny creatures began to swarm us.

Radiating shadows blasted from behind me, and the legion of red blips turned gray. Wiped out.

"I grow weary of these minor inconveniences." Maebe crossed her arms and waited for anyone to object to her assistance. She smiled when there was none. "I will be assisting in the fight with the black Dragon too—if there is one."

"Fine by me." James shrugged. "We got anything to eat up in this bitch?"

"It'll get soggy, so no." Yohsuke sighed. "But there is that tea that I put into a waterskin. Though it would help us to sleep, and I know we have enough time on the spell to make sure we can. We will definitely need to wait for the food. I think there's a good chance that we should take our rest now and have a snack once we find some place dry. Yeah?"

We weren't happy about it, but it made sense. The rest of us nodded.

"All of you rest. I will take first watch." Maebe turned toward the opening and all but ignored us outright in her focus.

I kissed her on top of her head and laid against her back so that if anything came, we would be ready.

I slept as best I could through the night—my friends let me sleep rather than making me get up because of all the swimming I did for us.

In the morning, or whenever everyone was ready, I cast Water Lung once more to keep us all going strong on being able to actually breathe, then spent a minute recovering my mana before we moved on.

We moved further along the cavern, traveling steadily toward the surface—or what we hoped was the surface. As

Jaken's buff began to wear off, we took turns alternating Purify until he was able to get it back on to us.

Another hour and we came to a room with actual air and a way out. I checked for signs of life, and nothing came back, so we popped up and deactivated our water-breathing spells. I was pleased to see that the others—except for Maebe—had the same visceral reaction to the spell that I had and a lot of salt piled next to the water.

We stopped to enjoy an actual meal, letting Yohsuke cook while the rest of us explored the space. The stalactites were enormous and of varying colors and shapes that mesmerized me even though it was so dim in this place with light from our cooking fire.

"Why are we cooking?" James asked Yoh. "We have rations. We can eat those and move on."

Yohsuke blinked at him, slowly, before he shrugged, "You don't wanna eat my food? Don't. You wanna go into a Dragon's lair without resting? Go ahead, dragon boy, be my guest. The rest of us are going to park our asses here in a bit and enjoy a nice meal before we go meet a giant lizard."

James looked taken aback but mumbled, "Sorry, I was just wondering."

"Shut up, you know I'm not, not going to feed you. Go away." Yohsuke went about his business, and the rest of us moved off.

Every time I moved, I cast Sense Life. I caught rats, lizards, and occasionally, low-hanging bats but nothing hostile, and none of the animals seemed interested in speaking to me, though I could tell they were curious. The place was probably a hundred and fifty feet by a hundred and ten, give or take a dozen feet. I was never the greatest at measuring distances.

As I was exploring, I also noted a rivulet that led to the water. It smelled acidic, and when I took a chance and touched the vitriolic slime, it burned. I purified my fingers and growled at myself.

"Found the runoff from the Dragon." I told the others as I warily walked back to the group.

After exploring and finding nothing of great interest, we had all returned to the cooking fire for food. The smell of roasted meat and freshly warmed and buttered bread was almost intoxicating after having not eaten anything substantial.

We wolfed the food down as it came, muttering words of praise and gratitude to a surly—but smiling—cook.

"Food," I heard muttered next to me. I looked and saw nothing, initially but looked down to see a rat.

And another. And more. More kept pouring from the shadows around us. Now, to our credit, none of us screamed, but Muu was on a fucking warpath unlike anything I had ever seen.

I watched—startled—as the Fighter began to stomp and crush the rats that came too close.

"Don't." Stomp. "Like." Deep growl of resentment. "*RATS!*"

"They're just hungry!" I tried to explain before I felt tiny teeth sink into my breeches. "Oi! Fuck off!"

I willed the shadows at my feet to heed my desire and sent a wave of darkness slicing through those loosely clumped around my legs. A notification popped up, but I dismissed it offhand. Combat wasn't a place for this. I lost a healthy 135 MP with that experimentation.

I sighed as I looked out toward the darkness, and a seeming tidal wave of tiny rodent bodies began to roll toward us. I cast Fireball into the coming shit show and watched as several larger rats began to surge forward from the dead. Their teeth were large and crooked in their mouths, the fur singed, but they seemed even darker and more dangerous than the others.

"Watch those ones!" James ordered from behind me. He fired a ki blast at one, and it crumpled. The others beside it stopped to begin eating it as more piled forward. "I can promise that a bite will be shitty. Think of the trench rats during the Second World War!"

"Oh, fuck *that*," I heard Jaken growl. A torrent of arrows flew out at the rats in front of me, then a nimbus of gold flashed next to me.

"This is gonna be bad!" Yohsuke grunted. "Maebe! You want to help a little more?"

"I think I will." She stepped next to me and touched my shoulder. "They will overrun us if you fail here. Tell the shadows to form a wedge-shaped shield in front of you, and hold it as best you can."

I looked at her, and she shoved my head back toward the problem at hand. With a clap of my hands together before me like I was diving into the water from a diving board, a surge of instinct washed over me, and I shouted into the void, "*Bend, straits between the stars and answer my will. Sunder the living before you and shield us!*"

As I finished that, I snarled and opened my hands so they formed a wedge-like a snow plow against the coming tide of vermin five feet in front of us. As soon as they touched the freshly-made shield, the loss of mana made me groan. I was instantly at 200 MP and falling steadily by large numbers.

I gritted my teeth. "Can't. Hooold." I began to see stars; my mana went back up a little and began to fall once more.

More bursts of arrows and ki to my left. A burst of muted-black light and a burst of blood and black snow lightly from Yohsuke. I saw some rats freeze. Then burst.

My vision began to fade. I fell to my knees. Someone fed me a mana potion, and it helped a little, but the rats were everywhere. I heard a giggle, "Good work," and suddenly, the pressure was gone.

I gasped and fell over—looking for the impending pain of teeth and slithering rats' tails, but finding nothing.

"They are gone," Maebe stated simply. "Touch the shadows. You will know what happened."

I blinked, not wanting to move, so I called the shadows closest to me over and dipped a finger into the blackness.

They were there, alive and frightened, and the shadows around them *loved that.*

"What will happen to them in there?" My voice sounded hollow, even to me.

"We will see, in time, but for now, they are in stasis, much like my art." She offered me a hand, and I took it numbly. "You did well with that shield. I am certain that in the future, you will only get better."

I nodded, exhausted. I felt a hand on my shoulder and turned to my left to see Muu there. His somber face looked relieved, and he nodded once before turning and walking away. I saw him stamp on another rat corpse as he went, then noticed the others.

Some were a little bloodied. Yohsuke's legs were bleeding, and he seemed a little paler than normal, but Jaken was seeing to him. Bokaj seemed to be casting Purify on Tmont; the panther laid mewling piteously on the stone before him. Her stomach looked slightly distended; likely, she had devoured the rats without thinking of what they might have consumed. James floated in a meditative trance—likely gathering his ki, and I was sitting there like I was in shock.

Was manashock a thing? Going through that much all at once? I had never really gone through it like that before, but it seemed to be what I was feeling. Distant thoughts. I felt cold. My hearing was slightly impaired and my vision—fine for now —but I had only taken in my friends one at a time.

As I contemplated this new sensation, warmth crept into my being from Coal. The flame wolf was obviously worried about me, his ears flat against his head and his tail tucked. I thanked him silently and closed my eyes to the world around me. I took solace in that warmth. Basked in it and tried to circulate it throughout my body before I looked at the two new notifications I had.

***Shadow Scythe – The caster summons and expels a close-range sweep of shadows that carve through the enemy. Cost: 57 MP. Range: 10 feet. Cooldown: None.***

*Void Shield – Casting your thoughts into the nether, the caster wills a malleable barrier into existence. Base Cost: 203 MP (Mana points are expended as damage is taken unless the shield is grounded at a specific amount of MP.) Range: 5 feet. Cooldown: 10 seconds.*

Those were really cool new spells. I would have to see if I could mix them with anything else.

I looked over at Maebe, her arms crossed under her chest as she watched me with obvious curiosity.

"You would have helped if I hadn't been able to do it, right?" I asked her quietly.

She took a step closer and looked me directly in the eyes. "I care for you, and this may even be something akin to love. But those emotions have no place in what has just occurred. If you had not taken the threat seriously and relied on my assistance—or anyone else's—then you would not have been able to truly use that spell to the effect you needed to." Her green eyes stared coldly into mine. "Never forget that you are the truest source of your survival. Never forget that in times of duress—it will be you who must save your friends."

I blinked. That was true. She had been as calculating—as cold—as she had been when we first met in the Fae Realm.

"Thank you." I reached out and touched her cheek, and the frost in her eyes melted slightly.

"Thank me if we survive this." She kissed me on my shoulder. "Do not fail yourself. Do not fail your friends. Do not fail your Queen."

I nodded in response and turned to my friends, who seemed ready to go. We packed the rest of the food and cooking equipment away before walking toward the rivulet of detritus material leaking into the water.

Carefully, we traveled up the ledges beside it. Jaken and James took the fore, Maebe, Yoh, and Tmont in the center, and Muu and I took the rear. The walk was slow at first—the air was slightly noxious—but as we continued on, it grew more and more difficult to breathe. After an hour, we had to take turns purifying each other once more. James seemed largely unaffected by the growing toxicity in the air.

As we crested the next rise, another tunnel greeted us, splitting from our current route.

"We could follow the acid and poison, or we could check out the new area." Jaken turned to James, and the black Dragon-kin just looked uncertain.

"The Dragon knows we're here." He glanced at the path to our left. "If I wanted to lure anyone into a trap or where I wanted, I'd offer up some kind of easier route, then lay the trap there."

"Yeah, that makes sense, but then again, who knows what a Dragon is thinking?" Muu shrugged. "Ampharia led me to believe all kinds of things while she was training me, then completely surprised me with the opposite. Or the very thing she told me would happen. There's no real knowing. So we go in cautiously no matter which way we choose."

I saw his face light up, then he grinned. "You get a point of wisdom?"

He looked smug and stated, "Two."

We all smiled and began to make our way behind James toward the right where the noxious gas kept coming from. It wasn't long before light graced us, though it was a small amount, and we came out of the opening slowly.

The cavern we were in now was clearly a hollow in some kind of mountain or something. Mounds of glowing fungus and lichen dotted the floor and the ceiling high above us. Off to our left, there was a bend in the stone and light shone dimly against the gray outline of rocks and weakly growing fungal pods hanging from the walls.

*This won't be fun,* I observed to myself.

There was motion in my peripheral on my right, and I looked over in time to see James slinking toward a large pile of something.

*Bones.* He stopped to look over them. *Dragon's bones.*

*It's fucking dead?* Bokaj's dismayed question made all of us more than a little angry.

Not at him but that we hadn't been able to get to the Dragon before it died.

*Well, whatever happened, let's at least try to get some loot from the place before we check out.* Yohsuke's sigh was audible, but he continued telepathically, *No telling what could be around here, though. So, let's keep our eyes shifty and our thoughts to ourselves. Be cautious.*

The rest of us gave a thumbs up and began to slowly move around the area. The ground was littered with some sort of powder, likely from the fungus in the place—old spores maybe? —that kicked up into tiny clouds as we moved about.

There was a back room to the cave that led deeper in— surprising, I know—that we began moving toward. James began to use hand and arm signals as though out of instinct. He held a closed fist up with his right hand, his arm bent at a ninety-degree angle.

"Do not hide, intruders," a loud, bass voice rumbled at us from behind us.

I turned to see this behemoth shadow in front of the dim light of the cave mouth around the bend.

"How rude of me," the being tutted itself. "*Light.*"

The lichen on the walls and the mushrooms around us glowed brighter and brighter until they could have been house lamps without shades on.

"Better." The black Dragon grinned.

Its form, easily rivaling Winterheart's bulk and dwarfing Ampharia's graceful form, was what I noticed first. The large wings that would span twice as long as its body lay folded neatly against the ebon-scaled back and sides of the mythic beast. It leaned down to look closer at us. The head—the size of a modern-day utility truck—tilted to the side. I noted scars running over the length of its snout and the jagged and hewn scales along the ridges of its eyes, maw, and chest.

The horns, like that of a bull's, jutted out before it, one of them chipped and the other whole and so dark it seemed to eat the light. Red eyes, the irises engorging as the pupil slitted to take the rising level of light.

"Much better." The hot, fetid fish breath reeked as it washed over our bodies.

James stepped in front of the group and squared his shoulders at the beast.

"We've come seeking your assistance in protecting this world from—" he began, but the beast cut him off.

"War." The Dragon opened his mouth and blew the monk over on to his ass. "The voices said you would come. Some said to trust you. Others to kill you on sight. Some still think that a game would be fitting for the first time a group of adventurers like yourselves have found my latest lair," it looked around dramatically, "but all I seek is the solace of the end."

"Death," James said as he sat up from the ground. "You seek the final reprieve."

"Yes. I came here and fought the red Dragon you saw over there in hopes that she would provide the ultimate thrill before the end—but she failed. Like so many others." The great black looked genuinely saddened before looking at Muu. "But you smell of kin. Tell me, little cousin—where is she?"

"Safe, but why don't you tell me something?" The green Dragon-kin stepped next to James and threw his hands out slowly. "This huge cave and no hoard? Are you truly ready to move on? To bite the big one?"

"My hoard is safely hidden from prying eyes." The great red orb swiveled to regard the tiny being before him. "You need only concern yourself with the entertainment you will provide me—or you can tell me where the Dragon you know is. That will earn you a swift death."

*This is gonna get bad really fucking fast*, Muu growled through our heads.

*I got the front line. Get close so I can buff us all and then get to it,* Jaken ordered. We all shuffled as if uncomfortable, drifting closer together.

"I came seeking a blessing to help a friend. I need that. Give it to me, help me how you can, and we will leave," James insisted.

*Bokaj, do something!* I hissed at the training Bard inside my mind. *Seduce him or some shit.*

*You have got to be fuc–* Thumph—the Dragon smacked his tail on the ground in annoyance.

"You have one more chance to tell me before I start killing your friends, cousin." It looked to the rest of us then. "Or maybe one of you knows?"

"I know," Yohsuke admitted hurriedly. The rest of us looked over at him in confusion.

The gray Elf stepped forward and waved toward the rest of us. "They don't matter. They don't know the sheer awesomeness of the creature in front of us, but I have two requests."

The Dragon seemed to weigh its options before nodding once for the diminutive creature before it.

"Let us see the light of day once more, outside in the fresh air," Yoh motioned towards the entrance behind the Dragon, then continued, "and the second is let us know the name of the great and mighty Dragon who brought our adventure to an end."

The black Dragon's teeth flashed as it began to hiss with laughter. "Such a humble creature. You do well to recognize the end. Fine, my name is Riktolth. March forth outside my lair, morsels. Enjoy your final moments, and prepare to part with your information."

Riktolth stood and shuffled to the side so that we could file past him.

*Don't freak out—we need room for Muu and all the rest of us to work. In here, we're way too confined,* Yohsuke explained as we walked.

That made a lot of sense. It took a couple minutes for us to trudge outside, to take in the scenery. The trees outside were dead as all fuck. They were blackened and twisted. Mutated, likely by proximity to the Dragon who inhabited the cave inside now. The ground was blackened and blasted with craters, and gashes dotted the stone entrance to the place and the ground before it. Claw marks.

"This was the scene of a magnificent battle," Jaken observed as he took in the scene himself. He turned to our host and asked, "I take it that you took part in this?"

"It was a… pitiable battle." He closed his eyes a moment—lost in the memory of the fight, most likely—giving Jaken time to cast his buff. The Dragon's eyes snapped open, but it noticed nothing that seemed off. "She fought well. Even managed to scar me, but she was no match in the end. Tell me. Where is this Dragon?"

"She's in a jungle to the south of here. Her name is Ampharia," Yohsuke said and threw a branch he had picked up to the side of the trees. Riktolth's eyes followed the object until it landed. I heard a shuffle and then nothing before he glanced back.

"Thank you, morsel. Your death shall be swift." His maw opened in our direction, the beginnings of a blackened fog.

Yohsuke's hands shot forward, firing twin balls of dark light. I knew those spells well—Star Burst. One must have been stored, and he cast the other to fire into the jaws of the beast. If Riktolth got that breath weapon attack off, though, the spells might not have the desired effect.

Arrows clattered against his right eye, and Jaken moved off to the Dragon's left side and banged his shield to get his attention. When that didn't work, he simply threw his longsword at the Dragon's head.

Riktolth snapped his mouth shut and jerked back. A plume of smoky spittle rained from his mouth. I smiled as the Dragon roared in rage. A tooth had been knocked loose there, and I was sure as fuck going to capitalize on it.

I cast Aspect of the Ursolon on myself and brought Magus Bane into my hands just as a whistling sound reached my ears. I grinned savagely as Muu's short spear thundered into the Dragon's rib cage just above the base of the wings.

"Yes!" Riktolth cried. "Struggle more! Give me the fight I have longed for!"

I growled and rushed forward—time to fuck shit up. As I ducked beneath the Dragon's body to do what damage I could, I started by trying to hamstring the beast, going for the rear legs. I got one solid wack on the left leg, but the Dragon's tail walloped the ground near me, and I took it as a sign to get the fuck out of Dodge. As I was moving, I saw our prey breathe deeply and arch his back.

Riktolth launched himself into the air and blasted the ground in a dense fog of putrid breath. Our buff held the debuffs I knew would have been there, but it still hurt. I was down to sixty-five percent health, and I couldn't see the others' HP at the moment, so there was no telling how they were doing.

I brought out my other great axe, Storm Caller, and held one in either hand. Magus Bane in my left, and Storm Caller in my right. Both of them were pretty light thanks to my higher strength and one of the abilities I could use, but they would be unwieldy one handed, and I wasn't truly planning to try and divide my damage like that.

This was a means to a grisly end.

I sprinted out from under the beast's stomach and activated my ability Feather Axe. Both of the weapons in my hands immediately felt like they weren't there. I used Wind Scythe, an ability that allowed me to throw my axe accurately to a certain range, but I just needed it to go far. I shouted at the exertion of throwing Storm Caller as hard as I could.

The weapon arced close to the Dragon's right wing, and he juked out of the way with a sneer. I laughed and activated Blade Shift. I appeared above Riktolth with my hand on Storm Caller's haft. I put the weapon back into my inventory as I began to fall and prepared to strike at his exposed back.

I heard another shriek of air being parted as Muu finally began his descent with his lance. The Dragon-kin laughed maniacally as he flew by; he drove the icy weapon wreathed in vibrant green venom into Riktolth's back at the connecting joint to the wing.

The airborne beast bellowed in pain and rage as it tried to get his wing to work but succeeded only in overcompensating and partially turning mid-flight to bat at Muu with a wickedly clawed forearm. The Dragon-kin took the hit with his shield arm and flew away with his lance in his fist at seventy-five percent HP and falling due to a bloody rent in his armor.

Riktolth noticed me as I activated Cleave and dropped on to his stomach to chop like I was splitting wood, the attack slowing my momentum greatly. A gash appeared in his underbelly where I had to hope his diaphragm would've been. The Dragon tried to grasp at me but hit the ground with an island-shuttering crash. The jarring impact knocked me off to the side, but I managed to roll rather than land straight on my side. I took a couple points of damage, but it was negligible. Still, I cast Regrowth just to be safe, leaving me at 650 MP. Still sitting pretty.

James hopped up on to the Dragon's throat and began an assault of fists and feet that was awe-inspiring. His normally calm and precise jabs were replaced by powerful swings enhanced by his ki and rage.

"I'll take my blessing from you, then!" he spat as his hands erupted in flames and lightning.

Jaken and Yohsuke began working on Riktolth's arms in their own ways. Jaken's long sword was floating and harrying the Dragon's face as the Paladin set to work with his greatsword. Bokaj worked on trying to blind the grounded bastard with his bow.

Yohsuke dug his astral blades through the ligaments around Riktolth's arms, likely trying to make that one useless.

I summoned Coal; the flame wolf came out braying at the Dragon.

"Light him up, Coal—but stay out of the thick of things!" I ordered as I made my way toward the tail. I was about to try and take that shit.

The Dragon flicked his tail up and knocked Muu out of the air just as he was about to strike again. Muu grunted at the impact that swept him to the ground with a solid crunch and a shout of agony. His health plummeted, and he didn't seem to be moving much.

I held a hand out and cast Heal, then Regrowth on him. Golden energy coalesced with my green healing mana, and the Fighter was back up to full and trying to get up, but the tail was still on him. Jaken grimaced before nodding at me and turning to roar angrily at the Dragon.

"Come on, you scaly shit!" Spittle flew from Jaken's mouth, and Riktolth seemed to take offense.

I walked up to the base of the appendage and grinned evilly. I closed my eyes and focused everything I had into my swing; with a grunt, my weapon sunk deeply into the Dragon. My mana leaped up by seventy points as well. 646 MP with my current regen plus the mana Magus Bane stole. I left the axe in the tail as the Dragon thrashed and howled as it tried to stand. I cast Stone Weapon to make a great hammer and smashed the hammer into the hammer portion of Magus Bane.

The axe bit deeper into the flesh before it, and Riktolth screeched. The rear leg behind me—long forgotten in my stupidity—smacked my shoulder and sent me careening through a dead tree. The sound of a crack and severe pain in my rib cage let me know I now sported a broken rib. I cast Heal on myself, raising my health back up to sixty percent, and another Regrowth assisted in getting my regeneration into overdrive.

Rather than going straight back into the fight, I noted that Magus Bane was stuck fast in the Dragon's tail. I jogged around to the side of the beast where the hammer's head would be, then dismissed Aspect of the Ursolon in favor of Aspect of the Belgar.

*Get here, Yoh!* I bellowed to my friend through our earrings. *To the tail!*

My skin and fur hardened, graying slightly, and my snout

tickled and itched fiercely as a horn grew from my flesh. My muscles grew denser and more powerful. The only trade-off was that I became exceptionally nearsighted. Luckily, I was facing my desired target.

I took my first steps, then ten feet later, I was in my stride and charged my shoulder into the hammer of Magus Bane. The weapon dug deeper and deeper as I kept charging through.

I heard footsteps and had to trust that it was Yohsuke.

I heard flesh beginning to sizzle and heard Yoh grunt, "Always gotta get the tail when you hunt monsters."

At that point, the foot came again, but I was only pushed away by a few feet this time thanks to my added bulk and higher defense.

"Halfway through, man. He's trying to get up!" Yohsuke warned.

I heard a shout from Muu of, "Fuck *you!*" It sounded close.

A grunt of pain from the Dragon, then a wheeze.

"Muu!" I called. I pulled Storm Caller out of my inventory and threw it into the air. "Give us a hand!"

*Tail!* I barked into his mind, and he let me know he was on it.

"Two steps left—no, three more now—and back straight up," Yohsuke ordered me. I did as he said, and as soon as I was where I needed to be, he shouted, "Now!"

I charged once more and drove my shoulder into the hammer with a sickening crack, my shoulder dislocating despite the enhanced defense. I gritted my teeth and shoved past the pain, thinking quickly, I reached into the shadows and flung a Shadow Scythe into the flesh in front of me to help. I heard a roar and Muu's manic laughter before the squelching of blood and a heavy, thudding noise.

"Tail's down! Back up!" Muu's voice was panicked as it floated away, and rather than defense right now, I needed to see.

I grabbed Magus Bane and dropped this aspect before I began hopping backward as Riktolth reared up, bloodied and angry. His HP was down to a little under half, and he was bleeding heavily from his neck.

"You think you can best me?" he screeched.

Coal's glowing body was next to a tree, outlining Bokaj as he continued to fire arrows into the Dragon's weak spots and wounds.

As he stood on his hind legs, Riktolth reared back, dodging a few arrows and took a deep breath. I took a calculated risk, thinking that I'd need to start slinging spells soon—and cast Aspect of the Owl.

The world took on a largely different hue as the details of everything stood out to me differently. The added ten to my wisdom would help me recover my mana faster.

A little of the Dragon's breath leaked out of the wound in his throat, but the wound was closing swiftly. A lance of pure darkness, radiating cold energy, jabbed it through the right knee, making the breath weapon swing wide and rake the stone above me and Muu.

Which gave me an idea that could work.

*I need everyone to distract this fucker. Bokaj, you got any of those Fire-ball arrows left?* I looked over at the Ranger, and he shook his head.

*I got Lightning ones though. This one is pretty weak. Will it work?*

I nodded once and explained my plan. Thanks to the earrings, it only took a few seconds, but that was precious time to get things set up. And two seconds after that, I had enough mana to enact the plan.

*Now!* I mentally shouted.

All hell broke loose before me.

James set about trying to clamber up Riktolth's back with his weapons damaging the beast as he went. Yohsuke had forsaken his weapons for spells. He cast Astral Bolts at the Drag-on's injured knee, then switched to Hellfire Arrows.

For Bokaj, it was business as usual. He fired arrows into the slowly closing wound in Riktolth's throat. To further the distrac-tion, he used the last of the elementally charged arrows that I had made him, shocking the beast and allowing the next portion of our plot to take place.

Jaken bounded over to us with both of Muu's weapons in hand and handed the Dragon-kin his lance. Jaken took the spear and ran farther to our right to get away from us. He hefted the weapon, and it began to glow a deep crimson before launching it at the Dragon's exposed underbelly. Then he moved in close to tank the beast.

Riktolth's health was down to a fifth, and he looked to only be growing more irritated and enraged.

"Hope you know what you're doing, man." Muu sighed. "These are my last two for the day."

I just gave him a thumb up and shapeshifted into my fox form. I watched as he took a deep breath, brought his lance up like a javelin, and used his bracelet to add extra strength to the throw. Once it was clear of his hand, I leaped into the now-empty palm, and he repeated the motion, using the bracelet's ability one final time to launch me as well.

The lance hit first, the icy weapon creating a rim of frost around the deep puncture wound. Seconds before I was close, I shifted back into my fox-man form and cast Void Shield with a flat, round surface. The surface acted like a hammer to Muu's weapon—the nail—driving it further into the dragon's body.

The force behind our strikes made the Dragon stumble, and as I fell, I watched James stab his Dragon's Fang fist weapon into Riktolth's eye and drive it in up to his shoulder with a bellow of rage.

### CONGRATULATIONS
### Level Up!

I grinned and allocated my points swiftly for intelligence only. My mind seemed to grasp at the world a little better, and I felt a little more at ease with my spells. Coal grew to level 15. His natural point went into wisdom. So I spent his three remaining points evenly for strength, dexterity, and constitution.

Coal was now easily the size of a dire wolf, his shoulders almost even with my own as he stood. His features were brighter now, the heat radiating from his body as he panted happily as his tail thumped my leg.

"Oh, you *know* we're going hunting for loot, baby." Yohsuke grinned at the rest of us.

"Sure," Bokaj smiled back, "right after this word from our sponsors."

The Ranger fell to the ground laughing as the rest of us joined him. The running noxious fumes from the corpse were beginning to affect us. I laughed as I wandered over to the corpse. James huffed breathlessly on the gashed chest as he tore the flesh away, exposing something inside. He growled when he didn't find what he was looking for, then moved further up the neck toward the base of the throat, near the skull. He wiped his hands on something from his inventory and held a book to his face then tracing along the flesh before him.

He nicked it with his bladed fist weapon and closed the book before throwing it into his inventory. I blinked, the toxicity of the Dragon's closeness abating slightly due to my shock at his actions and the breeze from the ocean floating through the area.

Like a surgeon, James dug his blade into the fleshy jawline of the corpse, creating a large gash in one side, then the other, then took his weapons off completely and slipped them into his inventory. He reached inside the first gash and pulled out an oblong-shaped organ the size of his torso that pulsed with a faint, purplish light.

He sat the one gently on the ground before stepping over to the second gash. This one seemed to give him a little more trouble than the last; he had to balance the item in one hand and use his clawed fingers to dig it out.

I decided it was time to investigate, so I began to move his way, bumping my dislocated arm on the corpse. I hissed at the fresh pain and carefully made my way over to him.

"Do me a favor, since you're up and about?" He looked over at me as I spoke and nodded. "Help me relocate my arm in the socket so I can heal it right?"

James stepped closer to me, his bloody hands grasping my

wrist and the shoulder and pulled before the bone shifted and sat in the socket correctly. I cast Regrowth, and my health began to truly replenish.

I watched as he tore several of the black scales from the corpse; some were large, and others were small. He took the blade of his hand, enhanced it with ki, and made a Ki Blade before cutting a tooth and a claw from the body.

"What're you doing, man?" I asked as he positioned the items in a rough circle around him. He took the blood on his hands and rubbed it on his chest, reached inside the gash of the last organ he had dug out and rubbed more on his face before sitting in the center of the rough circle.

"I plan on taking his strength for myself," he responded simply. He closed his eyes and began to intone a mantra that sounded oddly like the chanting of a spell spoken harshly.

I watched in morbid fascination as his form began to glow and lift into the air, levitating as he might normally, but then the items around him began to lift into the air as well. As the chant began to repeat, the fang and claw took on an ethereal appearance and began to fade. Then the scales. And the blood. Finally, the two organs burst in a shower of fetid black rain that stopped short of me and the area surrounding the monk floating between them.

The liquid began to turn to fog and flit toward James, spinning around him like a nimbus of doom. I was beginning to freak out a little, and if he hadn't looked so calm, I would've tried to intercede. The fog swirled thinner and thinner until it covered him completely in an oval shape, like an egg.

Then the fog grew dense and slowed until it was a solid wall of darkness. It lowered until it sat on the ground and stilled completely. Runes began to crawl all over the outer layer of the item, and I lost my fucking mind.

My friend was stuck in some kind of egg.

# CHAPTER ELEVEN

"So our friend is stuck in an egg?" Bokaj looked as confused as the others had when I told them what had happened, but the evidence was right in front of him.

"So do we have to crack this egg to get to the punch line of this yoke or what?" Muu asked with a cheesy grin on his face.

"Shitty time for a pun, man." I sighed.

"Can you put him in your necklace for now?" Yohsuke looked over the runes but found nothing he could understand that I could see.

I touched the shell and willed it into the necklace. It resisted, but then went into it with no other issues. Inside the necklace was a sort of stasis zone to protect a willing creature. The egg must not have been conscious enough to choose, so it went in.

"We need to get rid of the body somehow, but first, we need to get some of the scales, the claws, fangs and anything else that can be used." I looked to my friends. "Muu, you wanna pick it as clean as you can while we go and try to find the loot?"

"I doubt my knife will be able to pierce the hide." He pulled out his skinning blade and held it out to me. I still had some diamond powder in my inventory, so I enchanted the blade with a diamond's hardness and to be sharp enough to cut stone. I hoped it would work on Dragon hide.

"Do as much as you can, brother." I looked back at the others in time to see Bokaj walking over to the darkened trees. "What's up?"

"These are infected." He touched the one he stood in front of, then grinned wolfishly. "I'm gonna take some of this wood and craft some arrow shafts from them. Should make for some fucked up attacks. Mind chopping this one down for me? I'll cleanse the area while you guys go look around. T' and Coal can look out for Muu and me while you guys go."

I shrugged. It wasn't a bad idea. I took Storm Caller out of my inventory and sliced cleanly through the thick trunk in two good chops and a final Cleave.

I left the two crafters to their tasks and walked back into the cave with Jaken, Yohsuke, and Maebe.

"He said it was hidden. You think it could've been some kind of lever pull? A false wall?" Jaken had wandered toward where the tunnel we had used had been as he spoke.

It would make sense, but I didn't think that would be the case. They would likely have had to have humans or humanoids build that for them.

"Probably hidden by magic." Yohsuke looked over the bones of the red Dragon, picked clean of all meat and sinew. He took his Astral Blade and began to slowly saw through some of the fangs and claws. "He did something with the fungus in here, willed it to be brighter."

A command word. With my True Sight, I'd be able to see through any illusions, but that didn't mean I could see through stone.

*I'm a fucking moron*, I growled to myself.

I shifted into my earth elemental form and began to feel along the wall closest to me. The stone I touched felt dense and seemed to connect to the outside. Over the next half an hour, I walked the walls until I couldn't find anything.

"Where the fuck could it be?!" Yohsuke threw a stone at the wall. It clinked loudly, echoing longer than I would've thought.

"Well, if it isn't down here, maybe up top?" Jaken suggested.

We looked at him in confusion, and he sighed before pointing up at the roof of the cave hundreds of feet above us.

"Think about it. You have a ledge that only you know is there? No one can see it because it's stone—the same as the material around it. False walls are a common thing in a lot of haunted houses and mazes."

I walked right up to him, put a hand on his shoulder, looked him dead into the windows of his soul, and I said, "I love you, you crazy bastard."

"How else could a huge-ass Dragon have snuck behind us without knowing that you could see through illusions?" He shrugged.

I shushed him softly. "No more words, evil genius. Save that for later." I slapped his face playfully, and he laughed at my antics.

I shifted into my owl form and flew toward the roof of the cave. Sure enough, there was a false overhang with a rather large hideaway in it. There were mounds of treasures, piles of gold and jewels, some weapons—some of them looked more ornate than others—but the whole place was rife with it.

I shifted back and called back down. "Get out! I'm gonna shove all this over the side of the ledge!"

I waited a second before one of the two responded with, "'Kay!"

I gave them a few minutes to get out of the way as I worked my way toward the back of the pile. I blinked, and suddenly, Maebe was there. She surveyed the piles with a sly smile.

"Take your pick, my Queen." I bowed my head.

She lifted her hand toward a pile of gold and items, and the shadows consumed it. The majority was still there; there was simply too much to get rid of all at once anyway.

"That will suffice," she stated. "What was it you were planning to do now?"

I couldn't help the shit-eating grin that split my face as I set my mana expenditure at 500 MP for this Void Shield. "I'm gonna make it rain, baby."

I cast the spell, the shield becoming a large line of shadows. I took a breath and walked forward, shoving the shield into the mounds of gold and items. It was slow work, and this time, Mae helped bolster the spell.

After a few minutes, we finished clearing the loot from the overhang. I did a final walk through, slowly searching for anything we might have missed. I didn't note anything, but Maebe stopped me from leaping over the edge and going down.

"Time for another lesson." She touched my face and pulled me close. "I want you to reach out to the shadows with your conscious mind and feel around."

I stared at her oddly but did as she said to, closing my eyes and casting myself out into the shadows. It was weird at first, warmer than it had been before. But this? This was weird. Then as I rose with them, I gasped.

"There is another overhang." I nodded to her once and jumped as high as I could with a lazy try and shifted into an owl to get up to the next level.

What I saw there was enough to make me both sad, over-joyed, and sent me into an internal rage so deep that I couldn't comprehend the full range of the anger I felt at the black Dragon that had taken this cave as his own.

Sitting in a nest of melted gold, gems, and platinum nestled three red Dragon eggs.

I shifted and fell to my knees, cursing softly as I took the view in. Were they alive? Did they stand a chance of making it? If they did, how would they care for themselves? They'd die.

"Mae," I whispered. Tears crept from my eyes. If I had known these were here, I would've been much more brutal in killing that Dragon.

I felt a hand on my shoulder as she grasped me in shock, the pain of her grip somehow centering me. I needed to be strong now. I could mourn later. There was a chance these guys could make it.

"Can Winterheart care for eggs?" She seemed to think about it for a moment before shaking her head.

"Not three. He's not going to be around for too much longer," the thought made her sad for a moment, the pain flickering across her features, "but he might be able to help raise one."

"We need to see if they're even still alive." I gritted my teeth and prayed that Mother Nature was looking out for these guys.

Maebe and I stepped forward into the nest and were rewarded with a wash of intense heat from inside, as if I had just opened an oven and it was at the perfect temperature to bake something.

I touched the closest egg. Unfurling my fingers wide as I felt toward the little Dragonling inside—I just *knew* it was devoid of life. The warmth of the shell outside was a lie that made me curse vehemently.

"This one yet lives, Zeke, but it is weak." Maebe removed her hand, and I felt for a sign that let me know she was right. I sensed it—a tiny heartbeat. A shred of warmth. I pressed a Heal through the shell into the little baby and hoped that it would help. The beating heart felt a little healthier, and I sighed in relief.

I turned to the last egg with a determined gaze. *Please be okay*, I prayed.

I touched the egg, and the pulse that greeted me was leaps and bounds stronger than the other egg. I cast Heal on the other egg once more and looked to Mae just before a notification burst into my view.

**QUEST ALERT!**
**Secret quest now available.**
**Great Egg Scramble - Mother Nature loves all her creatures, and Dragons fall into that category. As a Druid and as a special breed yourself, these young ones' plight falls to you for assistance. Find someone**

*suitable to bring these creatures into adulthood, or their line will perish, and the world will be poorer for it.*

*Reward - Unknown, favor with Mother Nature.*

*Failure - Loss of two great powers in this world and a severe loss of favor with Mother Nature.*

*Do you accept? Yes / No*

I accepted readily, though whoever was naming these quests was seriously demented.

"If you put them into your shadows for transport, they may die, right?" I asked Maebe. She thought for a moment, then thought a little harder.

"I do not know." She touched a shadow and pulled a living rat out. "This one lives because I will it, but it is mutated and cold. The shadows would steal the warmth from these eggs."

I sighed to myself. "Come on. Let's get to the others and explain what's going on."

We both left the overhang for the time being. I landed on the floor to find my friends gathered around the treasure, mouths hanging low and eyes wider than I had seen so far. Muu and Bokaj must have opted to come when they heard the cacophonous crash of coin and items hitting the ground.

Coins and items were scattered throughout the room, but information needed passing on now.

"Bad news guys." I cleared my throat to get their attention. When they all finally looked at me, I continued, "That fucking asshole killed a mom. Mae and I found her clutch. Three eggs. One egg was gone, another was well on its way to joining the first, and the third seemed healthy. We gotta find them a home."

"Can't you take one as a companion or a familiar?" Muu asked as he started shoveling coins into a bag.

"No, you *GREEDY FUCK!*" Without thinking, I advanced on him a little. He stopped what he was doing, and I cooled down a little. "Sorry, man. There's a kid dead up there. You think Ampharia would take one?"

I didn't know if I could handle having a Dragon as a pet. It was bad enough having Kayda, a giant fucking bird who was a creature of myth in her own right. A Dragon too? And *feeding it.*

Look, the gamer in me has some serious doubts in my lineage right now. Like, I'm pretty sure the only thing that part of me hasn't called me is a wheelbarrow, which is upsetting. But logistically speaking? That big of a mouth to feed would be a huge drain on us.

"A green Dragon raising a red?" He scoffed at the incredulous thought. "In a jungle she sees as her home? No. Not likely. They have a tendency to want to *burn* things, man. What about Dinnia?"

That suggestion gave me pause. She was strong, at least as strong as I was, and she knew a lot about nature in general. She could do it with help, and Sharo would help. He would likely complain—but he'd help.

"Okay. Yeah, that's a solid idea." I motioned toward the pile in front of him. "Let's get our loot on and then get to getting. We need to dispose of the body and then get these eggs taken care of. Right away." I took a second then to think before looking at Muu. "Did you and Bokaj finish what you were doing?"

The Ranger nodded, and Muu did too. "Got about a hundred pounds of scales that should likely be armor quality. I think we should just take the tail itself back to the village so that the smiths and the enchanters get to look at it and scour for components."

"Yeah, and I sure as *fuck* ain't cooking that nasty-ass Dragon for food, y'all." Yohsuke crossed his arms resolutely, and I had to agree that I didn't want that fucker anywhere near my mouth.

I went outside with Yohsuke and began the slow process of burning the corpse away and purifying the ashes as we worked through the body. Coal helped us where he could. Then I had a face-palm moment—the shadows!

I cast my will out and gathered the darkness in the world

around me, beckoning it to me. As it swirled, I redirected it toward the corpse and said, "Consume."

The nether slowly crept over the corpse and ate away at it, joyfully sucking it into nothingness. It took ten minutes, but the darkness consumed all of it, and there was nothing left of the Dragon but the tail off to the side where we had left it.

We went back into the cave and helped the others gather loot. At least the loot that would be the most useful. The money would always help, and with some new items, we would be set for items to enchant. I noticed a small glint of light refracted off something and reached down to pick up a skeletal hand with two rings on it. One was a ring of diamond and the other of sapphire—both wholly made of the precious gems.

Both were exquisitely made, and they weren't enchanted, so I would take them for now, and if anyone had any objections— I'd hear them out then.

We spent some time throwing weapons, armor, accessories and other things into piles while Muu and Maebe gathered the money into large sacks.

After a mind-numbing amount of time, we finally just decided to stop; if we needed money, we could come back. Nothing was going to come here and take anything unless they were brave enough to risk the waters around this set of islands. If they were? They could have our leftovers.

We gathered the tail and had Muu throw us up to the first ledge above us. With my intelligence at seventy-five, I'd be able to Teleport with up to fifteen creatures. That meant my full party of five, Maebe, the tail, and the eggs if I took Coal back into my body—with plenty of room to spare.

We spaced ourselves out and touched each of the desired items, making sure that we were also in contact with each other before we teleported to our first waypoint. There, I would let the cooldown pass and finish the trip. We would be most of the way to the village with seven hundred and fifty miles per Teleport. When we arrived, I realized we had accidentally brought the nest of precious metals. Half an hour later, we stood in the center of a wildly surprised village.

I cast Mental Message and called to Dinnia, "Dinnia, we have a huge favor to ask of you. We will be in the center of the village."

"I'm flying there now," I heard her respond through panting.

I blinked in surprise. I didn't know she could respond while shapeshifted, but ten minutes later, a falcon crested the roof south of the square, and she shifted as she landed.

"What in the Hells and the eternal Heavens have you brought to this village, Zeke?" Her voice was tight with some kind of emotion that I couldn't seem to place, but she was completely rigid and looked ready to scrap.

"When we found the black Dragon, it had killed a red and left these ones motherless. One of them is gone. The second is just barely hanging on, and the third seems to be healthy," I explained, then stepped aside as she rushed toward the nest.

"Get the dead one out of the nest. Dragon eggs can drain the life from each other if they aren't kept at the proper temperature." It took me, Muu, and Jaken all lifting and shifting the egg left and right to get it out of the hole that it was buried in.

Once it was gone, Dinnia had Jaken and I cast multiple healing spells into the fading egg while Coal stood in the nest and superheated himself.

Dinnia closed her eyes, and her lips moved rapidly. She snapped her eyes open and looked at us. "Help is on the way."

A dull *chuff* came from over next to Muu where he stood watching the goings on when Ampharia, the green Dragon who had helped train him, appeared standing next to him.

"What the fucking *fuck*?!" He stumbled and fell on to his ass to the crowd's amusement and his chagrin.

"Hello to you too, Muu." The elder Dragon, in her Dragon-kin form, grinned at him sweetly before turning her head toward the nest. "Well Druids, both of you seem to have a habit of cutting into my napping."

Dinnia bowed to the Dragon respectfully, and I just gave her a big smile. "We don't mean to. You do nap a lot, though."

She eyed me reproachfully, then walked toward the eggs and spoke under her breath, "Oh this will be annoying." She looked to Dinnia. "Touch them. Feel their life force and feel which of them calls to you."

Dinnia looked at a loss for words as her mouth moved with no sound, but she finally took a deep breath and did as she was told. She touched the stronger one first, but Ampharia sighed and picked Dinnia's other hand up and placed it on the other egg as well. Now she touched both and closed her eyes.

There was no outward sign of decision other than Dinnia taking her hand off both eggs and then touching the weaker of the two with both hands, saying simply, "Him."

"Goody." Ampharia's smile was sardonic, but she walked toward me and pointed at the nest, "They will need exceptionally powerful flame to keep them alive long enough to hatch. It won't be too long, I'd say about a month or so, but with so little heat sustaining them for who knows how long, it could be longer."

"I'm not sure I can get you that kind of power without help," I replied honestly, my newly-made right hand clenching at the thought.

She glanced down and lifted it to her eyes for inspection, then sniffed at it. Her eyes closed, and she shivered.

"That is powerful magic, and it could be helpful. The scent that clings to it. That creature is here. Somewhere in this village." I nodded, and she grinned wolfishly. "I want it."

"Xiphyre is a citizen of my court and is not for loan to anyone but this village," Maebe supplied sweetly, but I could see the darkness surrounding her, the shadows under her feet—and those of the items and villagers around here—deepen menacingly.

I interceded swiftly, "How about I pay for him to make you an item? As payment for the help with this?"

Her grin only deepened. "Two, and I will take the other

Dragonling with me and leave your village unmolested. I'll even offer to come at your call should you ever need me. Do we have an accord?"

I sighed. We were flush and rife with money, so it was a hit we could afford, and it would work in our favor down the road too.

"We do." I offered my green and purple hand to her, and she seemed confused.

"I want my own items, not one that you are already wearing, Druid." Ampharia seemed offended.

Before I could explain, Maebe put a hand on my shoulder and excitedly told me, "Wait." She looked back to the Dragonkin before her and motioned to my hand. "This is a customary symbolism that an accord has been struck of many different types of humanoids in this realm. I do not know about a lot of other cultures, but Zeke and his company seem to hold fast to this belief. Though I'm not sure if saliva was involved with this one or not."

I almost laughed at the disgusted look that passed over Ampharia's features, her teeth bared and snout wrinkled. "Saliva? On your hand? For any other reason than licking away blood? Barbaric."

"There's no need to swap saliva." I shook my head and offered my hand again, palm shifted up so she could see there was none hidden.

She took my hand in both of her own and inspected my palm before grasping my hand with her's in a startlingly rough grip.

"Let's go see the smiths and enchanters then." I motioned for Ampharia to follow me and left the others to their devices. Maebe wanted to visit the children and check on her people.

The others wanted to rest and restock as best as they could.

She lifted the still Dragon egg in one hand and followed me without anything to say. I wasn't going to be the one to tell a Dragon I thought of as a friend what the hell to do with a

Dragon egg. It took a moment to get to the forge, but once we did, I stilled.

The building was changed completely. The outside of it was now black stone, similar to the stone I had seen Thogan make in the Fae realm.

The elves that Maebe had ordered guard the forge stood at their posts stoically, casting nervous glances at the Dragon in Dragon-kin form behind me.

They crossed their weapons, spears with long blades like a glaive at the end, in front of the doorway. "If she is with you, Master Erebos, she can enter—but only if you vouch for her." The Elf looked nervous. He was right to be.

"She's cool. We're here to buy some love from our crafters." I patted his shoulder, and he stiffened, then relaxed. "Thank you for all of your hard work. It's appreciated."

The Elven sentries looked to me, then at each other before they lowered their heads and weapons to allow us entry.

The first thing I noticed was the sweltering heat; then I saw that all of the wood had been replaced by stone. The interior racks of weapons had been covered by stones with metal studs placed on the corners with runes that glowed.

The dry, sauna-like air instantly made my fur itchy, shitting all over my day, but I wasn't alone. Ampharia clawed at the scales of her neck ferociously.

"Why don't I bring them out to you?" I offered, and the Dragon snarled at me. "Just a thought." I called out over the din of hammering, "Thogan! Rowland? Xiphyre. Get your asses over here!"

Rowland poked his head out from around the doorway to the forge area itself. "Oi!"

"Hail, Rowland, owner of this smithy!" I teased, and the Dwarf merely winked before ducking his head back out of sight.

"Thogan! Pixie! We got comp'ny!" The hammering stopped, and a rush of angry curses and the sound of something receiving a throttling reached my ears.

I bounded toward the doorway and caught the end of Xiphyre punching Rowland in the chest with a grimace.

"Call me pixie again, you pebble, and I'll curse you so hard that your own *God* won't even recognize you." I hadn't seen the crazy Fae pissed before, but he looked ready to kill someone.

"You aren't a pixie?" I asked, partially to fuck with Xiphyre but mostly because I thought he had been one.

A tiny fist smacked me right in my gob, and I stumbled back a step, a fourth of my health gone from the strike.

"Pixie heads are too big for their tiny bodies." He stood with his hands on his hips, his cheeks flushed in outrage. "Does my head look proportionally challenged?"

"You don't want me to answer that." I grinned wolfishly. If he was gonna be a bitch, I'd play. "What are you then?"

"I am a Ragalfr." His little chin pointed into the air haughtily. "We are second only to the Celestial Fae and powerful."

I rubbed my sore jaw and winked. "Sure you are, big guy."

"Thogan, Rowland," the smaller man looked to the other two men in the room skeptically, "I believe he is addled. Perhaps I struck him too hard?"

"He's teasin' you, Xi—means he sees ye as a friend. Aye, Zeke?" Thogan chortled when I winked in his direction. "What's ye come ta get, lad?"

"Is that a *Dragon egg*?!" Xiphyre stiff-armed past me to stop in front of Ampharia. "Where did you get it? Give it to me!"

He reached for the large item, and the green Dragon simply snatched him out of the air by his throat and shoulders, her fist almost engulfing him completely somehow.

"You may be second only to the Celestial Fae, tiny one, but you will never come close to the majesty of a Dragon. Never assume to take *anything from me*." She blinked once, her eyes shifting ever so slightly as she cocked her head to the side. "Do you understand your place in my world now?"

Xiphyre gurgled helplessly and choked out, "Yegh!"

Thogan looked ready to fight, his axe in one hand and a

hammer in another, and Rowland placed himself in front of his equipment.

"Ampharia," I grunted. The Dragon looked my way, and I motioned for her to let him go. "You're here as our guest. He's a friend, and he meant no harm. Let him go. Besides, if you kill him, he can't enchant your items."

A cloud of green mist flared from her nostrils as she thought for a moment. I heard a small snap, and Xiphyre grunted; then he was free and fell limply to the ground, his left arm hanging broken at his side.

I tapped him and cast Heal to help him mend, then Regrowth.

"A Dragon's toll," Ampharia growled. "Speak to him, Druid. I find this heat... irritating."

"Thogan, Rowland, and Xiphyre," they all tore their gaze from the Dragon and listened to me, "I'm requesting that you make two items of similar value to my arm for Ampharia. Enchanted, please."

I saw complaints and lack of interest, so I held out a hand.

"I bring components, scales, bones, and fangs of dead Dragons, as well as gold. Do this, and I will compensate you handsomely." That got their attention. Xiphyre was already flying again, running his greedy mitts together vigorously.

"Please me with them, and this egg is yours." Ampharia showed the large red egg off for sweetener. "Possibly add in another item? To pay for your lack of sound judgment earlier?"

"Done!" Xiphyre and Rowland shouted in unison. Thogan simply sighed and accepted his role in this.

"No specifications, and no requests other than what has been stated?" Thogan eyed Ampharia carefully.

"I have none." She lifted my right arm and motioned to it. "I do like this material though. It feels warm. Almost alive."

"It is, but that's an enchantment that I made, Your Scaliness." Xiphyre quipped, then seemed to reign himself in as Ampharia stepped forward. "I meant that with the deepest respect. Dragon scales are highly prized by enchanters of my level as components, and having only ever met one Dragon before your magnificence, I see that there is reason behind this now."

She huffed, and I saw her look directly at me before giving me a drawn-out wink. She was fucking with him now! Excellent. Weird, but excellent.

"We will begin immediately." Thogan patted me on the shoulder, and I called to Jaken through our earrings to get him to bring most of the bones and things that we had collected to the smiths. As well as the tail. I also had him be sure to keep some back for me and for Vilmas.

*Already on the way. Muu gave me an order that he would like to get done while we're here, and I think Vilmas has something for you.* Jaken grunted and growled, *This tail weighs a metric-fuck-ton.*

*You'll get it, bud.* I chuckled as I imagined the finger he might hold up in response to that and nodded to the others. I opened a notification I received and grinned.

### SECRET QUEST COMPLETE!

**Completed - Great Egg Scramble - Mother Nature loves all her creatures, and Dragons fall into that category. As a Druid and as a special breed yourself, these young ones' plight falls to your assistance. Find someone suitable to bring these creatures into adulthood, or their line will perish, and the world will be poorer for it.**

**Reward - Unknown, favor with Mother Nature.**

*Well, makes sense that I wouldn't know what it gives right away, annoying, but long game is okay, I suppose,* I grumbled to myself.

"I'll be going to meet with Vilmas now." Rowland perked up at her name and smiled to himself. Odd. "If you guys have anything interesting, I'd love to see it later. Drinks?" I asked, and the Dwarves looked so eager that I had to run before I was carted to the tavern for drinks I would likely have had to supply.

After I fled the room, Ampharia hot on my heels, the Dragon left to explore the village with her newly obtained egg in hand and a promise, "I will not injure anyone else unless they start it."

I had to take her at her word, and a short walk later, I was standing outside Vilmas's door in the tavern. I knocked, and a loud clatter and mild, squeaky cursing rang out. Vilmas, her hair messy and unkempt, opened the door a bit until she saw me.

"Zeke!" She reached out, grabbed a handful of clothes, and tugged me swiftly into the room. "I am so happy to see you!"

I felt her wrap her arms around me. I smiled and patted her head as I looked about. The place was a mess of components, a crudely-made workbench, and some items on the desk.

"What's been going on since we left? It's been a week or so?" I sat on the spot she cleared on her bed that had diagrams and designs all over them of varying sizes and complexities. "Holy fuck, Vilmas, what is all this?"

"Research!" She picked up several designs and shoved them at me. "Master Xiphyre has taken me under his wing and has been giving me lessons on how to create higher tier items and enchantments!"

She held out a small, metal raven made completely of Fae Iron with small diamonds for eyes. The detail in the work was unreal, as if the feathers would ruffle out then settle back against the chest under my gaze and the head peek to the side.

"Look." She shifted the item so that I stared at a complex series of runes engraved into the raven's breast. "The enchantment allows you to cast a Sending to anyone you know on your current plane of existence for only 100 MP, and they can respond for a full minute!"

"That's great, Vilmas!" She handed it to me, and I pocketed it for later. "What else has been going on? The wall for the village working well?"

"It is, but there's nothing to truly test it anymore—which is good!" she added hurriedly. "But there hasn't really been anything. Vrawn is out training with the newest recruits, and I went on a date with Rowland the other night to the mine where you found the Fae Iron."

*A date?!* I smiled at her and raised my eyebrows, making her blush.

"He was a perfect gentleman. Brought a pickaxe he forged especially for me, designed to help work through the minerals around the metal that are so much harder than normal stone and earth." A dreamy look settled over her gaze as she stared out the window, her normally well-thought speech patterns dipping toward traditionally Dwarvish brogue. "It were dark. He laid out a pan to sift the dirt away and gave me a chilly mug of ale he brewed himself. Never passed anyone's lips before mine, not even his own. Zeke, it were the sweetest I ever did taste, and you know what he said?"

I was damned near giddy at all the thoughts that were racing in my head that he could have said, but I shook my head excitedly.

"He took a long pull of his mug, and he threw it down—right upset—and he said, 'won't never be sweet as the sight o' you, Vilmas. Never as bold as yer figure, nor as delicate as yer smile. I'd need ta be a brewer me whole life ta come even close ta capturin' yer beauty in a barrel.'"

The woman's cheeks reddened furiously as I cackled in delight. Holy *fuck*, Rowland was smooth as hell!

"It was so sweet, what he said, do nae be laughin' at him!" She rebuffed me as her fist connected with my arm. There was no damage.

"I'm not teasing anyone, Vilmas. I'm not even laughing at him!" She seemed confused, so I put a hand on her shoulder comfortingly. "I'm proud of him. And you, for being so brave as to go with him. Other than that, what do you think of him?"

She hid her face in her hands for a moment, and I worried she wouldn't respond when she took a deep, steadying breath.

"He's handsome and a good crafter. A good friend. A hell of a miner." She smiled slightly before continuing a little stronger spoken, "His laugh is infectious. He's a fine brewer.

And have you seen him swing a hammer?" A lusty look passed over her features, making her blush. "He's so different from any of the other Dwarves in Djurn Forge."

"And that's a good thing?" I leaned a little closer to her.

"It is. He doesn't see my clan or my abilities as a curse. He sees me as a crafter and as a woman, proper." She looked up at me, tears beginning to fall from her eyes as she smiled and whispered, "He's so sweet and shy. Gentle. I want to court him."

I clasped her shoulders and called to Thogan with Mental Message, "Thogan, my friend—send Rowland to the tavern for me? Right away. Tell him you need him to grab an item from Vilmas, and don't mention me."

"Well then, he will be on his way!" Thogan chuckled conspiratorially.

"Hold on to that resolve then, Vilmas." I smiled and shifted so that I stood behind her, facing the door.

"He's coming?" She tried to rise from her seat, but I put a steadying hand on her shoulder. "What if he thinks I'm moving too fast?"

I laughed softly, remembering how struck stupid the smith had looked when he first laid eyes on the other Dwarf for the first time. "I don't think you'll have to worry, but it's okay."

A couple minutes passed with Vilmas nervously wringing her hands before I heard panting and a light knock on the door. I scented the air and caught the scent of burnt metal and sweat. And fox?

"Lady Vilmas?" Rowland knocked softly.

Vilmas looked to me, then when I nodded, called, "Come in!"

"Ye sent for me? Hello, Zeke." I could see a little disappointment cross his face, his lips turning down slightly and his eyes dropping a bit.

"I did," I smiled at him and cleared my throat. Vilma's looked up at me, and I looked pointedly at Rowland.

She blushed and hid her face.

"Ever'thin' aright, m'lady?" Rowland took a step forward, then another before kneeling beside her, opposite where I stood.

He took her right wrist in his burly hands gently and prized it into his grasp. "Is there somethin' heavy on yer heart, lass? Can I help ye?"

Vilmas's lips quivered slightly, and her shoulder shook. Rowland looked horrified.

"No!" he whispered, tugging a perfectly white kerchief from his pocket with a flick and began to wipe her tears away. "Donae cry, m'lady! What's got ye upset?"

"Nothing, at least not anything outside meself." She sniffled, then took her other hand away from her face. Tears fled her eyes, and she wiped them away swiftly. "I've been searchin'."

"Searchin'?" Rowland prompted as she turned introspective and silent for a moment.

"For the words ta ask somethin' of ye." She looked at him, and he frowned.

"If I could fetch ye the stars, m'lady, I'd build the ladder meself." The smith smiled reassuringly. "If I could give ye the most precious thing yer heart desires, ye need only ask."

That made Vilmas start sobbing in truth with small, hiccuped giggles. Rowland gently padded the water from her cheeks. It was almost too cute, like watching a romantic comedy where you get all giddy and embarrassed and have to look away from the screen so it's slightly less painful.

Hey, I watch all kinds of things—get off my back, okay?

"What's weighin' on ye?" Rowland asked her softly.

Vilmas put a hand on his cheek, his beard sliding against her fingers as she cradled his face. Rowland looked alarmed, and his cheeks actually flushed at the contact, but he sat still, motionless as she stared deeply into his eyes.

"You." She sniffed. "You have been weighin' on me. Thoughts of you and yer kind words. And yer sweet smile. And yer laugh, and I want ye ta know that I like ye too."

Her speech went, her composure went, but the entire time, her face grew steadily more determined.

"Rowland, I wish ta ask ye—if ye would like to court me proper?" Vilmas shyly tried to hide her features with a hand as she finished the question, but Rowland had none of it.

His huge grin, nearly splitting his beard, made me smile in return.

"I'd never be more honored ta have a beautiful, proper lady such as yerself ta court. I'd sooner shave me beard daily for a decade as hurt ye on purpose. I'd lose me will ta forge if ye were to think me unworthy." He stood and started to move his hands toward her, then stopped suddenly. "If'n I might be so bold, could I give ye a hug?"

Vilmas looked startled and muttered, "I'd like that, but I'm still a bit too shy about it. Could I offer something else?"

Rowland nodded, a serene look of understanding settling over his features, and he offered his hand, palm up.

Vilmas looked askance of him, but he merely waited until she put her hand over his. He knelt, slowly—so he wouldn't startle her—then placed his forehead on it.

"I promise, Vilmas, that I will treat ye with respect and dignity 'til ye choose me over another, or ye'll have naught to do with me—I so swear on the Mountain."

Vilmas's demeanor straightened, and she returned, "And I Vilmas, will endeavor to prove to you that I am worthy of your affection, until such time as you deem me fit for a bride or will have naught to do with me—I so swear on the Mountain."

"I bear witness to your oaths to each other and bind it as kin. An oath to bind as sure as the stone under our feet and along all of our Ways. May each of you find happiness," I spoke, the foreign words pouring from my mouth unbidden. I felt a divine hand had been in this, and the awestruck looks on Vilmas's and Rowland's faces were enough to confirm that Fainne had inspired that somehow.

Weird.

Rowland bowed to his lady, and Vilmas waved him out of the room so that he could go and continue to hone his craft. But they had promised to dine together that evening. I loved it.

Vilmas thanked me, and I noted that she looked a lot less harried than she had.

"You're welcome, but could I ask a favor?"

"Indeed." She looked at me as I pulled out the full sapphire and diamond rings. Her eyes widened, and she snatched them out of my hands. "Where did you get these?"

"In the Dragon's hoard?" I grinned, and she looked ready to steal them for herself. "Could you possibly enchant those for me? I'd be happy to pay you for the service."

"What did you have in mind?" She bounded over to her desk and swatted the clutter out of the way in favor of a clean sheet of paper and a quill.

"Well, I was thinking that maybe something that could give me an edge in the Hells?" I pointed to the diamond ring, then the sapphire one. "These are high quality, right?"

"No." She shook her head and smiled. "These are uncut, but if I were to cut them properly, I could give you high quality rings. I have a couple of things in mind. Leave me, and I will have them done tomorrow. Let me have that bird back?"

I dug the raven out of my pocket, and she tapped it. I yelped as the bird came to life and flapped its wings, looking at Vilmas expectantly.

"Master Xiphyre, if you would—please join me in, oh, say, three hours' time? I have a couple of items you would love to help me enchant." She finished the message and tapped the bird once more. A spectral image of the bird separated from the raven in my palm and the bird stilled—wings spread wide. A few seconds later, it moved, and the wings fell back into place at its sides.

"That is how you can tell the message has been delivered," Vilmas explained when she saw my look of open curiosity.

"That's amazing!" I lifted the item to observe it again, but it was as still as it had been before. "Is there a cooldown?"

Vilmas shook her head. "No. Just the cost. It was meant to be a powerful boon, as Maebe had requested."

"Thank you." I gave her a pat on the shoulder and left with

a smile. It was nice having friends who would work with you like this. Do so much to take care of you.

So nice.

I dropped by my own room to change out of my bloodied clothes and put on a fresh pair. I thought of having the shadows come and clean the blood from me but opted to at least wash my face in clean water. The water in the basin in my room was changed daily, somehow, so I stripped down and went to it.

The water was serene, still, and silent. A preference I was happy to acknowledge after having been fighting for my life in the ocean only recently. With a sigh, I dipped my hands into the water, and my conscious mind went with them.

# CHAPTER TWELVE

I blinked. The water all around me, clean and cool against my being felt nice but foreign. I began to panic but realized that I could breathe despite being underwater. I looked around at my surroundings, taking them in slowly.

The bottom of an ocean greeted me. It looked like something one might see in a deep-sea documentary where the oceanic floor was supposed to be dark and murky, but this one was light. Coral reefs dotted the horizon outside the room I stood in, their colorful structures as large as whole buildings and skyscrapers on Earth dotted the horizon, but the coral that made this room was bone-white and shimmering somehow. Pearl, maybe?

*Finally, droplet.*

I turned to see a throne made wholly of coral and seaweed spun of golden light. On it sat a small figure that looked like a woman, her human features flowing somehow from a young to a middle-aged woman. Her hair was sea-foam green, and her eyes were a crystalline blue like the Caribbean. She wore a toga of sand, seaweed, and small sea creatures that shifted in the water but stayed together.

"Primordial Water Elemental?" I asked, knowing damned well that I was looking at her.

*I am, and I also am aware that I do not resemble the Flame nor the Earth and Wind Primes. They are not the caster that I am, nor did they have the beginning that I had. Now, for your gift.*

**QUEST COMPLETE!**

**You have completed the quest: On Cleaner Tides – The Primordial Water Elemental has ordered that you find the Dragon and rid the area of it in whatever way you deem necessary.**

**Reward: What the Primordial deems "Handsome" and a hefty monetary sum.**

I dismissed the notification and watched as the Primordial stood from her overly-large throne and walked toward me, her features changing slower and slower until she looked to be in her mid-to-late twenties now. Her facial features were soft, not fat, but just soft. Unfinished or undeveloped. The rest of her was hidden beneath her toga of moving oceanic life and findings.

*You did not fail me, and your reward will be handsome.* She lifted her hands to cup my face before she dropped them. *This will be rather invasive and probably painful but worthwhile. Please, shift your form to that of a human.*

I did as she requested, and then she cupped my cheeks again. The water around us swirled as she stared into my eyes.

*The water gives life, and without it, the flow of the lifeblood in all creatures large and small turns to dust. To understand the depths that my magic runs, you must experience the loss of it.*

It was a weird sensation, the hydration of my body—the seventy percent of it that was all water—fleeing from my skin. First, the racking pain of cramps in my muscles, my legs and toes fighting to curl in on themselves. My arms folded into my body, and I cried out, desperate for any kind of relief from this pain.

My voice came out a shattered gasp as no air could leave my

body with enough moisture to make sound—even my vocal cords were dusty and barren.

The water around us darkened and swirled faster, tendrils of it slashing forth, eating what little of my HP bar that remained after being turned into a husk of my former self. My muscles continued to deflate and waste. Finally, my body gave way and collapsed, but the Primordial held tight to my face. My life ebbed from me, and I knew nothing but agony.

*Now, understand the truth behind the gift and use it to your advantage.*

I felt the water pressing around me. Into me. Then I felt something soft against my mouth and opened my eyes to see the Primordial pressing her lips against mine. Her lips parted, and more water rushed from her to me. I noted that my HP was refilling faster and faster. My desert-like muscles and sinew regrew and moistened, coming back stronger than they had been before.

Relief flooded my mind and with it—knowledge. The ebb and flow of tides. The ebb and flow of the water in the body— in all life—that all of it was capable of being manipulated and used to make the body healthier. Stronger. Even the spells that I knew already could be changed and manipulated—made stronger and more deadly now.

*I have strengthened your healing magics and other spells. When you leave my realm, take this flask and have your friends drink from it. Then pour the rest into a large hole outside the village. Dig it yourself if you must, but it will be worth the effort.*

She pressed a flask into my hands as I listened to her speak and nodded when she finished. Dumbly staring at her, I clutched the item to my chest.

*You may leave now, droplet. If you have need of my aid, simply call out. If I need you—you will know. Do not grow stagnant, but cut and carve your path in the stone foundations of this world's history. Go.*

With a slight smile, she shoved me backward, and my conscious mind slid out of her palatial home and up. I blinked and brought my now-human hands out of the basin—the flask coming out as if it had been there before my dive in.

I shook my head at the disorientation, and vertigo suddenly plaguing my mind and body. That had been real. Not only that, but I had come out stronger for it. Right?

Looking, none of my actual stats had changed, but my water, ice, and healing magic were much stronger now. I grinned boyishly.

Better distribute the quest reward then.

I slid the flask into my inventory, washed my face with the water in the basin as I had meant to originally, and beckoned the shadows forward to clean my body. They slithered over my body and ate the salt and grime away, then left me standing nude and clean. I dressed swiftly and fled the room in search of my friends.

I found Yohsuke pouring over a cookbook and had him drink from the flask after a brief explanation. His eyes went blank for a second, then he returned to us and grinned.

"Oh, that's cool as fuck!" He gripped his fist and growled, "The Overlord's powers grow ever more!"

"Fuckin' nerd." I snorted, and we laughed together. When we finished, a thought hit me, "Hey, man—what did the shadows give you?"

He frowned, then held his left hand out, the arm of his shirt pulling back. There, along his gray-skinned arm, was a long band of curling, inky-black shadow.

"It's like a whip." He shifted his arm and focused on something.

I felt the tendril wrap around my own wrist and jerk me toward him before letting me go.

"Did you not see me using it to avoid being crushed during that fight with the Dragon and the fish before that?" I shook my head, and he shrugged. "Yeah man, I been using that for a minute. It's pretty fucking nice."

"And what about this?" I shook the flask in front of him.

He shoved his hand on to my chest, and I felt a pulsing ebb of strength fled my body, my HP bar shrinking by about twenty-one percent.

"Gave me an ability called Sanguine Tide." I hid the wonder and jealousy I felt at that name and waited for him to continue. "I can already leech health through a spell of mine called Vampire's Touch, but that increases my understanding of it and therefore strengthens it." He tapped his own chest. "Had I been hurt, more than half of that health I stole from you would've been mine."

"That's sick as fuck." I cast Regrowth on myself and was surprised to see a tinge of blue to my green druidic healing energy.

But the spell was vastly more powerful now. Going up more than double what it had been. Before, it had returned 3 HP per second for thirty seconds. Now? A full 6 HP. That would mean going back up by 180 HP after a mere thirty seconds. That was nice. The best part? There was no change in the mana cost. Still a flat 30 MP.

"I'll be back later, man. I gotta go find the others and share the love."

"Later then, puto!" Yoh called after me playfully.

I called to the others telepathically, *Where are y'all at? I have our quest reward.*

*Muu and me are at the forge. They're making him his order, and it's fucking hysterical,* Jaken answered.

*I'm borrowing some tools from Sarah to work this new wood into some arrow shafts,* Bokaj grunted into my head, and I smiled. I'd visit him first.

I knew Maebe would be with the children somewhere. The thought of it was both super endearing and troubling. I missed my son. His little smile when he thought I wasn't paying attention. His inquisitive spirit and his immense sense of adventure. I missed Kayda too. The big, feathered pain in my ass.

I scratched my chin, realizing I was still human, but not caring enough to change back to my fox-man form, I walked toward Sarah's carpentry shop.

I heard laughter inside and smiled. I walked in and found

Sarah trying to help my friend dislodge a rather painful-looking splinter.

"Seriously, just pull it out!" the ice Elf hissed at the human woman.

Sarah, Rowland's pride and joy, laughed openly at the sight before her, her black hair swaying as she laughed; it bounced as her head moved. Her smile deepened when she turned to see me. "Hello, Zeke."

"Hey, Sarah." I waved a hand and cast Regrowth on my friend. Rather than the desired effect, he shrieked in agony, and his health fell by a huge chunk.

"It's the WOOD!" he cried. I bounded forward and—sure enough—the splinter looked to have grown more savage looking and dug deeper into his flesh.

I took my right hand and grasped the sliver with my nails, gently at first—but rougher when I could hardly grip it—and pulled sharply. The thing fought like a motherfucker, and I had to pull with my whole strength before it finally gave. What was left was a bloodied hole in his hand and blackened lines running from the hole into his finger.

I cast Purify on him and watched as the angry, black lines burned away. He groaned, and I cast Heal to be safe. His health leaped back up.

Damn, man, another good return. Instead of the flat 100 HP healed, it was 200 HP now. Nice!

Sarah came closer to us to see what was going on, her dark eyes sparkling curiously.

I shoved the flask in his face, and he drank from it. The same blank stare fell over his face before he came back with a smile.

"Deeper understanding of ice. Nice!" He looked at his hands. "Healing too. I'm not handling that shit without gloves now though."

I patted his shoulder once, looking him somberly in the eyes and said simply, "No glove—no love."

As he cackled and Sarah stood confused, I walked out the door laughing too.

The forge was next on the list of things to do. I called to Muu and Jaken from outside. When they didn't respond, I repeated the call over our earrings.

They wandered outside, and each took a pull from the flask. Jaken got a boost in healing strength—duh—and Muu received a new type of skill that he said he would have to play with to fully understand, but it involved a more flow-heavy kind of fighting style?

Fighter shit. Weird, right? Oh well. Now, for the last member of the party before Maebe.

Hey—she fought too, and she helped us out. She counts.

I walked into the center of the village where Ampharia sat watching the eggs with Dinnia.

"You guys wanna help me scramble an egg of my own?" I raised an eyebrow at them, daring them not to laugh at my humor. Ampharia simply blinked, and Dinnia looked confused.

I sighed. Sometimes genius goes to waste. Willing the egg containing my friend out of the collar around my neck, I did my best to set it on the ground gently.

"What is this?!" Ampharia was suddenly next to me. "James?"

She touched the egg with her hand, then pulled it back with a deep hiss of pain. "This is dark sorcery, Druid," her intense gaze fell on me, "and you say your friend—the monk—is inside?"

I nodded, keeping my words to myself. Had James resorted to dark magic to get the strength he felt he needed? It sure seemed that way.

"You will tell us what it was that he did before this happened," Dinnia's voice came from my left shoulder. Her hand hovered over the eggshell and pulled away.

I did. I told them about the items he had pulled out. The scales, teeth, blood, and what I had to believe had been the breath glands. All of it.

"We must get him out," Dinnia stared fiercely, "and find out what tome he was using."

"But he's in a damned egg." I pointed at it for the effect it deserved.

"So we break it." Ampharia closed her eyes and scented the item before her. "He has matured greatly already."

"Then why don't we just wait until he comes out in his own?" The thought of forcibly breaking him out bothered me. Especially since I had already done so once for a loved one.

"You do not understand, Druid—what comes out of that egg may very well not be your friend." Ampharia grasped the egg with one clawed hand and shifted into her true form, her draconic body taking up the whole of the square. "Take the egg and follow me. Druid Dinnia, come."

She lifted off, the turbulence from her sudden, rapid motion almost knocking me from my feet. I tapped the egg and willed it into my collar before calling to the others through our earrings.

*All call, James is possibly in trouble. I'm going with Dinnia and Ampharia to sort it out.* I growled as the others were leaving me behind. Fuck. *I'm going with them toward the east. Catch up when you can!*

I didn't have time to get Maebe as well. I just hoped that maybe someone would grab her. I hopped into the air and shifted to follow them.

After flying for a solid fifteen minutes, we landed in a flat area of the woods. I summoned the egg, and we thought for a moment on how to do it.

I gave the others a more detailed path to get here, and they said they were coming.

For shits and out of curiosity, I cast a fire spell on it. The flames engulf the egg, then seeped into it.

"Magic resistant. Great," I muttered.

"Truly." Ampharia's huge teeth flashed, and she reached her clawed forepaw down to grasp the egg. "Both of you, gather your strongest healing abilities. I will crack this."

A rush of fear and adrenaline burned through my veins,

and suddenly, I had to speak, had to say something—anything —to break the tension.

"Man, if an idiot makes a joke about an omelet in the middle of the woods with a Dragon, a Druid, and a gigantic egg—is there anyone who would understand how hurt I am right now that no one could hear that?"

The others stared at me, and I grunted for them to carry on.

Ampharia hissed as her flesh came in contact with the egg, and after a sickening crack and the release of the putrid-smelling contents, it started to come apart.

I moved closer to start sending heals into my friend when a large shard of egg smacked me in the chest and knocked me down. I'd lost a negligible amount of health, but I was surprised to see that the egg had burst apart like a grenade.

"Why have you disturbed my work," James growled. He eyed me, then Dinnia, and finally Ampharia. "You should have left me alone."

"Are you playing with matches, asshole?!" I fired back. He looked to me, and I continued, "Where the fuck did you get that book, and what the hell were you trying to do becoming an egg?!"

Now that the light was hitting him, I realized that he was larger now—more than six feet, muscular, and covered in scales the color of midnight.

"Taking what is my right." James smiled, his sharp incisors flashing. "He wouldn't give me his strength, so I'm taking it. And that book was in the library. So don't worry about it."

"Researcher or not, you aren't fucking invincible, man." I stood up and began advancing on him. "Show us the book."

"You aren't the boss of me!" His eyes took on a blackened hue and wings shifted from his back. He blasted forward and had me by the throat immediately. "You think because the elementals favor you that the rest of us can't touch you?"

I saw the manic look in his eyes reach a peak, and I noted a darkness that hadn't been there before. I put both hands on his arm and began to charge Purify. After the ten seconds of him holding me by my throat, my vision began to blur as he gripped tighter. I released the pent up spell, spending the 600 MP for the spell to hit him.

He blinked once; his grip loosened enough for me to extricate myself and flop to the ground, sucking in air greedily. My head felt fuzzy and light, but I didn't have time to dwell.

"That's—gah—the Dragon talking," I gasped as I stood unsteadily. He brought his hands to his head and groaned. I pulled the flask out of my inventory, and he was back to being a foe. Luckily, a large vine burst from the ground below him and wrapped around an ankle, then slithered up to his hips. He tried to cut himself free of it and made it through some of the grasping vines before a clawed hand swatted him down on to the ground with a sickening crunch.

"Fuck!" He groaned, and I lumbered over to pour some of the contents of the flask into his mouth.

He tried to bite at me, his teeth appearing sharper than normal. Larger as well. I took that opportunity to do the deed and clamped my hands down around his mouth to force him to swallow his medicine.

I felt the water hit my hand as if he were trying to spit it out, so I socked him in the stomach as hard as I could with my left hand. He gasped and in his pain, swallowing the water. I backed away, but Ampharia kept two of her claws on his lower body as he thrashed.

Wracking coughs and retching made me almost turn away and vomit from watching James heave bursts of black ooze and blood. His health was falling slowly, but I cast Purify on him once more, and he seemed to get whatever it was in him out a little easier.

I summoned the shadows around us and had them eat away the ooze as it gathered. It was done in seconds, and James seemed to be feeling better.

"Give me the book, James," Ampharia ordered. Her claws dug into the ground on either side of the fallen monk.

He opened his inventory with his pinned arms and

summoned the item. The book, a small tome, slightly larger than a comic with maybe a hundred pages inside, fell to the ground.

Ampharia relinquished her crushing hold on James, and he stood slowly.

He came over like he wanted to say something, but I waved it away. No apology necessary. Seemed to be a common thing with our group lately.

The Dragon shifted into her Dragon-kin form and took the book in her hands. Opening it, she hissed vehemently.

"Dark magics like this—abyssal." She regarded James coldly. "Where did you find this?"

"It was on the shelves in the Djurn Forge library. It was the first book I found there when I went to start researching things." He shrugged and pointed at the book as he moved closer to her and it both. "It taught me a lot and always let me read it perfectly."

"That's the sorcery behind an object like this. It's an ancient artifact that brings the reader under its influence slowly." She looked him in the eyes, hard. "It needs to be destroyed."

"No!" James lunged forward, but a large bear reached out and grasped him as he struggled. "Let me go! That book has helped us so much! I can keep it under control! Please!"

"You finding and killing the Dragon and needing power was likely the perfect catalyst it needed to take control." Ampharia began to tear the pages from the item as James screamed, fighting against Dinnia in her bear form ferociously.

The pages began to flutter in her clenched fist as if they were trying to fight back as well.

"Stop!" James bellowed, his wings thrashing a little. I stepped in and put a hand on his chest to keep him away. "It can be saved! It can be useful."

Ampharia then held the pages out before her, and a green flame enveloped her hand, eating the pages greedily. An other-worldly screech pierced the air making all of us but the Dragon groan in anguish.

The screech stopped, and a demon-like shadow dissipated in the air above the Dragon, her smile cruel and triumphant. "It is done."

James felt to the ground on his knees at a loss for words. "That book helped us. Made me stronger."

"It did. I can see it obviously worked. Right?" I tapped his arm, and he smiled. "But you're better off. What kind of stat boosts did you get?"

"Oh yeah. I'm stronger, faster, and my defense is way higher now. Let's see," he opened his status screen and started figuring slowly, "I'm five points stronger, two more dexterous, and my natural defenses have gone up to plus thirty! But it says here that the transformation was incomplete. So I could've gotten more."

"You would likely have been fully changed and taken over," Dinnia added quietly. The rest of us looked at her, and she pointed to the shell.

What was left of it was beginning to decay rapidly and slough on to the ground in liquid and gelatin-like chunks of sludge.

I motioned toward the disgusting item, and the shadows went to work happily, devouring it all whole and leaving no trace of evidence.

"That's fair. Thanks for helping me out of there. And that water helped a lot. But that was all, I think."

After thinking about it, James likely had coughed the majority of the water out as he got whatever was infecting him out, but I didn't want to risk it, and even trying to summon the Water Primordial seemed stupid. We would just have to be satisfied.

"I'm gonna recenter my Ki, then walk back to the village on my own." He must have seen the worry in my features because he added, "Just go, man."

He sat on the ground where he stood, then closed his eyes, tuning the rest of us out.

"I'm going to collect Sharo. Then I will return to the village.

It should take no longer than an hour or so." Dinnia shifted into her own bird form and flew off swiftly.

Ampharia just looked bored but laid down, "I will watch over him. There is much he needs to learn of what it means to be a Dragon. I should have offered him knowledge despite his scales when first we met. Go, Druid."

She closed her eyes, snorting softly and began breathing steadily.

I shook my head and gave James a last glance. He looked to be doing fine, so I took off.

*Things are fine. He's okay but wants to be alone with his thoughts,* I called to the others telepathically. *You guys can head home.*

*Fuck!* Muu shouted. I flinched. *You took me away from my nap for that? I'll get mine!*

*Shut the hell up, fool,* Yohsuke growled. *You sure you guys are cool? We're like, two minutes out.*

I grimaced. *Yeah, buddy, it's kosher. He needs to deal with some stuff. Ampharia is with him so he'll be okay.*

I lifted into the sky on warm thermals and headed toward the village.

As I circled the place, I noted something going on in a large clearing to the east of the village, just outside the wall that had a fence attached to it. There were dozens of children of all ages sitting enraptured as shadows moved and fought each other.

As I closed the distance, the figures became the black Dragon Riktolth and my friends and I fighting him. It was wild to see from a different perspective, but now that I could—I realized even more how badass my friends were, how far they had come, and how crucial they were to all of this.

"Then Master Erebos chopped into his tail, and with Master Yohsuke's assistance—helped carve far enough through it that Master Muu could help sever it completely."

As she spoke, the shadow marionettes reenacted the battle almost perfectly. The only thing missing was the actual danger. She made it look as though we were invincible. Untouchable. She made it look as if getting kicked by that Dragon hadn't

almost killed me or that getting back up hadn't been excru-
ciating.

At the time? Nah. Being in a life or death fight—especially
against a Dragon—had the ability to slightly dull pain for a bit.
It's not really needed in the moment.

But seeing my friends getting smacked around—battered,
crushed—was painful in a different way but also cathartic. We
had made it through—together—and that was awesome.

I landed on a large limb where I shifted from owl to fox,
then to panther so I could lay comfortably to observe Maebe
moving through the children and narrating events.

Their cries of amazement and anxiety over what was going
on before them reminded me of watching my boy enjoy a
movie. The pain of losing him—of maybe never seeing him
again—hit me hard. I didn't know it was possible to cry as a
panther, but I was.

I sighed as I finished my wallowing. I would always worry,
but there was nothing I could do now other than do what we
came to do.

I came back into events as Maebe was finishing, "And so,
the party vanquished the horrific Dragon and saved the island
and oceans around it!"

The children stood and clapped loudly. Some of the elder
ones whistled and all of them crowded closer to the narrator to
ask questions. The smallest among them, a tiny human boy of
maybe six or so, grasped at Maebe's hand.

The Queen of Ice and Shadow bent toward the little boy
who asked, "What was your favorite part? And how did they
win?"

Maebe thought for a moment before smiling at him. "My
favorite part was sharing the story with all of you, and I
think they won because they work together a lot. They may
not be perfect, but they work hard. And I think if you wait,
one of them may be here to tell you something about that
himself."

I felt the cool embrace of the shadows behind me nipping at

my tail. A purr rumbled in my chest as I slunk down on to the ground from my spot.

Several children gasped at the sight of me in my panther form, so I shifted into my fox-man form, and they relaxed immediately—the little boy especially. His face lit up with wonder.

"Hello, everyone." They waved as I did, and the little boy, still clutching Maebe's hand, stared wide-eyed.

"You had a question for him?" Maebe prompted him.

He stepped forward and kicked the ground nervously.

"It's okay. I think I heard it." I motioned for everyone to sit down, and I sat in front of him. "You wanted to know what her favorite part was and how we won, right?"

He nodded and sat down in front of me as I spoke, "Well, my friends are all *really* strong. And Auntie Maebe is right—it's because we work together a lot, but do you know why that's so important?"

Some of the older kids may have known where I was going with this, but they stayed quiet. I was grateful for that.

"Because when we work together, things are easier. See, I'm only as strong as all of my friends are, and it's the same for them with me. Think of it like a chain, right?" The kids nodded. "One link alone isn't all that strong, but if you have a whole bunch of links working together—they can hold really heavy things!"

"That means you have to be strong too, right?" a voice in the crowd called.

"Yeah, but it's not about me." I rubbed my chin for a second, then snapped my fingers. "I'm really good at healing and shapeshifting, I'm kinda strong and kinda fast, and I have decent magic," they nodded along as I listed my strengths, "but Yohsuke is so much faster than me, and he can hit someone with a spell so hard that they get dizzy."

I rolled my eyes and spun my head wildly; the children giggled at the display. "And Jaken is so good at healing and being a shield for us that we stay healthy for a long time. And

Muu? He can jump *reeeeeally* high! Like a bird, but he's all scales. And he's really strong. You saw how he threw his spear at that Dragon, right?

"Bokaj can fire lots and lots of arrows in a matter of seconds because he's so fast! Not to mention, he's a really good singer, right?" They nodded; one little girl mimicked an air guitar, and it was the cutest thing. "James is so fast, and he punches really hard. I should know. We spar together to stay strong. And our other friend Balmur is so sneaky that he can move through shadows."

"Like a kitty cat?" the little boy in front of me asked.

I chuckled. "Like a kitty cat."

He puffed his chest out proudly, then his head quirked to the side. "So, if everyone else is so good at one thing, then how do you win? Don't you have to be good at everything?"

I grinned at him. "Nope!" He frowned, so I continued, "It's because we all work together and know when to let our friends do what they know best that we win. Remember—together, you're stronger. Like, if you have a friend who is good at playing the drum, you know how to sing, and that guy over there can play a string instrument well. Individually—alone—you might sound okay, but together? Oh man, together, you can make some really sweet music."

More than a dozen children nodded slowly; the boy before me was awestruck.

"That's enough for today children," I heard a voice call. An Elvish woman I didn't recognize right away ushered the children toward the village.

"She's one of the guards I brought through. She is here specifically to shepherd and care for the young ones," Maebe explained as she laced her fingers through my own.

"How did you know I was here?" I watched the children leave, romping and flitting about.

"Who didn't know?" She eyed me teasingly. "I heard you sniffling. Even as a panther, you were an audible mess. Are you unwell?"

"We can talk about that later. For now, drink some of this—it's a reward from the Water Primordial." I handed her the flask of water.

She sniffed the liquid, then looked me in the eyes as she tipped it past her lips. Her eyes closed as she drank deeply. At last, she stopped, and the temperature around us dropped so steeply I could see my breath and hers.

Her green eyes opened, and I swore I could see a snowflake in them. Maebe's clothes fluttered in an unseen wind, and a blast of frost and ice shot from her feet toward me. I bounced back out of the way, just barely getting clipped by a jagged spear of frozen water. A massive chunk of my health sheared off of my health bar, and I growled at the suddenly-numb feeling in my leg.

I cast Heal on myself and negotiated the swiftly melting ice. "You okay?"

Her eyes glowed for a heartbeat, blazing with icy-blue power, then returning to her normal, deep green coloring. "I have never felt better."

She closed the distance between us, the cold following her noticeably. "You do exceptionally well with children, though at times, you can be a bit clueless."

I had to laugh at the observation—it was true at times.

I had always felt so out of my depth with my son; though I knew I loved him more than anything in the world, I always felt inadequate. I couldn't help the hard look in my eyes, the self-doubt and hurt there.

She grasped my hand and pulled me closer as her eyes searched my face. She took her other hand and pressed it against my cheek softly.

"I forget that you are a father already at times." She pulled me into a hug then let me go. "We will sit together this evening, and you can talk about him tonight. I would enjoy hearing of this little one."

"I'd like that," I replied simply. "Now, I need to dig a hole near the village."

Maebe eyed me, then shrugged when I did the same in response. We chose a large portion of open ground between the tree line and the village's wall. It was roughly eighty-five yards between them and likely a perfect spot to build our hole.

Using the shadows and some of her newly strengthened ice magic, Maebe and I dug our hole.

We treated it with care, being so close to the village, we didn't make it very deep at first. The closer to the wall we got, the more shallow it was, and the further away—it grew steadily deeper. Not too deep, though—only enough that a tall person would be about chest level with the water.

Once that was finished, I upended the flask into the hole and watched as a torrent of water gushed from the mouthpiece. It kept coming until the water almost reached the sides of the hole. Magically—because you know, magic—the water stopped.

The water was crystal clear, and seconds after it settled, steam began to rise from it.

I felt a tap from inside me, and my tidal tattoo itched fiercely.

*This is a reward for all of you. While you were in my realm, I noted that your people had a source of pure drinking water, but nothing like this from your memories. This water promotes not only relaxation but healing as well. It will stay pure, but being exposed as it is, it will invite trouble.*

"Thank you. This will help the village greatly." I hesitated, and the Water Primordial interjected.

*The great monetary sum was the Dragons' hoards. There will only be another reward should you prove your worthiness to me once more. Do not push your favor, droplet.*

A cold chill ran through my veins, and I simply answered, "Yes, ma'am."

Maebe blinked at me and pointed at the water. "This is the reward?" I nodded. "That is all?"

I nodded once more, and she pursed her lips. "I suppose the monetary gains promised came from the Dragons?"

"Sure did," I answered tersely.

Maebe's smile over that was unsettling. "I like the way she thinks."

I shook my head, and we began walking toward the village gate. The walk was short, thankfully only a five-minute stroll. The gate, a large metal affair made wholly of steel as thick as my arm and shot through with veins of Fae Iron, stood closed before us. There was a glaring crystal next to the gates on the right side.

Two human guards watched us walk up to it, obviously noting that we could see the gate, them, and the wall.

"Good day," one of the older guards spoke casually. "Please, place your palms against the crystal."

This was new but not unexpected—though I was worried. Had I been included in the spell to protect the village? I mean, I could obviously see it.

Maebe smiled and took my left hand and pressed it against the crystal. The large gem warmed against my skin, and the guards relaxed a little. Maebe did the same, and we were admitted into the village.

"We collected some of your blood from the bandages. There were many." Her tone was playful, but I sensed the reproach in it. Noted.

We headed back through the square, then headed to the Tavern. I cast Mental Message to Sam Wildheart, the village Mayor, "Sam, it's Zeke. We have a gift for the village near the spot outside that the children go to for classes. Don't ask where it came from, but you may want to get someone to cover it and include it in the fencing."

A few seconds later, he replied, "I will go now to observe what fresh wonder befalls this village." The man chuckled. "Thank you, my friend."

I smiled as we stepped inside. The room was well lit, and the air was rife with the scent of well-cooked food and booze. There was music playing in the corner, and I was surprised to see that Bokaj was playing his guitar—no song I knew but strumming a playful tune despite the look of consternation on his face.

His fingers danced along the cords, and his strumming seemed well paced. I wasn't going to interrupt him.

I grabbed some drinks from Willem and ordered the special for myself and Maebe.

That night, as my friend played the confusion in his soul for all to hear, I told the woman I cared for about my son. She listened intently and laughed when he would be obstinate, which could be a lot. He got his stubbornness from somewhere.

It wasn't long before we went to bed, and darkness took me. My thoughts on him and turning toward the north where we were going to be heading soon. Someone among the high elves knew of a way into the Hells. And we were going to find them. One way or another.

# CHAPTER THIRTEEN

At breakfast, the group ate while the task before us came into focus.

Breaking into the Hells to get Balmur meant a trip to see the high elves.

James sat at the table, now wearing a vest to keep his wings from flaring out behind him too much. The others had been surprised and happy to see him, and they were definitely happy that he wasn't evil. Muu was still slightly miffed about a ruined nap and a seemingly wasted trip, but he dealt with it.

We both decided to leave out the whole fighting thing, just as a point of keeping the drama down. It did nothing to tell the team what happened because it didn't matter now.

"When are we leaving?" Bokaj asked, going straight for the throat.

"Xiphyre promised my new weapon would be done last night. He mentioned something about Vilmas needing his help too." I grinned as Muu mentioned the two enchanters working together.

"What're you smiling about?" Yohsuke asked.

"Vilma's promised to enchant a couple rings for me, and

I'm going to ask them about a design idea that I want to do before we get to the Hells." I began to wolf my food down hurriedly when I felt a thud on my head.

"Muu, your weapon is completed at the smithy with Thogan and Rowland. It was too much to take it from them after they had worked on it so lovingly." I turned to see Xiphyre, fresh and rested, fluttering behind me. "You enjoy your food properly, tails. I brought the items. Vilmas exhausted herself last night over these, so you be sure to write her a nice thank you note to find when she wakes up."

I coughed and nodded. He pulled the two rings out of thin air, as if by magic, with a flourish and handed me the diamond ring first.

*Mage's Well*

*Stores up to 500 mana. 0/500 available.*

*A ring made by the earth itself.*

*Ring crafted by Time, cut and enchanted by Grand-master Enchanter Vilmas Brighteyes.*

"She's a grandmaster now?!" I whispered to myself and raised my eyes to a proud Xiphyre.

"And it was the other ring that did it!" Xiphyre tossed the freshly cut but unadorned Sapphire band at me and I caught it deftly.

*Clarity*

*50% resistance to all charisma-based charm spells and mental attacks.*

*The wearer of this band becomes resistant to the wiles of the mind placed by another. When attacked the band is even said to glow as a warning.*

*Ring crafted by Time, cut and enchanted by Grand-master Enchanter Vilmas Brighteyes.*

"Holy *fuck!*" I slipped the rings on to my empty left hand.

*Warning!*

*Finger accessory limit has been reached. 4/4 rings. Any additional rings added will not work.*

Huh. Well, that would've been nice to know sooner, but still, we could work with this.

"Bokaj, try to charm me." He looked at me like I was an idiot. "Fucking do it, man!"

I saw him focus on me, then he sighed. "You know you can be so stupid sometimes?"

I felt the hair on my arms and neck stand for a fraction of a heartbeat. "Yeah I know. I can be like that sometimes. I'm sorry, ma– Hey, my ring's glowing." I looked up at him, and he was grinning from ear to ear. "You asshole! It worked! Well, it didn't, but it did!"

"Awesome, man!" He smiled. "I take it that ring is supposed to help with charms?"

I nodded. "It's a warning system too. Also, four ring max for items. Xiphyre," I looked at him, and he raised a brow in question, "can you make everyone a ring similar to Clarity?"

"I could," he shrugged, "but you'll need rings with sapphires on them, and they will need to be of a higher quality."

Muu whipped out three silver rings with sapphire stones in settings on them. Of those, Xiphyre took the best one. I pulled out five similar rings, and three of them were sufficient. Yohsuke pulled out a platinum ring with the entire front of it a solid sapphire—that would work. Jaken pulled out a silver and gold pendant from around his neck that had a large sapphire stone nestled in the center with the ring around it to hold it in place.

We stared for a second, and he shrugged, "What? It was really pretty."

The rest of us laughed at his expression, and Xiphyre just rolled his eyes. "I understand you have an interest in enchanting, Zeke? Listen, and I will explain as I work what I am thinking when I work on these items. Same as I taught Vilmas."

And he did just that. Xiphyre explained that for the enchantment to take on this kind of item, they couldn't be visibly engraved. It had to be done inside the band. I looked inside my own, and sure enough, there was a tiny engraving that I couldn't even begin to know what it was. Still, the knowledge was useful.

"The intent to this is to increase the wearer's mental faculties enough so that they can rise above the attack." He reached over and tapped my ring. "We also want to add the aspect that alerts the user to the attack, just in case. This can be useful in case of someone else being targeted specifically."

He worked methodically but not slowly. Each time he touched an item, his focus was laser dialed. Even as he explained the nuances to the craft and the different things to look for in the items to check quality, he worked perfectly. It was awe inspiring.

No wonder Vilmas had gotten to grandmaster; under his tutelage, I could probably get to master swiftly.

After he finished, the others happily equipped their new rings. Muu's was the lowest percentage at forty-two percent, James, Bokaj and the extra ring we took for Balmur each had forty-nine percent resistance, Yohsuke's was fifty-five percent, and Jaken sat pretty at seventy percent due to the high quality of his pendant and the gem within.

I was a little jealous of the other two, but then again, it was Xiphyre. There's no way Vilmas could compete as a fresh grandmaster. The Fae was likely centuries old with decades upon decades of experience that she just didn't have yet. Perfectionist or not.

I looked at Maebe, wondering if her glamour would set the ring off, but it sat against my furred finger with no light at all.

"Clever boy, this one." Xiphyre patted my shoulder. "It will not allow you to ignore a glamour unless said glamour is hostile or meant to lure. She has no desire to do so that I'm aware of."

The queen bit an apple and looked at Muu. He suddenly went slack-jawed and began to walk forward toward her with his left fist glowing like a beacon. Then he stopped, just as confused as before.

"Oh! A test. Good idea!" He laughed nervously. "Well, time to go get my new weapon! Later!"

He fled the tavern without so much as a glance back.

"What did you make him see?" I asked her as the others began to gather around Xiphyre excitedly with questions.

"What you see." Her dark green eyes met mine, and I swear I saw the stars on her skin begin to glow and move as if in orbit.

"That's cruel." I swallowed heavily.

She finished her apple and stood from her chair slowly before coming to stand in front of me.

The warm scent of the fruit on her breath was enticing as she whispered, "The cold and dark are always cruel, mortal. Even when there is warmth, they are watching. Waiting."

Her finger touched my nose and drew me out of my sudden stupor, my left hand a beacon now as well.

Her smile was triumphant. "I like that they work so well."

"When we get on the road, I want to try and consolidate what we've got going on spell wise. I know it's something we try to do when we level up, but it may help us plan a bit better." I turned to watch Yohsuke stand and look at the rest of us. "We can't go into potential enemy territory the same way we have been. Also, we up our training to include team tactics. Three on three."

"What sparked this?" Bokaj wondered at him with his hands in his pockets. "Not complaining about it, I agree, but why now?"

"We've been here months treating this like some kind of fantasy story," he waved at the emptying tavern, "like some kind of movie. This is a game. We're gamers. We should be acting like it. We have our bearings. We're a helluva lot stronger than before, and Balmur needs us to refocus. *We* need us to refocus. That fight with Riktolth sparked that in me. We keep getting fucked up because we allow it."

Not for the first time in both my time on Earth and here in Brindolla, I saw Yohsuke's eyes flash dangerously. "We got shit to do, and these assholes won't make it easy. We work on our shit, fix it, and fuck everyone else up" He punched James in the shoulder and pointed at me. "That means back to basics for the three of us. We need to make sure our civvy friends can hang. They don't have to be Marines, but they will sure as fuck train with us like they are."

For the first time in the years since I had gotten out, I uttered, "Oohrah."

James nodded, and we left the tavern to go get Muu.

Getting to the smithy wasn't hard. We found Muu on his way back with a big grin.

"Well, let's see it." James motioned for Muu to show off.

Muu reached behind his back and pulled out a nasty-looking battle hammer. The handle of it was the same green Fae Iron as my right forearm and hand, though it was wrapped in a familiar, black leather hide.

Muu began to point things out starting there, "So this is the Dragon's hide that I was able to skin. Untreated but enchanted so that it will stick in my grip. The Fae Iron haft connects to the Dragon's tooth by being hammered into it and around it. The joints of the metal starting at the center toward the pick portion are covered in scales from the tail that have been treated with a special resin to be harder than they were on his body, and the ones on the end are sharpened."

He motioned to the front hammerhead portion of the weapon. It was filed down a bit but not too much. It was roughly eight inches in diameter and covered in what looked like a black and red metal cap against the yellowed fang.

"The cap is made of a mixture of some of its blood and a certain, crazy-poisonous wood resin that I happened to find lying about." He whistled a little, and Bokaj smiled.

So they had used sawdust created by the wood that Bokaj had collected? Or maybe it was sap? I wasn't a woodworker, so I didn't really care, but the idea was interesting.

"It'll make things being healed hellacious." Muu's grin widened, and I felt my own lips quirk.

"We ready? Everybody stocked on potions and whatnot?" I

raised my eyebrows, and Bokaj held up a hand to show he had them. "Cool. When we get there, we can put on our new gear—no. Now. Let's do that now."

I opened my inventory and began to look through the gear I had available. Yohsuke clapped me on the shoulder and slid an object over to me. It was a green, hard leather cuirass that would fit over my current armor, but just barely, it seemed.

**_Druid's Blessing_**
**_+20 defense, +10 to Nature Spells_**
**_A green leather cuirass touched once by the Mother. It is said to keep her chosen from harm, so wear it well!_**
**_Leather Cuirass crafted by Grandmaster Leatherworker Lymanil Gresh'n and blessed by Mother Nature._**

"Oh shit! Thanks, brother." I pounded Yoh's fist and reached into my own inventory and slid him an item in trade. It was a wicked-looking dagger called Nocturn's Sanguine Slasher. This was an area I would need to improve on. I had originally taken the item to study it and see if I could figure out how to make it better—or something similar for my own weapons—but Yoh could use this more.

**_Nocturn's Sanguine Slasher_**
**_+13 to Life Stealing spells_**
**_Sanguine Syphon – Two (2) times daily, wielder can summon the freed life essence of those around them to recover their own._**
**_Dagger created by Master Smith Samron Shillyorc and enchanted by Master Enchanter Lilith._**

"Fuck, man." He shook his head as he looked it over. "It's cool and all, but I don't use normal weapons."

"I think it would be better for you to have it than one of us because you have those kinds of spells. Not to mention, you would be able to have a spare weapon in case we don't have access to magic," Jaken advised as he slipped another longsword and sheath into his belt on his left hip. This one sat above his current weapon.

"What's that, man?" I asked curiously.

"It's a new sword, duh," he teased before pulling the blade from its home. The silvery sheen of it was almost physically painful even from a few feet away. "It's called Righteous Brand. It bumps my healing and holy abilities up by twelve each, and it's a bane weapon too, so if something is weak to silver or holy damage, they become poisoned."

"Ho-Ly *fuck*," I cursed. "That's badass man, but let's be careful using that around me."

"Hell no." James smacked my back. "That's what he will use when we spar against each other. There's only one way to learn to fight shit like that. By doing it. Play like we fight, fight like we play."

I had to admit, the prospect of facing a weapon like that, even if it would be wielded by our Paladin, made me nervous.

Bokaj had a new bow already, but he pulled out one that had blades on the ends of the limbs with a mercurial string that tied on a rounded hook on both sides. "Blade Bow." He grinned and moved it so fast it carved through the air with a whistle. "It's not enchanted, so you can enchant it later for me."

He also pulled out a few accessories and flashed them at me. "You'll be put to work on all of this shit as well. We need to be up on our gear, and you're going to make that happen." He eyed my right hand, then raised his eyes to mine. "Without blowing your shit up this time."

I flipped him the bird with the prosthetic hand he was just eyeing, and he just laughed back with the others. Maebe began to say something, then decided not to and just giggled with the others. I wasn't really mad. Just irritated that I hadn't seen it coming sooner.

Once all of us were dressed and readied, James in his new Djinn Bracers that raised his elemental resistance, Muu promising me he had work for me later, we were ready. Rather than walking anywhere, I Teleported us to the place where we had first met Coal.

The snow whipped around our feet, displaced by the sudden magical shift in masses in the immediate vicinity. The large fir trees towered above us, spaced almost evenly around us with a massive field of white behind us. The site of the carnage that had taken place here had likely long since been covered by the snow that was prevalent in the area.

All I could smell was the crisp scent of fir and snow, and that was all. Nothing else was in the area, and nothing floated to me on the wind either.

"We're heading further northeast from here." Bokaj panned his map so that the location was visible to us. "Looks like there's some serious forest between us, at least a week of travel, and there's no telling what's in the area, except maybe those wolves that had helped Coal out."

I nodded, and we set off, all of us carefully observing our surroundings. Both of the Dragons of the group wore their cold weather rings on top of their coats, which was good because the cold was terrible.

Everyone but Maebe and Bokaj shivered in the freezing eastbound wind, only sparingly broken by trees that we were loathed to leave to move on to the next.

The skies above us maintained a murky sort of white that I began to connect with bullshit weather.

There were no songbirds in this frozen waste, no plants other than the trees and other hearty shrubs that appeared to be dead. As we moved through the forest for the next couple hours, with only the sound of crunching snow for company, the temperature dropped even farther.

"Fuck this place." Muu's teeth chattered despite the ring and coat he wore.

"Seconded." I muttered, and James nodded along vigorously.

There had to be a way for us to be comfortable when we

stopped for the night, and as an enchanter—I could try to figure that out.

I brought out a ruby that I had taken from Riktolth's hoard. *This would do nicely*, I thought to myself. It was about the size of a small stone, little more than an inch wide but maybe half an inch thick. Cut round, the many faces of it reflected the light well.

"Jaken, you have any copper on you?" I asked after I was finished inspecting the ruby.

The Paladin blinked, then checked his inventory, and shook his head. "A bunch of rings I thought might be gold. Any of you?"

The others checked their inventories, Muu pulling out a large sack of copper coins. "Will these work?"

I hadn't thought of that. I looked at Jaken in question, and he took one out.

"This one is high-quality copper." He began to sift through the sack and tossed the bad coins to Muu, who stuck them into his inventory.

After a while, I had more than two hundred copper coins in the sack at my disposal.

"Awesome, when we stop for lunch, I'll work on this idea of mine. I'm going to try and make us a comfortable place to be, and I swear, the first one to mention blowing anything up is going to *eat* this ruby."

"Early lunch?" Muu asked Yohsuke with hope in his voice, cautiously not mentioning what I knew he wanted to.

"Hell no. We march on. Watch the trees for signs of life, and you might not be so damned cold." Yohsuke looked at me and nodded.

I understood what he meant. We needed to toughen up, but there was a limit to that. If we got sick, we would be useless. Better to try and help when I could.

While we moved on foot so that we could train and learn to work together more deeply, I began to gather the intent and necessary focus for the enchantment. What I would try to do. After that, the engraving came to mind easily.

We stopped to eat, and while everyone huddled close together, I began my work. First, I summoned a thick, hollow rod of stone with a claw at the end that looked like a weird back scratcher. I then channeled my flaming mana into the coins that I had Jaken pour into his bucket with my hands until they melted, and the liquid copper poured down into the hollow rod.

While I did that, Maebe used her shadows to dig a cooling trough for me and filled it with snow that I melted. I packed some cool dirt into the end of the rod when I had filled it to the point I wanted it to. Then I placed it in the cooling water until the water stopped bubbling to quench.

"May want to do that again with fresh water to be safe," Jaken advised. "The water didn't touch it after it cooled right away, so portions could still be hot or even molten.

He splashed the water out, and it froze almost as soon as it hit the snow, turning to ice. We used more snowmelt to quench again; then I let the spell dissipate.

In the water was a thinner replica of the stone rod, a foot and a half long, with the four claws coming up over it. The metal looked rough in places, but Jaken took the item from me and began to go over it with a file. A few minutes later, he handed it back, filed perfectly smooth.

"Thanks, brother." He waved it away, and I began to work on my design. On the base of the rod, I put a symbol for flame —not the Flame Elemental's crown—fuck that. Just a normal flame. Like a bonfire. From there, I put three lines that swirled from the bottom equally spaced apart until they reached the top where the ruby would sit in the setting. I dipped my finger into the setting and applied enough heat for Jaken to take a slim hammer and beat a dent into it for the gem to sit comfortably in.

Once it was set, I heated the claws, and we bent them until they held the ruby still and it didn't budge. Once that was completed, I ran the engraving lines up seamlessly on to the gem and had them stop at the line of a circle on top of the ruby. The circle ran the whole of the top facet of the gem, and that was it!

I took a breath to clear my mind and got to work on the enchantment I envisioned, adding a small pinch of Fae Iron shavings as the component to lend the object strength, flexibility, and whatever else the item would take from the metal.

**Mobile Spring Rod**

*The warmth of a new year has been packaged in such a small rod. Within this item's range of effect, the weather is pleasant and warm with a sweet-smelling breeze.*

*For a small mana cost, the temperature can be increased and the breeze turned into a thermal gust. For a heftier cost, the area affected can be increased for a short time.*

*Area of effect: 35 ft diameter.*

*Temperature increase: 50 MP*

*Thermal Gust: 100 MP*

*Additional AoE: 150 MP per 10 ft diameter per 30-minute increment.*

*Item created by Craftsman Enchanter Zekiel Erebos.*

The results were immediate. The temperature around us rose considerably to a comfortable level, and an aromatic breeze passed through the area that reminded me of a babbling brook.

"Nice dude!" Yohsuke smacked my shoulder. "That's the shit I'm talking about! We just gotta refocus."

Well, at least we were less at risk of catching a cold.

I felt Maebe's hand on my shoulder. "May I?" I handed her the item, and she looked it over. "This is good craftsmanship. I think I may have you make things for me some time."

I smiled at her and whispered, "Happily." I cleaned my hand in some of the swiftly melting snow next to me and then ate a sandwich Yoh handed me. It was good and just what I needed to get up and walk for another five hours. This was going to be fun.

---

Travel had been uneventful so far, thankfully, which let us focus on building our communication, both verbal and telepathic. We would point things out to each other and try to pinpoint the information as exact as possible. It took some getting used to, and there were misunderstandings at first, but it got a little easier by the end of our trek that day.

The only truly interesting bit, to me at least, was watching Maebe create snow that would cover our path of melt left by the Mobile Spring Rod. She did it effortlessly.

When we set up camp, Maebe erected her shadow barrier but much larger than normal to accommodate our group sparring session.

Splitting us was a little hard due to the fact that our specialties were so different that it was almost impossible to make the teams fair. But that was okay.

First, I was split with Jaken and Yohsuke on my side. I summoned Coal as well, no point in him not getting some practice in. This was going to be interesting.

Rather than me charging the rod, Maebe did, and the sphere of influence grew until it covered about a hundred and eighty feet.

"No holds barred. Just don't kill each other," Yohsuke warned. "Let's say that the first to ten percent health loses and the others carry on?"

The rest of us nodded.

In my head, I heard Yohsuke speaking once more, *Bokaj is going to be the worst problem. He can pretty much fuck us up immediately.*

I sent a mental command to Coal that he was to watch Tmont and not kill anyone. He understood, though he was eager to play and made no promises about the trees.

*You guys know that they're coming straight for the healer, right?* Jaken focused on the group before us and watched as they were likely strategizing on their own.

*They may, but they're going to come hard and fast. First thing you need to do is make sure that you get that shield up. Muu is going to throw as soon as they say go.*

"BEGIN!" Maebe barked once, and all hell broke loose.

Sure enough, Muu threw his spear but straight at Yohsuke, and before I had time to see what he did to counter it, I was tapped multiple places by sharp fingertips that left me stiff and sluggish. James had gotten to me.

I growled, the red haze filling the corners of my vision, and for once, I welcomed the rage. I was a lycanthrope—more specifically, an Alpha-and there were perks to that. I was going to make this fight my bitch.

As the fires of the change swept through my body, I felt the resistance of the pressure points loosen enough for me to break free of them. I stopped myself from changing and cast Aspect of the Ursolon.

While my form enlarged, I noted that James was now moving in on Jaken who was hiding behind his shield to avoid the arrows raining on his position.

*I'm coming, buddy. Watch for James!*

I bolted forward and just barely managed to grab James by his right wing and around the throat. With a great grunt of effort and a twist, I lifted and tossed the monk away from our Paladin and into the line of Bokaj's fire.

Instead of crashing into the squirrelly Ranger, James spread his wings to buffer himself and slow his momentum. Still, he took several shots to his back, and his health dropped to about seventy-three percent. He flashed with golden energy just before a dark Astral Bolt slapped the side of his head and dropped him to the ground, dazed.

I heard a yowl of rage and turned to see Tmont batting at Coal as he scampered away from Bokaj.

I stepped toward them, hoping to put the panther to sleep with a solid whack to the dome when an arrow took me in the thigh. It put me down to eighty-two percent, and I looked over at Bokaj who was now safely in a tree somewhere, and Muu was nowhere to be seen.

*The sky!* I shouted telepathically to the others.

I jerked the arrow from my flesh and began healing my wound with Regrowth, shifted into my owl form, and lifted into the air, hoping to find Muu.

I heard a whistle, and the owl screeched, *Bank! Left!*

I dropped and banked left just in time to avoid Muu's spear.

*Fucker's in the trees by Bokaj. We need air support,* Yohsuke growled.

*You got it!* I flew further into the air until I was more than three hundred feet up outside of the dome and into the biting cold. Once I was there, I shifted back into my fox-man form and dropped as I charged Winter's Blade.

*Don't be near that tree. I'm dropping some special mail on them.*

The others took that to mean turn up the juice, and they did. Yohsuke sent his spells flying, and Jaken began glowing red. Two blue specks shone in the trees.

I held it for thirty seconds, then shot the gigantic, twenty-foot sword at the tree where the two of them had been. Once it was fired, I went owl and flew down toward my friends.

Yohsuke had moved in on James and was blasting him in the head from close range with Astral Bolts to ensure he stayed dazed.

Jaken glowed red again to try and gather the hate for himself, but the spell struck the tree and exploded in a burst of icy shrapnel that pierced the trunks of the trees around them.

I thought I saw Muu go down, but I couldn't be sure because it was that time that an arrow ripped through one of my wings, and the owl screeched as I did when we crashed to the ground.

Tmont was on top of me a second later, and it took all my focus to shift fox-man and slug her in the chest. She crumpled just long enough for Jaken to heal me, and then James was there to kick me in the face. The first one pissed me off, the Werewolf's haze returning stronger than before.

The second one weakened my resolve to keep that rage in check. The third one, I caught in my clawed hand and used Predator's Call. James's left hand glowed with blue light as his ring lit up in warning, but the ability took, and he froze. I took his leg and threw him to Jaken with a roar, and Jaken caught him on his sword the same time as Yohsuke threw an Astral Bolt at him.

His health dropped to seven percent, and he was out of the game. Jaken cast a regen spell on him so he was out of danger, and Maebe called shadows to drag him away.

Time to start fighting like I meant it.

I reached out to the wolf inside me, slavering and baying at the walls of my will, and metaphorically took it by the throat.

*I'm in charge. You work for me.*

It looked me in the eyes, the black-furred left side and the white-furred right, one ice blue eye and one red. It stared back and answered.

*We are one.*

I felt the shift take me and stood in my hybrid form.

"Yo, Z, you good?" Jaken's startled tone caught my attention.

"Always," I growled back. And the power coursing through my veins right now? I would always feel the truth in that statement.

An arrow hit me, nicking my arm and healing almost instantly. I spied my prey and dropped to all fours to pursue him. I slapped Tmont out of the way as gently as I could, but she still spun away. I dipped beneath another arrow as Yohsuke's Star Burst took a good-sized chunk from the tree that Bokaj hid in.

I snorted at the air and found a scent trail that to me looked like it may as well have been a chemical trail in the sky to follow straight to Bokaj.

I dug my claws into the trunk of the large fir and launched

myself at the branch my prey hid in. When he was close enough, I took a swipe and received a burning arrow in the gut.

"*Roaaaaargh!*" I howled as the burning spread. I clawed at the offending shaft, and a dull slam in my right shoulder sent me flying away from Jaken and Yohsuke and on to the other side of the tree.

I landed, and the shaft of the arrow snapped, leaving the burning sensation inside me. I cried out again, and Coal was there beside me, whimpering. The Werewolf wanted to lash out, but I knew he meant no harm. The worst part was that my health was plummeting fast, and the regen I had as a Werewolf was gone.

*Silver? Fuck!*

Yohsuke called to me through our earrings, *We're coming for you, man. Just give us a second.*

I grunted, *Don't, it's a trap!*

*Shut up,* Jaken barked.

If they came over here, Muu and Bokaj would ambush them.

*Coal,* the flame wolf looked at me in worry, *I'm going to pull the wound apart. Get the arrow out, okay?*

He whimpered again, but I wouldn't let him refuse. Gritting my teeth, I dug my claws into the wound and pulled it carefully apart until the broken part of the shaft was visible.

*Now!* I barked at Coal.

He dipped his head into the wound, the heat uncomfortable against the muscles and inner walls of my stomach, and gingerly gripped the arrow with his teeth. He pulled once, and I gasped. He stopped, and I told him to just keep going until it was out. He jerked his head back once, twice, and after I heard the squelch and tearing of flesh and muscle, the arrow was out.

Looking at it, all it had been was a silver coin tied to the head with string.

*Crafty fucker.* My Werewolf form dissipated, and the burning calmed a little but not by much. I cast Heal on myself, and two hundred health returned with a sigh of relief.

INTO THE HELLS

I pulled Magus Bane from my inventory and stood. I activated Cleave and sliced through the branch that Bokaj was
sitting on, firing at Yohsuke and Jaken. The branch fell, and
with it, the Ranger. He landed on his back, and before I could
bring my weapon around to strike at him, I heard a shriek of
laughter. I watched in horror as Jaken took the brunt of Muu's
drop from the sky, and his health dropped to half.

The Fighter took out his hammer and smacked him in the
head twice, dropping him to ten percent exactly before turning
on Yohsuke.

I heard a groan behind me and saw Bokaj begin to sit up
with a loaded arrow, just as Coal fell on him and savaged his
shoulder, trying to drag the Ranger away from me. Tmont
limped over at me, hissing and snarling at thirty-five percent
health. I decided she wasn't worth the distraction and turned
back in time for Bokaj to release a Volley straight into me from
almost point blank range.

I went down hard and fast. Lights out.

# CHAPTER FOURTEEN

When I finally came to, the others were chatting over bowls of noodles and veggies.

"Holy shit, man," I grunted as I sat up. I was sore but not too bad. "Nice shot, Bokaj."

"You made it kind of easy." He clapped me on the shoulder, and Tmont eyed me dangerously.

"No hard feelings, pussycat?" She rolled her eyes at me and ate her own dinner, a large side of meat that she shredded easily.

"So, that was a start." Jaken slurped some of his noodles noisily and looked at us. "There was a lot going on there, and the planning and communication—while not perfect—were there. Right?"

"They weren't perfect," I answered. "There were times when I acted alone when I think I should have focused more on helping you guys rather than trying to neutralize the threat."

"This is true, but that is a balance that anyone rarely finds," Maebe added. "You did well to bring low one of your enemies, especially one so dangerous as James, but your true target should have been to ensure that Yohsuke could align an attack on Bokaj."

"How do you mean?" James looked from her to Yoh. "What, you would've tried to snipe him the same way you did me?"

"Yeah. Bet your ass." Yohsuke took a bite as he stared at Bokaj for a second. "He shoots so fast and often that getting close would only truly be ideal if it was you closing in. I can slice shit up, sure, but that just means I have to focus on defense until an opening comes, and that won't happen unless I can get him to stop firing."

"Excellently put." Muu belched rudely. "Knowing each other as well as we do means that we can see each other's weak spots. It makes it more difficult to fight each other."

"Which is why I can summon enemies for you as well," Maebe offered.

James clapped his hands. "A warm up for the day, and then we can focus on fixing things that went wrong in the evening?" His sharp teeth flashed. "I think that could work."

That night, I took the first watch while the others slept. Maebe sat a little ways away from me, so I could focus on the lesson she was giving me while we had this time together.

She was currently teaching me to press my awareness into the shadows around me so that I could sense danger—a minor ability, she had called it, but the first hour of my shift had been spent working out how to do it.

Now, by hour two, I was able to send my awareness into the shadows around myself, my friends, and even beyond our bubble of safety that Maebe erected for us.

While I was moving my mind along the shadows, I felt a brush of movement, almost small enough to think it had been a muscle spasm, but then I felt it again. I homed in on the offending motion and found a small creature, a hare, snuffling at the shadows south of where I sat. His presence gave me pause, and I wondered about something.

"Hey, Mae." I kept my eyes closed, but I knew that she was

paying attention to me now. "Is it possible to move things through shadows?"

I felt her awareness push against mine inside the shadows around our position and knew she had seen my reason for asking.

"Yes, and it is a simple thing as well." I opened my eyes, and, suddenly everything around me went dark, then reappeared, and I was next to Maebe.

"How did you do that?" I asked in wonder.

"Tell the shadows to surround your target wholly in a ball, then pull the creature or object to the shadow nearest you." She put a hand out in front of her, and a small amount of snow appeared in a perfect sphere in her hand. "Be sure that the shadow around them is solid and that your focus does not waver. Try it."

I blinked at her, worried I might fuck up and kill the animal, but I did as I was instructed.

I brought my awareness into the shadows and built a ball around the rabbit so tight that I worried about it being able to breathe for a moment, but then I yanked it toward me into the shadows about three feet from where we sat.

The ball of shadow appeared, then dissipated, and the hare stood immobilized by fear. Suddenly, it shrieked, "Where am I?! Who are you? What was that? *Don't eat me!*"

I tried to smile reassuringly, but that didn't help, and I worried that the animal's crying out would wake my friends.

"It's okay!" I whispered calmly. "We won't eat you. I'm a Druid. I only wanted to talk to you and practice an ability—which you have already helped with!"

"What about her?" It sat back on its legs and motioned to Maebe. "How can I be certain a big predator like that one can be trusted? I can feel the weird coming off her. Like she's waiting to eat me."

"Because she is my... mate," I added as the hare's nose began to twitch nervously, "but she won't eat you either. I promise."

It calmed down significantly, and Maebe pulled a carrot out of the shadows on the ground to offer to the hare. He bounded away from it at first but soon figured out it was a peace offering, then began eating greedily, stopping to observe his surroundings. I dug a small bowl into the ground and transported some snow into it so that it would melt and I could practice.

***ABILITY UNLOCKED!***

***Nether Transport (Minor) – Caster uses the shadows to move small objects and animals through the void. Cost: 50 MP. Range: 150 Feet. Cooldown: 30 seconds.***

That was a pretty cool ability, and I could see having to do both portions of it to unlock it being important. It helped set limits. I liked that.

The hare drank the water with gratitude, and I watched it for a time, wondering if the form would be worthwhile. There didn't seem to be a limit to the animal forms I could take, so why not?

"Would you mind biting me?" The hare looked at me oddly.

"I am not one to convert to the predator side of the food chain, Druid," it replied flatly.

I had to chuckle, and it stiffened. "I wanted to see about acquiring your form, and it seems the swiftest way to do so. Though I could just hold you for a couple minutes if you like?"

It blinked at me and then bounced up and clawed at my open hand before biting me.

"Ouch!" I cast Regrowth with a grumble. "You came in swinging, huh?"

"I had to be certain you hadn't changed your mind about eating me!" It nibbled the carrot, warily eyeing us.

Maebe and I just watched it in silence as I cast my senses back into the still darkness around us. The rest of the night was silent and enjoyable.

That morning, we ate breakfast and sparred first with a large shadow beast in the shape of a gorilla that was basically on PCP. No matter how we beat the damned thing, it didn't seem to hurt it, and it kept separating us from each other, so our grouping tactics were foiled. It would grab me and throw me into Jaken, then whip around and toss James into Bokaj, breaking his line of fire.

Yohsuke would attempt to call us all back together, but the beast slapped him senseless enough that we had to distract it rather than grouping together to beat it. And don't even get me *started* on Muu's attempts to spear the thing to the ground from above.

Our normal tactics just weren't working, and as I would steal glances at Maebe, I knew exactly why it felt like the beast was cheating.

It was because it was. She was.

As we traveled after breakfast, our travels went much the same as the day prior, but we focused on trying to incorporate hand and arm signals from the Marine Corps into our communication. There had been too many times of late where our earrings hadn't worked for us not to learn from that.

We would swing our fists slowly up and down to garner attention, then motion toward what we were seeing or put a fist up next to our heads to signal a dead stop—a hand straight up, fingers closed for caution, then the same with splayed fingers multiple times to fan out.

While we moved, I stepped closer to Maebe. "I saw that this morning."

She cast her gaze my way, a mischievous glint in her eyes. "Do you disapprove?"

I shook my head. "It's what we need." I watched the others moving cautiously in practice. "We have to break the mold. Think outside the box."

"What is this box?"

I blinked at her, then scrambled to put together a coherent explanation. Leave it to me to forget that I was speaking to a Fae Queen.

"Think of the box as being how things are normally done. You get comfortable there. It's structured. Safe. But inside it, things can grow stagnant." I motioned to my friends. "Without innovation and thinking outside the norm, we can't improve. We can't develop. Not to our best anyway. Does that make sense?"

"Perfectly." Maebe's eyes shifted toward the sky. "That is a very clever term, not to mention idea. You are very wise, indeed."

I waited to see if there would be a wisdom increase. There wasn't. Look, I'm wise okay? Real wiseass here.

I shrugged. "It took someone much wiser than me to figure that out. It's a common phrase from where I come from, but saying and doing are always a little different, aren't they?"

Her smile at my response was breathtaking, and it was a moment I would likely remember for some time to come—her dark, star-speckled cheeks against a backdrop of our small bubble of spring, snow in the background. I felt a welling in my heart that made me smile ridiculously, and I had to turn away to keep from stumbling over a root.

As the warmth of the moment began to drain from me, I began to think about Kayda once more. We were in the north; I should be able to feel her presence. Right?

So why couldn't I? I know that the distance our bond covered was small, maybe a mile or two at most, but still, I hoped she was okay.

I turned my attention back to our travels and on we went.

That night, and the few days that followed, our new routine set in. Scouting was dangerous with the trail being sent to us when someone on foot would return, and the errant gusts and quick shifts in temperature would freeze my owl form swiftly.

It was line of sight and craftiness for us as we moved forward.

We fought each other in the evenings, and the next morning, we fought a shadow beast. To keep things interesting and varied, we would switch out on certain exercises and fights. Sometimes we fought one to one, and the others would offer advice; sometimes it was two to one—three to one.

That last one still left me a little miffed because I had gotten my ass handed to me. There was absolutely *NO* reason they had to do me so dirty like that.

I mean, sure, getting smacked with a hammer while distracted by a floating sword? That could happen to anybody, but having me go flying over James who was waiting behind my legs so I couldn't catch myself? Those dirty bastards.

Well, the joke was on them. Remember when I said I would get my revenge for them fucking with me for Vrawn?

Here. Some. Came.

As I picked myself up off the ground, I cast my newest aspect spell.

*Aspect of the Hare – The Primal Warrior's body lengthens and shifts slightly, making them as agile and springy as a maddened hare.*

*-15 strength, +20 dexterity*

*Hearing and movement speed greatly increased.*

I could feel my legs lengthening, and though my muscles became a little sprier and stretchy, I noticed the lack of strength immediately. My ears lengthened slightly to that of a hare, and I could hear so much more than I normally would.

But if I was going to get the shit kicked out of me—I was going out kicking.

I tensed my legs; they were bent weirdly, but even if it felt unnatural at first, I knew I would be able to move quicker. I grinned savagely and released myself.

It was hard to compensate for the sudden burst of motion I had going. I'd only get a short amount of time before they caught on to my tactics or the spell ran out of time.

Time to play.

I realized I was bouncing over James as my foot caught the back of his head and shoved down almost of its own accord. My right ear twitched, and I used the kick to my friend's dome to shift my momentum slightly to avoid the hammer that swung beside my head. I brought my left leg up into a front kick that disarmed Muu.

The hammer flew into the watching crowd and smacked Bokaj in the chest by accident.

"Hey!" I heard him groan.

*Clang!* A shield smacked into my hip throwing my legs into the air, taking seven percent of my HP with it. I punched Jaken in his exposed shoulder, making him shift back, then kicked him in the face, snapping his head to the right.

The Paladin glowed golden with some kind of healing spell, and then James was punching me in the gut. I socked him in the face once, twice, and as I went for the third, he turned and hip tossed me on to my back. I was down to seventy-seven percent health now.

I reached out and cast Lightning Bolt. The shock flung James away from me, and I shoved my way off the ground. I ducked under Jaken's sword swiftly and moved away.

As soon as I was in range of Muu, his short spear readied, I dipped my hand into my inventory and brought out my simple great dagger—one of the first weapons I had bought from Rowland—and I shoved it straight toward his heart, hoping he would fall for the feint.

He dipped left and brought his shield in to parry as his spear shot forward almost inhumanly fast. It caught my left bicep as I flung myself toward his legs in a forward shoulder roll. Now, I sported seventy-three percent health.

As soon as my feet were beneath him, I kicked up as hard as I could and shoved him into the air with a grunt, then cast Water Sphere. A large ball of water sucked Muu in, where he struggled mightily, and as I was about to cast a lightning bolt, James and Jaken crashed into me. The pummeling they gave me was worth it.

After all of our wounds were healed, I was still laughing.

"Why are you laughing, fool?" Yoh raised his eyebrow at me. "You just got your ass beat. Why didn't you use your axe?"

"It was my first time using that aspect. I didn't know what exactly to expect beforehand." I held my hand up to stop him. "I take that back—I knew. I just didn't know exactly how much it would be to get used to. I figured, in the moment, the dagger would be better because it would let me get close and use my legs without throwing off my balance or new-found speed."

Maebe seemed to find my answer satisfactory, but Yohsuke shook his head.

"We can play all we want later—for now, we focus. Do you think that form would be decent in a fight?"

"Hell yeah." I didn't wait for him to tell me to elaborate. "I might lose a significant amount of my strength, but I can close with an enemy almost as swiftly as James or Muu. With my spells, I could shove a Lightning Bolt into a caster's throat before they can fire off a spell. I could be shoving Falfyre into someone's skull one second and then helping one of you a second later. I can jump higher too, I think. If they didn't expect me, I could storm an enemy line and hamstring them before you get there."

"All of those are viable options," James agreed. "Those punches were fast, and that kick hurt. If you had your axe for that, it would've been hard. We would've been hard-pressed to get close to you."

"So then maybe he fights in aspected forms to get used to them?" Muu offered. "Like I had to get used to heavy-ass armor so that I could jump higher."

I shrugged. That was a solid idea, and getting used to fighting in the many different aspected forms I had would be advantageous. It was time to do so.

I could clearly see myself hopping around the battlefield as a jackrabbit version of death and destruction gifted at the blade of my axe.

It was added work, but we began to squeeze that into our routine as well, a warm-up before our fighting, then as a cooldown after our evening sparring sessions. It hurt to fight each other, but I felt like we were better for it.

The next few days flew by. Every now and again, I would get little blips from our surroundings, showing that we were in the pack's territory, but they kept their distance for some reason.

I was okay with that. Being around the pack, or at least thinking about it, made me want to fight. I don't know why, but the Werewolf wanted to subjugate them in the worst way.

The trees, larger by far than they had been when we first arrived in the area, began to thin, then give way to a large, open plain of frost and snow with jagged winds swirling the snows into flurries.

"That's going to suck," I observed to the others.

Bokaj looked at us and snorted derisively. "Wimps."

"How are we going to stay together?" James asked as he shivered just looking at the vast expanse.

I felt a hand smack my shoulder and turned to see Jaken grinning at me. "Zeke is going to break the wind."

"Look, man, I farted a mile or two back, and I heard Muu gag." I looked to the astonished Fighter. "Sorry, man."

"No, man—break the wind. You'll be our barrier. You take your Ursolon form, and we just walk beside you. That way, we can't get separated by the gusts and snow." He tapped the Mobile Spring Rod in my grip. "I don't know how well this will work, but we don't want to leave too big of a path behind us, and without the trees to block the wind, it will still be rough going."

That was some damned fine thinking.

"Improvise. Adapt. Overcome." Yohsuke clapped the Paladin on his shoulder and nodded. "Good, man."

So, I stood as a barrier for my friends. Could Maebe have stopped the biting cold and stinging winds? Yes. She could've, but I figured that going into whatever we were, she would need to be fresh. If the high elves had treated her so poorly when they numbered so few, how would they treat her in their own halls?

Better safe than sorry.

The wind entered the rod's area of effect and warmed slightly, but it wasn't enough to keep me from shivering a bit, even in my bulkier form.

Bokaj didn't seem to be bothered by it in the slightest. At

times, he would scout through the snow, seemingly embracing his ice Elf heritage and scouting into the distance before returning to report his findings—nothing.

The second day of wandering through the snow, me as an Ursolon and the others by mount so they were out of the swiftly melting snow, saw us to a freak, gigantic snowstorm that just suddenly began as we trudged on.

"Uh, the fuck is going on here?" I growled to the two people with the most experience with the cold. The snow was hitting our bubble of spring and melting, drenching us in stinging, semi-cold droplets.

"This will pass." Maebe held a hand into the air, and the snow did seem to stop swirling so violently around us.

"It turned us!" Bokaj cursed. "Turn left. We're closer to the city than I thought. It looks like it's closer."

"Then we forge ahead!" I smiled to the others. Finally! We were closer to our goal!

We trekked through the torrential waves of snow-turned-rain water, the drizzle hitting us to the point that I could feel the cold fingers of madness beginning to clutch at my mind, wondering when the next gust of cold-turned-slightly-warmer-water drops would tap my skin. Finally, after a couple hours that had seemed to stretch endlessly, the blizzard began to billow less and started to slow. As the radiating flurry before us opened up, the party gasped collectively.

The snows behind us became more of a barrier in my eyes as the sight before us unfolded. Boulders lined a valley just in front of us, cutting off a little of the view, but what it didn't cut off was breathtaking.

A sprawling city lay in the valley below us that looked to be well in the throes of summer, somehow. Rivers flowed easily through the hills, and the homes appeared to be made of some kind of white material that grew from the ground itself. There was even a larger, milk-white structure in the center surrounded by a rainbow of colors.

There were no walls. No sentry posts that I could see. It was well protected by the near impenetrable snows—we had been lucky to have Maebe here to help us—it looked like security was lax.

"State your names and your purpose with the high kin!"

Well, fuck. So much for the lax security.

To our right and slightly ahead of us, a High Elf sentry stepped out from behind a boulder. He wore leather armor, surprisingly well suited to the surroundings as it was dyed to match the grays, browns, and sparse greenery of the upper portion of the area we were on now.

Several others in the same uniform joined him around us, some leveling bows in our direction, and more than a dozen astral adaptors flared to life.

"Queen Maebe, ruler of the Unseelie Fae, and if you continue to keep me from seeing my former subject and my emissaries, you invite death and cold into your fair city below." Her brows arched as some of the sentries stepped forward like they wanted to start some shit.

"My lady," Bokaj began. "While you could easily slaughter them all or turn them into living statues of ice doomed to stand guard for the rest of time," I noted a few of them gulping, "this isn't the time to waste yourself on rabble like them, right? You killed a—what was it again?"

"Greater fiend?" I offered to help him, seeing that the others agreed with nods and calm expressions.

"Ah, thanks, man—a greater fiend, in less than ten minutes?" He shrugged before motioning to the now-nervous looking group of sentries before us. The leader looked decidedly pale. "They would last, what—a heartbeat?" Bokaj moved to stand in her way and knelt before her theatrically. "I beg you, my Lady, find it in your heart to forgive them for even daring to question you."

Maebe's eyes twinkled at the show of fervent placating on before her and laid a hand magnanimously on his shoulder. "Rise, youngling, and know that their reaction is fitting of a city guard. They stand here day and night, toiling and guarding for foes who may seek to attack them. They do their home and people proud."

It was *so* hard not to laugh as the sentries before us stood a little taller. And the best part? None of us had been able to feel Bokaj using his charm against them if he had. I'd have to ask when we weren't around company.

A telepathic conversation right now might draw attention. There was no telling what kind of abilities these guys had.

In came Maebe with the right cross though, "They do so well, in fact, that they stop a visiting queen who seeks an audience with their ruler."

The guard who had addressed us first paled once more and put his bow down before whistling a shrill note and making several motions with his hands and arms. I thought I made out one that was meant to act as a gathering before he pointed to our location.

I brought Magus Bane into my hands just in case. I saw my friends pulling their own weapons. Yohsuke's hood almost fell, but he fixed it before letting his hand slip swiftly back into his sleeve. That had been odd.

"Majesty, we will have a number of guards to serve as escort to you and your party—unless you wish to send them away?" He waved dismissively at us as we clutched our weapons menacingly. "Clearly, they are mercenaries, rabble unfit for the high Elven city of T'agnolian Val."

The other sentries hadn't put their weapons away either, but seeing us clutch our own had resulted in a similar return.

Before any of us could so much as blink, Maebe levitated in front of him, clutching him with one hand on his throat and his feet dangling.

"You question me. You question my guard—*my champions*—and yet I allow you to still draw breath." She regarded the others who had begun to react at last coldly, "Do not be like this one."

Ice burst from her grip and surged down his body until it held him aloft where he was. His head was the only portion of his body free, his lips quivered, and I could hear his teeth chattering from twelve feet away.

"Does anyone else wish to insult a monarch whose name is synonymous with death?" Muu asked loudly.

Maebe waved the rest of us forward, and we brushed past the guards in a tight formation around her, as though we were really her guard.

As we walked through the sentries, their attention split between us and attempting to free their leader, there were some seriously hateful glares. And I heard a few things they muttered to themselves. Getting even. Mongrels. Faithless. Heathens.

Maebe went rigid, but I whispered, "It's okay, Highness. They mean nothing."

As we continued on, the others began to speak via earring.

*Lesser beings,* I heard Yohsuke grunt into my head. *These fucking assholes have no idea.*

*Oh, I know. By the way, did you charm that guy, Bokaj?* I asked as I observed our surroundings. Just below us on the path down, a troop of ten sentries marched forward toward us.

*Nah, he seemed nervous already. I was just ensuring that they knew who they were fucking with. She would have killed them if I hadn't stepped in.*

I sighed. I could understand that.

*She was almost itching for it,* Jaken added softly. *I think she's missing her more brutal side. She's been pretty soft with us, man. You think she needs to flex on some people for herself to make sure she knows she's still the shit?*

I blinked at the thought. We had been working our asses off, and I had to admit, the side I saw most often was indeed kinder and gentler—the children being much more beloved to her than I expected. Was that true? Was she getting the itch to run rampant? To show people that she was truly one to be feared?

*It is possible. He did just disrespect her choice in who she surrounds herself with, though.* I looked at the others. People I had fought with and bled for. *If she hadn't done something, I might have.*

*Calm yourself, man.* Muu punched my shoulder lightly. *You would've killed one, and it would've gotten us attacked and probably fucked over. Even with the queen of hot and heavy here.*

*What the fuck did you just say?* I looked at him out of the corner of my eye and saw him look away pointedly.

"Hail!" a voice greeted us from a distance. "I see that we are to escort you to her Royal Highness!"

"You are, and your friend will likely need help for being an imbecile," Bokaj replied.

The sentries who closed on us turned and began to walk in front of us as the other five waited on the side of our forming parade. Once we passed them, they took their place at our rear, and the fur on the nape of my neck stood on end.

I didn't like the fact that they were behind us and I couldn't turn and watch them. Or could I?

*Muu, I'm gonna catch a ride on your shoulder to watch our backs.*

He held a thumb up out to where I could see it with my peripheral vision, and I jumped a few feet into the air before shifting into my owl form to watch the high elves behind us. I alighted on his shield arm's shoulder, facing them fully.

He seemed uncomfortable at first, but it was a necessary evil.

*You do realize that we can turn our head almost completely around, right?*

I blinked. *Of course I know that. That's why I chose this form. Duh.*

I felt a flutter in my mind and a hooting kind of chuckle I hadn't heard before from the owl instincts.

*Then why not face forward and stare at them like that to make them uncomfortable?*

Oh. Yeah, I liked this new side of the owl instinct, but I kind of wondered what changed to make him come around like this.

*I like your take on being a dick,* I sent a mental, metaphysical nod to the voice in my mind. I turned on Muu's shoulder so that I was facing forward like the rest of the party.

"I thought you were gonna—oh my god it turns that far?!" he whispered and shrank back a little bit. "Fucking birds."

I now watched with my head turned in a complete one-eighty, tilting it from side to side. One guard seemed pleased to see an animal. The others? Not so much. They were slightly concerned, but their hands stayed off their weapons, and I was all about that.

As we moved along, I snuck glances at our surroundings. The lands outside the main host of the city looked to be farmland that farmed standard crops, fungus, some kind of bushes, and there was a vast grove of trees off in the distance that seemed to span acres of land.

The interesting part to me, though, was the lines of metal that intersected the rows of different foods. With the owl's perception and long gaze, I could see a series of engravings and runes on them that could have been anything. My suspicion, though, was that these were meant to help the crops grow faster, healthier, stronger, have more yield, and keep them safe from insects and disease. At least, that's what I would have thought.

*Coming to some kind of arch in the path here, great spot for an ambush*, I heard James speaking through our minds.

I whipped my head around and saw what he was talking about. I tried to respond but couldn't, instead receiving a system message.

***Error!***

***While in animal form, speech of all kind is beyond you. While you can understand others, they cannot understand you unless they're under the influence of a speech-type spell such as Nature's Voice.***

*Oh, that is such bullshit*, I growled to myself. The owl stayed quiet, thankfully.

I observed the arch and began to panic. Those runes looked nasty. I wasn't sure what they did, but I didn't want the party to pass through them without knowing what they did. I took off from Muu's shoulder and fluttered ahead of the group.

"DO NOT FLY AHEAD!" one of the guards bellowed.

I saw an archer poke his head from atop the archway, and an arrow whizzed beside my right wing. I dropped from the flight path I was on and rolled as I shifted into my fox form. I was ten feet from the arch, and I could feel the power radiating from it.

I scrambled through a hail of arrows and shifted into foxman to touch the stonework.

I heard scuffling and angry words behind me, but the arch was all that I needed to get to at that moment.

The arch was beautiful, a deep maroon with gold runes etched and filled in on the inside.

**Portal of the Whole Truth**

**Information concerning all equipment, statistics, abilities, and spells on every individual who passes through this arch are cataloged and available immediately to the ruler of the high elves.**

**Within this archway, the seen and unseen become apparent to She Who Rules, long may she reign.**

**Architecture carved by grandmaster stone mason Carver Pumpkil and enchanted by grandmaster enchanter Brelm Silverthroat.**

"Oh, *FUCK* no!" I turned to see the others halted around my friends with weapons ready for a battle. "We aren't going through there."

"You will if you want to see the queen!" the archer above the archway screeched. His voice cracked as he said the word queen. "All visitors must pass through it! It is the law!"

"What does it do?" Yohsuke asked.

"Catalogs details on everything about us, our equipment, abilities, and spells—*all of it*—so the queen can have it." I eyed the guards who seemed unsurprised by this revelation or that I could tell what it did since it was an item. "It's your law, but it's bullshit. We mean you no harm unless you try some shit first, and this is the second time that your people have offered insult rather than hospitality!"

The red ring of my Werewolf rage made itself known in my vision, and my breathing began to quicken with my pulse.

These guys wanted a fight? I would beat their asses myself.

*We could turn them all and flood the city with our kind. We could rule.*

The voice was intoxicating, and I immediately knew that this was the Werewolf speaking. I battered the rage aside and spent precious seconds to steady my breathing.

I opened my eyes, and three guards had astral adaptors at my throat.

"We will pass beneath your archway," Maebe calmly stated. She looked pointedly at me, and her gaze held warning. "Allow my warrior to return to me, and we shall pass beneath your gate, so swears Maebe the Queen of the Unseelie."

The guards' eyes widened, and I could see them dismissing the Fae warning that they would all have received, the same that I had received before.

As they allowed me to pass, I stepped close to her and mumbled, "I hope you know what you're doing."

I felt her hand cross my face, the strike louder than it was painful.

Her gaze was cool and outwardly furious. "You do not question your queen, warrior."

Did I just get bitch slapped? This was going to be a bad time later on if that was the case. Could I beat her ass? No.

But I would damned well be hurt in her general direction! Smack me in front of all these people and without saying surprise. Sure as hell wasn't my birthday either.

The guards began to walk through. As they did, the runes flared, and then the world went dark just before we passed under the archway.

"Act as if nothing happened," Maebe ordered quietly.

We blinked at her, and she ordered in a low whisper, "And step!"

We all stepped forward as the light returned to us, and then the guards before us stepped through the archway.

I heard a muttered, "I swear I saw something odd, Belthios. They seemed to *flicker* in the shadows."

"It's just play of the light, Nictol." An older sounding guard sighed. "You've been jumpy ever since the other night. Maybe you ought to go see the wizard?"

"Creeps me out worse than seeing things." The first guard shivered. "Play of the light. That's all."

An act. And she must have kept her word somehow because no one seemed the wiser about it. Had it been an act then?

It took us another twenty minutes at a quick pace to get to a line of metal that had been coated in an oily substance attached to the side of the chasm wall that fell into the valley at a slow decline. There was a large basket that reminded me of a device I saw in movies all the time at home, cable cars that ferried people in mountains and hard to reach places.

"This will ferry you to the ground where another set of five guards will join you." The leader of this set of guards looked at us and smiled, his angular features stretching. "Do try not to fall out."

He caught himself leering and bowed curtly to Maebe. "Your Majesty, welcome to our magnificent city."

Maebe ignored him, two of the guards had gathered inside the basket, and the others bowed slightly to signal we should get in. The ground seemed steady now, but the basket, even only slightly raised from it, swayed precariously as we climbed aboard, then joined us.

Seconds later, one of the guards on the cliff face touched his palm to a rune that I had been too distracted by the huge amount of air between us and the ground to notice.

Now, I know what you're thinking—you have the ability to shapeshift into an owl? Why are you being such a fucking wimp? It's not wimpy to be aware of your mortality. Right?

Don't get me wrong, I had flown back home too, I flew on CH-53E Super Stallions, MV-22 Ospreys, hell I even got to fly in a CH-46E Sea Knight before they were completely phased out of the Marine Corps. I had flown with some of the best pilots to do that damned thing, and it had been wild! But I'd always had a gunner's belt. That lifeline that wrapped around my chest just beneath my arms and attached to rings on the floor of my aircraft of the day.

This damned thing didn't have one fuckin' gunner's belt. No

rings. And sure as fuck wasn't piloted by some of the best in the game. The five assholes other than us who were in it right now looked amused to see that I was sweating a bit more than normal about this, but I wasn't really worried about them. If shit went sideways—they would die too.

And my friends as well. I could save one of them, thanks to my collar, but not all of them. And that was highly upsetting.

I felt a small tug on my sleeve and saw Maebe take a deep, calming breath and did the same myself.

It was a ten-minute ride, as the basket traveled swiftly, before the figures on the ground began to resemble more than ants.

I began to see a shape that looked like heat on the road when I used to run in the summer that ran the entire edge of the valley. Some sort of barrier?

Five minutes after that, before I could make out faces and the same energy, but this time, a cool blue with earthy brown undertones around the outskirts of the city. Some sort of wall?

I sent a mental call to the others to let them know. They let it go without comment—they couldn't see it.

And finally, three more minutes after that before we gently alighted on the ground.

The youngest guard I had heard earlier, Nictol, opened the basket and offered a professional smile that showed no teeth. "Please, your Highness, mind your step as you disembark."

We filed out after him, and Maebe came out last. After that, we began our walk through the city.

We moved into the inner wall, our lush green surroundings proving that there was a deep, natural magic at play here, and the enchantments that enhanced that natural magic around them were intriguing.

Sure, it seemed these guys were asshats, but there was some ungodly talent here. If I could get some extra training from these guys, getting the next couple ranks in enchanting would be an easy thing, but it would be a problem to get them to part with it.

That and we were needed elsewhere. My desire to improve my craft could wait if it had no immediate value.

The outer portion of the city seemed to grow from the ground itself. Large, tree-trunk-like protrusions with wide, almost acorn-looking rooftops seemed to make up the outer ring. There were windows, doors, and other home-like additions that made it seem quaint.

High elves of all sizes and ages stopped to watch us as we passed through. Signs hung above shops built from large leaves the size of a Dragon's head with various items in windows, elves spoke to each other in hushed tones that ranged from passing conversation to heated debating or haggling.

Those who did watch with more than passing interest seemed to be interested in the Fae-Orc, the Celestial Fae, and the weird fox. The Dragons were intriguing too, especially James and his wings, but I kept hearing hushed, angry whispers about gray skin.

Whatever. I knew they were talking about Yoh. Why? I didn't know, but fuck them.

Haughty dicks.

"This place is crazy, man," Jaken muttered. "It looks like they grow all of their buildings."

Nictol piped in, "We do!" When none of the other guards stopped him, he continued, "We're most in touch with nature and the magic of this plane. Favored by Mother Nature and the elements of long past."

"What does that mean? I thought the elementals had rescinded their favor from all the casters in all the planes?" I looked at him to see him narrow his eyes distrustfully, but he looked ready to answer.

"Not that one, Nictol," grunted the guard next to him. "Not your place to teach history, not your place to speak for the elementals. Or the queen."

The young guard nodded, a frown of thought on his face before he turned and simply stated, "Just wait for the queen to state what she is willing to share."

Smart kid. But now I was curious—why did no one seem to know about this? And how were we only just now finding out? I mean, the high elves had boasted about stopping human Mages from enslaving the elements and had punished them for their heinous magical experiments that resulted in the Beast-kin.

Had they been rewarded for doing so? It would make sense.

As we marched toward the inner city, crystalline structures grew in seemingly random places. They appeared to be hollow, and although they looked transparent, they obstructed view inside making each one beautiful and desirable.

The colors ranged from crystal clear-ish to radiant golds, purples, reds, greens, blues, and other colors in between. It was truly a magnificent sight to behold, but the truly bewildering thing of it was the castle carved out of a milky-looking material. The arches, buttresses, and columns were odd but had a truly Elven feel to them. They were carved in the shapes of trees, leaves, and other vines and plants.

The walls had grasping vines that looked so real that a stray wind could—wait. They moved. *The plants were real!*

"It's beautiful," I whispered.

"Yeah. It's really fucking pretty," James agreed.

The towers had spiraling tops that looked to be topped by gems the size of my head which seemed to scrape the sky.

"Come along," the elder guard who had rebuffed Nictol droned, motioning us forth toward the grandiose entrance to the palatial place in a borderline impatient and annoyed manner.

Maebe stepped toward the front of the group, and I shrugged away the building wonder I could sense mounting inside my heart. This place was truly amazing, and I wanted to see more of it sometime, hopefully.

We stepped through the doorway, the three guards in white robes outside eyeing us carefully and continued forward into the unknown.

Inside, the building was breathtaking. The colors that surrounded the outside were amplified and spun throughout the inside a hundredfold. It was so colorful and vibrant that it was close to physically painful to look at one area for too long, partially due to the lighting but more so because as your eyes shifted and moved, so too did the colors.

The entryway itself wasn't a hallway, as would be expected, but seemed to come directly into a meeting hall the size of a large convention room. Along the side walls, there were murder holes with arrowheads glinting, warriors next to each one with dual astral adaptors naked in each hand. Their eyes murderous, even covered as they were in their helms.

At the head of the room, a chair grown from a large tree carved from crystal and padded by leather and leaf. It took half the center of the room, around twenty feet wide at the base and rose far out of view.

Four figures cloaked in white stood next to the throne, their cowls hanging over the majority of their features, their sleeved hands hidden from view.

Whatever was going on, it was painfully obvious that these guys were ready to throw down big time.

"Welcome, Queen Maebe, Lady of Shadow and Hoarfrost," a voice that rang like chimes in the wind rang out toward us. A dull blue glow emanated from my left hand, Clarity, signaling the possible attack.

"Silvanas, Queen of the high elves, Lady of the Stone Carved Tree of Life, descendant of the True Fae," Maebe returned. "I see that you have built yourself quite the home."

"Thank you," Silvanas answered as she stepped from behind the throne.

The figure was lithe, athletically built and alabaster-skinned. She wore a ceremonial style robe that fell well past her legs on to the floor and dragged behind her dramatically. As she stepped, she seemed to dance along the base of her throne to the seat; she eyed all of us, her warm, honey-colored irises shifting slowly. Her pink lips parted softly, bowing at the corners in a small grin. It was captivating. Her hair was as white as the rest of her, though there were strands that reminded me of

Maebe's own hair with the many different colors that high-lighted the front; they were tucked behind her high, pointy-tipped ears that looked to point almost directly up to the top of her head.

"Tell me, great aunt, what brings you all the way from your realm, your place of power? Why have you sent emissaries to us after centuries of cold silence?"

"Change, niece—glory to the Unseelie, a new path forward for our kind." Maebe paused, taking the time to slowly consider the elves around us. "Most importantly, for now, is that I have thrown my lot into current affairs of all Brindolla and the realms attached in facing this new threat to our very existence."

"Ah, then I take it these are those summoned to our world by the very gods who can do nothing to keep War and his ilk from taking over?" Her suddenly pointed question was discon-certing.

"The Gods are trying their best, your Highness." Jaken bowed his head respectfully. "They brought us here so that we could hunt where they cannot and so that they can focus on the threat at hand."

"I am well aware of the foolish notions you believe in, mortals." She waved her hand dismissively. "I am also well aware of the fact that you truly believe you stand a chance at doing anything in a world you know nothing of. Of how you are siphoning power from Brindolla's people and threatening our way of life." She looked pointedly at us. "I know well the threat at our door, and the ones who should answer it are we."

I knew damned well what was coming next, but whose mouth it came from surprised me.

"The true Children of Brindolla!" called a familiar, wizened voice.

An older Gnome with gray, balding hair over sparkling, storm-gray eyes stepped from the other side of the throne, dramatically striding to stand beside Silvanas. His serious and wrinkled face hadn't changed, but he did seem slightly more spritely than before. He wore a red shirt with metal links on it that looked like silk from a distance but clinked ever so slightly as he moved. This tucked into black trousers and boots of deep brown.

He carried his same white, wooden staff covered in a single stripe of metal spiraling from a cap at the base to the top handle. The metal had runes engraved throughout it. It looked almost unchained but for an all black metallic addition just beneath the top of the item.

"Tarron *goddamned* Dillingsley," I growled and began to stride toward the little bastard.

He looked at me with his trademark unimpressed scowl, unthreatened and unbothered. I would've finished crossing the now red-ringed room but for the cry of thunder above made that ground me to a halt.

Kayda, now easily almost twenty feet tall and huge by all previous standards dropped from high up above.

"Kayda!" I cried in greeting, my brothers calling out to her in equal joy. She landed before me, and as soon as she landed, her right wing snapped out and threw me back ten feet.

I couldn't feel our connection, and she had willingly struck me.

That's when I noticed it—a jet black ring around her throat that matched the one on the little bastard's staff.

"*What the fuck did you do with my baby?!*" I roared, openly fighting both the rage that threatened to take control over me and the urge to try to go to her again.

# CHAPTER FIFTEEN

"A new kind of collar for the insufferable bird that just so happened to arrive before I did." Tarron strode over to stand beside her massive bulk. He touched her on the side of her leg, and my blood threatened to boil over. "See how attentive she is? How she doesn't shock or attack her betters?" He looked me directly in the eyes. "She knows she's much better off with a *true* Brindollan."

*Dude, you do what you have to to get tweets back,* Muu growled behind me. *The rest of us are ready to back you.*

I ignored that for now and instead turned my sights to the person I felt was truly responsible for this.

In Druidic, I shouted aloud, "MOTHER NATURE! What the *fuck?!*"

Kayda's eyes blinked at me from above, and the sudden shift from cold blue to violet purple was evident.

Mother Nature's voice crept into my mind, *I did not know that this would happen, Druid. It shames me greatly that Silvanas would think this way and be taken in by someone so consumed by their own petty hatred. I cannot take my blessing from her or her people and have it be of use to you right away—but I can tell you that for this instance and this instance only,*

317

*I will lift the restriction of how many aspects you may have active to two. Consider it a trial.* I felt a breath of power circulate into me before she continued in a deeper tone, *I will also let them know of my extreme displeasure in my own way. Use this distraction to your advantage.*

I focused for a second on letting the rage clear from my mind before telepathically speaking to my friends, *Mother Nature fucked up, and now she's going to help us get Kayda back. She's going to make a distraction. I'm going straight for that matching black band around his staff.*

*We've got your back, brother. Get the damned bird back. I got shit I need her to eat for me,* Yohsuke replied, surprisingly calm. *We'll keep the guards off you. James, Muu, don't kill anyone unless you have to.*

*Aww man,* Muu groaned, and James just grunted.

Bokaj took over from there, "Looks like the Lady you worship is pissed off about this."

"How could a lowly creature like you know what Mother thinks, Outsider?" Silvanas purred. Bokaj's ring glowed, and he shrugged before pointing to the top of the crystal tree that shifted; the leaves I had thought were true crystal began to wilt and fall, shattering on the ground.

I used the wailing and surprise of the elves around us to cast Aspect of the Hare, then Aspect of the Owl just as the gnomish bastard looked up as well.

**Error!**

**You can only have one aspect active at one time!**

**Error Lifted!**

**The Primal Warrior has been granted great power by the Mother. Fight well!**

I didn't wait to move. I completely ignored the changes sweeping through my body as I brought Magus Bane into my hand. Using my enhanced perception and superb hearing, I was able to avoid the worst of the falling crystal leaves. I stepped left, then *blurred* toward my target.

I stood next to him a heartbeat later, his surprise apparent as he looked at me, but he seemed to be moving so slowly. I planted my right foot in his wrinkly face as hard as I could to try and separate it from his body. At that moment, I didn't care if he died.

But he only slid into the base of the tree, a small sliver of his health gone and a growing, cocky grin on his face.

*We found our enchanter and backer for the Children of Brindolla!* I shouted mentally to the others.

*Moving on the staff!* I heard our Fighter growl through my mind.

Muu's spear shot straight beneath my left arm between my body and weapon and lodged itself into the crystal tree next to Tarron's head. The gnome cried out despite knowing he would likely be okay.

The best part was that he dropped his staff. As he bent to collect it, an arrow struck the weapon and sent it skittering out of reach.

*Get it, goddamnit!* Bokaj shouted.

Kayda screeched, and I heard wings beating the air.

James called to her, "Here birdie, birdie!"

A rent in the air that sounded like a sonic boom crashed off to my left, and I happened to see the two queens standing in front of each other, casting their hands toward each other.

Jaken materialized on my right in time to block something. I heard a dozen pings of metal on metal, and he shoved me. "Go!"

I nodded once and pushed myself forward, my insanely increased dexterity pushing me faster with each step. I bounded at my third step, flipping over a section of slowly arcing arrows with the staff in my crosshairs.

My fur stood on end, and I whipped myself to the right using Magus Bane like a rudder as a silvery bolt of lightning rocked the area a foot from me. I wasn't able to get out of the way fully, and the attack struck my left leg. My HP bar dropped by a fourth, and my leg went completely numb. It felt like I had been sitting with my legs crossed watching something and had tried to get up, that all-too-familiar feeling of dead leg taking over.

Kayda screeched in outrage at missing her target; still, our connection was closed, and that spurred me on.

Twelve feet from the staff, it began to slide back toward the throne, then stopped abruptly.

*Take a silence, you little bastard!* Bokaj chortled into our heads.

I brought my right leg under me and skipped toward the staff. James flitted into a crowd of gathering guards on the other side, barely avoiding their swipes and stabs with their astral weapons as he began to flow effortlessly from attack to defense. He parried and swirled, flowing from attack to attack, then defending. His body began to glow with his ki as he moved, and the longer he went, the more ki he would gain.

Poor bastards had no clue what was about to– *CRACK!* Yup, he just put his ki-enhanced fist through one of their mana shields and tossed that guy into six of his buddies.

Finally, I brought Magus Bane up and back in an overhead chop that I strengthened with an activated Cleave. The great axe crashed on to the weapon, once, then again, and a thin barrier crumbled to dust, filling my mana back up to 500 MP! FUCK!

That was a huge return. I flipped the weapon and activated Devil's Hammer, the ability that let me use a blunt portion of the axe to stun an opponent. In this instance—I wanted to break the fuck out of this damned thing.

The hammer connected with the top of the staff, and I heard the wood give, the ringing of metal on metal peeling through the air in a clear note.

I struck once more, denting the metal deeper this time. As I went for the strike I thought might end it, a gigantic bird crashed into me and sent me careening into the wall in front of me, my great axe dislodged from my grip.

As she slammed me into the wall, I fought to turn around in her clenched claws. I just managed to turn around and fend off her strikes and jabs with her massive beak. I cast Heal on myself and began to try and muscle the damnable collar off myself.

Here's hoping I whacked it well enough to loosen his hold.

As Kayda struggled against my grasp, pecking at the armor over my stomach, stealing slivers of my health despite it, I pulled and tugged for all I was worth.

After what seemed like a stretching eternity, I heard a single voice among the mayhem, the cacophonous crashing of spells being cast, cursing and vile words, and the sound of battle.

"*ENOUGH!*" bellowed Muu, his voice somehow amplified. "I am sick of this mother*fucking* bird ignoring her mother*fucking* daddy!"

He hefted my great axe above his head and slammed it down on to the staff before him with the full benefit of his eighty-five strength. The item cracked and resisted still. A guard came too close, and Muu flung my weapon into him and shot the offender into the wall behind him. The Fighter angrily whipped his own hammer up with a tight flourish and brought it down one final time against the staff and black ring, destroying it with a mighty grunt; the heftily enchanted weapon's magical discharge flung him back with a muted *whompf*.

The fight stilled, and I tugged one last time on the collar around Kayda's neck. It crumbled to dust, dirtying her feathers slightly but falling away harmlessly.

And then the brush of her consciousness against mine.

I could see her memories. Tarron had told the truth. Kayda had come here first. It had been a week of her learning things from Silvanas, and she was an apt pupil. She learned that she could indeed control her abilities; she just needed to be smart about it. So Silvanas taught her things that would help her keep her wits even when instinct took over.

She also learned to fuse her cold and lightning abilities to startling effect. It took a good deal of mana, but she could do it, and that was what was important. A little more teaching and she could return to me.

But then the gnome had arrived to speak with her instructor. She had been forced to be hospitable when Silvanas offered him sanctuary to hear his plight.

He *lied*. And she had been taken in. She had even arrested the nice Dwarven lady who had pet Kayda so nicely when I had been in Djurn Forge.

Silvanas helped him collar her when she refused to help them in their fruitless fight against War and his Generals. The collar, a gift from a mysterious benefactor, Tarron had called them, had clouded her mind and stolen her intellect. Her will. But it was back, and she craved blood.

Especially after what he had done to the Dwarven lady.

The entire exchange between us took maybe three heartbeats, and I was as pissed as she was. More so because the little bastard actually thought he was in the right, and even Kayda didn't know what the gnome had done to Shellica.

He was standing now, right beside Silvanas's throne, where he had fallen and then been silenced.

The queens seemed to be done fighting for now, as the High Elf queen touched the tree and frowned, tears beginning to fall from her cheeks.

"Queen Silvanas," Tarron croaked, his voice seemed to be hoarse but returning. "Come, we must rid your lands of these violent interlopers. It is time to truly take the next step to freeing Brindolla!"

Silvanas turned her head toward Tarron, and as the tears fell, her white hair began to gray. Her features, once pristine and beautiful, sagged slightly and wrinkled. Her age began to show.

"I will not." Silvanas looked hard at the little man. "You may believe what you do is right, but the higher powers know better." She held a hand out to her people and then pointed at the gnome. "Arrest this charlatan. His crime is high treason against the gods and this plane. He has cost us everything."

Tarron Dillingsley spat on the floor in front of the throne, then turned his gaze toward us. "Then the high elves are as weak as the others. Do not worry. The true Children of

Brindolla will see that your end is swift when we take our lives back for ourselves. This is not over."

He pulled out a bead from his pocket as guards, beaten and bloodied, began to close in closer to him and tossed it on to the ground. A wisp of white smoke rose and obscured him, and he was gone. No sound of footsteps scurrying away. Nothing to see with my True Sight. He was gone. Just gone.

And that was more than enough to bring my rage about.

"*Fuck!*" I roared. The guards nearest me leveled their weapons in my direction, fear on their faces.

"Calm down, man. It's over. They're cool now, right?" James looked at the guards who slowly lowered their weapons. "Queen Silvanas has seen the truth."

"Truth be *damned.*" I stalked forward toward her slowly. My voice a guttural growl as I asked, "What did you let him do to Shellica?"

When she didn't answer right away, I howled, "*Answer me!*"

"You do not order a queen, *fox,*" the closest guard to me barked with his astral blade bared and flashing toward me menacingly. "You *will* show proper respect to your betters!"

I didn't even so much as move as I funneled my mana through my hand and cast Lightning Bolt. The spell hit his chest, and he fell to his back, unconscious I hoped, but I would not appear cowed in this. Not right now. I continued forward, the guards taking up positions of protection in front of their now-frail-looking queen.

"Zeke." I felt Maebe's sure grip on my shoulder, and I shrugged out of it.

"Don't try and stop me, Queen Maebe. This concerns family."

"I know," her voice whispered next to my ear. "Please, let me help you before you start a war and she is lost to you possibly forever."

That reality splashed over me like cold ocean water, unnerving and leaving me feeling all kinds of salty.

"We can speak on this later," I promised her softly, "but thank you."

I blinked away the notification of my word given and stared at the queen across from me. She slowly made her way into her throne, collapsing into it. Kayda, ignoring the guards and me, hopped over to her side and looked her over quizzically.

Despite my anger and outrage, I was touched that she readily forgave her teacher, though it would've been against her nature to include someone who was mildly blameless in this charade.

Well, she could've been, but she just chose to hold all that anger and hatred for Tarron.

"He experimented on her. To see if he could pull knowledge from her about Dwarven takes on enchanting, engraving, mana, and the like," Silvanas's voice crossed to us tiredly. "Then when he found out that she had trained you personally, he tortured her, from what my guards tell me."

I felt several hands on me, and instead of rage, I felt sorrow. Crushing and pathetic sorrow. Yet another person who had self-lessly helped us, and this cause had been victimized. Wasn't it enough that their very lives were at stake—all of them—if we didn't stop War's minions and Generals? Apparently, we needed to put some of the idiots here in their place as well. Fuck.

"Where is she?" I asked, my voice hollow sounding, even to me.

"I'm here, lad," Shellica's tired voice rang out to my left. I turned and saw a hallway of crystal of deep purple. She was beaten. Bruised. Her lip was cut, and she looked thinner than normal, but her manic grin seemed even more stuck in place than usual.

She was immediately buffeted with healing spells from me, Bokaj, and Jaken. Hard to tell who put her up to full, but it was good to see her healthier. Yohsuke walked over to her and offered some kind of wrap and a flask to her, and she bit into it gratefully. Decorum was gone at a time like this.

Who the fuck cared what anyone thought.

"Are you okay?" Muu asked her softly. He reached out and tapped her shoulder, making her flinch once, but she nodded.

"Aye." She stared at us hard. "He couldn't break me. He could pull a few things from me here and there, enchanting wise that is. Even managed to get me to cut a gem for him with his fell magic and persuasion. After a few days, I remembered his name from our conversations."

I sighed. I could only guess what she was going to say next. I was right.

"And I let him *have* it!" She threw her head back and cackled before biting into her wrap again. She swallowed and continued, "'Don't matter how much you pull from me,' I said to him. 'You're enchanting is shite anyway! And you're a shite teacher!' And I laughed in his face for hours."

"So you let him torture you?" Jaken asked in wonder.

"Wasn't goin' anywhere, was I?" She shrugged. "I might be old, but I'm hardly daft. I learned a bit from him as he worked, and something wasn't right with that one. Seemed almost a man unmade. More dangerous."

I turned to the others, but they didn't seem to catch the turn of phrase. Was there a chance that this whole thing had been orchestrated by a General? This budding alliance against us and shift toward Brindollan righteousness?

It was likely, and if that was the case, we would have to be careful everywhere we went.

"Melthorn, gather the royals, we crown a new ruler," Silvanas ordered, her voice was still weak. Rather than wait, she held her hand up for silence. "The Mother has taken our blessing. Rescinded her touch on our lands. Our blessing will die out in three days' time unless a new ruler is crowned. And my vitality will not return. I am dying."

Damn Nature—you scary.

One of the archers fled the room swiftly.

Silvanas looked to us. "You owe us nothing, but you helped us to see the truth, even if it was done in disrespect and desperation. You are welcome to stay and witness the coronation."

"Thank you, but no." Bokaj stepped forward.

"I will stay and witness on behalf of the Unseelie Fae of my kingdom and hope that this garners us a special thought in a future possible alliance." Maebe stepped away from me and began to approach the throne, only to stop a few feet away. "This may be a time of great change, but you will not need to be alone in this. Our people can be united again."

Silvanas bowed her head, then raised it to see Bokaj beginning to speak once again.

"We came here seeking a way into the Hells, and this," he pulled out a drawn copy of the symbol the Celestial had drawn us, "is something that we had hoped to find here. I guess that it has something to do with an entryway to the Hells?"

The queen chuckled once and shook her head. "No. That is a tattoo, a mark of those especially beloved by Mother Nature. The only person here other than myself who has that is my own Druid."

One of the casters that had been standing next to her throne before the battle, bloodied and limping, stepped forward and showed their wrist. There, against the pale skin of their wrist was a brilliant green and purple replica of the leaf symbol we had copied on the page.

The figure pulled his cowl back, his vibrant, golden-honey eyes taking each of us in turn.

"Tomorrow morning," his soft voice sounded like a mix between a wheeze and a growl. "We will have our enchanters make a keystone, a waypoint for you to return to in our plane of existence. They are highly experienced in this. It is merely the material components that you pay for. Do you know where in the Hells you need to travel to?"

I heard Yohsuke muttering something, then he looked up from inside the shadows of his hood, careful not to expose his features.

"We need to go to the third outer circle," he offered the answer cautiously. "The information we seek is there."

"Anything farther than the fourth would have been beyond

my means, so this is good." His hand pulled back into his sleeve. "Take the rest of your time today and early in the morning to prepare how you can or will. We have many shops and artisans that you are welcome to peruse, though people may treat you oddly. I will have my familiar guide you while I prepare things on my end."

He turned toward his queen. "We will not be charging them for this service, will we?"

Silvanas's head lifted, her eyes appeared more sunken in than before. "To? No. From? Yes. It will cost them one thousand gold. Plus the cost of the components you need."

"Done." Bokaj didn't hesitate in the slightest. The amount was worth it to him, it seemed, and honestly, we could afford ten times that and still be flush. Not to mention, we would have all paid it happily to get to Balmur.

The Druid waved his hand, and a small, green and white spotted cat popped out from beneath his cloak. It looked up at us from next to his legs and meowed at us, seemingly friendly.

"His name is Fern, and I am Questis. When you are finished, we will provide you shelter for the eve in my quarters and begin in the morning," Questis turned his attention to his familiar. "Please, take them to some of the shops and wherever they need to go to obtain what is necessary. Also, Fern, please do not pester the vendors and merchants for food, you rotten kitty."

I cast Nature's Voice, and the cat's response was artful. "But they worship me, Questis. Who am I to keep my adoring public from pleasing me—their favorite."

Oh good, our guide had a god complex? This cat would've fit in well in old Egypt.

Bokaj laughed, and my guess was that he had cast the same spell to listen in. Speaking of Bokaj, I hadn't seen Tmont since we had come through the blizzard.

I looked at the ice Elf a little closer and noticed that his hood, down on his back and shoulders, seemed to be full of something. As I watched, a black tail swished through the air and then flicked back down into the hood. Ah, the little asshole was sleeping and had slept through all that? That fucking cat was something, man.

"Good day, and do not worry, Fern is a good cat. He will not lead you too far astray, but please, do not feed him over-much." Questis bowed his head before turning and wandering off.

"Maebe?" Looking at her, she looked like she was going to be sick as she watched Silvanas quietly.

Or like she wanted to put the slowly deteriorating queen out of her misery.

I stepped toward her, watching the queen's difficult to read, deep-green eyes tear themselves from Silvanas. "You okay?"

"I must be, for now." Her terse response was enough for right then, and we followed Fern from the place.

The carnage—I felt a fight of this magnitude had earned that description—was surprisingly small. There had been no casualties, though the guard I had zapped looked mighty butthurt when I walked by him, which was fine by me.

Was he being a good citizen to his queen? Sure. Had he been a dickbag about it? Fuck yeah.

"Later, Sparky." I waggled my fingers at him with a huge grin cemented to my face.

While we followed Fern into the city, people stopping once more to ogle us, I turned my attention to Maebe.

"Thank you for helping stop me from needlessly attacking Silvanas, but you looked… off. What's wrong?"

Her voice was soft, so soft that I had to bend closer to hear her.

My perception and hearing thanks to the two simultaneous aspects I had cast had faded after combat, not nearly as long as normal, but it was two spells. And I hadn't been trying to kill anyone.

"When I was a girl, I watched my mother send Silvanas and her people, as well as various other sylvan creatures such as the Kitsune, through a portal to this realm. That has been millennia to this realm, and she had not been back since. We corresponded, but they had largely, and to our dismay, declared themselves free of us and our reign." Maebe sighed wistfully. "To see someone who had been so brave as to tell my mother that she was free and so too were her people had always made me look up to her, in a way.

"To see her in such a state because her powers have begun to wane thanks to an outside force has been... educational to me." Her voice took on a note of pure anger. "That will never happen to me or mine unless I so will it."

"I won't let it, if I can stop it," I offered, and the anger contorting her features faded slightly.

I could have felt bad. I could have let Mae's sadness make me feel guilty for my small role in bringing down her former role model. Was I going to? No. Silvanas had picked the side that she had thought was right and had paid for being wrong. I could respect her choice in trying to take this matter into her own hands, but it wasn't in me to feel bad for the choice she made and the consequences now.

"Thank you." She took my hand into her own cool palm and cradled it for a moment before she spoke again. "An illusion. That's how we passed under the arch without them knowing our capabilities. I used the shadows to pull us under it, true to my words, and the illusions went through. That is how we kept our element of surprise."

"That was really badass then, Mae. Great work!" I pulled her into me and kissed her head as we walked.

"And you as well, regaining your composure like that was both wise and took strength, I am certain." Her voice was controlled, tight.

"I may have wanted blood at that moment, but I don't want your people to pay. Or the people of this realm."

"And that is part of why I chose you as a champion. Your potential is great, but you show wisdom and discerning judgment at times that surprises me." I eyed her as she spoke and couldn't help but tease her.

"You calling me a stupid hothead?"

She whipped her head toward me with a startled expression, and her perfect lips turned down in a frown. "Are you just now learning this about yourself?"

I clasped my heart in feigned hurt. "Oh, you wound me, my lady."

Maebe smiled briefly before the somberness of the situation returned, and we moved on to try and catch up to the others.

"Fucking love birds, right?" I heard Muu grunt to Bokaj. The ice Elf made kissing noises, and the two of them laughed.

"Talk shit all you like, lizard slayer," I called and watched as Bokaj's cheeks flared red. "That's what I thought."

A large shadow passed over us, and I saw that it was Kayda; her mind touched mine, and I sighed.

She was hungry.

"Hope you can restock on food, Yoh." I saw my friend turn a bit to listen. "Your favorite eater is quite hungry."

"She can wait until it's all done later! I gotta shop and get her fat ass food." He flipped her the bird playfully, and I passed along his message.

She wasn't happy about it, but she could always wait for his cooking. Greedy thing.

The first place we stopped was to collect potions and something I had been hoping to find—holy oils.

"These sorts of things are typically used when trying to commune with nature and the Gods, but I suppose if you were to be going to the Hells, they could be useful," the shopkeeper, a studious-looking High Elf with the left side of her head shaved smooth and the right side long over her right eye, said. "I could part with the stock that I have blessed currently, about a liter in a small barrel, for about four gold and five silver?"

"I'll give you an extra two gold and five silver if you will divvy it out into vials for us," Jaken offered.

"It will take a little bit, but I can do that. Stop by after you complete your other business, and I will be happy to give you your purchases." She took a quill and scribbled a few things down. "And you require healing and mana potions?"

Yes. We were sure as FUCK getting those. We nodded, and she pulled out three different bottles.

One of which I had seen before—it was the medium healing potions we had seen previously. Those were a gold each, so we nabbed twenty of them. The second vial was called a strong healing potion, and that was double as effective as the medium. It returned a full 100 HP instantly—we bought her out of those at two gold apiece for thirty vials.

The final vial was called Sylph's Vengeance. Sure, it sounded threatening—I should know, being the badass sylph that I am.

Pump the guns baby, *woo!*

The potion gave the user insane regenerative abilities for two minutes, both mana and health. She had only one of those, and we bought that for Jaken at twenty-five gold.

Next, we went to browse through weapons, and I had to admit, these Elven weapons were forged excellently. They were light, and there were a few daggers that were made of a crystalline material that reminded me of the stuff that made up the buildings around the palace that we had been in.

I bought that, as I had some things in mind for it, and Bokaj bought two of his own for me to enchant for Balmur. We would be in the Hells, and he needed to have some new weapons too just in case. Total, we spent seventy-five gold there. Then we went to see about food for us all.

I know, I know—we have a Dragon's hoard. A *literal* Dragon's hoard at our disposal. We were so rich it really wasn't funny, but spending like it's hot is how you lose it, right? So yeah. We would still try to be frugal.

The amount of food we got really was borderline reprehensible, it was. Yohsuke had our collective fat asses spoiled, and all of our purses were paying for it. And the amount of food we had to get to feed Kayda alone?

Well. She was a growing, bigass girl. You can't see me right now, but the look of pride on my face? Priceless.

"Fuck, man, eighty gold worth of meat for that fuckin' bird?!" Yohsuke shouted.

Okay, okay. So there was a price after all.

"I got that, man." I stepped forward, but he shoved me back.

"Fuck you. I buy the food for now. I need the ingredients to try and get my cooking level up." Yohsuke pulled out his money and began counting, "Five. Ten. Fifteen..."

That reminded me of something, and when we went to look at more accessories, I bought a thousand gold worth of high quality items—earrings, rings, bracelets, a nose ring, and a shit ton of purified silver.

I had to try and give us some kind of ace up our sleeve. Jaken took the small metal ingots, about five hundred gold worth. Hopefully, it was enough considering that it was roughly sixty-five pounds of silver ingots.

We left and made our way back to the potion maker's hut. Fern wandered from us a little, just far enough to call loudly to vendors. He rubbed up against one Elven woman who harrumphed loudly, turned her head, and in her 'displeasure' she 'accidentally' knocked a whole section of fish and bones on the ground.

The greedy cat scarfed down the morsel and rubbed magnanimously against the woman's leg. She tried to play it off, but she *definitely* enjoyed the contact, and I had to say it. I had to.

"Yo, I think that cat has higher charisma than Bokaj, man."

Jaken blinked at me, turned to look at the cat who had found another person to mooch off of, and then looked back with a grin.

"Looks like that's completely true. He has this city on *lock*." The Paladin laughed, and the others joined him.

Bokaj didn't even seem to care. "Hey T', why don't you come out and we see who big man on campus really is. No reason to keep stressing for now—our goal is in sight. We can relax for a minute."

Tmont, her sleepy face popping out of Bokaj's hood, blearily glanced about before putting her head down.

"There's food out here," Bokaj taunted, and Tmont's head shot back out of her hidey hole.

"Food?" The cat's purr sounded a little lighter than normal, but as soon as she cleared his hood, she began to do the same as Fern, the other cat having not noticed his new competition.

One stall caretaker offering jerky actually squeaked in surprise and delight that Tmont was in front of him.

"Who is this?!" he cried. He picked T' up and stared into her eyes. "You're beautiful! Are you a friend of Mr. Fern?"

Tmont, unbeknownst to her admirer, responded, "I have no recollection of this Fern, but feed me, strange Elf. And I will forgive you for picking me up."

"Hey, man, since when can T' get so small?" I asked Bokaj as I tried not to laugh at his cat.

"At first, I didn't know she could." He scratched his head, "I thought it was only for travel, but when she got really cold and wanted to hide, she just shrank so that she could fit into my hood. She's the size of a normal cat now. If she wanted to, she could likely go back to her fighting size."

*Huh. Could Kayda do that?* It was a decent question.

Oh man, I was going to be so mad if that could happen. I had a twenty-foot-tall bird with a serious appetite, and we were going into the Hells. Maybe I could ask Questis about it.

I didn't dare disturb him if he was working on our key home. Perish the damned thought right there and then.

I did, however, enjoy watching Fern and Tmont begging for food until Fern realized that he had company.

"Who are you?!" The green and white cat's fur bristled and stood on end. He began to pace around the interloper.

"My name is Tmont, and I am my master's protector," the black cat replied coldly. "I take it that this is somewhere you think belongs to just one cat?"

"Yes!" Fern yowled; a crowd had begun to gather and coo over the two felines who seemed intent on a throwdown of some sort. "They're my subjects, this is *my* city, and I *will not share.*" That last was hissed.

"I am not concerned with that. All I want is food." Tmont began to sway past Fern, but the other cat hopped into her way with his back arched.

"And I'm telling you it's *mine!*" The cat hissed violently, and Tmont stared at him for a second before deciding to back away.

I honestly thought that she had finally learned not to be an idiot. Genuinely, I had.

Rather than conceding, though, she grew to her full size and swatted the now-smaller cat aside like she might swat a ball of yarn.

Fern nimbly leaped back on to his feet and began to grow as well. He was easily the same size as T' but kept growing and growing until he was larger than her by two feet, his great green and white spotted pelt stretching over expanses of muscle that made the panther before him seem like a kitten. His incisors grew so long that I instantly knew that Fern was some kind of saber-tooth cat.

He roared once, long and hard, and I felt it deep in my chest.

"Hey, woah, guys, this is all in good fun, right?" Bokaj tried to talk over the clapping crowd.

Apparently, it wasn't unheard of for Fern to wander the city in this form as well? Fuck. I needed that cat form. For reasons.

"Looking a little long in the tooth, eh Fern?" I stepped closer to Tmont; her body was rigid and tense—ready for a fight. "Didn't Questis tell you not to do something like this?"

The saber-tooth Fern regarded me with little interest before turning his gaze back to Tmont. His voice, much deeper and accompanied by a growl, "Back down."

*I got T'. You wanna take care of the other one?* Bokaj sighed into my mind.

I put my left hand behind my back with a thumb up. *Yeah,*

*man. Good luck. I wanna get his form, so none of you freak out and kill him.*

The others remained quiet, so I took that as assent.

The two cats were beginning to yowl and spit at each other as they padded back and forth across from each other.

As Fern leaped forward to attack Tmont, I pushed Tmont aside and threw my arm into Ferns maw. It hurt. A good deal, actually, taking fifteen percent of my health and leaving me with a bleed effect as well.

"Well, Fern, thanks for that," I grunted as he dislodged his teeth from my forearm. "Tell you what, you don't say anything or attack my friend's panther, and I won't tell Questis or the queen what happened here. Deal?"

Fern growled deeply and eyed me angrily before huffing finally, "He knows already, we share memories the same as you and the bird. However, the queen does not need to know. Be certain to tell my admirers."

Bokaj took the cue, scooping a struggling Tmont into his arms where she shrank until he could put her into his hood. "Stop struggling, you stank kitty!"

The people around us seemed concerned for the ice Elf's sanity, but when Fern began purring and tickling people with his tail, all seemed well.

"No one saw anything that could potentially prevent Tmont, Mr. Fern's friend, from coming back, right?" I asked as I cast Regrowth on myself.

Several people shook their heads before returning to their work. Others brought food for Fern, and a few people even offered the Ranger a few scraps to give the angry Tmont as a treat. That seemed to go a long way toward easing her lingering resentment.

We went back to the potion shop and collected our holy oil. While we were there, I bought five of every plant she had available. I didn't even bother asking what they were or what they did because I didn't get a system message from them weirdly, but the vendor said that it was because I didn't know any kind of herb lore. And that seemed fair. Identifying plants seemed like a Druid type thing to do, but I wasn't really too interested.

These were for our own potion makers back in the village. It would be nice to be able to rely on them for potions rather than having to come here for the good stuff.

The vendors had seemed wary of selling any kind of astral adaptor to Yohsuke, seeming downright hostile when he asked, and we didn't dare show them the ones he already had. We would need to see if maybe Questis could send someone to buy one for us.

That seemed reasonable.

The rest of our time in the city was relatively uneventful, other than people giving Yohsuke odd looks here and there, but none of them seemed to care enough to do anything about his presence with Fern here.

As we neared the palace, I called Kayda to me, and she allowed me to put her into my collar; thankfully, she still fit.

The great cat crossed between the guards to the palace entrance without a second glance, and we filed in behind him.

Maebe brought me out of the monotonous trek back to the palace as we entered. "I am going to be with Silvanas for a little while. Be safe, and if you need me, send for me. Otherwise, I will come to you when I am done."

"Okay, be safe, and give her my regards." I touched her shoulder, and she kissed my hand before she left with a small, somewhat sad smile.

My heart ached for her. She was watching someone she held in high regard die. Fuck that. I had gone through something similar with my grandmother. That woman had done every-thing for me, for her family, and all she had wanted for herself was that I sit under a blanket on her chair and heat it for her while she made her strawberries with sugar that I loved so much.

She had passed away, withered before me, and though I knew that something was wrong, I could never have fully comprehended it. Not then.

But I did now. And this was very similar.

He led us down a red and green crystal hallway that led to a series of rooms furnished with various plants and some small sofas and tables with charts and tools littered across them haphazardly.

"Ah, Fern, new friends, welcome to my humble offices." Questis stepped out from behind an ivy green lattice covered secret passage. "I trust that my kitty was not too much to hand— Fern, you greedy thing, why would you be so full of yourself in front of our guests?"

The cat sat with his head high and looked down imperiously at Questis. "You have known me since I was a kitten, Questis. How could you possibly not know that I would defend what is mine?"

The Elf blinked at him once. "Because it is not yours?"

"Simply semantics—Silvanas was a figurehead for my reign, and you know it."

Questis laughed heartily, wiping a tear from one eye. "She let you sit on her throne when she was cold because she likes cats! You really do have fur where your brain should be, my friend."

Fern just stuck his tongue out and padded toward a large cushion in a corner before shrinking to his original, house-cat size to snooze.

"Forgive my thoughtless friend, please." Questis turned to us and smiled. "You are welcome in my guest chambers if you so wish. There are plenty of rooms for each of you to sleep comfortably."

"Thanks, man." Bokaj smiled. "I'm going to try and get some rest, maybe make some more arrows with that wood as the shaft. If we can, let's try and get some holy spells held in them?"

Jaken clapped him on the shoulder. "Zeke and I will work on that. You and T' go rest. Why don't all of you go get some Zs? I think Zeke has some things on his mind for me and Questis."

"Me too," Yohsuke grunted.

Questis regarded him, taking in his cloaked form, but waited until the others had left the room to ask, "Why do you hide yourself? You are purportedly not of this world, therefore the shame that would befall one of your birth would not be felt."

"Because everybody has their reasons to hate the abomination I chose. Just because I found this avatar advantageous doesn't mean I enjoy seeing other people unnecessarily uncomfortable. Their reaction as a people is expected. Unavoidable." Yohsuke pushed his hood back and let himself be seen for the first time since we had come here. "Happy?"

"No," Questis replied flatly. "Seeing you like this fills me with anger and pity for my brother who was the product of the same kind of union. He thinks much the same as you, about the necessities of his hiding among us, though he sees not the pain of his existence in himself but others. You have my respect for your answer. Thank you."

"Enough respect to possibly have someone purchase an astral adaptor for him?" I blurted hopefully.

Questis blinked at me, taken aback for a second. "I did not see you using an astral adaptor during our spat earlier. Are you capable?"

"I am." He took out his first astral adaptor and held it out, blade engaged, the flowing black mana making the blade look similar to a katana.

"This is garbage." Questis broke the thing in half with a small grunt and began to poke inside until he found what he was looking for. A small, blackened object the size of a small nail file. "See how the crystal is blackened and charred?"

We nodded, and he continued, "The amount of mana being passed through it was too dense, and it wasn't strong enough.

When a user's mana is too high for the weapon, it degrades faster. Much faster. If you had used this possibly once more, it could have burst on you." He shook his head ruefully. "Never pleasant business, but you have how much mana?"

"Seven hundred and fifty," Yohsuke answered, and I whistled. That was a good deal.

Questis thought for a moment then shook his head. "You will be hard pressed to find a good fit out in the city with that much mana. I have a friend here in the castle. He dabbles in enchanting. I believe he was also tutoring the Dwarven enchanter before her studies were so *rudely* interrupted?"

"Could he make something tonight?" I asked excitedly.

Questis shrugged. "Perhaps. The art of making adaptors is lost on me. I prefer my plants and enchanting other items."

"Cool, so where do we go?" Yohsuke asked.

"Your friends must stay." Questis motioned to us. "He is reclusive, and too many people around make him… volatile."

*You guys cool with me going it alone?* he asked through our earrings.

*We have to be.* I shrugged as if we were simply having a nonverbal conversation through glances and body language. *Just be careful, and if shit gets bad, holler and make a big boom for us to follow to you.*

Yoh smiled and turned back to Questis. "I'm in. When do we roll?"

"Fern!" Questis called over his shoulder. The cat ignored him pointedly. "You will earn your dinner tonight, you spoiled cat. Take our guest to see Zell. Then wait there until he is ready to return."

When the cat didn't move fast enough, one of the many plants surrounding his plush pillow began to stretch impossibly long and began to reach slowly toward his leg. The cat opened an eye as if warned by instinct and hissed menacingly at the plant before eyeing Questis.

"Hmph. See if I let you sleep tonight, Elf." He stretched his body a little as he stood, then eyed Yohsuke. "Come along then, tormentor. The sooner you are there, the better."

"He will take you now." Questis ignored the threat and waved Yohsuke after the disgruntled cat.

When they were out of earshot, I asked, "How did you come across Fern? He seems…"

As I was trying to find the right words, Questis chuckled. "Impetuous? Surly? Self-entitled? He has been that way since he was a kitten. The fact that he is a saber-tooth and larger than most of the other great cats gives him confidence beyond his ability at times. The city spoiling him because we do not have many animals here also does not help his… disposition on just how special he is."

I had to laugh. There was a saying back home: it takes a village to raise a child. A community can nurture and care for a whole family, and not everyone wanted to be a part of that. But it seemed like these guys all wanted to be the good guys for the cat, and that wasn't necessarily bad, but it had to make things rough on Questis at times.

"That's rough, Questis." A thought occurred to me. "How is it that Fern and Tmont can shrink from their original sizes? Would Kayda be able to do the same?"

Questis blinked. "The roc?" I nodded hopefully. "I suppose she could. It is a thing that she could do herself as your familiar. All it really calls for is for her to envision herself growing smaller, and then from there, a small mana sacrifice. Fern does it almost without thought. Then the reverse to grow once more."

Huh. That was interesting. I released Kayda safely in an open space and, with Questis' help, walked her through the process of shrinking to the size of a large parrot. Once that was accomplished, I had her stay out for a while. It was nice having her be this small again.

He nodded, then Jaken tapped my shoulder. "You bought all this silver for something. What do you have planned?"

So I filled him in. I wanted to make Muu a new spear, but with this one, I wanted it to be a demon slayer spear. It needed to pack enough of a holy punch that it would act as a deterrent and as a viable threat to anything we might uncover that wanted to fuck with us in the Hells.

"That's going to be a little rough on you considering your… aversion to silver." Jaken blinked sweetly, trying to dance around the Werewolf in the room.

"Are you trying to say that he is a lycanthrope of some flavor?" Questis looked even more interested now and must have noticed the looks of surprise and apprehension on our faces because he added, "I could smell you, Fern could smell you, as soon as you entered into the palace. We weren't sure who it was at first, but when you started to express the signs of lycanthropy and I was close enough to truly smell the beast on you—I knew."

I blinked at him, and he smiled softly. "Look, I realize that you think my kind are uptight and stand on some sort of moral high ground, but I am—how might I put it?—not a prick?"

"Oh, I like you." I laughed. And honestly? It was true.

The dude hadn't tried to fuck us, and he seemed to be genuinely cool.

"Now, I believe you had an issue with your ailment? Have you need of tools?" Questis asked.

"Nope!" Jaken grinned sheepishly before pulling a lidded bucket out of his inventory. "I forgot to give this back to Granda when I left. It's the one I use, not the one you made him. It should suffice, right?"

I blinked at it. It looked like it might hold maybe four ingots at a time.

"I mean, this is going to be a pretty gnarly weapon, man." I scratched my head. "What do you think?"

"I have scratch paper if you would like to work on the design?" Questis offered, motioning to paper and coal shaped like a pencil.

This is a wonderful time to reiterate to you all that I am a *shitty* artist, man. Can't draw myself out of a paper bag. Terrible.

But I tried. Moving slowly, I tried to get the dimensions and designs that I had in mind blueprinted on the sheet so that they could see it.

The design was, truthfully speaking, simple. It wasn't a short spear in need of balancing with a counterweight. It was a traditional spear, but the head of it—the bladed portion—was the Celestial pictograph for the word "holy." A single feather, nib pointed skyward, with seven beams of light radiating from a halo around it. The halo connected midway to the base of the feather so that it seemed like one solid piece.

"That will be intricate work for a metal worker of his caliber," Questis observed. "Forgive me, Jaken. I mean no disrespect."

"I'm well aware that this is beyond me," he shrugged, "but if I could make a suggestion?" I flipped him off and tossed the charcoal to him. "Thanks, bud. Silver isn't the hardest metal. Sure it's potent against the forces of evil, but it's not going to be able to stand combat. So, how about if we upped the holiness of it by including an equally holy metal?"

"You have some?"

"We all do, man. It's platinum." He pulled out several of the coins, and I wish I was flexible enough to shove my own foot in my ass. How had I not known? "Metalwork isn't your thing, man. Like he said, this is beyond me, but I can work platinum. If you make the base how you made that rod, I can add the cutting edge to it, and then we can use something sturdy to lend it durability during the enchanting process."

"Hell yeah!" I punched the Fae-Orc on the shoulder and grinned.

"I would like to be involved in the enchanting process, if I may?" Questis spoke up, and when I turned to regard him, he had a hopeful look on his face. "I also know of a metal worker in town who is quite talented. She would be willing to come help for a price. It has been some time since I have heard someone so passionate about a project like this, and I wish to be of further aid. My other work for the eve is already completed, as is your key to return. It is just sitting in a safe environment attuning to this plane."

I looked at him skeptically at first but held up a single finger. "Only if you let us pay you for your work. We've had gifts in the past, and I don't think it's fair for us to take advantage of a new friend's hospitality like that. Do we have a deal?"

"We have a deal then. I have just the things in mind!" Questis clapped his hands and began to flit about his office then stopped. "Ah. Fern is gone. I will have to summon her myself."

# CHAPTER SIXTEEN

It was the wee hours of the morning by the time I finished projects I had in mind for our trip to the Hells. Jaken and Questis had taken over the weapon when I finished my portion of it.

Being around that much silver made me queasy. Blurgh.

As to the other items I had enchanted for my friends? Well, I had to admit, I was pretty damned proud.

For me personally? I traded my Infernal Band, it gave me a huge boost to fire damage and added hellish fire damage— probably not useful in the Hells—for a new ring. It was a platinum affair with a simple diamond setting. Perfect for my needs.

*Radiant's Binding*
*+10 to healing distance and potency*
*Additional healing never hurt anyone, right?*
*Ring crafted by master jeweler Nift Ranger, and enchanted by Adept Enchanter Zekiel Erebos.*

That was going to be super nice where we were headed. For Yohsuke, I had to get him another ring as well.

*Vampire's Kiss*
*Steals a maximum of 50% of the wearer's HP from*

a target as long as they are touching. Once that limit has been reached, the ring is inert for up to three hours.

*The kiss of the walking undead isn't always pleasant but is necessary to survive. Thankfully, they can be sated.*

*Ring crafted by grandmaster jeweler Yuckto, and enchanted by Adept Enchanter Zekiel Erebos.*

You know what? You guys probably don't care who made or enchanted these things do you? Should leave that bit out? Okay. But just for this part, okay? I got *busy.* Ahem. Back to gushing over gear we go!

James got two new rings, as his other ones, the mental resistance and the healing, were still decent.

**Samhain**

*+10 to physical attacks*

*One of the more well-known creature's to visit the realms was the violent demon this ring shares a name with, and he liked to punch things. A lot.*

**Ring of Stone Skin**

*Allows the wearer to cast the spell "Stone Skin" once per day for half an hour.*

*Sometimes getting beaten up makes you tougher; other times, you get tougher to return the favor.*

Those had been fun to make, but it got a *little* tougher for Jaken and Bokaj. They needed some serious upgrades, and I was really starting to get why people might think I was ignoring their needs.

**Wild Regeneration Band**

*Wearer regains 3% of their health per second for ten seconds but has a chance to fall into a Rage state for thirty seconds. Three uses per day.*

*Sometimes in nature, getting bitten can teach you a lesson, sometimes it pays not to bite the crazy thing one bite away from snapping.*

**Defensive Signet**

*+15 to defense.*
*With the symbol of the shield engraved in this ring, getting smacked around doesn't necessarily feel so bad anymore.*
*Ring of Recovery*
*Wearer regains 5 HP per second for thirty seconds. Cooldown: 1 hour.*
*Feel that warm rush of healing energy!*
*Calamity Band*
*Teleports user to a spot that they can see within 200 feet. One use.*
*That spot over there sure looks healthier! Hope you can get away!*

Those last two I hoped Bokaj would find useful. I doubted he would want to throw any other ring on if he had one, but he could always have one of our old ones in a pinch. Was it lazy of me? Probably. Do *you* have a bigass mana headache? No? Thought not.

Moving on.

Muu? That asshat was the worst one for me, mana wise. He needed a royal mess of items done, and I couldn't phone these ones in. He might be physically stronger than us, but he was still lower level, and we needed him healthy. So I ponied up some new rings and a necklace that I thought was hilariously named.

*Shield Band*
*+18 to defense.*
*Ouch! The hand that guy hit you with sure looks swollen.*
*Ring of Spell "Heal"*
*For a mana cost, the wearer of this ring can cast the spell "Heal" on themselves. Cost: 50 MP. Cool Down: 1 hour.*
*You got mana? You got healing!*
*No Bake Necklace*
*70% Resistance to fire damage.*

*Doesn't matter how hot this kitchen is, something sure smells great!*

Those had been fun, and painful, to make. And my head was *pounding*, but I had a couple more things to enchant. First, my own crystalline dagger meant to replace my great dagger. Then the ones that we had procured for Balmur.

*Redemption's Mercy*

*+13 damage to evil beings, +8 to damage against demons and abyssal beings*

*The crystal doth sing as it cuts through sin—sweet release.*

Ooooh man. I'd have to call this baby Mercy for short. Though, how much of her namesake I showed would depend.

*Bright Sear*

*+13 damage to evil beings, +7 to fire damage*

*Holy flame, cleanse this evil before us. Amen.*

*Moon Bane*

*+11 damage to demons, Evil's bane – wounds to evil creatures fester and cause damage over time.*

*By the glinting silver of this crystal blade, your end is nigh.*

Those two were badass as well. I was honestly lucky to have my Paladin friend here to cast holy intent into it with me. Because of him, the holy damage skyrocketed, and the silver on that last weapon at his behest was a slick idea.

All in all, my work had some great rewards. I was now level 43 in enchanting. Hell yeah!

After collecting a tired and grumpy bird into the gem of my collar, I stumbled into the room that Questis had told me about to lay down and see about some shut eye when a wash of cool air rushed over me. I opened my eyes to see Maebe sitting next to me on the bed. Her eyes were downcast, and her shoulders were tense.

"I take it Silvanas has taken a turn for the worse?" I asked softly as I sat up to be closer to her.

"She is much the same, but my outlook on things is not."

She paused to collect herself. "She has told me of their original reason for coming here, and it was not what I had once believed. Rather than coming in an attempt to take control of resources and send them to us in the Fae realm, they were banished here by my mother and Titania for their practices that made them somehow closer to the lands they were on. The monarchs feared that if they were beloved by Samir, Silvanas would overthrow them and upset the chaotic balance of the realm. And that realm would cease to be."

"Does this affect your governance?" I asked quietly, still a little confused and more than a little tired.

"No. My people are still mine, but it was good for me to learn of this as it is something that I must now consider." I could see her eyes narrowing in the shadows that played across her face. "There are spies of the Seelie here, living among the high elves, and I think they could be learning how to commune with the world the same as those as they dwell with. If this information were to get back to the Seelie in my realm, my world would be thrown further into peril."

*QUEST ALERT!*

*A Champion's Duty – Queen Maebe, leader of the Unseelie Fae, has informed you of a potential plot to throw her world and her people into great peril. Assist her by rooting out the spies living amongst the high elves.*

*Reward: Deepened standing with Unseelie Fae, further tutelage in the art of wielding Shadows, and further favor of Maebe upon acceptance.*

*Will you accept? Yes / No?*

I accepted without a second thought. She was my girlfriend, I cared about her, and her people. Not to mention, I still had a lot to learn.

"I'll help, we all will, to find these guys. So don't worry overmuch, okay?" I kissed her shoulder, hoping it would help draw out some of the tension. "As soon as we get Balmur back here, we will look for them. Okay?"

She nodded once without making a sound, then took a deep breath, released it, and looked to me. "I am sorry I cannot come with you to the Hells."

"So am I." I tried to play it off, but I would miss her company. "I understand that you have a duty to your people and that being so far away could be detrimental. I respect your resolve and your dedication to them."

"You are a part of them, you know."

I couldn't help the cheesy grin that crept over my face. "I'm your champion. Of course I am."

I felt her hand on the side of my neck, her palm sliding up slowly to cradle my cheek. I looked her in the eyes to see a single tear in her left eye.

"No. You are the man I have come to love." I felt a thrill of chills envelope my body, and she kissed me gently. Imploringly.

It felt like that brief brush of lips said so much more than anything I could have at that moment. As my brain fumbled for sonnets, for epic poems of how I felt for her, my body reacted on its own.

I kissed her back. I kissed her back, and I felt that tear fall against my cheek.

I knew then and there, I had to come back to this woman. I had to. And I would fight all of the Hells to do it.

———

I woke up to Maebe watching me from inches away, but I didn't jump this time. I was used to it by now.

"You will come back to me." Not a question. Not an order. Just a statement.

"We're coming back come hell or high water, and we'll bring Balmur with us."

Her full lips pressed against the side of my head, and her eyes sparkled at me. "Good. Go get your friend."

With a renewed sense of purpose, a bit of a bounce in my step, and my clothes and armor freshly in place, I stepped out of the room. Maebe followed after a moment, and we were on our way to see the others with Questis.

They sat around a table eating, joking, and trying to plan.

"'Bout damn time, man," Yoh greeted us. "We won't be gone long, so there's no reason for the sappy-ass goodbyes."

"I will miss you as well, Yohsuke." Maebe smiled at him, and he just sighed in return.

Rather than waiting, I handed out the items I had enchanted to my friends. Everyone took them gratefully and slipped them on to their fingers, switching out older items for the newer ones.

One item I had made last night while she meditated was for Maebe—a nose ring.

***Reminder***
***The wearer of this item is reminded of their love's embrace for four hours. Cooldown: 4 hours.***

Was it sappy? Sure. Necessary? No. But if I could give her some kind of comfort going into this terribly uncertain situation, I would.

Gods knew I could use it myself. But our friend needed us, and we needed him back.

"Thank you." She clutched the item in her hand, then blinked. "Here. Take this as a token of my affection."

She reached into her shirt and brought out a simple handkerchief of dark material and lace. All was as it seemed with it, but I had to admit, I felt like a knight with his Lady's favor at that moment.

She leaned forward and whispered simply, "I love you."

The sound of those words sent a thrill through my being, and I mouthed the same to her in return. The mood was somber, despite the pent up excitement in all of us. Muu held his new spear.

"What's it called?" He offered it to me to touch, but I just stared at him before he took it back.

"It's called Saint's Grace. Huge damage bonuses against evil beings. Holy damage like crazy. Thanks, man. I'll try to be worthy of it."

I took another look at the weapon. The silver made up the base, true to my original design. As Jaken had suggested, the cutting edge was made up of platinum, but rather than the feather bearing the brunt of the attacking, he had used the symbol to hold two thick, platinum cutting edges that looked like angels wings. They swept from the shaft of the spear and met just at the tip of the feather to support it.

That was a sick addition, and I was more than a little pissed off I hadn't thought of it myself.

"I added a little—the original design was great, but one wrong move and a ray of light might have broken off. That could have made the weapon's enchantment defunct." He pointed to the spearhead, and Muu relinquished it to him. "I had a little bit of divine inspiration for this, and Questis' enchantment was badass. He added both crystal for higher durability and holy oil to make it a bane weapon. It's highly potent stuff."

"That's more than badass, man." I gave him a fist bump before looking to Questis. "Thank you. How much do we owe you? For the weapon and the key?"

"Jaken paid for the weapon himself, so that is no worry." He looked to Bokaj who forked over a large bag of gold. "And I will not count this sum, but trust that more than two thousand gold is here?"

Bokaj dipped his hand into his inventory and pulled out another smaller bag and tossed it to the Druid. "There is now."

"Then we are settled. Who will take the Key?"

"I will," Jaken replied as he stepped forward.

Questis pulled out a small satchel and handed it to Jaken, then whispered a word I couldn't hear into his ear before leaning back. "Be certain that everyone you want to bring with you is touching. The limit is fifteen beings that can be transported. Be safe, please."

Questis backed away, Fern at his feet. He looked at all of us, stepped toward the doors to his rooms, and motioned that we follow him.

All of us stood and followed dutifully. The guards at this wing of the multicolored crystal hall didn't acknowledge any of us as we trudged through. I wondered why they were here but soon found out why.

In the large room behind them was an archway similar to the one we had fooled outside, but this one was made of gold, platinum, and crusted in precious jewels along the outside. Inside, glyphs, sigils, and runes moved, dancing and shifting back and forth along slate-gray stone that was indecipherable to me, and assuming from the whispered words of awe coming from the others—they had no clue what they meant either.

"This will be your doorway; it is what the key is attuned to. Do not lose that key. Do not give it up. If you do and the demons get ahold of it, they can send their strongest here, and I shudder to think what will happen if they do."

So, that was a thing to worry about. Damn. Okay. Focus.

I hugged Maebe one last time, and she turned to the others.

"Be safe, my friends." Her formerly sad face was now serene, a mask of support and elegance.

"You too." Jaken smiled.

Bokaj gave her a salute. James gave her a nod and a thumbs up with both hands. Muu offered a soldierly salute with his fist over his heart and heels clicking together.

Yohsuke walked over to her and put a hand on her shoulder. "You be safe too." In a whisper that I was close enough to hear, he added, "We'll keep him safe and make sure he comes back."

"I should hold you to that," she smiled sadly, "but this time, I want all of you to return."

I scoffed, but she seemed to appreciate the gesture; whether it had been a playful ribbing on his part or not, she took it seriously.

She stepped back and observed with us as Questis began to tap the shifting symbols and hum a tone that sounded like chanting at first, then a song. Finally, he barked a single word, "*Inferni!*"

The symbols he touched glowed golden, then red and shifted from the stone to the center of the open air in the center of the archway. As they spun, burning and leaving trails of light in the air, Questis stepped aside and slapped the stone three times before the flaming symbols halted and burst.

The heat was unbearable at first, then began to abate.

"Go now!" the Druid shouted over the sound of the now-open doorway into the Hells.

And we did.

# CHAPTER SEVENTEEN

The transport was instantaneous. One second we were standing in the Prime plane, safe and well, and the next, we stood in a darkened, red-hued landscape with flames that cast shadows over barren grounds. Craggy mountains that reminded me of skeletons or long-dead corpses grew in the horizon and a sky of light gray.

And the bones that littered the area. There were thousands that almost seemed to be as much a part of the ground as what we stood on.

"Oh, what the hell is this shit?" James muttered as he lifted his feet in disdain.

Muu looked at him, blinking once exaggeratedly. "Why it's the Hells, sweetheart. Did you expect snow?"

Rather than wait for them to bicker, I looked to Yohsuke.

"You know where we're headed?" I raised an eyebrow as I fished in my pocket. "Think we should try to get in touch with Balmur?"

He nodded. "Give me a second to try and find out on my end as well." I could see Yoh's mouth moving as he did what he could.

I pulled the raven out of my inventory and poured a hundred mana into it before speaking, "Balmur, buddy, we're here, and we're coming for you. Can you tell us where you are?"

The raven flapped his wings, then a purple, spectral version of it took off and disappeared west of our position. "It's heading west," I advised my friends.

"That's where we're headed, according to the demon I'm contracted with. When we get closer, he will have further instructions," Yohsuke stated. "Let's get moving."

"… and that's probably why your mother dropped you as a child," Muu finished, and it looked like James was too stunned to even come up with a comeback.

"Would you two shut the fuck up?" Bokaj growled. "We're in the Hells, and we're on our way to get my best friend. Get your shit together."

The others had calmed down significantly after that tongue lashing, but the heat did little for our moods—until an idea occurred to me. I took out the Mobile Spring Rod, and instantly, the heat around us cooled significantly.

"That thing is fucking genius, man." James sighed in relief. The sweat that had been building in the fur of my forehead and on the others began to abate a little, and I checked to see that we left no trail. "Seriously hadn't thought that would do the same thing here but opposite, you know?"

I blinked at him. "Yeah. I gathered that, man."

"I'll just shut the hell up." I gave him the finger guns, and he waved me off. As we walked, the small, spectral version of the raven reappeared in front of us and landed on the figure.

When it opened its mouth, I heard Balmur, his voice rough but resolute, "You get out of my head! I know you demon assholes are fucking with me, and when I see you at the negotiation circle, I'll end you all!"

"Fuck." I filled the others in on what I had heard, and things looked bleak. "What do you think is going on?"

"I don't know, but it sounds like they've been able to get inside his head," Bokaj growled. "There's no telling what he's been through. Better to just go radio silence until we get close to him."

I nodded and put the item away. "Let's get moving then."

We moved cautiously, every now and again seeing figures in the skies that looked like perverted versions of birds with many eyes and grasping claws. The sight of them made me almost ill, but I didn't dare shapeshift into an owl. I did let Kayda out of the collar, still in her parrot-sized form, and had her watch the skies and our backs so that we would be prepared. She sat herself on my left shoulder, and although I was now blind on that side with the sight of her feathers, I trusted her to see for me.

After a couple of hours, the sight of a growing cityscape dawned on the horizon. An hour after that, we broke for some food and a little planning.

Yohsuke, sitting among us, gave us the skinny on what was about to go down, "The demon I'm contracted with lives in that city, and I've been in contact with him since we got here. The deal is still good, and he's got information for us. Once we get there, he will give us detailed instructions on where to meet an imp who will take us to him. He was explicit that we not have any of our holy weapons showing. It's okay if we're attacked, but outright brandishing them will get us unnecessary attention."

"Anything about what to do if we're attacked?" Muu asked around a mouthful of food.

"Dude, we may be in hell, but manners?" I grunted.

He looked at me dryly, but Yoh answered before he could speak, "What I said would happen when I made the damned deal—if they get in our way, they die. Period."

"Okay. Looks like we get to go on a rampage!" Jaken grinned ferociously.

"Woah there, holy boots." Yohsuke tutted. "Pump the divine brakes for a moment. If they actively keep us from getting to Balmur, they die. If they're doing their job and shit, only if they absolutely have to. If anyone tries to fuck us over or attacks us,

you can take the first swing, but I need you to keep yourself and your religious smiting in check. Cool?"

"Yeah, yeah. Just Paladin, you know?" He pointed to himself, then our surroundings. "Everything about what I do is meant to fuck this place up."

"We get that, but you gotta stay under wraps with it until it's needed. Now, let's move on." Bokaj stood up as the others finished eating, and we prepared to move once more.

It was well past dinner by the time we reached the city proper. All of us arrived surprisingly unmolested but dirty and hungry.

The wall around the city was more like a wall of spikes with bodies and other things hanging from them in various states of decay or undeath. I saw one figure reach out from several feet up, only for one of those bloated, creepy-eyed birds to land on it and begin pecking at the exposed flesh and soft bits.

*Do not throw up now, damnit. Don't. Do. It,* I growled at myself angrily as bile began to rise in my body.

I could take a lot of shit, but holy hell, that took the cake, man. The blood room the lich had going to his evil-ass basement was a water park compared to this.

The guards, two hulking demons, their skin a deep maroon with goat-like legs and cloven hooves for feet, stood beside the gates. Their features reminded me of Tim Curry's character from the movie *Legend* with the high angled cheekbones, narrow chins, and gaunt cheeks. Their horns were filed down to nubs though, rather than his Minotaur-like ones.

Both of them stood almost nine-feet tall with great swords planted in the ground before them.

Each of them had a title and their level displayed above their heads. Left being the lower level.

**Guard 1 level 73.**
**Guard 2 level 75.**

The one on the right spoke first as we approached, "Ah look, Byla, more souls to corrupt," the figure on the left, his name changing above his head, snickered but remained quiet, "and what, pray tell, are you doing here without your master or masters?"

"We don't have a mas–" Muu began indignantly, but a flying figure slapped him cleanly across his face, shocking him into shutting up.

"Speak out of turn again, slave, and you will see the enforcer's whip!" A small, blue-skinned imp with a single horn sprouting from the left side of his head flapped his tiny wings in front of us. He turned his attention to the guards. "Byla, Scrot. You two knew I was expecting something for my lord. How dare you attempt to claim those who are claimed. *Again.*"

**Imp level 34.**

By this time, the little imp was inches from Scrot's face. The larger demon looked bored but sighed, "Can't blame me for trying, can you, Zirex?"

"I expect nothing less of a no-horned goon from the guard," Zirex spat, but I thought I saw a wink. "This is the last shipment today. Shouldn't be any tomorrow, but next week may be more fruitful. I hear tell that a certain pillar captain is expecting a fresh batch of meat, five of nine—if you catch my drift, that is?"

"Awful kind of you, Zirex," Byla answered, the deep grumble surprising us. "Go on, you lot, and don't do anything stupid."

As we walked by, I heard Byla speak to Scrot, "You see the tails on that one? And the Fae-Orc? Reckon he's some kind of gods-touched Paladin. Poor bastard what owns them has their work cut out for them. Hope the one Dragon gets sent to the pleasure district, be fun to tear the wings off…"

I shuddered and tuned them out, instead looking to the blue imp, Zirex as he flitted about herding us into a caged cart. "Get in, get in. No time to dally."

"If you think I'm getting in that thing, you have another thing coming," Yohsuke growled. The beast that sat in front of it, tied to the thing, observed the scene with what seemed like a placid look. It looked like an ox of some kind but larger, and the fur was a coal-like color with bits of red here and there. It had eight legs and four eyes. Weird looking thing.

The imp dropped in front of Yoh, and they were dangerously close to touching noses. "The demons and other creatures of this city will take you from me if you are not in chains or a cage—which do you prefer. Chains? Or cage? The latter will not be locked, but I have no qualms about taking you to my master the other way. The way *I prefer*."

*Let's just get in the damned cage, man.* Bokaj patted him on the shoulder and opened the door wide, testing it. *I may not be Balmur, but I can pick a lock, and I'm pretty sure Muu can just kick the damned thing off the hinges.*

*Fine. Muu and Bokaj get in last,* Yohsuke grumped.

We got into the cage that was more than large enough to fit all of us comfortably before Zirex slammed the cage shut with relish and the cart lurched forward.

While we moved forward into crowded streets, we watched and took in our surroundings. The first things we noticed were the grotesque, hideously twisted forms of some of the demons and creatures that inhabited the city. Some of them seemed more like gelatinous blobs of skin with many faces stretched impossibly in agony and torture with a main face that seemed normal in comparison. There were creatures of bone with long, lanky limbs, fangs inside their skulls and milky sinew that held the bones together, their long, sharply-pointed fingers reaching and grasping.

Some grasped at meat hanging from hooks outside what looked like a butcher shop with a tall, ogre-like creature that I swore looked like an oni of Japanese myth. They had long faces with huge fangs and insanely muscled bodies. It cleaved the meat before it in one slam of the butcher's knife in his great, meaty hand.

The others had been too far to see their levels, but the one butcher? Fuck me.

**Butcher level 83.**

Don't get involved in *his* meat market. Got it.

Weird that all these levels seemed to be so readily on display here. It was like it was the opposite of the Fae realm.

I mean, in a lot of the books I had read about both worlds, the Fae were a chaotic and alluring people, designed to trick and be mischievous as a whole. Demons, though evil and vile and despicable as a rule, upheld some kinds of lawful order. If it was law, they obeyed.

Didn't mean they didn't find ways to work around it, but they stuck to their deals, and if you worded things well enough, then you could get a decent deal. Yohsuke had managed it.

The buildings around us, for being in a hell realm, were well made. They were brick, brass, and sometimes bone, but only the shoddiest looking places had bones in them. After half an hour of navigating the roadways, we crossed into a nicer part of the city. These buildings were made of large sections of stone that reminded me of castles with finer cuts and mortar made of... what the hell was that?

You know what? Not going to get into that. Didn't wanna know. Nope. Noooo. Not me. Fuck that.

*This place is tripping me the hell out, man,* Bokaj groaned to us. The rest of us agreed, and we decided to stop being so observant of our surroundings and simply watch for threats. Even that was unpleasant, but that's life.

"We will be arriving in a moment. Look lively!" Zirex called back to us. We all simultaneously flipped him off. Damned demon. He just laughed, his high-pitched voice grating on our nerves further.

A few seconds later, we were shepherded through a large gate into an open yard with several creatures watching patiently under cloaks, their forms hidden from sight. The only things we could make out were their eyes, glowing multiple colors or missing completely but the vacuous space seemed even more terrible.

All of them were just out of our range to see their levels, but I figured it was safe to assume they weren't weaklings.

"Welcome!" a voice that was familiar greeted us from a balcony.

Other than the lavish clothes he wore, the white shirt stark against his deep-red skin, the demon looked the same as he had in the Fae Realm where Yohsuke had summoned him with Maebe's help. He stood an easy ten feet tall, not including the scaly, curved horns that jutted out of his forehead coming to a pointed tip a foot above him. His face was stunning, staring at us with glowing, red irises, blackened, pouty lips that let a little bit of fang peek through almost as if practiced. His jawline and cheekbones would have made a male model jealous and most women weep with joy. His body was slim and athletically muscled, but I knew for a fact that he had some serious supernatural strength going on—I had read it in dozens of books and seen it in all kinds of movies and shows.

"Amazing that you all have made it a point to stay alive," he pointed at Yohsuke, "and you keep drawing more and more from my power. I like your hunger, child. You are an excellent warlock, though you do waste your time with that sword."

"You remember our contract, demon?" Yohsuke called back to where the demon stood.

"Yes, mortal, I do. For now, you may call me Archemillian."

"I'll call for my information—where's Balmur, and how do we get to him?"

The demon hopped over the side of the rail, his large wings fanning out behind him majestically and slowly descended to the ground before us.

***Demon lord level 124.***

Fuck. I blinked and fought my body for it not to go rigid.

*Holy Hells, that level!* Bokaj grumbled into our minds.

*Not now!* Yohsuke barked.

"You always were a straight dealer," Archemillian pouted. "That's hardly any fun. How about this? I'll sweeten the deal a little—your soul, and I will tell you where he is right now and how best to reach him without being seen."

"Fuck you," Yohsuke spat.

"That wouldn't cost a soul, but alas." He bent until he looked into Yohsuke's eyes. "Tomorrow morning, he will be in the negotiation circle. It's how we higher-born demons and evil entities settle deals and bets without dirtying our own hands too much."

"So, then we wait and go to this thing tomorrow and then bust him out," Jaken growled and punched a gauntleted fist into his other hand.

Archemillian tsked softly. "Ah, therein lies the problem. You are masterless non-demons with nothing to negotiate and would be denied entry. Likely taken into slavery and eventually sold for various reasons." His pout became a smug grin. "But I can offer you the deal of a lifetime. Two, in fact."

"We aren't giving you our damned souls." James huffed loudly. Several of the smaller demons and creatures around us stared at him, making him visibly shudder.

"For this, I will forgo the souls and skip to the deal—I want you to fight for me." He motioned to the group of us and continued, "I want to be in a much more powerful position than I am currently, and the only way to do so is for one of you to fight the other demon lord's negotiator. In this case, your 'Balmar'. Did I say that right?"

"Balmur," Bokaj corrected, then looked at us and spoke telepathically. *It sounds like this is the best shot we have.*

*Only because the sonofabitch made it seem that way,* Yohsuke grumbled in return.

"What do you get out of this?" Muu asked after a moment.

"Power, green one." The demon swept over to stand in front of the Dragon-kin. He took one clawed forefinger under his chin and pulled it upward, then left and right. "You would fetch a lovely price at auction. Ah, yes—power. My status among my peers would grow, and with it, my strength. The number of damned souls my house would receive would increase, we would get to choose the choicest of slaves and meat that arrive to the city, and not to mention favor of the current Lord of the City for taking down this usurper."

He saw us frown and clapped in delight. "Oh how glorious, you haven't pieced it together yet." We eyed him quietly, and he seemed to deflate a little before sullenly informing us, "The creature your Balmur is enslaved by is none other than the one who has been causing turmoil on the Prime plane with all of the demons that have been sent there. That incubus? Hardly the worst he has sent.

And tomorrow, he means to challenge the Lord of the City for his seat. So, if I can prevent that, I will be rewarded handsomely, you can take your friend, and then you will have free reign to do what you wish from there to ensure this never happens again." The demon's red eyes twinkled in devious glee.

"Explain tomorrow then. How does the negotiation circle work?" The others looked at me oddly, but I didn't care. We needed the info.

"The Lord of the City can only be challenged after any other grievances have been aired and… settled." He smiled, his perfect lips bowing in delight at the thought. "To win, all you must do is neutralize your opponent. If you lose? Well, that can be *quite* unpleasant."

"What aren't you telling us?" Jaken growled. "And why not send these guys? They're all higher level than us."

Archemillian clapped his hands and spun about, taking a step back. "Oh, but the poetic *justice* of it all! Think of it this way—you show up, take on your friend, and when he sees you, he hesitates. You capitalize on that hesitation and.."

"He means kill." I sighed. "We would have to kill Balmur."

*Do NOT let him know that we have the ability to bring people back,* I ordered the others telepathically. *That's what I had expected. Let's make it look like the idea upsets us and then come up with a plan.*

"I know of your kind, Paladin." Archemillian stepped in front of Jaken. "You would have been a fun one to see broken and corrupted." He regarded the rest of us. "Is this deal amenable?"

Bokaj didn't wait for us to confer before nodding and responding aloud, "Deal."

### QUEST ACCEPTED!

*What the fu—* I started, but as I looked at the notification, my heart sank.

*Hostile Negotiations – The being you know as Archemillian has struck a deal with a party member (Bokaj) that your party will do your best to see his bid for power through in the negotiation circle into fruition.*

*Reward: Increased opportunity to abscond with your friend (however that may be) and increased power for one of your party members.*

*Failure: The loss of possibly all of your immortal souls should you perish, to Achemillian and his horde of torturers for all of eternity.*

"The verbal contract has been set. I will not offer you power, as one of you already benefits from sapping some of my strength, but I will allow you safe lodging in my home this evening." Archemillian snapped his fingers. "Our food is not something you could stomach, and I did not prepare you anything, but the lodgings are yours. Prepare yourselves for tomorrow. Rest well."

———

The rooms we had been given were filled to the brim with things that were likely meant to convince us to sell our souls for them. The rest of us were still too sore at Bokaj to really give a shit about the mounds of gold, a surplus of beautiful weapons, and master-crafted armor enchanted so heavily that looking around made my mouth water but my head ache.

Finally, after an hour of sitting in sullen silence, Bokaj spoke, "You guys done being mad about shit that any of you would have done for someone else here today?"

James was the first to make a response to the Ranger's outburst, "It's our immortal souls, man! You could have at least let us all talk about it."

"Would any of you have said no?" Bokaj tested as he stood and began to pace. "Yoh, would you not have done the same thing for Zeke or James? Muu, if Jaken had been taken rather than Balmur? Fuck, Jaken would have done the same for any of us. Look at him!"

We grudgingly did so, and the Paladin's face was resolute. "He's right. I would have. There's no point in saying that none of us would have done the same because we're all here right now." The rest of us blinked, and I knew he was right. He continued, "We can be butthurt about the specifics, split hairs, all that stuff later. We need a solid plan of attack for tomorrow. I think we know who will be fighting."

Each of us stared at Bokaj, who nodded once. "Me."

"Okay, now with that out of the way, what do we have left to get ready. Everyone has better accessories, better weapons, and better spells. What else?" I asked.

"Anyone who hasn't been spending their points in their combat tabs," Jaken eyed me knowingly, "may want to do that. Who knows what we're getting into tomorrow."

I smiled. I had actually been saving my points for just such an occasion. Now, could I have used them earlier? Yeah. Hell yeah. But now I had sixteen of them at level 31. Time to play!

So, since it's been a while since we played with the combat and weapons tabs, let's review, shall we? The weapons tab opens at level 5, and when it opens, you get a single point to spend on a weapon proficiency. For me, I had purchased Great Axe Proficiency, which gave me an additional 1% damage and a little more skill with the weapon overall.

From there, you gain the ability to choose weapon skills and abilities. I had chosen three of them at one point apiece that I used to deadly effect often.

***Wind Scythe - Throw your Great Axe into the enemy accurately up to 30 feet. One additional foot per 5 strength (max 40 ft). 15 - 30 base damage. Cooldown: 1 minute.***

*Cleave - Boosts damage of the next attack by 100%. Cooldown: 3 minutes.*

*Devil's Hammer - Slam the butt of your axe into the enemy. 50% chance to stun target for 30 seconds. Cooldown: 2 minutes.*

And then some that I used less but were no less important.

*Charge - Allows the user to close the distance to an opponent of up to thirty feet away, almost instantaneously. Cooldown: 30 seconds*

*Feather Axe - Lowers the weight of the weapon used by two thirds. (Current weapon weight 30Ibs; will now be 10Ibs) Duration: 10 minutes. Restriction: Weapon must be a Great Axe. Cooldown: 15 minutes.*

Not to mention that I had also spent an additional two points to get to the second level of proficiency and a total of two percent additional damage to my attacks with a great axe, then another three to get to the third. As the proficiency raised in level, the cost rose accordingly. So to get to level four, I'd have to spend four points for the next and so on. It didn't stack, which sucked, but that was okay.

Sixteen points to play with, and I would play. First, I spent nine points to get my proficiency up to level five, with an additional five percent damage boost.

A flood of knowledge and surety drowned my senses. I didn't have my weapon in hand, but I *knew* I would be that much more deadly with it.

Next, I took a gander at some of the skills I had available to me now.

*Executioner – Your axe becomes the judging end of your foe, may the Gods have mercy on their soul—for yours is swift and brutal. 20% chance to finish an opponent with 30% HP or lower. Cooldown: 10 minutes.*

*Bladed Storm – You are the maelstrom of pain and the flurry of metal blows. You are the storm. Movement with a Great Axe is greatly increased, weapons strikes are faster and less predictable for a time. Duration: 1 minute. Cost: 200 MP. Cooldown: 3 minutes.*

*Epicenter – Where your axe strikes, the earth crumbles and shatters. Weapon damage is greatly increased for a single strike, while weapon weight is quintupled. Cooldown: 5 minutes.*

*Ravage – Your strikes rend flesh from bone, but these strikes dig deeper, leaving bone decimated and blood in your wake. 70% chance to cause a hobbling wound and damage over time to an opponent.*

*Cost: 50 MP. Cooldown: 2 minutes.*

Holy. Fucking. Shit.

Okay, take a breath. Release. Repeat. That's how that whole breathing thing goes, right? At three points each, this would be a tough decision.

The no brainer was Executioner. That would be super helpful, despite the ten-minute cooldown. The other three had their uses, of course. Epicenter would be wicked, but I didn't need to have to lug around an axe that weighed hundreds of pounds. Ravage was fucking wicked sounding, and to be able to hobble a creature *and* do damage over time?

Beautiful, but in the end, I had to go with Bladed Storm. To be able to move faster and strike faster would be amazing. Not to mention, I could likely use that in conjunction with other skills. Cleaving, Charging my opponent. All of it.

There was nothing worthwhile for my last remaining point to go toward unless I wanted to pick up a single level for daggers, but I was already kind of skilled with them from my obsession with bladed weapons as a kid. And in the Marine Corps. How many hours had I spent making the same slicing, cutting, stabbing, and parrying motions with a blade since I was a younger teen? Countless hours. I would wait until I had more points to sink into my great axe.

The others looked like they hadn't done a damned thing except Muu, who scratched his scaled head.

"What's up, buddy?" I asked him from my seat. It was hard

to resist the urge to get up and finger some of the valuables that bastard Archemillian put around us as temptation.

"Well, as you guys know, I get five points per level to put toward weapon proficiencies and abilities." He began to tinker with some settings, and his screen popped up.

*Name: Muu Ankiman*
*Race: Half-Dragon Beast-kin*
*Level: 28*
*Strength: 85*
*Dexterity: 65*
*Constitution: 50*
*Intelligence: 15*
*Wisdom: 14*
*Charisma: 14*
*Unspent Attribute Points: 0*

Righteous. His stats were fucking amazing, but what he was showing me now was even more interesting. Of all the weapon proficiency points he had received, he'd only spent ten. So he still had a hundred and five to use.

"That's fucking criminal man," I muttered jealously. Jaken nodded, and James snorted.

"What I'm wondering is where do I pour these points?" Muu looked to us for guidance, and I just shook my head.

"I couldn't tell you, brother. You're what, level three in your spear proficiency? Why not bump it up to like, ten?" I started doing some math in my head, wishing for a calculator. "That would leave you with fifty-six points to buy skills or up your other weapon proficiencies."

Muu tinkered a bit, a look of consternation on his face; then he went completely slack for a moment before returning as if nothing happened. "Okay, there, that's done. I upped spears to ten. That's normal spears and short spears because they weirdly count as the same weapon since the counterbalance is there? I don't know—it's weird."

"What was that?" Yohsuke asked.

"What?"

"You looked like you had like an aneurysm or something. You okay?"

Muu blinked at Yohsuke. "Yeah, it was just a lot of information to take in." He tapped something else a few times. "Hammer is up to level three now too. There are six points gone. Fifty left… *oh my god!*"

"What?" we asked.

He turned his screen to us once more, and on it, I had to admit, was something I didn't expect to see.

***Nightmare Thrust – You are an opponent to be reckoned with, but those who are struck by this attack know true fear. Duration: two days with a 50% chance at the sight of the wielder, they may become paralyzed by fear. Cost: 22 MP. Cooldown: 6 minutes.***

***Magicked Missile – Your weapon sails as if spelled and homes in on your desired target. Objects in way may divert path. Cost: 57 MP. Cooldown: 2 minutes.***

***Gale – Your strikes and thrusts are so swift, the air splits and moves with your weapon. Gusts of wind will pierce and slash your opponent or anything in their way up to 30 ft with an additional foot added per 5 strength. (Max distance: 47 ft.) Cooldown: 2 minutes.***

***Sky Sunder – Your weapon will split the skies and your foes. Vastly increased damage of attacks against opponents from above. Cooldown: 10 minutes.***

"Those are fucking sick, but that five-point cost is rough, man. What will you do?" Bokaj whistled as Muu turned the screen back around grinning. "You just bought all of them, didn't you?"

"I like to plan, sure, but those are too good to not have in our arsenal." Muu dismissed his screen and the remaining thirty points he had to spend. "Besides, tomorrow, the majority of the fighting will be done by you, Bokaj. Are you going to be okay?"

"No." The ice Elf shrugged, Tmont climbed out slightly

from her hiding spot in his hood to headbutt the side of his face comfortingly. "I've been best friends with him since we were kids. We live together. He's seriously family to me, but I'm going to do what has to be done. End of story."

"Well, that's fair." James yawned and began shoving shit out of his way so that he could move to one of the beds hidden under piles of awesome stuff. "We should get some rest. Gotta be fresh for tomorrow."

We all laid down for the night, Tmont and Kayda taking turns watching over us with the elves who needed little rest.

Who knew what these negotiations would bring. The only thing that I was certain of was that we weren't taking "no" for an answer where Balmur was concerned.

# CHAPTER EIGHTEEN

"Truly, would you all relax? You're here as my guests for this event. Just don't be imbeciles, and you'll be fine." Archemillian sighed for the umpteenth time.

We had been watching fighters duke it out for the last two hours for smaller things. Stolen goods, slaves, besmirched honor. This whole watching other people fight while surrounded by hundreds of thousands of evil creatures made my skin crawl. Not to mention the closeness of these things. They smelled *awful!* And the sights? Super awful.

Especially when I was seeing a constantly shifting sea of levels around us at all times. It was starting to give me a migraine. Ugh.

The place was a stadium that made the Ohio State Football Stadium look like a children's playground. The battlefield below was gigantic, at least one-and-a-half football fields long and one wide because the creatures that fought in it weren't always small or weak.

I had seen an imp with a really nice staff dismantle a crea-ture that looked like a furred ogre that had flames all over its skin and four arms. The little thing had cast a single spell that

looked like some kind of meteorite that dropped on her opponent and crushed him so thoroughly that when the spell faded,
there was merely a smear of brackish black and red left.

And don't even get me started about the half dozen ape-like
beasts that had fought in it after them. There are really only so
many times you can watch an audience member get doused in
flaming fecal matter before you start wondering if you can
step in.

And the entire time, I had to think about Balmur fighting
these things, about him trying to survive in this very place. The
thought of it made my tongue feel thick in my mouth and bile
rise in my throat. I didn't pity him, I don't think, but I knew that
things would likely be different.

*I just tried to get a hold of him via earring—nothing.* Jaken looked
away from the now-concluding fight in the center of the
stadium.

*He just sent me a Mental Message. You guys, he's been here for a year
and a half.* Bokaj's voice broke in my mind. I could hear the
strain in it now. *He said, "I know you probably can't hear this, and
that's okay. It's been more than a year and a half since I saw you, and it's
getting harder to keep them out of my head. They want me to do things.
Terrible things. I just… I miss you, man. I hope you don't come. Stay
away. It's not safe here. Not safe. Not.*

A biting sting and tightness took my throat. Cold rage
seeped into the pit of my stomach, and I wanted to just start
massacring these damned demons right then and there. As soon
as the thought occurred, the crowd around us, across from us,
began to cheer, boo, hiss, and spit. The range of emotions on
top of what I was already experiencing was discordant, and it
made me angrier.

"It's him!" I heard one slave hiss aloud from somewhere
behind me to my left.

"Your friend comes," Archemillian muttered to us, and we
stood, though we had basically front row seats to the action in
the center of the stadium.

In the center of the now-bloodied, grayish sand of the

center battlegrounds, a red portal opened, and a large, brutish figure stepped out. His purple and red mottled skin just barely covered its muscled figure, covered in chains, a loincloth and a thick belt around its waist. The large, heavy-browed face scowled around it as it reached back into the portal and pulled out a chain. It stepped further from the portal momentarily so that it could give a mighty tug on the creature at the other end.

Out of the red portal, a significantly smaller figure covered in nothing more than rags and bound heavily in chains and barely functioning stumbled out.

Balmur. His once tanned, fiery flesh was now covered in scars that seemed to take up all available space. The demon hauled him further from the portal and then began to unlock the cuffs around his wrists as the crowd began to howl and chant.

"Talgov! Talgov! Talgov!" they chanted in some guttural language.

"What does that mean?" I asked Archemillian over the din.

"It means, loosely, in your tongue, 'die.'" He leaned back from me as the crimson of my rage bloomed at the edges of my vision.

By now, the hulking figure had managed to get the cuffs off, and rather than simply stepping away, he drew his hand up by his cheek and backhanded our friend so that he fell sprawling to the ground. As the brute strutted back into the portal, two smaller creatures—imps—flitted out of it with weapons—Balmur's Mountain Fangs.

From what I could make out, they were chipped and on their last legs, but as soon as they were dropped in front of him, he was up and in motion.

He swiped once, lashed out with his foot and then stabbed with his other weapon, and both lesser demons were dead and laying at his feet. He began to sprint at the portal, but it snapped out of existence. He came to a halt, a cloud of dust and debris behind him, kicked up from his mad dash.

He snarled at something and then bellowed angrily.

A loud, booming voice belted against our ears, laughing, "Do not worry, my pet, you will be able to destroy more soon, fret not."

I blinked and scanned the sides of the walls, trying to pinpoint where the sound came from but didn't find anything outright until Bokaj tapped my shoulder and pointed. Directly across from us on top of some sort of box, like a closed in portion to watch from, stood another hulking figure.

He basically looked like a twelve-foot-tall carbon copy of Archemillian, but this demon was all kinds of roided out. His muscles had muscles. He wore a black suit of armor with gold filigree on it in the shapes of screaming figures. The helm on the ground beside him had room for his horns to jut out, and his eyes were pitch black.

"Demons of this fine city, of the third circle of the Hells, thank you for your attention!" The figure waved to boos and hisses from our side of the stadium, while more and more on his side cheered and applauded. "Yes, I know we are not united yet, but we shall be. Too long have we been warring against ourselves, fighting over scraps! Waiting to be summoned by some horrid creatures to do their bidding, make *them* more powerful. No more!"

The crowd on his side of the stadium went wild. Balmur spat, his weapons clutched in scarred hands. His left eye—the one that he had chosen to sport a scar on for the look of it when we first arrived—was now well and truly gone. A huge gash was still healing over it in a mirror of what he had thought looked aesthetically pleasing.

"We will unite, and then we shall make them all *ours!* Then we shall take out our displeasure on all of the realms—not just the Prime but also the Fae, the elemental, the abyssal! All of them!"

"Oh, he has General written all over his big dumbass face," Yohsuke spat.

"Yup," James grunted.

"Ytteriol! Lord of this City, I challenge you for your right to rule! Send your champion against mine and let us see who negotiates stronger!" The figure shoved his fist skyward, and the crowd lost their minds. All of them. I took that to mean this didn't happen often.

"Would that that could happen, Melvaren!" Archemillian called, his throat glowing slightly as his voice radiated outward. "However, it will be you who answers the challenge today."

"Archemillian, you vile *rat*. You *would* wait until now," the other demon spat. "You stand so staunchly in the way of progress—in the way of new leadership and the way things *ought* to be, that you are too blinded by petty power to recognize real opportunities when you see them."

"If you would please keep your tripe to a minimum, pretender, it would be appreciated. You are merely a demon possessed by something who knows how to manipulate. I believe it was called a 'General of War?' And I have on good authority a way to soundly see you out of meddling in our affairs."

"I'm more demon than you are," Melvaren postured with his hands out to his sides. "Who is it that has sent more demons to the Prime realm in eons? *Me*."

"Yes." Archemillian nodded sagely before pointing an accusatory finger at the other demon. "By way of *lesser beings*! Beings unfit to summon our true power. The demons you sent forth *died*—painfully—only to be robbed of the souls they garnered in unsanctioned deals by *you*."

The crowd around us and even on the other demon's side became rather close to rioting, shrieking and spitting curses in multiple languages.

"People of this fair city!" Melvaren, clearly angered at the accusations, bellowed to the crowd. "I assure you, these slanderous words are simply untrue. Unfounded! I assure you, my innocence is clear."

"Funny thing for a fucking demon to say," I grumbled sarcastically.

"Prove it!" I heard an imp to our right bellow.

Some bone-like demon above us shouted, "Blast him to the inner circles!"

"I challenge you for the right of right!" Archemillian challenged. "Your champion versus my own. Winner has the right of these findings. Should your champion out negotiate mine, you can freely challenge the Lord of the City."

"And if he doesn't?" Melvaren's eyes went cold. Calculating.

"Then you are guilty of all accusations against you and are subject to the same laws as the rest of us, though you are a pretender and a charlatan of the vilest sort." Archemillian smiled, his face taking a smug look.

"My champion is undefeated." Melvaren raised his horned head.

"And my own is untested." Archemillian spread his hands as if to show all. "You would truly be an idiot not to answer this challenge," the taunting demon raised his brows in mock surprise, "or did you want to add 'coward' to the list of things you're accused of?"

"Fine!" the pretender called, "but if you lose, I get those mortals in your care."

To his credit, Archemillian didn't even flinch. Or had he known this would happen?

"If you win, you may break them all here in this very place with no one to stop you," as the crowd began to stand and applaud, Archemillian held a hand up to quiet them, "but should you lose—they will break you on the Lord of the City's behalf."

Another booming voice surrounded us all, "I find this turn of events both fortuitous and entertaining. Archemillian, Melvaren, this thing will happen and has my favor. Winner take all the other has. Melvaren, should you lose, you lose all standing, possessions, and souls. The only way to regain some semblance of dignity will be to face Archemillian's guests and win. Should Archemillian lose, he loses his guests and all his holdings, souls, and anything to his name. Are both parties satisfied?"

Archemillian nodded his head once, and Melvaren followed suit, although he looked considerably more shaken.

"Then let the negotiations *begin!*" the voice—I assumed that it belonged to the Lord of the City—roared and the crowd went nuts.

Bokaj nodded to each of us, a look of nervousness replaced by determination on his face before he hopped down into the sandy area and began to cautiously approach his best friend.

"Hey, buddy… how you been?" he began softly, hands out to his sides.

"Slave!" Melvaren spat. Balmur's head snapped to him with a deep, guttural growl. "No mercy, or do you want to visit my Hall of Tender Graces again?"

The nearly feral Dwarf growled again as he turned back toward Bokaj.

*He's not gonna be fuckin' gentle, guys,* Yohsuke warned. *Bokaj, get that bow out and stick to the plan. You can do this. He needs you to be hard in this moment.*

*That's what she said,* Muu interjected to the rest of us.

*Dude, now is so not the time,* Jaken reprimanded softly.

*Sorry.*

"I'm half tempted to fall for that disguise again," I just barely heard Balmur over the din of chanting around us. "You wouldn't be the first of these dicks to come at me trying to feign my friendship. Lying to my face."

"It's not a lie, buddy. It's me, Bokaj. You and I have been friends since I don't know when," Bokaj offered, still refusing to outright draw his weapon. "I even have T' here. I know you miss your fiancée, and I know you miss Gatsby. You remember your little dog, right?"

Balmur roared and just fell into his shadow and disappeared. Not good.

*Move!* I bellowed at Bokaj through our earrings.

Luckily, the Ranger's reflexes were on point, and he was able to dodge both swipes at his legs as Balmur burst from his shadow beneath his feet. The blades of his Mountain Fangs caught the edge of Bokaj's shirt and sawed through slightly.

As Bokaj rolled up on to his feet, he had to dash away from the pursuing feral Dwarf. Gone were the precise swipes and jabs he had shown us once earlier. They were replaced by a blood-thirsty drive to destroy and kill his offender.

*You all can't see his level, but I can and holy fuck!* Bokaj began and dodged out of the way of another attack, just barely getting out of the way. *Level 35!*

*Our boy's been busy. Damn it.*

Tmont bounded out of Bokaj's hood and yowled at Balmur. The Rogue blinked at the cat, her form growing but her look of pleading unchanged.

"Master's friend!" I could almost feel Tmont's heart break seeing Balmur this way. "You're back! Don't hurt Master. He loves you! I love you too. Come feed me and rub my belly like you used to."

Balmur's legs trudged forward as a haunted look fell over his face. "Not her too. Not again. Not T'. I expect everyone else but not her too."

"It's cool, man," Bokaj tried to soothe his friend as he walked toward the panther.

"Don't worry. I'll free you T'. You don't have to be played by some cruel demon ever again, baby." As he closed the distance, the Rogue fanned his arms out, flames wreathing his weapon in his ancestral Heart Flame ability. I had seen him use it multiple times before, but he was brandishing it at his best friend's pet.

"Don't you do it, Balmur!" Bokaj cried. I looked up in time to see three arrows soar through the air from his Wild Bow before they met Balmur.

Balmur's body moved almost as though without thought, slicing cleanly through two of the arrows and lifting a foot to *guide* the last arrow toward Tmont.

The panther hissed as the arrow passed narrowly beside her face, slicing her cheek and shaving three percent of her health away. Tmont didn't sit and just take that, though. While his attention was off her, she pounced and pulled him down to the ground. Her piteous whines of not wanting to hurt her Master's best friend punctuated by his unintelligible cries of anger at the beast holding him down.

Two arrows sprouted from his shoulder. He grunted in pain before looking at Bokaj and making the shape of a gun with his right hand and 'firing' toward him. I recognized the spell instantly.

*Fireball! Move!*

Bokaj threw himself to the left and still got caught in the blast radius of the spell. It tossed him ten feet into the air, and Balmur melded into Tmont's shadow before she could savage him any further. Bokaj was hurt, his health at seventy-five percent. Not too bad yet, but I had a feeling it would get worse.

*He's going to go for her again, get there,* Yohsuke pointed out.

*Keep the commentary minimal for now. He's so much stronger than before. Fuck,* Bokaj panted into our heads.

*Then use your bardic shit on him. Make him stop!* James implored.

Balmur was up again, screaming out of the cloud of smoke after Bokaj but throwing one of his Mountain Fangs at Tmont.

No. He wasn't about to use that, was he?

The Dwarf's form shimmered and blinked from his previous position behind Bokaj and reappeared feet from Tmont.

*Fuck,* I growled mentally.

Tmont's form grew, doubling the size of her already large panther form, and she batted at Balmur as he closed the distance. He took a solid blow to the dome, but he used the momentum to shift out of the way as her second clawed paw swung toward his legs. He hopped on to her back near the shoulder and hacked into the side of her leg once with one weapon, her angry roar turning into a scream of agony as he stabbed the bladed portion of his other weapon into her neck.

"TMONT!" Jaken, Bokaj and I shouted in unison.

I felt a burning hand on my shoulder. Archemillian looked

down at all of us. "If you interfere now, they perish and so do your chances of winning. Sit!"

We grudgingly did as we were bid and sat down.

By the look of hurt and understanding that dawned on Bokaj's face, he knew that the kid gloves had to come off.

"That's it. You leave her alone and come for me!" he roared, fear and desperation beginning to show in his features.

Balmur looked up from where he stood on the now-shrinking panther's shoulder with tears streaming down his face. "You took her from me! You monsters make me kill my friends every other day for more than a *year* so that I could fight for you in some *fucking* petty power struggle!"

He stomped off Tmont, her health ebbing from her body slowly but steadily from the massive wounds to her shoulder and neck.

Balmur continued his lamenting, "I can't even kill myself to make it stop! I *tried* to, and you keep bringing me back. *Making* me kill things. Messing with my head." Bokaj tried to move closer, but the crazed Rogue wouldn't allow it.

He stopped only a few feet away from Tmont and motioned back to her. "So after I kill that thing, I'm going to kill you because at least when I win, it takes them a little while to work up the will to torture me with having to watch my friends die."

Balmur turned his back on Bokaj and wept as he walked toward Tmont. She tried to crawl away from him, but he threw a Mountain Fang into her back; she screamed into the air.

The crowd roared, their bloodlust close to being at least partially sated.

Suddenly, I heard something shatter, *felt* something break, and as I wondered what it could be, I watched Bokaj step in front of Balmur and put a hand on his chest. He had used the ring I'd made!

"Freeze," he ordered, and Balmur did. Bokaj threw his hand back toward Tmont, and greenish, pale-blue light enveloped her. Her health shot up to half, and the bleeding lessened as her wounds closed.

Bokaj looked back at his best friend and pulled him into a hug before driving three arrows with black ribbons tied around them into his back.

Balmur's health plummeted, then began to siphon out of his body. Faster and faster somehow. Then I looked down into Archemillian's hand to see a vial of growing, red liquid cupped secretly there.

He saw me notice it and simply held a finger to his lips. "Shhh."

I watched as Balmur's life faded, and before he faded, recognition flitted into his eyes.

Bokaj, cheeks slick with tears, whispered something I couldn't make out as he slowly knelt with his friend's corpse in his arms.

When the body rested on the ground, the roar of approval from the crowd was deafening.

"You may go to them now," Archemillian whispered. "Make what preparations you can while I stall them, and do not mention this. This was a gift. All will be explained later, should you survive."

We didn't wait to hear the rest. A roar of denial came from Melvaren as he watched what was happening.

"There is some sort of trickery to this! There is no way my champion was bested!" he howled and stamped his foot.

We booked it straight to Balmur and Bokaj. I cast Heal on T', then Regrowth to be safe. Her health bounced up rapidly, and she meowed, "Thank you."

Jaken set to work on Balmur immediately while Bokaj fiddled with the Dwarf's hand. I watched him put his bow over his shoulder and say a little prayer as he slid the three black ribboned arrows into his inventory.

*Surround me. This ain't gonna be pretty if they realize what I'm doing before it's done,* Jaken ordered. We complied.

I heard him praying. Lifting his thanks to Radiance and asking her to guide this lost soul back to his body. I heard him grunt as his mana drained, then his sigh of relief when the spell seemed to take hold.

*He's back, but I don't know what kind of shape he's gonna be in.* Jaken sighed. He pulled out several of the medium mana potions and downed them. His mana flowed back to full in seconds, and with a belch, he groaned.

"Bad idea, that." His sour look worsened as he heard what was said around us.

"Well, Melvaren, it seems that your negotiator has lost his edge and life. And you are wrong. Now, hold to the terms of our negotiations and prepare for your *lesson*." Archemillian's smug tone slid over my nerves like a cheese grater over an open wound.

Fuck that guy, his schemes, and this place.

But I could curse him later.

*You guys ready?* I asked the others.

*'Bout as ready as we can be. Save the holy weapons for when he's in here. If he comes in here.*

Sounded reasonable.

"Well, Melvaren, time to prove if you're worthy to stay among us!" bellowed the Lord of the City.

A figure stepped in front of us on a box up above the edge of the fighting grounds. His figure was easily more than fifteen feet tall. He wore a small crown of gold atop his golden head with a weird sigil in it. His skin was as white as the winter snow, his smile showed sharpened teeth, and the gold of his eyes swam in a deep red.

Rather than the leathery, bat-like wings the other demons had, his were made up of ebon feathers that looked to be singed but still moved easily.

He wore a simple but elegant golden loincloth that hung low beneath his hips, the weighted front of it held by an ivory flask of some sort. He held out his hand and made a great show of grasping nothing with his left hand. The muscles in it bulged, and he moved his hand to place a struggling Melvaren before us.

"Lest we forget, you were proven to be an intruder here, as has been deeply suspected in your rise amongst our ranks," the Lord of the City's lips didn't move when he spoke, but his head did shift back. When it did, I thought I saw small, budding horns from just beneath the hairline and above the crown. The look of contempt in his features was plain for all to see, the joy he took in bringing this pretender low in front of all these demons and slaves.

"Your power is that of a pretender, you insufferable offspring of an angel!" Melvaren spat. He turned to face us. "I will break you all, and in War's infinite mercy, I will give you to him. Maybe he will allow you to help when it comes time to break your own world. *Come!*"

He stomped closer, his level becoming apparent, and I gulped involuntarily.

**Melvaren level 145.**

"Ah-ah!" Archemillian tsked, this time took on a joyful sound. "Your strength was garnered and gained through *ill-begotten* means, Melvaren. That means they are no longer your own, and all you hold in this realm is now *mine.*"

The white demon held his right hand out as the other hand took up his flask. He took his thumb and flicked the lid off of it, and this horrid screeching and sucking sound emanated from the opening.

Nothing happened to us, but Melvaren dropped to a knee, holding his head with a wavering groan of anguish.

"Gaaaaah!" he cried. Blood seeped from his eyes, nose, and ears. His pores opened along his skin, and little bits of white and red began to dribble out of him slowly at first, then more and more rapidly.

A vortex of the stuff funneled from the General on his knees into the flask, and then the lid was on it once the process was complete.

**Melvaren level 56.**

Much more manageable. The asshole struggled to his feet,

panting, and trying to open his mouth as if his tongue were too thick.

"This is nothing," he grunted and looked to the other demons in the crowd. "Do you not see how they manipulate you to keep you weak and complacent to the status quo?! They *need* you to think this is the only way, but join me, and we can crush them together. We can make a new world and take it to War!"

Demons began to howl and laugh, but as I watched, some began to slowly make their way toward the lower levels of the stands.

*You think they could be minions?* Muu asked, his voice sounded panicked. *'Cause there's a lot of the fuckers moving in from back here.*

*Same over here,* Yohsuke growled. *Balmur up and at 'em? We're gonna need him.*

*He's conscious, and his ring is glowing like a motherfucker.* Bokaj let us know, and I turned to see one of the rings we'd had made on his finger.

By now, the demons who were taken in by the promise of power began to drop over the ledge of the wall.

"Those who join him in this are subject to punishment as he is!" The Lord of the City roared angrily.

Some of the tide of newcomers stemmed, but still, there were hundreds of lower level demons in here with us now, and they were joining Melvaren on his side of the field.

"Ha! He's simply upset because he cannot hope to control you all!" Melvaren's hands spread wide. "He is *afraid of you!*"

I mean, I couldn't blame him, but that didn't seem to be the case looking at the Lord's openly angry face. He seemed more pissed off than afraid.

"Mortals," the great demon bellowed, "you are free to destroy those who attack you, and make the imposter *suffer*. Make them all suffer. Fight well, and if you die, I will enjoy tormenting you."

**Quest Alert!**
**Hells Hath No Fury Like a Demon Scorned – The**

*Lord of the City, Yttriol, has given you free rein to murder the demons who have defied him by joining in this sanctioned punishment.*

*Kill any demon you like so long as they stand in the sand pit.*

*Reward: A longer lifespan than if you didn't, multiplied EXP, and increased favor with the demons loyal to Yttriol.*

*Bonus Reward: If you make any of them suffer, to include Melvaren.*

*Failure: Failure to kill Malvaren, resulting in your death, will likely mean a terrible, horrid torturing until your soul and consciousness fade into nothing but agony and pain. Running away will also cause a severe fall in trust with demon kind and a halt in growth to one of your party members—as well as demon hunting parties sent to find you and bring you back.*

*Due to events unfolding in the way they have, you have been forced into accepting this quest. Good luck!*

I was really going to need to have a sit down with whoever the hell did the system messages in this world.

*We gotta be ready for a brawl. There's too much experience here not to be taking advantage of it.* James dropped into a low stance, preparing himself.

"Wha's go'n on?" Balmur asked blearily. His eyes opened, fluttering slightly as he took us all in. "Oh, not this shit again."

Jaken smacked his chest with the back of his shield. "We don't have time to prove that we aren't demons, but Melvaren and a horde of assholes are coming, and we *need* you."

Balmur's eyes narrowed slightly. "Name something Rowland told us when we first started apprenticing with him."

"Really?!" Jaken grunted as a demonling lobbed a ball of flames for him to deflect. "Now of all times?!"

Muu and I rounded on him with a shout, "Just fucking do it!"

"He told us that if we had our heads up our asses at any time, we'd better make room for his boot because he'd be crawling up there to knock sense into us for wasting ingots!"

Balmur smiled, his scarred visage relaxing. "Got any other weapons? These won't last long."

"*That was all it took?!*" Bokaj groaned.

"Talk about this shit later!" Yohsuke barked. "Focus on the demon horde gathering?! *Please!*"

"Fine!" Bokaj and Balmur grunted together.

I looked back and noticed that Bokaj had slid the Rogue his new daggers and that Balmur looked like he was finally happy.

"Time to get my revenge," I heard him grunt.

"My slave yet lives!" Melvaren roared, turning his back to us, stupidly.

*Holy weapons out. Let's make it rain blood, lads!* I ordered the others as I called Kayda from her place in my collar and summoned Coal. Both seemed so pleased to be working together once more.

"Yes, it seems that after he lost and was killed, that cursed Paladin brought him back," Yttriol observed.

"Then he can still fight! The negotiations aren't over!"

The Lord of the City smirked. "One death was all that has counted in this city, nay this *circle*, for eons. Just because he is the first to return and escape you does not mean your loss is overturned." The white demon looked to Balmur with a sly, knowing look. "Besides, I would hardly call that one yours."

Melvaren turned and glowered at us, Balmur specifically, and his scowl turned into a toothy smile. "I would."

He stepped forward and put a hand out, his fingers grasping. "Return to me, slave. Return, and this slight will only be mildly punished."

Balmur's ring didn't glow, but I could see the struggle in him. I put a hand on his shoulder. Bokaj did the same.

"We got you," was all that was said, and his body relaxed before his burning, green eye opened with hatred.

"Let's end this," the quiet man seethed before he looked at us.

His left hand glowed blue—a mental spell was being used against him—but his determination seemed set. He reached into his inventory and pulled out his own Telepathy Earring, then clipped it into his ear with a sure hand.

*Muu and Jaken, anything gets close to the casters and Bokaj, you fuck it up. Usual tank fare,* Yohsuke began to hand out roles. *James, Balmur, you can cause as much general mayhem as you please, but stay close. Bokaj, me, and Zeke, we will bring up the rear here and cast spells at anything that so much as fucking exists. You get low on mana, melee until you recover or drink a mana pot. Questions?*

*What about the big fucker?* Muu asked.

*We move on him if he decides to get too close, but if you wanna harass him from afar, be my guest,* Jaken answered for Yoh. *Just help me keep agro off these guys, and we're good.*

"Fine," Melvaren spat. "You will be broken under the bodies of these demons until I deem you worthy of my attention. Break them!" Melvaren turned, and some of the more powerful demons that were closest to him looked at him expectantly. "All of you, go for Archemillian and Yttriol."

They seemed hesitant at first, but when he picked one up and crushed its head in his hands, the others moved away to do as ordered.

*Go!* Yohsuke hollered into our minds as the demons began to rush toward us.

Level thirty and lower demons scrambled over each other to get to us, only to be slashed and stabbed with holy weapons. The only reason we weren't overrun then and there was the fact that the demons were scared of them, but they still charged in.

We grouped together in a tighter formation. Muu and Jaken were in front to tank, but both had exceptionally strong holy weapons, so the demons that got too close took a thrashing.

Bokaj fired arrows into the coming waves as though they were meant for anyone. And they were. The beasts clambered so closely together that to get near one with a shot was to hit another. Any target would do. Tmont hissed and bounded at those who managed to get too close, swiping with her claws unsheathed.

More than a few demons fell to the duo and even more demons fell as Balmur rampaged just outside our tight, little cluster. His blades swirled, sliced, stabbed, sundered, and punctured any available surface, and all he did was flit from one target to the next. As he moved and weaved under claws, weapons, and through arrows with grace and feral tenacity, he would redirect some of Bokaj's shots as he had in their own fight, the projectiles finding homes in even more vulnerable and terrible spots.

The blood that covered him was ignored. Well, to be honest, I wasn't sure how much of it was a demon's or if he was hurt, but he seemed to be fine with a glance at his mostly-full health bar.

*Zeke! Nine o'clock!* I heard Muu growl into my head and instantly brought Magus Bane up to deflect a clawed blow followed by a flaming spear.

I grunted before mentally ordering Kayda, *Go show them what hell really is, hon. And Coal? Stay close to me, yeah? Maybe help kill anything I drop?*

Kayda took to the sky and burst into her full twenty-foot-height mid-rise into the air and screeched like crashing thunder.

Coal snarled as he lunged at my attacker's legs and caught one in his jaws. He yanked the bastard down on to his back, and I slammed my great axe down on to its neck severing the head.

**EXP withheld until the end of the Quest.**

Well. That was a first, but then again? It made sense. Had to have a tally to multiply the total, but to be really effective, we would need to be cruel. I slid my weapon into my inventory, pulled out Redemption's Mercy, and summoned Falfyre.

The crystal weapon radiated holy energy, and Falfyre had been referred to as a holy weapon. So, time to put both to good use.

The waves came, and as we fought, they seemed to keep coming.

I watched as James moved through a group of demons with his ki moving through his body at lightning speed. Lightning struck a demon that had snuck up behind him, and Kayda screeched in victory.

Muu had begun using his Rant ability; it allowed him to grab attention and makes those who heard it want to attack him. Our hands didn't light up, so it must have been a thing he had learned to control. If only slightly. This ability allowed him to run his mouth constantly and drove everyone nuts. I'd almost beaten his ass over it once.

Arrows sprouted from a demon in front of me, and I looked over to see Melvaren reach down and pluck a dead demon from the ground, whisper to it, and then throw it toward us. Mid-flight, it seemed to spasm and start to come back to life.

I was good mana wise, so I threw Falfyre, slicing through the thing easily, and I ordered the weapon back to me. It had cost only a few MP, but if this kept going, we were going to be in a rough spot.

Yohsuke shot Astral Bolt after Astral Bolt at enemies that seemed to be getting closer to our friends' flanks, but they didn't seem to care that they were being shot. These guys were likely all dead.

*He's bringing them back to life somehow, making puppets or something,* I warned the others.

*They're everywhere, and the fight with the demons against Yttriol and Archemillian is keeping them too distracted to intervene,* Bokaj explained.

*I have a plan, and no one is going to like this, but we need to get to him,* Jaken offered.

*What is it?* James asked as he ducked beneath a gorilla-like beast and blasted it with lightning-enhanced ki.

*We need to get him away from here. He's got too many corpses to bring back, and we can't keep this up for too much longer,* Jaken grunted and shield bashed a small demon that sailed at him with his shield then sliced through it with Righteous Brand. *So I think we should take him back to the Prime with us.*

*Dude, the elves will shit themselves if that happens.* Muu spun his spear to block an incoming flaming projectile and then thrust his weapon through a demon's torso. He lifted it, and the holy weapon carved slowly through the little beastie until it fell to the ground with a splat. *Gross.*

*We have no choice!* Yohsuke sighed. *My mana is starting to ebb, and I don't want to use my ability yet. The potions are handy, but you guys are offering openings left and right.*

To punctuate his statement, he sent an Astral Bolt at an enemy that tried to drag Balmur to the ground, hitting it in the face and allowing the Rogue to stab both weapons into the demon's throat and carve outward.

*We should go,* Balmur spoke finally. *I'll keep killing these things, but I'm getting tired. We need to end this on our terms.*

The rest of us gave assent, and Jaken took the lead. *We march forward. Muu, as soon as we're through, make us a hole in the crystal palace's wall so we can try to get him away from civilians. We all need to be touching, so Zeke, get Kayda and Coal in. Bokaj, grab T'.*

*Before we do this, we put the moves on him here a bit,* Yohsuke added. *If we go through this without hurting him, he may get suspicious.*

Jaken nodded and began to bang his shield loudly, drawing Melvaren's attention.

"Time to get yours, you fat piece of shit!" Jaken shouted as we moved steadily toward him.

More demons began to pour over the walls, seeing that the fight was going potentially poorly for their former rulers and picking a side.

Melvaren, a chuckle escaping his lips as he lifted his helmet on to his head, snickered, "You think you stand a chance? Fine. Come and let me show you what I, Anarchy, can do!"

Oh, for fuck sakes, man, who the hell was naming these guys? Anarchy? Really? Nah. Melvaren worked better.

We marched on and as we moved, demons died, were gored, and otherwise beaten back, but it was a near thing.

I had recalled Coal as we began, and as soon as Kayda was in reach, she fired one last frozen lightning bolt at the demonic General. He raised a hand with a demon in it, and the thing turned into a frozen, deep fried demon. Melvaren grunted and tossed it toward us in contempt. I pulled her into the collar and watched as James leaped into the air and kicked the popsicled demon out of the way.

*Hit him hard and fast,* Jaken ordered, *but stay close. Listen for me to call it, then everyone be touching someone else.*

Muu laughed out loud, and I sighed. Time to play.

As soon as we were close enough for him to become a viable threat again, we fanned out slightly. Melvaren slapped away Bokaj's arrows before socking James in the gut for getting too close. He looked like he was enjoying this game of cat and mouse, his chuckles and teasing feints beginning to wear on my nerves.

Then Balmur was beneath his legs, slashing with his new daggers and melting away before any reprisal could be made.

"You *insignificant, ungrateful lout!*" the demon cried in outrage, his health bar having fallen a little. I noticed a small skull that appeared under his name and saw it was silver. Bane had taken effect I guessed.

I broke left, slicing a demon with Mercy as I rolled through a gap between him and his buddy and then stabbed another in the throat with Falfyre.

When I came up, I angled the sword toward the still surprisingly-meaty fist that rocketed at me. The weapon didn't pierce, but it allowed me to slide under the blow and take it on the back at an angle. Thirteen percent of my HP bar gone there. Better to not get hit.

Jaken was suddenly in front of the demon General with his sword in his hands, driving the gold weapon into Melvaren's left knee.

*Now!* the Paladin roared. All of us lunged forward and touched the vile creature, Jaken, or one of us. I felt teeth sink into my left leg that began to tear and attempt to pull me away.

"Niffllepleth!" Jaken grunted as a small, shiny object reflected some of the radiant light emanating from his weapon.

"What the—" Melvaren started to try and shove us away, but a tear opened just behind Jaken, and gravity *shifted* so that we hurtled toward it. One second we were there in the Hells, and the next, we were back in the Prime plane.

I blinked and saw a high Elven guard blink and nod once. "I will inform Druid Questis, and *merciful bounty is that a demon?!*"

"Flee!" Muu shrieked at the guard before taking his hammer and slamming it against the far wall of the room. Spidery cracks spread from where his hammer landed.

The rest of us began to beat on Melvaren in earnest. Something tugged on my leg; the thing must have come with us and was still trying to rend me from my opponent.

I growled and turned to see a small demon with six legs that reminded me of a skeletal dog with patches of fur and muscle here and there gnawing at my leg, shaking its head back and forth. I stabbed down with Mercy and severed the spine just below the base of its skull. The animal went down, paralyzed. Rather than leave it to suffer, I brought my sword down into its skeleton skull and shoved myself back up on to my feet—six percent lighter on my health bar.

*Zeke, help us get him out of here and into the open,* Yohsuke called into my head.

*Belgar, coming up. Stay out of my way and keep his attention.*

I moved as stealthily as I could away from Melvaren and dismissed Falfyre with thought. The sword dispersed, and I focused on my Aspect of the Belgar spell. I made sure I was lined up and finished the cast.

The transformation took hold. My muscles grew denser, my fur hardened, and a horn-like protrusion sprouted from the top of my nose. My sight grew fuzzy, but my hearing grew sharper. More focused.

*Coming!* I settled into a sprinters position and dashed forward, settling into the Belgar's charge.

*Move!* I heard Jaken bark through the earrings; then I dipped my left shoulder and *WHAM!*

Not the band but the sound of me hitting that asshole like a freight train hauling ass whoopings.

Melvaren's body pushed through the buckling wall, carried by momentum out into the blinding sunlight.

"Agh!" he cried, throwing his hands into the air.

*There's a wall ahead,* I heard Bokaj begin to warn, but that spurred me on harder.

He was gonna love on that damned wall.

*Count me down,* I grunted and kept pushing. He started to try and wrestle out of my grip; his hands burned on the sides of my arms and shoulders.

*Three,* Yohsuke called. Melvaren growled and began to chant something in a guttural tone.

*Two,* Muu continued. The chanting grew a little more fervent.

*One! Shove him!* Jaken snarled.

"Orahej– ooph!" The chanting stopped, and I canceled the aspect spell before trying to shank the General in his kidneys with my own holy dagger in hand, but he launched himself backward, turning and swatting me away. My health dropped by twenty-seven percent, putting me just above half health.

I cast Regrowth on myself and checked the others. Jaken looked fine with being able to keep the others healed but was hovering around seventy percent HP himself, so I cast Heal on him to help out.

Time to get hands on. I put Mercy into my inventory and then pulled Magus Bane back into my hands.

*I'm going hands on,* I warned the others. *Cast your spells now.*

By the time I got in there, James was slugging away at the General's upper body, bounding off the side of the canyon walls as if they were a springboard. Balmur sprinted almost vertically up the side of the canyon and launched himself at exposed vitals as best as he could, but the demon swatted him aside.

"You pesky *flies!*" Melvaren bellowed. A ring of flame burst from him and pushed James and Balmur away as I was sprinting in from where I had been tossed.

Some of Bokaj's arrows burst into flame as they met the wave.

The demon summoned a large sword from somewhere and brandished it as we surrounded him.

*Zeke, Jaken, run interference,* Muu grunted, and I heard his armor rattle once. *I'm going to come down from above, but this will only work once.*

I activated Charge, crossing the distance between myself and Melvaren in an instant, then activated Bladed Storm, and my swings became erratic, almost to the point that I didn't even know where they were coming from—but the momentum and the hand placements, the swings and chops just felt so *right.*

I was carving into his health at a steady rate; he would parry here and there, but it was hard for him to maneuver the sword to deflect all of my blows on top of Bokaj's arrows and Jaken's dancing sword as it moved freely on its own off to my left.

Yohsuke moved in to help keep the monster distracted and took a slice to his left bicep for his trouble. His HP dropped to fifty-five percent instantly, and some sort of crippling debuff appeared beneath his HP bar.

James was there in an instant to deflect the blow, his scaled flesh covered in fine stone from his ring, to grab the fallen Spell Blade and drag him to safety.

*Bokaj, see if you can purify him,* James barked as he started toward Melvaren with his fists clenched. He shot a ki blast at the demon, who dodged it deftly.

I activated Feather Axe, and my weapon sliced through the air as if it weighed less than a ruler.

*Back away NOW!* Muu ordered.

I activated Devil's Hammer, took the blunt end of Magus Bane, and smashed it into Melvaren's left kneecap, hoping to drop him, but the armor he wore mitigated most of the damage. The demon was approaching sixty percent health. We were chipping away at it, just not enough at once. As I cleared from him to re-evaluate the situation, his scowl turned to a smirk.

"Getting tired?" He cracked his neck noisily, his armor creaking. "I'm just getting started."

A beam of light shot straight toward the top of his head with a shriek of sliced air that reminded me of a sonic boom.

Melvaren acted just in time, lifting the flat of his blade to intercept Saint's Grace. A clash of metal on metal followed by a pure note of resonance rang out. The holy spear fell to the ground just outside the crater that had formed around the demon from the impact of the blow. He cursed and threw his ruined weapon aside, a group of arrows raining at him from Bokaj.

Jaken stood defiantly in front of him, his shield tossed aside with only Righteous Brand in hand. "Still think you can take us, asswipe?"

"I'll enjoy breaking you, Paladin." Melvaren whipped a hand out, pointed a meaty finger at Jaken, and a bolt of sickly green energy shot toward our friend. Suddenly, Yohsuke was there to block it with his shield bracelet, the harmful magic fizzling against the spell barrier.

Another piercing sonic boom came, and as Melvaren tried to dive to the left, his right leg was gored by the still-airborne Fighter's ice lance, pinning him to the ground from above. In dropped Muu like a ton of bricks, short spear held by his head and a manic grin on his face.

"*Fear me!*" His weapon became covered in a black and red aura, and as soon as he was close, Melvaren trying to fend off the attack Muu used—what I could only assume was Nightmare Thrust.

The weapon slid through the General's left hand, into the arm, and then finally the chest before it stopped with a squelch and Melvaren's agonized roar. His health dropped a mere twelve percent, but that was *huge* damage from a weapon that wasn't holy.

And then Balmur was there with his twin daggers slicing

and dicing as he shouted, "How is this for vengeance? How is this for punishment?" He kicked the General in the side of the head as Muu went for Saint's Grace and the others moved in to assist. "You made me kill my *friends over and over again, you bastard.*"

Balmur took one of his blades and slid it slowly down the struggling Melvaren's left eye in a mirror of his own, the holy weapons burning and slicing the skin like a hot knife cuts through snow.

As he finished making a perfect line, Balmur slid his dagger beneath the eye there and cackled gleefully. "An eye for an eye is the demon way, eh, you sick *fuck?!*"

The Dwarf was weeping now, even as the blade scooped out the orb disgustingly—for all of us to see.

"Balmur, let's just end it, man!" Jaken barked, but Balmur wouldn't hear it.

"End it?" His eyes took on a crazy gleam as he shook his head, his good green eye flitting back and forth in challenge. "I *tried* to end it. Several times. Tried to throw fights," he motioned back at the General who's bloodied face slowly began to regain control, "but *he wouldn't let me.* He was the one that made me this," he gestured to his own missing eye, "this *monster.*"

As he hissed the last word, he drove his blades into whatever flesh of the demon he could find until finally, Muu and Jaken stepped in to assist him. He was at a quarter health at long last.

A wash of sulfur and the scent of rotting meat hit my nostrils just before the demon's right hand shot up and gripped Balmur by the throat. We were all blasted away; I smacked into the side of the palace and I noted that my health had taken a beating from that. I was at eleven percent, and the others weren't looking any better.

Balmur himself was only at seven percent. What the hell had that spell been?

"You are not worthy to end me," Melvaren spat. "I broke you, as War did me, and I will answer *only* to my master."

As the demon squeezed my friend, arrows pierced his flesh,

Saint's Grace jabbed into his side several times, and finally, he was at eighteen percent health. Yohsuke was there as well, stabbing with his vampiric dagger with both hands, trying to regain health, while I hobbled toward Melvaren after casting one last Heal on myself. I cast Regrowth on Balmur, took Magus Bane, and swung for the hills, activating Executioner. The weapon swung true and hit the big lug, but rather than killing him, it sheared through his outstretched arm.

"GRAGH!" Melvaren roared as Jaken stepped forward with Muu and Bokaj; an arrow sprouted from between his eyes at the same time the spear pierced his heart, and a divine smiting split his head in two.

The body fell to the ground, limp. Dead.

Balmur struggled to regain his breath. He cursed long and hard. Even as Jaken's healing aura surrounded him, then me, and the others, he let it go.

He let it all go.

"He killed me. He killed me. This is hell. It's finally over, but he killed me. I'm useless." The Dwarf curled into the fetal position and rocked himself back and forth as he sobbed softly, his mind broken.

Bokaj stood there, uncertain what to do but went to kneel next to him anyway. Tmont hopped out of her place in Bokaj's hood and cuddled against Balmur. Her soft purring lent a metronome to the Dwarf's rambling.

But they were both there. And so were we.

That's what friends did, right? Even when the going got tough and shit seemed to be falling from the sky around your ears, friends stood with each other. And that's what we did.

We would stand by our friend and help him recover. He had earned that.

I mean, he had been through hell, right? At least in hell, not sure how much he got to travel.

# CHAPTER NINETEEN

The gear that Melvaren had *surprisingly* dropped was garbage—
a broken sword, too large for us to try and get fixed and his
armor, which sported some badass stat enhancements, was so
heavily cursed that it was like being near radioactive waste, and
I had a feeling *none* of us would be getting superpowers that
were worthwhile from jumping into that mess. I didn't even
want to touch them again to show you the stats because
touching it had made me ill and knocked me down to like, five
in all my stats.

It felt nice not to be dim or almost so weak I couldn't move.
Having to have my friends drag me away from it on my face
had been embarrassing, but the necessary action won out.

So we just sat for a time and enjoyed our surroundings. The
place was dimly lit but nothing compared to the Hells.

"Hope bringing him back here from the Hells didn't fuck us
on that reward." Yohsuke sighed from where he laid down on
the grass.

"Same, but I'm just too tired to go through the notifications
right now. I mean, what're the odds we're going to have to fight

something else so soon after that?" James scratched his head and inspected his fingernails as he spoke.

"Highly likely at times, but here?" Bokaj snorted. "I don't think that's gonna happen just yet. Not too many high elves that want to actively kill us, right?"

"I'm trying to make sure I didn't shit my pants and that it's just demon blood I'm smelling, so if you all could shut up, that'd be great," Muu quipped sarcastically. The guy had a way with making us all shut up to question his sanity.

"We did it." Jaken grinned as he looked to us all. "I think there was something said about there only being five of them, and we just killed our second."

The grin that spread across my face was almost painful. I was sore, my brain hurt from all the casting, and I'm pretty sure I smelled terrible.

But we did it. The rest of us smiled and quietly basked in that victory.

We stayed there like that for some time before guards came to find us. I had notifications to go through, but they could wait. It was just so nice to just not be somewhere with every living being intent on using your soul as entertainment.

"Here they are!" I heard one voice call.

By now, Balmur had calmed down significantly and sat up, holding Tmont. As he slowly slid his scarred hands over her fur, the cat purred contentedly.

A retinue of guards in full battle rattle, Questis, and a young man who looked to be in his teenage years with silvery blond hair and a ceremonial style robe of green down the length with a bright purple shoulder cape that flared out at the shoulders marched in. It was him, the robed one, that I didn't recognize.

"Hello, Questis!" I called and waved.

"We are glad that you have returned to us," Questis greeted us. "And after so long of a wait."

Questis turned and bowed to the man next to him. "Your Majesty, King Telfino, these are the people your mother assisted in getting to the Hells so that they could rescue their friend. I take it the individual on the ground with the kitty is he."

"That would be correct." Bokaj stepped forward toward the young king, bowing at the waist. The guards made no visible move to stop him, so he stood and spoke, "My name is Bokaj, and these are my friends."

The young king stepped forward and pointed first at Bokaj, then to the rest of us in order and spoke our names, "Bokaj, Jaken, Zekiel, James, Yohsuke, Muu, Tmont, and I believe your Azer Dwarf friend's name was Balmur?"

Bokaj blinked in surprise, and we nodded for him.

"Welcome, formally and amicably," his light voice greeted us. He made sure to look each of us in the eyes as he spoke slowly and deliberately.

He seemed tense as he went on, "My healers will see to your friend and ensure that he is fit to be among us," he held up a hand to forestall our anger, "meaning he had not been somehow possessed. We will care for him, and while we do so, you are welcome among us."

His guards came forward with high elves behind them carrying a litter for the Dwarf. As they loomed closer, Balmur got a little twitchy, closing in on himself and eyeing potential targets.

Before they started to try and lift him themselves, Bokaj stepped in. "It's cool, Balmur. I'll be right there with you, me and T', so why don't you go ahead and stand up so we can let them carry your fat ass out of here to get you looked at?"

The Dwarf snorted and stood wearily but didn't make any moves to lash out. He laid down once he was on the litter, and T' rode on his stomach like a queen, her eyes were open and alert.

It was good to see that she didn't seem to be harboring any ill will against the Rogue for his actions. Likely, she may have understood that it was animal nature that he had used to survive.

"The rest of you, if you would be so kind, we would like to

have you all seen to in a similar manner, but we were most worried about his *prolonged* exposure, that there might be complications with his well-being. The rest of you, please follow my guard, and you will be looked over before lunch."

As the others walked ahead, dusting themselves off where they could. The king stood aside and waited until I was next to him to speak again.

"Master Zekiel, I have an urgent matter to speak with you about, if I may have your ear while we walk?"

I blinked. "Uh, certainly, your Highness."

We stepped out of the shadows of the palace and canyon wall into the light of a warm summer day. The city, despite the noise of our fighting, continued to function likely as it had before. Being this close to him, I could see the resemblance now to queen Silvanas in his nose and in his hair and build, but his eyes, which I had mistaken for a trick of his clothing, were a vibrant purple just like Mother Nature's. I half expected her voice to come out of his mouth, but he stayed silent.

The sound of life, normal life, was almost deafening compared to the dark and horrid hellscape we had returned from.

"Queen Maebe asked that I speak to you," the young king began, his eyes forward.

"I'd be happy to listen, but where is she?"

"She returned to her people more than a week ago. A matter of great import reached her, and she could wait no longer." He smiled and waved to a few of the people we passed.

"How long were we away?" I asked incredulously. Granted, Balmur had said he'd been there for a year and a half, but we'd been there a day or maybe a few hours more. "We were only gone for a day, day and a few hours, tops!"

"Ah. Then my calculations were correct—you've been gone roughly eleven days." He turned and looked me over once before continuing, "It seems that this time, time passed roughly eight to nine times faster there in that plane of existence compared to our own. Fascinating." I looked at him as if he were talking gobbledygook, and he smiled. "So while you were there for a day and a half, time moved faster for us here. That's the simple version. The more complicated version takes into account the distance between the veils that are crossed, planar shift and migration, and a myriad of other factors that I can tell from the look on your face are possibly a little more than what you can handle."

I blinked and closed my mouth, then blinked to moisten my bugged-out eyes and asked, "So it is possible for Balmur to have been there for more than a year while only a month or more passed here?"

King Telfino looked concerned but nodded once, confirming a lot of what I had questioned.

"Then is Queen Maebe okay? Did she tell you what was going on?"

"Only that the timeline for the quest she gave you has been hastened and that you are to speak to her as soon as you can." He motioned me forward into the palace. "She said that you are a Druid in service to the Mother. Is this correct?"

I nodded, and he began to smile genuinely. "Then I know I can trust you and yours with this urgent business of mine. My people are wary of outsiders. We are a proud people, but mainly because the last time we trusted outsiders, they stole our home from us."

I opened my mouth to respond, but he put a small hand on my shoulder. "I harbor no resentment against Maebe. She was not queen, nor was I even alive to know Samir as my mother did. I have known only this planet, and she nurtured our people as if we were her own. No. My problem is that some of my citizens have begun to disappear. There didn't seem to be any sort of cause at first, but after the fourth one had gone missing, we think we know why."

A thought dawned on me. "They're especially close to Mother Nature, aren't they?"

He looked taken aback. "Yes. Other than my mother's

funeral, it was why we held off on the solstice celebration. How did you know?"

I didn't want to let him know that Maebe was the reason for my suspicions, but I would give him a little. Better that he think it was a lucky guess based on my supposed hatred for the Seelie.

"When I was trapped in the Fae Realm, I was hunted by a group of people who tried to kill my friends and I. They would stop at nothing to achieve what they wanted, and that was when Titania was queen. Now, with their new king, he's more ambitious and ruthless than she *ever* was."

I scoured the area a moment to let him think on it before stating, "Wouldn't be surprised if he was looking for some kind of leg up over his peoples' long-time rival—however he thinks he can get it."

Telfino's face was a mask of thought. This kid would make a hell of a ruler.

"And you think he could be the one responsible?"

I shrugged noncommittally. "Maybe."

He sighed. "I will speak to my advisers and go over the list of subjects who have come into our village. I do not recall anyone but the ambassadors from each of the Fae monarchies coming into our city. Do you think I should pull them in for questioning?"

"No." The last thing we needed was to tip them off. "Put out the word for people not to travel alone and for people to watch for suspicious activity, but don't give anyone a hint that you may suspect someone specifically."

"Let that lull them into a false sense of security," he muttered to himself. "Yes. I *can* trust you with this. Please. Help my people. I will assist you in whatever way that I can, but this cannot continue."

*QUEST ALERT!*

*High Elf Highway Robbery – Someone has been stealing from the new king of the high elves, and that is just unacceptable. Find who or what is responsible, and either tell King Telfino or bring him evidence that they have been stopped.*

*Reward: Better relations with King Telfino and his people, ten thousand gold pieces, and a possible favor in the future.*

*Failure: Should you fail to find those responsible, King Telfino's people may choose to believe that you or Maebe could be responsible. You don't want that.*

*Accept? Yes / No?*

I accepted it for the group; it would be better that we do this as best as we could, as quickly as we could.

"Thank you." King Telfino sighed in relief. "Do not worry. You will have my assistance in this matter, and it will go a long way in helping to offer my people a chance to show them that outsiders are capable of good as well as harm."

"I hope to be of service." I smiled genuinely. The kid was alright.

"I must go and see that things are set in motion." He pointed toward the guards that were still leading my friends toward the palace but outside it rather than inside. "May the healers set you all quickly to rights."

"Thank you, Your Highness."

With that, he left. His hurried approach to the palace alarmed the guards at the doors, but he waved them aside.

Oh well. I caught up to the others and went to see about this 'healing' that really just consisted of being prayed at, doused in holy water and then a glance for horns and demon scales.

King Telfino must have told the healers about Yohsuke being an abomination Elf because they paid him little mind once he proved he could take his horns off.

They kept Balmur with Bokaj and Tmont with them for further observation, but they encouraged us to leave.

Yohsuke touched his earring before leaving to let them know we would be available if needed.

I filled the others in on the quests that I had gotten from Maebe and then King Telfino.

"So you gonna share these or what?" Muu asked.

I rolled my eyes and did so. They all accepted.

"We have leads?" James asked, taking out a notebook and enchanted quill.

"Yeah." Rather than risk being overheard, I switched to using our earrings to converse, *I suspect that it could be the Seelie Fae trying to get the upper hand over Maebe and her people. She suspected there were spies among the high elves attempting to learn how to commune with the world the way they do, but something must have happened to up their schedule because they may be kidnapping people with a special tie to learn it or take it.*

*So then we start looking for Fae that don't belong here. Simple.* Yohsuke shrugged.

*Dude, I doubt it would be that simple,* Balmur's voice interjected, startling us. *Sorry, you were talking to all of us, right? Anyway, Bokaj has been filling me in since I had my little... fit. They would likely know that you can see through glamours and have an item that could hide them from that. I doubt their enchanters haven't found a way to counteract the ability to see through glamours by now, so they could reverse engineer something. Sorry, shop talk. But yeah, they may have a way to hide from you.*

*Fuck.* Yohsuke kicked the ground. *Okay. So we have to investigate some other way.*

*Or we can draw them into a trap,* Balmur suggested.

Goddamn, it was good to have the whole team together again!

*We fucking missed you, man,* James smiled as he spoke to the other man mentally. *It's good to have you back.*

*Good to be back. They brought me something to eat, and I'm hungry as hell, so I'm gonna eat now. But we should plan later. Bokaj will keep bringing me up to speed, so don't worry.*

The rest of us had reached the palace entrance and walked through to find the King standing by his seat at the head of a large table filled full of food and drink.

"Please, join me for lunch. I am eager to learn more about

all of you." Telfino smiled sweetly as he motioned to chairs on either side of the table. "Sit, do not stand on ceremony."

*He seems like a good kid, but don't say anything about not being from Brindolla if he doesn't bring it up. I know that there was a big stink about it in the throne room and with the asshat gnome, but we don't know what he knows,* I warned the others as I sat down on the left side of the table.

The others sat down, and we chatted a little. Turns out that the king looked young because, by Elven standards, he was young, but for us, he was in his late sixties.

"My age was a point of contention among my mother's advisors, but they saw wisdom in letting someone also beloved by the Mother rule the kingdom." Telfino took a sip of his water before looking to us, then me. "Have you spoken with them concerning your findings and current quest? I saw that it was accepted by several others."

"I told them a little about it, but we were going to have a strategy meeting about it later, away from prying ears." I blinked as I lazily observed the servants and guards around us, then looked back to him.

Smart kid, but still a little overzealous or wet behind the ears. Either way, I think he got the idea.

"Excellent, thank you—all of you." He bowed his head, steepled this fingers, and closed his eyes. After taking a deep breath and exhaling, he was back with us.

"Are you okay, your Majesty?" Muu asked, the ridges of his brow wrinkling slightly in concern.

"Yes, Master Muu, thank you." The young king tried to look light and breezy, but I finally noticed the signs of exhaustion in him that I hadn't been able to note among my friends.

The kid looked stressed the hell out, and it was affecting him. Was he worried that he wasn't safe? Was there no one here he could trust? Could his people afford for him to? That was a lot to put on a kid. Sixties or not.

*Hey, man, they like animals here, right?* Yohsuke asked me.

I looked at him, confusion on my face, so he continued his

thought, *If they like animals so much, why don't you pretend to be an animal friend of his and keep watch over him so he can get some rest?*

*You can get the fuck out of my head now, thanks.* He snorted, and I looked to the king, chipper now as he stood.

"Thank you all for attending this meal with me." He bowed his head slightly. "It has been enlightening. I bid you all good day. Please, do not hesitate to ask the guard where to find me. They have been instructed to bring you to me should any of you ask for me."

"Thank you for that, your Highness. I must go on some business, but my friends will take great pains to find what they can while I am away. Good day, your Highness." I stood to confused looks from my friends, except Yoh, and stepped out of the room.

*Nobody fuckin' panic—I'm not leaving. I need to go talk to Maebe. Then I'm going to watch over the king,* I told the others as I was leaving.

*Could've said that first. 'Bout gave me a heart attack,* Muu grumbled sullenly. *Go do what you gotta do and let us take some time to level and think.*

I snorted. How many times had I seen him, or rather—*not* seen him in combat until he was rocketing toward the ground and an enemy at breakneck speeds? Yeah. Heart attack. What a character.

First, I went toward the canyon wall where it was secluded and dark so that I could contact Maebe.

I sent my awareness into the shadows and cast Shadow Speak.

A few seconds later, Maebe's form began to rise from the shadows, and her awareness touched mine. It seemed with my awareness in the shadows like this, more detail could be seen. I could sense her minute changes and flecks of emotion in greater detail than I could before.

That was pretty dope.

"You are alive," she said breathlessly.

I grinned. "I told you I would do everything I could to come back and make sure Balmur came with us. He's here, not exactly okay, but we're getting some help with that. How are things there? I heard you had to leave and go to your people?"

"I did. While I was away, some of my people began to disappear and were replaced by highly intelligent, powerful, Dofilnarr, a race of changelings that we had thought we hunted into extinction."

Oh boy. "And you think it was these Doflinor people who are doing this?

"*Dofilnarr*, dangerous beings Zeke," she warned, a tone of don't-you-even-dare in her voice. "Beings that almost took over my court centuries ago. Beings that did take over the Seelie Court completely years before that."

"Well, how powerful can they be?" Then I realized—oh. The Fae *hunted them almost to extinction.* "Scratch that. How do we figure out who has been replaced if there are any here?"

"That is what makes them so powerful." She sighed. "You cannot. Not unless you have... Fae Iron weapons!"

We had some of those. We had access to a lot of them, and not to mention, my arm was one.

"So what, you touch them with it, and they burn or something?"

Maebe shook her shadowy head. "You need to bleed them with it. A small prick will do, but it causes their form to drop for only a second. Otherwise, they adapt everything that their mark has to offer. Including some of their abilities."

Fuck. *Fuck.*

"Okay, baby, you good?" I asked, a new sense of dread creeping into my breast.

"I am well. What is wrong?"

"I need to be sure that my friends are who they say they are and then watch over King Telfino. His people are being kidnapped."

"Fuck," she spat vehemently. I was more than a little taken aback by her sudden use of foul language, and I would definitely be teasing her about it later. "Go. I will return to you once I finish checking for the spies here."

"Good luck, and I'll see you soon." There would be time for us to love on each other later. Rather than calling to the others, I called Kayda out of my collar and spoke urgently as she caught up with my memories.

"Go find King Telfino and watch him." She shrank down to her parrot-sized form so as to be stealthier. "If you see any of the others, do *not* stop, and just show me where they are, okay?"

She ducked her head and took flight, lifting effortlessly into the air and around the palace toward the front. She flooded my mind with images of Muu, Yohsuke, and James walking out of the front entrance to the place. I thanked her, shifted into my owl form, and took off much the same way she had.

As my friends came into sight, I dropped from the sky and plummeted silently. The first one I nicked was James, right on his neck, and nothing happened other than his hand snapping to the spot with an, "Ow, the fu—"

I shifted into my fox form and slid a pointed nail across Muu's hand along the back, and he grunted.

Then I looked to Yohsuke. He held his hand out, and I took my Fae Iron hand and poked his finger, observing him carefully.

Nothing happened. They did look pissed.

"Say nothing to no one. Once I make sure the others are good, I'll let you know what's going on. Stay together." I looked around. "Where's Jaken?"

"He went to go see Questis about something. I think it was about a design or something?" James said and pointed toward the entrance to the palace.

Damn it. "You guys go back to see Bokaj and Balmur. Act like nothing's up, but don't take no for an answer and don't tell anyone what's going on."

Yohsuke nodded and shepherded the others toward the healers' quarters. I shapeshifted, took off past the two guards at the front gate, blowing through their surprised faces.

I banked right and found Jaken on his way toward Questis' rooms with his sword naked in his hand.

I pushed myself harder to beat him to the door and sliced his face with my Fae Iron wing as I flew by. I didn't catch a glimmer, shake, or anything as I flew face first into a wall.

*Where the hell were you on that one, Owl!!*

The instinct simply snorted. *You have much to learn of aerial combat, Druid.*

Asshole. I shifted and stood slowly.

"You okay, man?" Jaken, too concerned about my well-being to care that I had just cut him, hustled over to me.

"Yeah, man, I'm fine," I mumbled. "What're you doing?"

"I was going to see Questis about upping the fighting time for my dancing sword and shield from what they are." He pointed at his long sword. "Why?"

"I can't say. Just put that away and get in my collar. We have a thing to do that can't wait."

He touched the collar and filtered in as gray gas. I shifted once more and took flight, the owl taking pity on me and helping me navigate the crystalline halls.

We arrived at the healer's quarters, and I flew in through the window, shifting and landing to let Jaken out with my friends looking at me expectantly.

I looked at all of them cautiously before stepping over to Bokaj and Balmur and pricking each of them with my green and purple hand. No change.

I sighed in relief. "Thank the Gods."

*You wanna explain what the hell is going on?* Yohsuke asked, slight worry in his voice.

I explained what Maebe had told me, and their expressions said it all. The same thing I had said.

Fuck.

*So that means we travel in pairs at a minimum,* James posed. *We keep constant accountability, and if anyone is alone, we check them. Zeke is the only one who should be immune?*

I poked myself, taking a point of damage as blood dribbled out of my left index finger.

*Okay. Pairs. Zeke pokes himself when we see him. Anyone sees something, they say something.* Jaken sighed. *This got complicated fast, man.*

I nodded. Yeah. It did.

*They were believed to be extinct though, right, so there can't be too many, but we have to be safe. You guys hatch a plan, and I'm going to go take care of the king. Maebe will be with us when she can.*

The others gave a thumb up and turned to talk to each other telepathically as I turned to fly away.

*Be safe out there, man,* I heard Balmur grunt. I looked back to see him eyeing me, evident worry in his features. I could say I felt the same. Getting a friend back after what had felt like so long and after so much trauma and watching them walk away… It had to be a lot for him.

I nodded once and took off toward the palace.

Kayda sent me an image of a lavish room, high in the rear of the palace where she sat on a rail.

I picked myself up and flew higher, arcing over a tower and under a walkway of some kind. I dipped lower, and after a moment, found what I was looking for.

I landed next to Kayda, my owl form slightly larger than her current size.

*Cute,* her mind touched my own, and I settled my feathers. I hopped off the ledge, shifted into my fox form, and wandered inside.

The room was as I had said—lavish, but not in the way one might think. This room was nothing if not covered in nature. The floor was a grassy meadow, complete with brilliantly blooming flowers in a rainbow of colors, shapes, and sizes. A tree, thick and tall, grew straight through the roof that was no longer there. As I looked up, I could see through the illusions and see that this tree was the true top to the palace. The tree below was merely a crystal knockoff of the true tree.

Bushes grew along the sides, holding platters of items and children's knickknacks.

As I walked further in, I could see that a portion of the tree was naturally hollow, like it had grown that way, with a mat of thick moss that grew inches off the ground with blue fungus at the corner that reminded me of pillows.

Across from the bed was a bookshelf with a toadstool that the king used as a seat at a small desk held by branches.

I wandered over and sat on the floor next to him, then shifted into my fox-man form and cleared my throat.

Startled, the king put a hand out, and a deep green bolt of energy flew my direction.

"Highness!" I barked and rolled aside, just barely managing to get out of the way.

He realized it was me. "Master Zekiel, you startled me. To what do I owe this visit?"

"My friends and I were concerned for your wellbeing," I started. I stood and walked closer to him.

He seemed to take my sudden closeness in stride, but he was slightly stiff.

"Highness, have you been sleeping?"

He blinked, smiling. "Elves do not sleep, Master Zeke, and please, when we are alone, you may call me Telfino."

"Sleep, rest, meditative state, whatever it's called—you need more of it." I took his hand in mine, much braver than I felt and lightly nicked his skin. He hissed and drew back his hand, but other than a pained look, nothing changed. "And now I can trust that you are truly King Telfino. We'd better chat."

I told him the gist of my conversation with Maebe, heavy on the details about the Dofilnarr and how I had made sure that the others in my party were good. He was interested in the bit about Fae Iron, but he was mostly worried.

"And you think they could be partially at fault for my people disappearing?"

I nodded grimly. It sucked. And it was going to be shitty.

"I know it's going to be hard, Telfino," I corrected myself before calling him some form of placating name or honorific, "but your people need you to get some rest. I'll watch over you and try to think of a way for us to catch whoever or whatever is at fault."

He eyed me carefully but seemed to acquiesce with a slight nod.

"Don't worry, Kayda and I are here for you." I thought about it and brought Coal out as well but had him sit out on the terrace. "Coal as well."

"Is he…?" Telfino couldn't find words for it, so I nodded.

"My familiar for the time being—with Kayda. He's a fire wolf. Rest. We've got you covered."

He laid on the thick moss and closed his eyes as I took a spot on the grass where I could see the door and the terrace. Kayda sat inside the little opening in the tree, watching Telfino sleep. As I sat, I opened my notifications at long last.

*QUEST ALERT!*

*Quest completed - Hells Hath No Fury Like a Demon Scorned – The Lord of the City, Yttriol, has given you free rein to murder the demons who have defied him by joining in this sanctioned punishment.*

*Kill any demon you like so long as they stand in the sand pit.*

*Reward: A longer lifespan than if you didn't, multiplied EXP, and increased favor with the demons loyal to Yttriol.*

*Bonus Reward: If you make any of them suffer, to include Melvaren.*

*Number of demons slain (total by party) – 147*

*Reanimated puppets – 234*

*Slow and painful kills – 27*

*Average EXP per demon slain by average level (25) equals 42 (294/7)*

*Average EXP per reanimated puppet by average level (15) equals 23 (161/7)*

*Suffering bonus – multiplier x 0.27 for base EXP rounded down to the nearest point.*

*Melvaren's suffering-filled death – 873 (688x0.27) x 5 equals 4,365*
    *Total EXP earned – 18,942*

I had to fight the urge to whistle. Also—where the fuck was all this math in all the other instances of earning experience like this?! Maybe the demon realm was more in touch with the rules of the game than the Prime or the Fae? Because in the Fae realm, game mechanics had all but been gone except leveling up. Maybe I could have a chat with someone who was much more adept at things like this someday and ask them all of these questions I had. For now, it was time to focus, so oh well.

With that much experience, I had leveled up *five times!* Holy crap, and a more than healthy two thousand four hundred forty-two points toward level 37. Holy damn.

Okay. Time to play with the stats!

Twenty-five points could do some serious damage if I decided to choose now to min/max my character. Kind of like some of the others did—once they reached a certain level, their stats would be really heavy in one or two areas, like Muu's strength and Bokaj or Yohsuke's dexterity. Both were crazy high.

But I thrived in being able to do what I needed where I was needed. So, I put four points in wisdom, ten in intelligence, five in constitution and dexterity, and the final point went into charisma.

*Name: Zekiel Erebos*
*Race: Kitsune (Celestial)*
*Level: 36*
*Strength: 52*
*Dexterity: 42*
*Constitution: 40*
*Intelligence: 85*
*Wisdom: 45*
*Charisma: 19*
*Unspent Attribute Points: 0*

Another cool thing was that Kayda and Coal had both earned half of the experience I had gained from that. So they leveled up as well. Coal had gotten five more levels to level 20, and Kayda was now level 21.

First, Coal. His five points that were naturally allocated per level had added two points each to dexterity and constitution. Likely all that dodging and fighting had toughened him up and made him a bit more spry. He also got an added point of intelligence, likely from having to discern which targets needed to be bitten to fuck. His other points, all fifteen of them, went as follows—ten to constitution, two to intelligence, and three to wisdom.

A notification popped up in front of me, and I dismissed it out of habit. I wanted to finish leveling Kayda, then I would see what's up.

Her four levels saw that she had gained two points in wisdom and constitution each naturally, and that left twelve points to use for her. At thirty-one constitution, she was pretty hearty, so I left that this time. I plugged four points into strength, four into dexterity, and four into intelligence. There. Looking pretty, birdie.

As I looked at her stats, I noticed that she had one ability that she could take for reaching a level past twenty.

***Blessed Rain – Caster calls on a healing rainstorm to heal allies and the land with a storm that will potentially harm enemies.***

***The Storm Roc now knows her calling, and her calling is to heal the land and all of the creatures upon it. But woe to those who have raised her ire, for Lightning and Cold are quick to strike at those she sees as a foe. Range: 1 mile radius on the caster. Cost: All mana. Cooldown: three hours.***

That was amazing. Like, really fucking amazing. And it looked like the ability she had used earlier was called Cold Lightning; it mainly mixed her two elements and threw it at an enemy. The cost was 75 MP, but there was only a ten-second cooldown. So that was sweet.

Now, on to this notification.

I opened it up, and my heart dropped.

***QUEST ALERT!***

***Quest completed - Enkindle the Elemental Beast – The Primordial Flame has asked you to oversee the growth of the flame wolf until it is strong enough to return to him.***

***Reward – 3,000 EXP, unknown.***

*It is time, little flame, for my beast to return to his place by my throne,* the crackling, hot voice swept through my being.

I groaned softly, so as not to wake the king, but I couldn't help but feel my heart rending in two. I hadn't known Coal all that long, but he had been a good boy. He had fought with me, risked his life for me and mine. Now, all that love and warmth he provided would be gone.

*Forgive me. I know that you have grown attached, and I feel also that he has as well.*

I looked over, and Coal stood, his body looking beefier and stronger than it had been before thanks to his leveling up. His deep, orange eyes looked at me with the same mirrored heartache that I felt. I stood, my legs a little unsteady and went to him.

As soon as I was outside the reach of the grass, Coal was bumping into my body, his tail wagging like crazy.

"I'm gonna miss you, buddy," I snickered as he headbutted me in excitement.

*Home,* he replied, his hot tongue licking at my cheek affectionately. *Family.*

He sent me a wave of emotion, warmth, a feeling of belonging. He sent me an image of my fighting next to him, of Kayda sharing her food with him, of the party in various states of play as we had been training. Chasing him when he stole food.

He loved us, but then he sent another image. A similar set

of emotions were tied to it. His mother. His family. His *true* master.

"You gotta go home, buddy. I can't keep you from that." I stood and patted his head affectionately. "I'll go trade places with Kayda so you two can say goodbye."

As I walked away from him, his sadness and longing coalesced and hit me together, but I refused to shut our bond. I would share this last memory with him, with this little family we had begun, and we would get through it.

*Go to him, sweetheart. He's hurting, and I know that you are too. Go say goodbye.*

Kayda fluttered past me like a rocket, and as I sat watching over the young Elven king, I lived through the breaking of three hearts simultaneously. It was rough, but finally, Kayda was able to fully convey how she felt.

*Love you, brother.* She sent him images of the two of them playing together, her watching him sleep, and protecting him from those nosey Dwarves. She loved him.

*Love,* he returned. I felt his warmth through our bond once more, and then the Primordial returned.

*I will take him now. There will be a small tear in the rift, but it will seal and likely not be felt for some time. Once I have him, I will return to you with your reward.*

I didn't respond outwardly. I couldn't trust myself to speak at that moment, but I did nod.

I felt a small shift, and then my connection with Coal was gone. It was like losing my arm all over—knowing something was supposed to be there, looking for it and finding it gone.

Kayda, the poor thing, mounted on the terrace where she had stayed for the whole thing cried in anguish.

*He is safely with me. I will not ask you this again, and should you ever find that you have great need, Coal will come to you once more. That is my gift to you. One final summoning. Continue to prove yourself to me, to all of my fellows, and we will continue to bless you and yours and help you to grow.*

"Thank you, Shining One," I whispered.

*You show courage in this. I have not forsaken you, and neither has Coal. Keep my gifts from before. I hope they continue to serve you well. Know that my interest in you is piqued, and I trust you, now more than ever. Burn hot, little flame.*

That last was said with a note of what could have been taken as affection that brought a wry smile to my lips.

I called Kayda to me, and we sat there, just being together. The three grand experience was enough to throw me over the edge to level 37; I spent three points on strength and the other two on dexterity.

I spent the rest of the time in the room, surrounded by nature training. But not in the normal ways. I began to try and see if I could send my awareness into the nature around me. It was hard, as everything seemed to have an awareness of its own, but the plants seemed to be happy that I was there and that I was trying.

That was comforting.

After a bit, I decided to look and see if there were any new abilities or spells that I had gained as a Druid or as a Primal Warrior. I had gained one for Primal Warrior, and it was a *doozy*.

**Beastial Fury – User enters a near-rage-like trance that brings the beast forth in the caster. Strength, dexterity, defense, and reflexes increased. Spell casting restricted for duration. Duration: 30 seconds. Cost: 235 MP. Cooldown: 15 minutes.**

The cost was steep, but I could see having *any* sort of an increase to my stats like that would be insane. The quickened reflexes would be great. I wondered if I could cast it under spell effects like the Aspect spells.

Definitely something to look into when I had some more time.

The others began to telepathically spout off their levels, and if they had gotten anything new. The majority was just powered up old spells, more mana and the like, but everyone was looking good. Muu had leveled up the most at level 35. Balmur level 40,

Bokaj, Jaken, and Yoh all got to level 38. That left James at level 37 with me.

We were getting up there. Kind of wondered what would happen at the next twentieth level mark for me. Balmur was quiet about it, though he did mention something about insanely boosted sneak attack damage. Was it the same as the first? Would we get some insane new abilities? I was eager to find out.

They were upset that Coal was gone, about not getting to say goodbye, or in Balmur's case, hello and goodbye, but they understood that it was time and the final summoning was something we could potentially use later on.

I sat for a while longer in silence. Finally, the King sat up, blinking his eyes. He still looked stressed out but not as weary.

"Welcome back," I greeted him softly.

"Thank you for watching over me." His head quirked to the right. "Something is different. It feels hot."

"My flame wolf Coal was finally strong enough to go home to his true master," I replied with feigned grace. I felt like shit about it, but I knew he was where he belonged.

"You did the right thing." He smiled, and his purple eyes flashed with mirth. "The Mother knows that you loved him. She is proud of you for knowing it was time to let go and for doing so without 'a fight' as she put it?"

I blinked. "How could you possibly–" then it hit me like a ton of shit to the face. "You're a Druid or cleric of some kind, aren't you? But instead of a god, you serve Nature."

His smile waned a bit. "That is dangerous knowledge in these times, Master Zekiel."

"I understand your being weary, but this could work in our favor somehow." I began to think of ways it may when someone interrupted my train of thought.

*Hey. Is the king awake yet?* James asked excitedly.

*Yeah, sup?*

*Ask him if they have some kind of celebration for Mother Nature.*

I looked over at the king and repeated the question. He nodded and explained, "Every year we have one near the solstice. I remember saying something about it before, but we didn't have one due to my coronation and my mother's... funeral."

I told the others, and this time, it was Bokaj who spoke, *That's how we do it. We have someone perform some kind of great thing to the Mother and proclaim that they're the closest to her or that her favor is with them, and then we watch them.*

I explained the plan, and Telfino closed his eyes. They snapped open. "This can be done."

"Good. Let's go spread the word then, Telfino." My vulpine lips curled over my teeth in a grim grin. "We've got a trap to set."

# CHAPTER TWENTY

King Telfino stood proudly on a platform balcony overlooking the entrance to the palace where hundreds of his people gathered to listen to him speak.

"My people," he began, his voice amplified by magic, "our hearts, broken as they are with the loss of our former Queen, my wonderful mother Silvanas, have cause once more to unite in more than just pain."

His gaze swept his rapt people. "They can unite in *thanks*, in gratitude for the Mother, for as one leaf falls, another yet grows in its place, and with it, so too can the love and bounty she shares with us.

My people, I know that I am young. I know that I am not the strongest among us—but I too know that I love each of you as my mother did before me. Join me, join each other, and join with the land as we have done for countless eons before me and countless eons after. Join me, and be my family now in this time of loss. Let us band together, *stronger than ever before*, so that we may continue to flourish with our Mother's love. My people, in three days' time, as is our custom, will you celebrate our new lives together with me?"

There was silence so deep and alarming that I didn't understand it. This kid had just poured his heart out to them, and they stood silently.

One voice, sweet and light came from a small Elven child near the front of the crowd to lift her chin high in concern.

"King Telfino, why are you crying?"

I looked, and he was. He was weeping openly in front of his people.

He smiled. "I have watched my mother speak to you all countless times before, seen her sway you with her words, her wisdom, and her experience. Her values were imparted to me, but I find myself sorely lacking in the rest. All I have to offer all of you is my love, and seeing you all here has overwhelmed me. Please, I beg your pardon, small one. I did not mean to show any of you this weakness."

Kayda, who had been perched in her full glory near the top of the tower, screeched and lifted herself from the crystal to fly over the crowd. In their faces, this sea of high elves below us, I saw fear. Uncertainty. But in more than a few of them, I could swear I saw hope.

As she crested to the top of where she wanted, a single, pure note emanated from her open mouth, a whistle, followed by a round of birdsong I had never expected to hear from the giant bird.

While she sang, a slight mist formed above her, deepening, and then a small shower of warm water began to fall like a spring drizzle.

The elves looked up, mesmerized, but it was the little girl who began to return her song in kind, swaying gently in the falling droplets. The grass on the ground grew slightly deeper green than before and trees seemed to thicken.

I watched, speechless as the people began to play, to shout and giggle and laugh as they just took in this song and dance of joy, and I found myself wanting to do the same. King Telfino, his tears swallowed by the rain, smiled up into the skies.

Rather than lightning crashing down and hitting random

spots, it flashed through the spectral clouds lighting the daylight sky with blueish and green lights, sparks and flashes. It was breathtaking.

As the spell ended, Kayda soared from her spot above and landed next to Telfino, her eyes the same color as his, and he nodded.

"High elves, family, will you join me in this festival of giving thanks to the Mother?!" he shouted with his hands up.

The little girl, her blonde hair swinging wildly over her shoulders, cried, "Yes! Let's play some more!"

The people cheered, seemingly healed by that burst from Kayda. I'd be feeding her some more for that later.

Telfino turned and thanked her softly before she fluttered over and landed next to me.

*Tired*, she grumbled sleepily.

"Sleep there then, my love. I'll call for you when there's food to eat."

*Food?* Her head perked up. Silly thing.

We went back into the palace and began to prepare things on our end. Kayda would stay here, watch over the king, and call to me should anything happen, and the others and I would go over some of the intricacies of the plan to capture these people. First, we would need to decide on the bait.

"How about Questis?" James asked around a mouthful of some delicious pie Yohsuke had managed to bake. The crust was perfectly flaky and the filling tart but still sweet. I had checked in on Kayda, and Telfino had food brought to her secretly on his plate.

"Needs to be someone they think they can get away with, someone who isn't an important figure," I reasoned.

"I don't know man, that's not necessarily the case anymore," Muu observed. "Maebe said it seemed like they were sending spies her way too. They want this. Badly, for some reason, and I don't doubt that they would take someone high profile if they fit their needs."

I had to admit that was a good point. If they thought that

they could overpower them or sweep them away before they could defend themselves, their victim could be anyone. Still, it would be rude to just throw Questis into that role without talking to him.

So we would go talk to him *after* we finished the pie.

I like pie, man. Leave me be.

Though before leaving, I pricked my own finger with my right hand to show them I was cool.

Once we were finished, everyone but Bokaj and Balmur decided to head over and see Questis. They stayed for the next round of 'observations' while the rest of us went to see if the Druid was open to being our mouse to catch these snakes.

These treatments for Balmur would end soon, and we would be able to take him home. At least to Sunrise and let him see everyone. It would be nice. We could get him some better gear, even though he was a higher level than all of us.

We walked the multi-colored crystal hallways with impunity now, King Telfino having had to order his guards to leave us the hell alone after some of them had detained Jaken and Muu for training together.

When we came to Questis' quarters, we found a strange person standing in deep brown robes with their hood up. Next to them stood Shellica.

"About time we met again, lad," Shellica greeted us warmly. The figure just stood statue still as we moved forward. "It's alright, Zell. They're good folk—personal friends of my clan. They won't treat you differently."

The figure spoke then, "If you say so, then, Shell."

They reached a gloved hand up and swept the hood of their cloak back, and I saw an older version of Questis, but the man's skin was gray like Yohsuke's—his eyes a hauntingly beautiful silver color and his hair a shaggy brown close to his cloak's coloring which hung down past his shoulders.

I nodded to the man before sweeping Shellica into a bear hug, stealthily pricking her shoulder, "Ouch! You blasted thing, let me down!"

She was Shellica all right. I then reached out to the cloaked figure but his hands were covered by gloves.

"Hey, Zell!" Yohsuke grinned and stepped forward to shake the other man's hand.

"Ah, Yohsuke, tell me how the weapon did for you." Zell's eyebrows shot up, and he seemed to instantly forget about the rest of us.

"Perfectly, but I did notice a wavering in the astral. I wasn't sure if you wanted to take a look at it?"

"Please, show me." Yohsuke complied to Zell's request, pulling the weapon from the strap on his hip.

The weapon was artfully made, and thanks to my own fighting, I hadn't been able to look at it in detail before. The hilt was essentially a normal looking sword hilt with a small cross guard to protect the which, but the weird part to me was that in the center of the weapon was a metal bar that was shaped like a sword but it was thinner, almost like a rapier, and short as well.

Yohsuke gripped his weapon and breathed out at the same time the weapon sprung to life. The astral warped out from the base of the cross guard and curled around it to engulf the full thing past the top of the center bar by more than a foot and a half. The whole thing looked kind of like a laser sword, and I was *so* jealous.

He took a few steps toward the unoccupied space behind us and began to take the weapon through a series of swings, chops, and thrusts. At certain points, the blade did seem to flicker slightly while he was bringing the weapon up from a lower position.

"Stop. I know what the issue is, and it's a simple fix." Zell stepped forward to take the weapon from Yohsuke.

Taking a set of tools out from his inventory in a tightly rolled bundle, he sat the weapon on the table and then took a seat in front of it. He took his gloves off, the long sheaths of leather folding next to the makeshift workstation.

"You don't have to break it, do you?" I asked, more than a little concerned about the loss of his craftsmanship.

"Whatever gave you that idea?" Zell looked at me, horrified.

"Well, because Questis had done that to look into Yoh's first adaptor," I explained a little less worried now.

The gray-skinned Elf held a steadying hand to his head. "I will be having a chat with my savage little brother about his care of weapons. Thank you, Master Erebos" He turned his focus back to the item before him. "Now, I need quiet, so please hold your questions, comments and observations until after I finish. Thank you."

Over the course of a few seconds, he took a small saw out and began to carve through the glue that held the leather on to the hilt near the pommel in seconds. Taking a couple minutes after that, he worked the leather strips off in quickening succession. He must have found his stride.

He took what looked like a wand and began to carve through the side of the bared portion of metal just below the cross guard, and with a *pop*, the metal released to show a crystal inside.

"Shellica, look at this and see if you can tell me what the issue is," Zell ordered softly.

The Dwarven enchanter walked over to the desk and peered inside, lifting the weapon and turning it to and fro. "The crystal isn't seated properly, and it looks like the only thing keeping it in is the minor rune on the inside of the setting and the sheer size of the crystal."

Zell's lips curled into a soft smile. "Correct. How do we get the crystal seated then? Explain as you go about it."

She motioned to the tools, and Zell stood to allow her to sit down.

"First, we slightly heat the metal of the improperly bent prong in the setting. Then we slightly hammer it back to allow the crystal to fall in." Shellica took a small tool that looked like it had a weirdly hooked hammer head on it and began to gently tap the cherry red prong toward her. "The crystal will then fall into place thanks to the purified rune of holding. Then we reheat and tap the prong into place, ensuring at the same time not to strike the crystal and conforming it to the facets."

As she worked, Zell closed his eyes, his ears shifting slightly like a dog's might. He frowned. "You struck the crystal, Shellica. Do be more considerate, please."

"Yes, sir," Shellica responded calmly. She refocused on her work, and I had to admit, while it was good to see the tables turned, it made me realize how much of a dick I had been in venting my frustration on her during my own training.

As she finished, she held the item out to Zell for him to inspect.

"This is wonderful work—Dwarven artisanal work is as superb as I recall," He pointed to a minuscule blemish on the crystal itself. "This can be fixed, but it is something to *always* be mindful of. A crack or chip in a mana crystal like this could explode and kill someone of Yohsuke's strength and mana depth."

"I will be more careful in the future, Zell. Thank you." Shellica nodded to him as she stood and relinquished her seat so that he could focus on putting the item back together.

That process was much simpler and a damn sight faster as well. After putting something on to the blemish, the opening was sealed with some kind of putty that melded with the metal perfectly. He applied a bit of strong adhesive glue to the metal as he perfectly rewound the leather about the hilt once more.

He handed the weapon back to Yohsuke, who went through the same motions, but there was no flicker this time.

"Hey, thanks, you guys!" Yohsuke grinned happily.

Before Zell could put his gloves back on, I crossed the distance between us and grasped his hand, my nails digging into the back of his in my 'excitement'.

"That's some amazing work, Zell. Have room for another apprentice?" I asked hopefully as I noted his demeanor only changed to that of an annoyed Elf when I touched him.

He lifted my Fae Iron hand in front of us and blinked at me

with his silver eyes deadpan as he asked, "How did this come about then?"

I blushed fiercely but ducked my head. "I got cocky and took on an enchanting project I shouldn't have. I'm glad that this was the worst of the damage, and that I was the one worse off."

"This was born of a carelessness that would cost you and possibly many others their lives." I had no doubts that he didn't need the exact details to know what he stated was the truth. "No. I cannot have such a reckless person under my tutelage in such a precise and exacting art."

He dropped my hand then, leaving me feeling more than a little defeated and embarrassed.

"It is nothing personal, young one, but I cannot accept any but a grandmaster in the craft in the best of times, and the only other I have taught of less than grandmaster rank was an especially gifted and studious child. She was a wonderful student." He broke from his small reverie and blinked at me again. "I assume that you still have Shellica to teach you so that you never make that same mistake again, but what she decides that you are ready to know is up to her and her esteem of you."

"He's a good student when he doesn't have his head lodged up his furry arse." Shellica beamed at me, but I saw a new emotion under her teasing.

Anger. She was angry with me. I'd have to weather that later.

"Do you guys know where Questis would be?" Jaken asked, seeing the tension beginning to go above what he was comfortable with.

"We had been wondering for ourselves that same thing, actually." Shellica scratched her head and looked around. "There are so many components strewn about here that it's making me want to enchant things. Come here, lad. Let me take a look at that contraption attached to you."

I did as she requested, and she grabbed it roughly. It didn't hurt really, but I still grunted. "Ow, you old bat!"

Her eyes whipped to my face, and her grip became crushing as she pulled me down toward her where she whispered harshly, "You learned a hard lesson, lad—harder still if ye think that it's over. Should you *ever* put ye'self in danger from lack of fore-thought for enchantin' again, I will beat yer hide until yer hide is as blue as yer eyes, and I'll nae teach ye again after. *Think lad. Think.* Use that lump three feet above yer arse."

Thoroughly chastised, I could see the worry in her features, and I answered her, "Yes, ma'am."

She slapped my cheek and turned her attention to the arm once more, "This craftsmanship is unrivaled, and the enchant-ment like things I've never seen. Where did you get this?"

"Queen Maebe called in a favor so that an enchanter she knows would make it." I flexed the arm and waggled the fingers for her to show her the range it had—how it was just like the hand I had lost.

"Cost you dearly, then with that experience cost, and I hear the one who made this is teaching Vilmas?"

"She's a grandmaster now!" Muu squealed excitedly.

"Oh, aye? Well, I always knew she had it in her." Shellica smiled proudly. "Just needed to break out of her shell is all."

"What are all of you doing here at once?" A disheveled-looking Questis shuffled into the room. "Brother, friends. How may I help you?"

I stepped closer to him, and as soon as I did, I wondered, "Where's Fern?"

Questis looked confused a moment. "Fern? He's out getting some supplies for me from vendors."

Unless all the vendors could speak to animals, how would they know what he needed to collect? And Questis hadn't had the neatest office, but this was still messier than the norm.

*Might have a Dofilnarr here, guys,* I warned the others.

*Do what you have to, man. We got the enchanters taken care of.* Jaken stepped forward with a smile. "We were actually here about the festival in a couple days. We wanted to know if you could help us with a surprise for the city."

"Oh?" He looked genuinely interested. The evil bastard. "What is that?"

I closed in on him casually, as though I was going to hand him something out of my pocket, and when I was about to drop this 'thing' into his open hand, I sliced down as swiftly as I could, bloodying the offered hand.

The fur on the back of my neck raised, and I ducked just beneath an astral weapon of some kind. I shifted into my fox form to avoid another swipe.

"Would you stop trying to kill someone in my apartments, Zell?!" Questis bellowed as he held his injured hand to him. It glowed with golden energy. "Thank you, Jaken."

"He injured you, Questis. That was malicious and uncalled for!" Zell growled as he stalked after me. My friends stepping in front of him.

I shifted back and looked to my friends. "No change?"

James shook his head, and Muu pointed toward my six. "Duck."

I sighed and ducked as the attack sliced a bit of the excess fur from my right ear tip.

"We're cool, Zell. I'm not trying to hurt anyone. We're on a quest from the King." That got him to stop, but his weapon stayed activated.

"Speak," the gray Elf ordered.

"We need to be sure we're not heard," Yohsuke stopped me.

Zell muttered some kind of incantation, and James was on top of him as he finished, just in case. A small dome the size of a tent appeared in front of him, and James smacked it, sailing through and losing his balance.

"Come in, and be quick about it." Zell's head poked outside the thing, and we wandered inside. "This is a dome of peace and solitude. A spell of my own design so that I can work silently. We hear dulled noises from outside, but nothing can hear us outside from in here. *Speak.*"

And I did. We told them about the Dofilnarr and how we were trying to help stop people from being taken. We left

Maebe's predicament out. Didn't know if these guys were team Unseelie or not, and I wouldn't risk that.

He blinked at me before asking, "What?"

"You look disheveled, the place is a mess." I motioned around us. "You okay?"

"It was Fern who did this. The naughty little thing has been acting up because he felt slighted over your last visit."

That did sound like Fern. The little asshat.

"Let me venture a guess—you wish for me to be the bait in this trap?" Questis asked as he ran his hand through his hair.

"Pretty much," Muu replied indelicately.

Leave it to the fuckin' Dragon in the room to be brutish about things.

"Okay, I will assist you as King Telfino has offered himself in service to this quest." Questis looked to his brother. "And you, Zell? You required?"

"I was coming to see how you were and to adequately introduce you to Shellica. She was taken before I could do so previously. She has many Dwarven techniques for gem craft and accessories that we do not. I thought you might like to speak with her at length about these kinds of things as a fellow enchanter."

Questis considered the spoken meanings and seemed to find them amiable. "I would be delighted to sit and discuss things over a meal, if you would be willing, lady Shellica?"

"I would be happy to, Questis," Shellica agreed. "What is this plan then, lads?"

"The less people who know, the safer it will be," Jaken advised wisely. "It's bad enough we have to put others in harm's way for this, but our options on rooting these guys out are limited."

"That's noble of you, but these are my people, predilections toward my parentage aside. I will assist in their defense." Zell raised his head in challenge, and it was Questis who took it up.

"Brother, you can help in your own way. Keep an eye out for things that we cannot. You remember the item you had been working on that detected portals?" Zell nodded with an uncertain look on his face. "We need you to work on that and see if there is anywhere that a portal has been opened within the city. Specifically, one to the Fae Realm. Can you do that?"

"I will assist you," Shellica stated. It was fact. She wasn't going to take no for an answer.

Good for her, and their doing that would keep them out of harm's way. Hopefully.

Hey—she might have just threatened me, but I didn't want her to be in any kind of danger. That threat had come from a good place.

"That's fine, so long as you are safe—we're cool," James spoke before I could. "And so far as your role, Questis, the king and Zeke will fill you in tomorrow when they meet."

"Thank you, I look forward to my role and will prepare in any way that I can." Questis bowed his head slightly, then clapped. "Ah, Fern, I trust the vendors found the note unsullied by your drooling?"

I turned to see the great cat sauntering into the room with a basket of components and crystals in it. The cat dropped it and growled, "You think your insult is clever, Elf? I will have my vengeance upon you."

"Such a wonderful kitty," the High Elf spoke to the rest of us as if the cat had no clue.

I snickered and heard the cat growl menacingly, "Druids." He walked away in disgust.

The rest of the day was spent in a blur of plotting, enchanting, and more enchanting.

Questis was a hard but understanding instructor.

"Your will and intent are good. Your mana control needs work, but you will have plenty of time for that." He looked over the sheet of metal I had used to practice the engraving I wanted to use on it. "Your engraving is... interesting. Why do you not use runes?"

"Uh, because I don't know any?" I replied uncertainly.

His head tilted to the side in a surprisingly cat-like gesture. "How do you engrave then? Simply by pictures and will?"

I nodded and motioned to my gear.

"How delightful." The Druid leaned closer to the item in front of him. "I could teach you some rudimentary runes, but at your level, incorporating them without formal training to understand the meanings could be a compromising situation that I do not believe you want to be in. Maybe when you are of adept or possibly even master level and have the time to commit to such a study."

"That would be nice, but what's the difference to having runes as opposed to having the small pictographs I use now?"

"To be succinct?" He raised an eyebrow. "Strength. A properly laid rune in a sentence form or even a Prime one would enhance your enchantments exponentially, but that is an Elven art that most do not know. Even Shellica was surprised, but she has proven an apt pupil under my brother's tutelage, and I can see her picking up runecraft very quickly."

"Yeah, she's a badass." I smiled at the memory of her teaching me—then shivered. "She's a hardass too."

Questis frowned as he looked down over me. "Quite. Your work here will be well enough. Please, continue."

So I did. I created some new arrows for Bokaj. Those were a lot of fun, though the majority were repeats. Three Fireball arrows, twenty-five Lightning arrows, seventeen Snare arrows, and thirty armor piercing arrows with his anti-healing shafts.

I did, however, have a few other… creative ideas that I wanted to try. And surprisingly?

They worked!

***Warp Trap Arrow (set)***

***+5 to damage, teleporting (minor) effect tethered to an anchor point within the range of effect. Distance from anchor to arrow based on intelligence of the enchanter. 20 feet base + (85 intelligence divided by five = 17 feet) for a maximum of 37 feet in range.***

***Warp Trap Anchor (set)***

*Anchor point for a warped enemy. This will not hold the person but gets them where you want, sort of.*

The next item I made on thin, three-foot square plates of metal and the engraving that looked like a spider's web.

*Pressure Prison*

*Once the face of this item is touched, the victim is held in place, frozen completely for a single hour. Use this wisely!*

I'd be lying if I said that I had thought of that last one on my own. Questis had questioned me about having a plan once they warped to the points unless we wanted them to split. So he suggested that. I made a supply of ten, praying that no more than that showed up.

But hey—we could always murder the extras. Hello, EXP! Sorry. Back to the story.

"Thank you, Questis. That's really awesome, man, and now I'm level 44 in enchanting!" I smiled and held my fist out to him.

He seemed to gather the notion and slammed his fist into mine excitedly. It hurt, but it was cool. We's bros now.

"I am glad that I can help you potentially save my life," he joked almost dryly. "Now, I have preparations of my own to make. Is there anything else I can assist you with?"

"No, thanks again." I stood and stretched my aching muscles as I searched for anything out of sorts. "The king and I are meeting sometime tomorrow. I think I might also have an idea for a type of arrow similar to the warp trap, but it's scrambled in my head right now, and I want to get it together before I see you next to discuss it."

"I am truly excited to see what this endeavor will be." He nodded to me as I left.

I walked too close to Fern as I was leaving, and the cat swatted at me in displeasure.

"Fern!" Questis reprimanded sternly. "Is that any way to treat a guest?"

"It is if said guest is an annoying Druid," Fern replied

434

angrily. "His tails look stupid."

I blasted the cat with a Snare spell and left as Questis howled with laughter. "That's what you get, you naughty kitty!"

I could still hear the threats from the yowling cat as I exited the palace. Today, I would go flying to see if I could find another worthy familiar—or companion, really. I wasn't going to force an animal to bond with me.

I let the others know what was going on, and James told me to be safe and stay high if I could help it.

As I flew in the late afternoon sun, finding precious little of interest, my thoughts turned to Maebe, and I wondered if all was well. I didn't want to contact her in case she was busy. Rooting out spies seemed hard if it was anything close to what we were doing presently.

Then my thoughts turned to the elementals. I would really need to start playing with the abilities they gave me. Earth and fire were both cool as fuck, and I think earth really liked me. Fire trusted me; he had to because he's allowed me to keep Coal safe and help him to grow strong. Wind was a douche, let's be honest here. And water—water was an enigma. She wanted to help, but she wanted to be feared? Respected? All of the above?

It was a lot. I needed a powerful familiar or one that would offer me a viable combat option, like Kayda had. I had the sky covered, so I needed something on the ground. Possibly a heavy hitter, but I didn't know what kind of restrictions I had for companions. Then again, maybe I didn't have any?

I mean, I had a fucking myth watching over Telfino as I flew about doing nothing but trying to find a way to grow stronger. This was real shit. I needed to stop thinking with where my heart was concerned and get my gamer ass in gear. Maybe I could craft one? Nah. Maybe not. Maybe Maebe knew of shadow animals I could talk to?

Were there any? Who knew.

Maybe I could have Maebe bring an Ursolon for me to have as a companion? Nah. Those things were big as fuck, smelled funky, and had tempers like a drunk who just found out that the kitchen at the bar was closed.

Nasty fuckers. Glad I had that form, though. Come to think of it, I had never heard the instincts of the Ursolon before. I hadn't changed into that shape since I had gotten my new subclass. I'd have to go introduce myself. I honestly would have to introduce myself to all of them. I had so many forms now.

Let's see, Ursolon, Sabertooth, owl, dire wolf, lion, belgar, octopus—that was a mini version—and spid...er. Ew. My bear and panther forms seemed to upgrade with the introduction of the two stronger forms of similar animals, so they were gone. And that didn't include my fox form, which was a natural form. Then I had fire, earth, wind, and water elemental shapes I could take.

A lot of forms. I had favorites, but it was a companion I needed now. Oh well, it'll have to wait.

I landed and shifted as I headed toward my room in the palace, the king's quarters, where Kayda confirmed he was studying. I stayed on the terrace a moment and called to the others through our earrings.

*You lot okay?*

*We've all been working in teams to be sure that we're good,* Yohsuke answered. *Getting pissed off that the cooks won't let me train with them, but it is what it is. Fuck them.*

Yup. That was Yohsuke for sure.

*Gonna be going down for the day. Bokaj, I got you some more arrows. I'll give them to you the next time we meet up.* A thought occurred to me. *Anyone taking care of Balmur's armor situation? Need anything enchanted?*

*Nah, brother,* Bokaj answered. *Got a set that he's going to like for now. Not the best, and we will need to get him some weapons the next time we're able that aren't strictly holy, but it will work for now.*

*Cool. Night y'all.*

The others gave their goodbyes before I turned to walk into the King's quarters. He had been so kind as to ask the room to make a bed of moss for me near the door.

No, I did *not* feel like a pet. That would be crazy. So no. Don't think it. Stop it. Okay, fine. Be that way.

"Master Zekiel," Telfino greeted from behind his book. "Is there anything I need to know?"

I reached out and pricked the finger he offered me after I gave him a knowing look. I pricked it with my Fae iron claw, and when he didn't change or do anything, I relaxed.

"Questis will be the bait for our trap." I took a seat on his bed. "I've enchanted some fun, new arrows for Bokaj, then made a few more that are designed to teleport the person attacked to an anchor within thirty-seven feet. Questis helped me make another item that traps the person who touches it."

Telfino raised his eyebrows. "Are you sure you wish for it to be Questis? He's pretty strong."

I explained our reasoning, and he seemed to take that as good enough. "Is there anything I can do for you?"

I offered him a sad smile. "You have a really powerful companion in here that I can take with me?" He shook his head. "Anything to help me grow more powerful as a Druid?"

"Mother Nature said to stop being a petulant child." Telfino grinned.

"She would. But yeah, I hear you." I sighed deeply. "We appreciate you being so cool. I think we've got this plan handled, but your role is going to be huge in this. You going to be okay?"

"I have no choice but to be." The king smiled sadly. "My people need me to be strong and to perform well. The Mother will watch over us all as best as she can."

"I know she will. I just want you all to be safe."

"Life is not safe, Master Zekiel," Telfino observed, lifting his book but staring at me. "Survival is a tenant of life among all of the Mother's creatures. All of her children. To survive, you must struggle and sometimes take risks. My survival is nothing if my people—my family—are endangered. You know this to be truth as surely as I do."

"The truth can still suck, Telfino." I looked at him, his

young-looking face mildly confused at the turn of phrase. "It's not good. The truth can still be unpleasant."

"You should have said as much." He chuckled at me. "I would have to give you that, 'to expect less would be folly on your part.'"

"Wow, you really are a wise ass." I had to smile at him. Young for an Elf, old for me. The kid was going places. "I'm going to take the time to rest before tomorrow. If you need me, let me know."

"Rest well, Master Zekiel." Telfino flipped the page.

"Hey, if you're going to have me refer to you as Telfino when we're alone, then call me Zeke. We're friends now, majesty." I gave the kid an exaggerated wink and my best, winningest smile. "At least that's how I see it. We both serve the Mother. To me? That's the start of brotherhood."

"Very well." He put his book down and stared at me as he mulled over his thoughts. "What would you say to telling me more about you personally? As a Druid, you seem… different somehow."

I quirked my head but remained silent.

"I don't mean to be insulting or to insinuate anything negative by it, but you aren't like Questis or the other Druids in our community." He frowned in thought. "Your power is off slightly. Your power radiates more beast than animal. More…"

He didn't seem to be able to find the right word, so I offered one, "Primal."

He smacked his hand on the desk and pointed at me. "Yes!"

I nodded, in Druidic I asked the Mother, "Is it okay to share this?"

*He is a cleric, the only cleric I have. He is more akin to you than any other Druid I have in my service because of how you both differ. You can trust him.*

I felt her presence around us, and my mind settled.

"Because I am different. My friends know that I am as well, but the significance of it I think is lost on them because they're pretty awesome too." I eyed him steadily, thinking of how to say things. Better to show, then tell. "I'm going to show you what I can do, and I want you to know that I mean no harm. Okay?"

"I trust you. So does the Mother."

I shifted into my Ursolon form. The huge bear, black fur with light, soft white strips along the body and stood to my full height.

A deep bass voice tumbled through my mind, *We gonna eat the little thing, or are you teasing me, Druid?*

*He's a king, though it is nice to meet you. I look forward to fighting with you some time.*

The ursolon's instincts grunted and retracted.

"That is magnificent. I read about animals like that in the Fae realms!" He stepped closer to observe me, but I shifted back, then spent the mana to shift into my air elemental form.

This was one I hadn't used before. The form was light, but I looked down, and my body resembled a dervish about my height and thickness.

"Amazing," Telfino whispered in awe. He looked closer and narrowed his eyes at the wind that loosed from me without thought.

I dropped the form, and he blinked in surprise. "This next bit is what makes me different."

I cast Aspect of the Ursolon. I grew taller, broader, and my body thickened as my muscles grew more dense. My vulpine snout shortened into a more ursine maw.

My voice, deeper and a little more like a growl trickled from my throat as I explained, "I am a Primal Warrior. The first of my kind. I use aspects of the animals whose forms I take to strengthen myself for combat. I am trusted by the elemental Primordials, and their trust brings power. Their blessings have aided my friends and me in combat many times. Without them, without Mother Nature or my friends, or the blessings of the Primordial Elementals and the shadows, I would be long dead."

"This is incredible." He seemed stunned. "How long have you been able to do these things?"

"A while for some things, less so for others. Though I think

I'm getting the hang of it, even if I could definitely plan better at times." I scratched my head and then dismissed the spell. "I can do other things, but I think because I'm not a typical Druid, I got a bit of a power-up for a subclass. I thank the Mother for that."

"You are welcome," Telfino said with a smile as he must have answered for her. "Thank you for sharing this with me. I have much to think upon, Zeke."

"Good night, Telfino."

Before going to bed, I decided that I would splurge with the points I had acquired and buy Epicenter. Who knew when a ridiculously heavy great axe would be useful for a single strike.

I listened for the king to turn to the next page of his book, then closed my eyes and let Kayda take the first shift.

———

The following morning, during breakfast in the king's chambers, we checked that everyone was good, then began to eat together. The spread was nice, though the conversation was somewhat heavy.

The main event, which was a ceremonial prayer to Mother Nature, was going to be orchestrated by the King, as was law. When he finished praying, he would ask that the crowd bring forth their tithes to the land around them. This would normally be in the form of a seed from a favorite kind of flower that would be planted in the central garden in a section of the city we had yet to see.

"The plan is for Questis to bring a seed that will grow rapidly like, on the spot," I explained. "Can you see that happening?"

"We will have our blessing," Telfino assured. "I will also ask that you dress so that your marking be visible to all tomorrow, Questis."

"Yes, your Highness." Questis bowed his head. "Where will my guardians be then?"

Bokaj spoke first, "Balmur and I will watch over Questis throughout the night in shifts with Tmont. Then T' and I will join the others in their places."

"Jaken, Muu, and James will be waiting in the orchard where the Mother will want you to go and pray so that she may speak with you," Yohsuke explained. "The Ranger group will meet them before sun up. From there, I will be a part of the King's Guard who follow you to the orchard. I'll be in ceremonial robes so that I'm covered, and no one knows who is there. The others will leave, but I will stay to see that no one bothers you."

"While you are en route there, I will be following you to the scene stealthily," Balmur advised. "I won't be seen, but I'll be close. So don't look for me."

Finally, I added, "I'll be providing air support, so that way, if anything weird happens, I can drop in. Kayda will be watching over the king."

"Setup will be concluded today, and the ceremony begins at dawn tomorrow," Telfino explained. He took a bit of his food, contemplating his next words carefully. "I thank you all for your assistance in this. It has been long in coming, but if this is a success, there will be a new era of hope among my people, an easing of our formerly closed-off ways, and I hope, an opening of their hearts."

"We're happy to do what we can, Majesty," Muu said after finishing a mouthful of fruit.

"We will see this to rights. Don't you worry, Highness." Bokaj grinned.

We ate the rest of our food in companionable conversation, Telfino spoiling Kayda with meats that she snatched out of the air greedily.

Once we were done with that, I stayed and began to train while the others went off to prepare in their own ways. I gave Bokaj his arrows, and the others smiled.

"How is it that you plan to train?" Telfino asked.

"Well, I was going to try and come up with some more

powerful spells and then practice my shifting." I stretched slowly —partially because I was stiff and just as much stuffed. Needed to get that full feeling to go away so I could focus. "Do you train at all?"

"I have trained to fight since I was much younger, but the act of it bothers me somewhat." The king motioned to a corner where a practice sword lay on a bench, collecting dust.

"The act of combat or the act of practicing to fight with a sword?" I asked politely.

The king looked at me oddly, so I continued, "You're a cleric. Your powers generally lean more toward healing, and you find hurting or killing things disdainful unless they're unpure or undead things. Sound about right?"

He blinked before nodding once with a blank face.

"Have you tried blunt weapons? Like a mace or hammer?" I hefted out my great axe, Magus Bane, digging into the floor a little.

"High elves do not fight with blunt weapons," he stated as if it were ingrained.

Which it likely was. Elves throughout most of the media that I've ever gotten my grubby mitts on were known for using their superhuman speed and accuracy as assassins, peerless archers, Mages, and all kinds of things, but I'd never really heard of an Elf using blunt weapons outside of a staff. Could I convince him to start?

"Elves may not, but a king?" I began with dripping skepticism. "One who clings too hard to a tradition that limits his people. Telfino, you're better than that."

"Well then, what would you suggest, oh He-Who-Knows-What-Is-Best?" The king dipped his head as he sarcastically bowed. It sounded like he was irritated.

I blinked at him slowly; he was adorable. "Try a blunt weapon for once. It's not cutting or stabbing anyone, and the harm can be minimal if you only knock them unconscious."

He seemed to study my face for a time. Likely trying to

decide if I was being genuine or not, but I gave away nothing because I was just trying to help.

He walked over to his tree and leaned his forehead against the wood before beginning to pray. When he finished, the tree began to shudder, and a thick branch began to grow from the place he had placed his head.

He motioned to my axe, then nodded to the limb. I snorted and offered it to him. He lifted it unsteadily, and I stopped him. I'd do it.

I lifted my axe and activated Cleave as I brought the weapon down as close to the trunk as possible.

I crashed straight through it, and the limb fell. I immediately cast Regrowth on the tree and patted it affectionately. It was a cool tree.

Not like I was gonna try to hug it.

I cast Regrowth on the limb as well. It was the size of a staff, just about as tall as the king, and the top was a large knot about the size of a small melon.

"Now what?" He raised his eyebrows in challenge.

"Now you practice with it until you get a feel for it, and then I beat your ass for doubting me." He looked taken aback, so I grinned and added a slight bow with, "Your *Majesty*."

I felt a thrill that I couldn't quite place and stepped to the left as the newly made weapon cracked into the floor where my head had been.

I looked up to see the king smiling. "I'll make you eat those words."

"Well, let's make that a little sturdier, and then we can start for real, eh?" I held a hand out, and Telfino slapped the weapon into my hand.

I used some mithral shavings to strengthen it, and I also added some increased damage to it. If he decided he liked blunt weapons, I'd try to get him a better staff or whatever weapon he chose.

I tossed the weapon back to him, and we began to spar. Once he got the hang of the weapon, he began to try and get fancy with it, and I ended up slapping him with the side of Magus Bane hard enough to send him crashing into the tree.

"Ow," he groaned pitiably.

"Get fancy when you're better with the weapon, Highness." I offered him a hand up.

He took it, and as he stood, he clobbered me in the stomach with it and bounced away from me.

"Little… shit," I grumbled.

"That was a low blow, Zeke, forgive me." He chuckled. "Will you show me how to use a weapon like this without 'beating my ass?'"

"Yup. Sure thing," I grunted as I stood to my feet.

After that, he and I spent a couple hours practicing while I offered him pointers on fighting with a two-handed weapon. The fundamentals were the same. Make sure you beat someone's face with the big end and use momentum to help yourself when crushing your enemies. Then we went over overhead, horizontal, and diagonal swings and how to properly use his hips when swinging so he could smack an enemy with his full strength.

By the end of it, we were both tired enough to just fall straight to sleep and meditation. It was nice to be able to help him some more. Him being able to defend himself without having to rely solely on magic was important.

# CHAPTER TWENTY-ONE

"Zeke!" the king called urgently.

I launched myself out of the bed. I had fallen asleep with my great axe in hand and began to look wildly around for a target to whack.

The king looked at me, halfway through fastening a silver and gold robe over his lithe figure and soft leather armor.

"If you don't hurry, we will be late." He tossed me an apple, and I gobbled it up greedily with a muttered thanks. I deposited Magus Bane into my inventory and kept lookout while he dressed. Before he finished, I jabbed his hand with a claw. Blood but no different.

"I will be immeasurably grateful when you do not have to do that," Telfino muttered.

"Me too." I tossed the apple core into my inventory to save the seeds for later. I'd try experimenting with growing plants.

You know, Druid stuff.

*You guys in position?* I called to the others.

*Unfortunately,* grumbled Muu. *The sun isn't even up yet. These people and their damn early mornings. Bokaj, Jaken, and James are here too. We have the high ground, and we're not visible—I don't think.*

Balmur chuckled into our heads. *You aren't. I snuck through and cast invisibility on you guys while you were speaking. I'm on my way back to the ceremony. The place looks great, by the way.*

*Thanks, buddy.* I turned to the king. "They're set."

*I'm with the guards outside the king's doorway now,* Yohsuke advised a second before a knock sounded at the door.

"Let us go then," Telfino spoke, his demeanor shifting more regal than it had been. He picked up the staff that he had used to practice and began to step with it as if it were a walking stick.

*Kayda, watch over him.* The bird in her parrot sized form fluttered over to land on his shoulder affectionately.

I nodded and shifted into my owl form then flitted to a limb above the doorway so that I could see the others as they gathered on either side of the king.

As they left, I ducked out the door as one guard closed it and fluttered along slowly.

The procession moved quickly, attempting to get the king to the ceremony as swiftly as they safely could.

They were down the hall and out into the pre-dawn light of day in a little under seven minutes.

*Got eyes on the king. Zeke has overwatch,* Balmur informed the others. *I'm standing by for Questis.*

The others remained quiet just in case, but Muu finally responded, *'K.*

Dork.

The king made his way with his guard unobstructed to a large plot of circular ground that looked to have been freshly tilled and watered by the dew of the night air.

Soon, elves began to crowd the area, lining up with fists clenched in front of them as they looked to their king.

*Questis is on the move,* Balmur advised.

I watched from a perch on a nearby roof as the festivities unfolded. With the sun still a little ways off, the people began to file around the plot, starting on the inside of the garden. They would place a seed, cover it, and it would sprout a little. Then the next. Hundreds of elves moved in and out in a single file line in mere moments; it seemed that a representative of each home was sent forth. Smart.

Almost like an intricate dance. They would bustle forward, do their business, and hustle away to watch. As the light from the east filtered through the clouds, the last of the line was dwindling and there stood Questis. Waiting.

When it was his turn, Questis brought a pine cone forth and lovingly planted it as the sun crested the side of the valley.

The sunlight streamed in, and as we watched, the elves swayed to a prayer, and all kinds of flowers began to grow rapidly. Small sapling trees budded, bushes, roses flared, and petals burst out of buds. An army of floral beauties blooming in full glory to the Mother's majesty and love for these people, but the plant that Questis planted, the pine cone, grew and grew.

The tree grew until it was full sized, and the growth surpassed all the other growths in the garden. Just as planned. It began to glow with a golden, then green, then purple light.

As the crowd watched in wonder, Telfino stepped toward the tree and pressed his palm on to the bark, closing his eyes.

The king opened his eyes. "Druid Questis! Come forward."

The Druid stepped closer to the king.

"Beloved by Mother Nature, strengthened by her favor, go forth to the orchard to the tree tied with ribbon so that she may speak with you her will for this season." King Telfino looked proudly to his people. "Our prayers are lifted and our bounty returns! Her love has not forsaken us!"

The elves cheered wildly! Families hugged each other, some folks wept with joy, others jealousy, but their spirits were lifted.

"Guard, escort our beloved to the orchard," Telfino pointed to Yohsuke in the front, "and you, stay with him while he prays so that he is unbothered. Escort him to me when he is finished."

As the guards filed away, I took note of some people leaving the celebration, but they didn't seem to be heading toward the orchard. They were heading into homes. Not too suspicious, I didn't think.

The guards, eager to please their king and get back to the

festivities that had begun—lively music and food were beginning to sprout from different places among the crowd—walked swiftly with Questis to the orchard. Once they arrived, I watched as they left him with a nod, and Yohsuke escorted him further into the orchard.

Yohsuke sounded into our heads, *See something, say something. Don't be shy about it, boys.*

*Yup,* Bokaj, Muu, and Jaken answered.

*Something from downwind of me smells like lilacs,* James advised. *I'll keep an eye out, but it feels weird.*

I had no clue where he was, but I wasn't going to abandon my post to go check out a scent that could be almost anything. I mean, hundreds of plants did *literally* just bloom in close proximity. It could be anything

I scanned the area, checking in with Kayda. The king was fine.

*Moving on the tree,* Balmur whispered.

Yohsuke stopped just outside the clearing that the tree was in. It was the largest and looked the most well-kept of all the trees in the orchard. Thick, juicy-looking fruits that I didn't recognize grew on it, and around the base of the trunk was a large, purple ribbon.

*Balmur, tell Questis that he needs to actually pray, just in case anyone is watching to lend it credibility,* Jaken broadcasted.

Questis knelt in front of the large tree, closed his eyes, and began to mouth words.

I settled on a branch in the leaves above him, within easy touching distance of a large piece of fruit. It was purple and green and looked to be almost orange-like in shape, but it was the size of a soccer ball. Wild fruits these.

We sat there for a time, periodically checking in with each other. After half an hour, we began to grow weary of waiting, wondering if somehow the trap had been a failed plot. After the first hour, we knew that if they hadn't come yet, they weren't going to.

*Alright, guys. Balmur, have Questis pack it in, and let's get back to the king.* Yohsuke sighed.

*Wait! I smell it again—lilacs. It's closer now. Stronger,* James butted in.

*Tmont smells it too,* Bokaj added.

I closed my owl eyes and began to cast my senses into the world around me, into the plants and trees; the tree I was perched on felt odd. Like there were two life forces inside it.

I opened my eyes in time to see a large dryad step from the tree and gestured grandly. "Your prayers have been heard, beloved of the Mother."

The scent of lilacs grew stronger, and I knew that dryad was a fake instantly. The last dryads we had spoken with spoke only in Druidic.

I pecked the stem of the fruit as it spoke.

"Come with me, and I will take you to her bosom so that she may know you better." The thing motioned behind it, and a portal opened to the left of the tree from my position.

*Got bodies coming from the south and the east. Slowly.* Bokaj counted aloud to us, *Seven not including the dryad.*

Balmur echoed his count. *And there's no telling where this portal goes to or if more bodies aren't coming. Bo—pick a couple off.*

*Got it,* the Ranger answered grimly.

I finally finished pecking through the piece of fruit and brushed it aside as it fell so it would fall behind the creature below me. It looked behind it, then up and saw me.

"Ho-ho hoot." I ruffled my feathers and flitted off in time for Questis to stand up and step back.

The quiet of the orchard shattered as Jaken, Muu, and James stepped out as if from nowhere to the side of it, and it growled.

"You dare interfere with what Mother Nature has planned for her chosen?" It motioned toward Questis who seemed as fed up as I did.

*One is gone. Bokaj made him go poof. I uh... made another one gone too.* Balmur tried to hide his killing someone with that, but we knew. That was okay.

"Tell us who you work for, and we won't kill you," James offered politely.

The dryad's wooden features screwed up as if in anger and outrage. "I am a dryad! I speak for the Mother in her wisdom!"

The scent of lilacs grew stronger, and the portal began to flicker slightly.

"Go through now, beloved!" the dryad tried to order. I looked from my new spot into the tree line and saw several high elves with weapons that sparkled and glittered in the light. One of them went down, hard, as Balmur dropped from a tree and on to his back, his daggers slicing cleanly into the arteries there.

A wild look on his face, he stepped back into the shadows, but one of the elves had seen him.

In Sylvan, she barked, "Portal Dofilnarr, *now!*"

An arrow struck her in the chest, and she was gone in a flash of blurred light. I didn't know where the Ranger had hidden the trap anchors, but it was close.

Time to end this.

I flew up into the sky above the dryad, trying to avoid detection, but it didn't happen.

"Kill them and take him now!" the dryad screeched as he reached down and tried to snatch Questis up in his wooden arms.

"Option two has *always* been my favorite!" Muu growled and pulled out his hammer.

An arrow and a spell whizzed at me, and the owl hooted, *Duck!* I rolled off the branch beside me as I flew and shifted into my fox-man form as I fell. I gripped Magus Bane from my inventory and dropped on to the dryad, knocking it to the ground with a cracking thud against the bark-like flesh.

"Fake dryad mother fucker." I whipped my axe into its side, then snarled and slashed down at it with my right hand, raking it a little, but the effect was instant.

A shiver ran along it, and for a single second, I was staring at some kind of gelatinous, horrifying monster from a game that I had played at home recently.

It hissed, "Fool!" as it shoved me away in my startled stupor.

I fell and tried to roll from the fall into a stance, but an Elven kidnapper barreled into me, shanking me in the ribs. I grunted, and a pulse of something entered my body, immediately making me feel queasy.

The Elf moved on toward my friends, and I cast Purify on myself before I cast Snare on him. Purify took 200 MP—fuck *me*, what the hell had that been?

He stopped in his tracks, and a lightning arrow hit him the same time as my axe on my next swing. It clipped him as he spasmed wildly, so I used the momentum of my swing, shifted my legs around a little further, and activated Cleave. The bastard's head sloughed off and on to the ground with a meaty thunk.

A panicked image from Kayda showed me a scene that I dreaded. The king, who had since retired from some of the festivities, had been on his way back to the palace when his guard turned a corner and turned on him. They had been kidnappers as well.

*The king!* I howled at the others. *Balmur, collar—get ready! You guys take care of these assholes. Don't. Die!*

*Shut the fuck up and go already!* Yohsuke ordered. He was dancing between two of the kidnappers with his weapon drawn, parrying blows and slashing in return.

I darted closer to Balmur and guided his hand to the collar, pulling him in before taking off as an owl in a desperate flight to assist Telfino.

I saw lightning crackling from the sky and heard Kayda's screech of anger.

I crested the small huts and homes to see that the fight was going manageable. They hadn't managed to make off with the king, but they were trying. There were eight of them, and they all sported those sparkly weapons. I dove from the sky and whipped into a barrel roll, raking my claws across one of the kidnapper's eyes.

I shifted mid-roll and let Balmur out with a snarl of, "Kill the guards, and mind their weapons."

"Happy to oblige." He set off to his grisly task as I smashed a foot into one of their chests.

"You gonna start swinging that staff or what, Majesty?" I asked as the young king struggled to free himself from one of the guard's grasp.

"Just help me already!" he grunted. The attacker was clearly stronger than he was, so I stepped forward, casting Aspect of the Ursolon on myself.

I had gained a little mana on the flight over but still lost the two hundred for the spell. I took my axe and smacked the butt of it into the captor's face, breaking her nose and loosening her grip.

Telfino ducked out of her grasp and walloped her over the head once, then whipped his weapon behind her kneecap and yanked, popping the knee brutally out of place as she fell with a gasp of pain.

All of the sudden, Balmur was just there, his dagger finding a home in her temple. "Good job, Highness."

Telfino looked like he was about to hurl, but he sucked it up and turned.

I looked on and noted that some of the others had begun to try and surround the three of us. Two of them laid dead, Balmur having taken care of them brutally but efficiently.

I felt that same thrill through my body that I had the other night and stepped to the left in time to dodge a sword that would have likely severed my spine. I whipped Magus Bane around and slashed at the Elf, but they parried, directing the weapon over their head and ducked under it.

That fucker. I activated Feather Axe, and the weapon in my hand began to weave faster in our dance.

"Behind you!" A clap of thunder drowned out the king as Kayda zapped the kidnapper behind me, and I elbowed him in the throat savagely. I took a slice on the arm for it, my health falling by eight percent and then another percent as whatever poison or buff they used took effect.

Then I felt a relief as healing energy enervated me, and I began to growl low in my chest as the kidnappers realized what I knew—we had a healer here.

I reached out, touched the one behind me, and cast Lightning Bolt, then Winter's Blade in rapid succession, killing him, I hoped, and then I refocused on the person in front of me, currently trying to stab me.

Their sword danced in around the haft of my axe and slid along my metal right hand before I let go and tried to snatch it from their hand. Their hood was over their face, so I couldn't see who they were, but their swordsmanship was on point.

A dagger appeared in front of their face, the head having whipped back in the nick of time to avoid the projectile.

"Damn it," Balmur cursed. I cast Void Shield as he turned from an enemy to try and go to it. Two swords whipped into the shield, shattering it, but he was able to take control of his fight once more. My mana was even closer to bottoming out. If this kept going, I would have to begin drawing on the mana from Mage's Well.

A clawed foot snatched my attacker by the shoulder and lifted them, whoever it was, screaming into the air. Then I heard an earth-shattering explosion in the distance toward my friends.

*We need to end this shit, like, a minute ago,* I said to Balmur.

He grunted, *You all okay?*

*Bokaj and James are down. James is hurt bad, and Bokaj is dead. Jaken is trying to get to him, but the Dofilnarr is keeping him away from his body. It's so fucking strong. It has so much more mana than Zeke,* Muu shouted into our heads. The panic in his voice sent a burst of adrenaline through my veins.

*Kayda!* I roared through our connection. The shout startled her enough to drop her prey from high enough that I knew they would either die or be severely hurt. *Get the king, and take him to the others,* now!

She screeched and dove toward us. "Telfino, Kayda is taking you to the others. We got this. Help our friends!"

He nodded once as he jumped as high as he could, and Kayda caught him by his staff in both talons and took off.

"After him!" one of the not guards shouted. I found that one and just fucking *clubbed* him with the hammer end of Magus Bane. I dropped Aspect of the Ursolon, crushed his head for good measure, then turned to the remaining four of the living kidnappers.

Balmur, his breathing growing steadily more rapid and shallow, was a blur of motion. The others had been moving to follow the king and Kayda, but they had discounted us.

Tell 'em. Go ahead and say it. Listen to ol' Zeke and just say out loud, "They done fucked up." Said it? Hold on to your britches, y'all.

"*Rrrrraaaaaaaargh!*" Balmur screamed as he launched himself after them. I was in his way, so he used *my* shadow as his personal doorway into the first ones, slicing her Achilles' tendons as he reared out of the void. His arms never stopped their flurry of motion and she was dead long before she hit the ground.

I bounded after them and activated Wind Scythe before whipping Magus Bane at the last of them. It hit with a solid crunch to the spine that populated a paralyzed symbol below his HP bar. I ripped the weapon from his back, taking another third of his life and then stomped on the back of his neck as hard as my fifty-five strength would let me. A sickening crack echoed from it but barely reached me through the blood pounding in my ears.

One of my friends had died—*again*, and I hadn't been there to help.

Balmur's forgotten dagger was at my feet, so I picked it up with a growl, the silver on the weapon burning my skin, but I didn't care. I launched it toward the Dwarf, surprisingly close to him, and he grabbed it on instinct. With another shout of furry, he sprinted after the others. I cast Aspect of the Hare and took off in hot pursuit.

It took another minute for us to catch them, me firing lightning bolts at them when they were close but missing by inches. Then having to keep tabs on them as they ran headlong through celebrations, tossing food into the air or shoving people aside.

One had even managed to grab a hostage long enough to give me pause, but a spurt of blood covered the victim in crimson as Balmur appeared from their shadows to slit the guard's throat savagely.

Gone was all thought of trying to keep things under wraps. Finally, someone thought to trip the fleeing guard, and Balmur and I reached him at the same time, my great axe severing his neck as Balmur gored his kidneys.

I put my weapon away and then called the incensed Rogue into my collar with a tap before taking off toward the orchard with breakneck haste.

Kayda had begun using her newest ability again, the lightning in it crackling and raining down here and there, the cooling and healing effect lost on me. When I reached the clearing, the scene was insane.

All but one of the kidnappers was dead, Questis and the Dofilnarr—who had taken my form—were at war, slinging spells at each other as Telfino cast healing spells at him while trying to help the others. I landed just outside the clearing from my last jump and released Balmur.

*Here. Stay out of Balmur's way,* I growled at the others.

The Dwarf looked for his next target and decided on her—this Mage looked battered but still relatively healthy and was shielding herself as she motioned with her other hand and chanted something.

Jaken lay on the ground, severely injured, but his hands were on Bokaj, his lips moving in prayer. Tmont stood over her master protectively as she batted at the Dofilnarr when he got too close.

James laid in a broken pile, his health just barely above a percent, Kayda's healing rain was helping a bit. Yohsuke was wounded, around forty-seven percent, and was busy fighting something from a freshly made portal that was trying to come through.

*Bokaj is up. Out of mana—drinking potions,* Jaken mumbled tiredly.

*Use the sylph's potion, man, now!* I barked and saw him pull the vial from his inventory.

I took out three of the medium mana potions and downed them in rapid succession. My mana popped back up by one hundred fifty, putting me at full.

I used my Charge Spell ability and held Mass Regrowth, a spell that normally cost 150 MP to cast normally. I held the spell for three pulses or fifteen seconds of my friends doing what they could. Then I unleashed the spell at the full 1,200 MP cost. I was down to 150 MP in the ring on my finger. I took one last medium mana potion to the gullet and cast Aspect of the Sabertooth.

**Aspect of the Sabertooth - +8 strength, +20 dexterity. Increased rate of attack. This great cat may be a little long in the tooth, but those who think that may find themselves gored swiftly.**

My canines lengthened greatly, my fur grew a little shaggier, but I felt my muscles grow denser and lither at the same time.

My friends' HP bars were beginning to rise, and as they did, so too did our fighting spirit.

"Room for one more, Questis?" I asked as I ducked under the creature's large, bear-like claw. It had taken Ursolon form. It looked exactly as I did, and that pissed me off.

"Ah, nice of you to join us again," the Elf grunted as he took a blow to his shoulder. Telfino healed him, and his HP jumped back up to eighty percent.

*Soon,* Kayda warned me, and I knew that she meant her

mana was recovering, and she would be able to join us in earnest.

An arrow sprouted from the Dofilnarr's shoulder, and it roared in anger. A crash of lightning sounded to our left, and I noticed that Balmur and Muu had finally worked their way past the Mage's shield.

*Bokaj, you good to go help Yoh at the portal?* I asked.

I watched as the Ranger limped by with Tmont as support. She hissed at everything.

*James good yet?* Yohsuke called.

*Mending his spine is going to take a minute,* Jaken muttered as if he were trying to concentrate.

"Telfino." I ducked away from a paw that swung at my face. Talking with fangs like this would take getting used to. "Go help Jaken, please."

I couldn't look to see if he had heard me, but I heard a shuffle of feet and muttering before a radiant green light began to flow into my vision from the right.

I didn't dare look right now. Rather, I buckled down and began to work into a good flow of axe forms—chop, swing, block, parry, step back. I heard the hiss of arrows being launched and then shouted cursing.

*"Anyone know how to dispel magic?"* Yoh hollered, the strain evident in his voice.

76 MP returned to me, helping ease the headache I was trying desperately to ignore.

Questis shoved me aside as the Dofilnarr Ursolon's head snapped forward. "Give me a moment, will you?" he asked softly.

I nodded once and batted the asshole's paw back to the side. Suddenly, golden energy flooded my vision, and there was a mostly healed James, his fists covered in ki so thick it looked like he held the sun in his hands.

We began to beat on the beast in front of us, its health falling steadily from seventy percent to sixty-eight percent. Its health pool was ridiculous, and there was little room to doubt why it had nearly killed two of us.

I heard a chant from the back of us, and once more, I felt my muscles begin to strain less. But more importantly, we all had buffs.

We were buff as *fuck* at that moment.

***Mother Nature's Love – Friendly creatures in the area of this prayer's effect receive a boost to mana and health regeneration of +3%. Duration: 30 minutes.***

***Mother Nature's Wrath – Friendly creatures receive bonus strength, dexterity, and constitution. Duration: 10 minutes.***

My mana began to go up by 93 MP now, putting me up to 169 MP. Good start. I dipped into my inventory and grabbed one minor mana potion and my last medium mana potion. I downed the two, and it threw me up to 294 MP.

Just enough to cast Beastial Fury. My muscles thickened, and the world around me seemed to grow a little quieter. Then I realized it was because I was roaring. My anger was fully realized.

I was rage incarnate, and the focal point in front of me just turned into a fox-man.

It opened its mouth to say something, but I was on top of it before it could finish. My great axe swung relentlessly fast, the angles of the slashes and slices becoming increasingly hard for the creature to figure out.

A dark figure, furred with claws flashing in mirrored rage and muscle, crashed into the creature before me and raked it with its claws. The tail was sporting a weapon striking like a scorpion wherever it would reach.

This was a friend. I brought my axe into an overhead chop, activating Cleave by second nature and carved through the attacker of my friend's arm. The limb fell off, thumping on to the ground and beginning to dissolve. The creature screamed loudly, and the furry friend continued her assault.

It was around sixty-one percent HP now and falling. Arrows

sprouted from it before a golden flash of light appeared around it. It had no effect, and the creature howled in anger.

Its body grew and thickened, the limb regrowing slowly, taking some of the health in its HP bar with it. Fifty-seven percent health left.

I heard a burst and scream from my left, followed by a cry of victory but couldn't afford to take my attention off the Dofilnarr. The beast had swatted the great cat away and began to move on me.

*Good, come closer so I can cut you easier,* I rumbled in my mind.

A being who glowed with a radiant gold and red aura stepped before me and struck the creature with his shield. A maw of metal and teeth appeared from it, grabbed the advancing creature, and it seemed to take hold. He swung it toward me, the back exposed, and I roared triumphantly.

Raining down chops and slashes with Magus Bane, my weapon began to refill my pool with mana that it stole from the Dofilnarr.

After a few hacks, I had the mana to use one more ability— Bladed Storm.

My weapon whipped back and forth in the air around me steadily, leaves and grass rustling with its passage.

"The portal is closing!" I heard an excited voice over the fury of my assault. I raked it with my clawed right hand. It lost its form once more.

The creature was at thirty percent health and dwindling.

A shield of ebon burst into life before me, and I kept hammering away at it. The creature then tore off his other arm, the one lodged in the metal being's mouth and push kicked both the bearer and the shield aside. It closed its eyes and disappeared for an instant.

I looked wildly around the clearing. One of the figures that had been fighting, a green one—friend—laid on the ground, unconscious but alive. The two who had been fighting at the portal mouth had been shoved aside, and the Dofilnarr began to flee through.

A *CRASH* of lightning cut through a Fireball rushing out of the portal, and I heard an anguished cry from the other side as the portal closed.

With the threat gone, my adrenaline began to flood from my system, and my mind began to take in more than the situation directly in front of me. My mana was recovering but not enough to be of much use.

I looked around. Yohsuke and James were bloodied, around thirty percent health despite the buffs. Muu snored on the ground, his HP bar around half but a sleep icon above his name. Across from him was the female Mage that had been fighting us.

Tmont limped over to stand beside her master who laid up resting beside a tree. He was pulling his guitar from his inventory.

Balmur… Balmur was nowhere to be found.

"Where's Balmur?" I asked, my mind a little muddied still.

"He went off chasing after an Elf that made it through the portal from the other side and then made it past Bokaj, James, and Yoh," Jaken answered as he fell on to his ass tiredly.

King Telfino sidled over to sit beside the Paladin. "That was hard. You all fight like demons."

"Thanks, Majesty." Balmur's gruff voice startled me as he appeared next to me, seemingly having forgotten his rage. "I was tortured by them daily."

Telfino looked uncomfortable for a moment, so I spoke first. "You find them?"

The Dwarven Rogue grinned savagely. "Yep. They didn't make it far."

Good. Fuck those guys.

"Bokaj, let's get ready to go get the ones we have held in the traps into the dungeon. Where'd you hide the trap anchors?"

He just shook his head, "Can't. The Mage there was able to dispel them in a motion, but it didn't matter. While we were distracted with that thing acting like it was you on steroids, she slaughtered them all and made another portal using their life essence somehow."

So we were up shit creek with no info and sure as fuck no paddle. Damn it.

"Salvage what you can," Yohsuke grunted as he sat up. His health was recovering more steadily. "Loot the corpses, and if we can, we'll revive one, but while I was fighting those assholes, I got shoved through the portal. It was the Fae, alright, and it led directly into some kind of fort or forward operating base. There were people everywhere."

He looked bleakly at Telfino. "I'm sorry, Highness—your people, the ones who were taken—are dead.

A large great cat, the size of Fern, sauntered over, and Questis shifted from it in a flash of green light. "There are no more in the area, your Majesty."

I prodded him with my Fae Iron finger, and he remained the same.

"We probably don't have to do that anymore, man," Bokaj grumbled.

"Everyone here gets poked. Protocol." Yohsuke shook his head. "Can't get complacent. Complacency kills."

That was true.

*QUEST ALERT!*

*Quests complete!*

*A Champion's Duty – Queen Maebe, leader of the Unseelie Fae, has informed you of a potential plot to throw her world and her people into great peril. Assist her by rooting out the spies living amongst the high elves.*

*Reward: Deepened standing with Unseelie Fae, further tutelage in the art of wielding Shadows, and further favor of Maebe upon acceptance.*

*High Elf Highway Robbery – Someone has been stealing from the new king of the high elves, and that is just unacceptable. Find who or what is responsible, and either tell King Telfino or bring him evidence that they have been stopped.*

*Reward: Better relations with King Telfino and his people, ten thousand gold pieces, and a possible favor in the future.*

"It is not the best result, but it is a result. You have upheld your quest and will be rewarded as such. Thank you for your assistance and for risking your lives for my people."

As I bled each of my friends and the king, I thought on it. Was this okay? We didn't need the money, not really. We'd had to slaughter those people—imposters—but still. Their families would be missing them.

I put my thoughts to the group, and they agreed, though Muu was still sleeping off the spell.

"Majesty." Bokaj stood cautiously and limped over to us. I cast Regrowth on him and T' just to be safe. "Thanks, man. Majesty, you saved us. The least we can do is have you take the gold and give it to the families of those affected. It's nothing compared to their loss, but we can hope that it helps them in their time of need."

"That is kind of you, generous even," Telfino started. He was sad; you could tell. "But it is my responsibility to see to it that those people are cared for, and they will be."

"We know," I offered, "but we want them to know that they have friends in us. And so do you. We won't swear fealty—but how about an alliance against those who seek to do you harm?"

"I need not even discuss this—my answer is yes." The king stood and clasped my wrist. "The high elves under my rule recognize the Unseelie Fae and Queen Maebe, The Frozen Shadow, as friends and allies. Long may our friendship bring our two peoples prosperity."

*Secret Quest Complete!*

*Diplomacy High and Low – King Telfino has recognized that without Maebe's aid through you, his people would be in even more grave danger and has agreed to an alliance.*

*Good work, champion!*
*Reward: Unknown*

Well, that was cool as fuck, but that left us with one question.

"So what's next?" Balmur blinked at us expectantly.

"Well, we need to get you some better armor and gear. Then we can follow our next lead." Yohsuke offered us a small bag of dried meat to pass around.

"And what's that?" Jaken asked before tearing a piece off.

"Going after the Drow," James stated. We looked his way oddly. "Farnik told us that they seemed possessed by something. Stronger. More brash. That could mean a lot of things, but to me, it seems like someone was pulling their strings and getting them to create some mayhem that would likely distract Fainne."

Seemed as good a place as any to start. And Gods knew we could use a break from this stuff. Balmur especially. I could try to find a decent familiar to partner with Kayda. And we could get closer to seeing this world safe.

Didn't mean there weren't still assholes out there that wouldn't stand in our way, but we were better off now. At least I hoped.

I surveyed my friends—beaten, bruised and covered in gore, some of it theirs, more that wasn't. And I couldn't help but smile wide.

It was good to have the team back together.

# AUTHOR'S NOTE

Hey guys and girls, your man Zeke here!

Just wanted to thank you for coming along on yet another wild ride in Brindolla with me and all my friends. Whoever is putting this thing into words has a lot more to say from me and the guys, and if he doesn't, he gets an ear full, but I want to tell you personally—we ain't done y'all. So come on back for some more fun, fighting, and general mayhem with your friends, y'hear?

# ABOUT CHRISTOPHER JOHNS

Christopher Johns is a former photojournalist for the United States Marine Corps with published works telling hundreds of other peoples' stories through word, photo, and even video.

But throughout that time, his editors and superiors had always said that his love of reading fantasy and about worlds of fantastic beauty and horrible power bled into his work. That meant he should write a book.

Well, ta-da!

Chris has been an avid devourer of fantasy and science fiction for more than twenty years and looks forward to sharing that love with his son, his loving fiancée and almost anyone he could ever hope to meet.

Connect with Chris:
Twitter.com/jonsyjohns
Facebook.com/AxeDruidAuthor
Patreon.com/StormCompanyandBeyond

# ABOUT MOUNTAINDALE PRESS

Dakota and Danielle Krout, a husband and wife team, strive to create as well as publish excellent fantasy and science fiction novels. Self-publishing *The Divine Dungeon: Dungeon Born* in 2016 transformed their careers from Dakota's military and programming background and Danielle's Ph.D. in pharmacology to President and CEO, respectively, of a small press. Their goal is to share their success with other authors and provide captivating fiction to readers with the purpose of solidifying Mountaindale Press as the place 'Where Fantasy Transforms Reality.'

Connect with Mountaindale Press:
MountaindalePress.com
Facebook.com/MountaindalePress
Twitter.com/_Mountaindale
Instagram.com/MountaindalePress

# MOUNTAINDALE PRESS TITLES
## GameLit and LitRPG

The Completionist Chronicles,
The Divine Dungeon, and
Full Murderhobo by Dakota Krout

King's League by Jason Anspach and J.N. Chaney

A Touch of Power by Jay Boyce

Red Mage by Xander Boyce

Space Seasons by Dawn Chapman

Ether Collapse and
Ether Flows by Ryan DeBruyn

Bloodgames by Christian J. Gilliland

Wolfman Warlock by James Hunter and Dakota Krout

Axe Druid and
Mephisto's Magic Online by Christopher Johns

Skeleton in Space by Andries Louws

Chronicles of Ethan by John L. Monk

Pixel Dust by David Petrie

Henchman by Carl Stubblefield

Artorian's Archives by Dennis Vanderkerken and Dakota Krout

# APPENDIX

## THE GOOD

Zekiel Erebos (Zee-key-uhl Air-uh-bows) – Marine who loves gaming as a civilian with his buddies who are still in. Class: Druid. Race: Kitsune, has a tail.

Yohsuke (Yo-s'kay) – Zeke's best bud/brother from the Marine Corps. Overlord, yeah you read that right. Class: Spell Blade. Race: Abomination (halfbreed Drow and High Elf)

Jaken Warmecht (Jay-ken) – Zeke's friend who typically needs help catching up in the games the group places together. Class: Paladin of Radiance. Race: Fae-Orc.

Bokaj (Bow-ka-jh) – A friend from the gym who loves video games and is in a pretty wicked band! Class: Ranger. Race: Ice Elf.

Tmont (Tee-M-on-t) – A panther with a taste for tails who happens to not just be a walking bag of assholes but is also Bokaj's pet. Mainly that first one, though.

Balmur (Ball-mer) – Bokaj's best friend and another good buddy of Zeke's who loves to game! Class: Rogue. Race: Azer Dwarf (Fire Dwarf) HIS BEARD IS A FLAME!

James Bautista (Really?) – Another Marine that Yohsuke and Zeke know and game with often. Class: Monk. Race: Dragon Elf.

Muu Ankiman (Moo Ahn-key-men) – Dragon Beast-kin with green scales and Zeke's roommate on Earth. Liiiiittle crazy, but he's okay. Class: Fighter. Race: Dragon-kin (it's shorter!)

Kayda (Kay-duh) – A pretty bird with a shitty past and hopefully a bright future. Recently turned into a Storm Roc. Very protective of a certain flame wolf.

Coal – A flame wolf that Zeke is taking care of for a bit on behalf of the Primordial Flame Elemental. He's got a good temperament—a little heated at times, but he's a cool pup.

## LOCALS

Sir Willem Dillon – Owner of the tavern in Sunrise Village (the starter town) and Paladin of Radiance. The first guy the group meets and doesn't try to kill. (Or do they? MUAHAHAHA— No really, do they?) Jaken's trainer.

Dinnia (Dih-nee-uh) – An Elven Druid who takes pity on poor Zeke and brings him into Mother Nature's good graces. Zeke's trainer.

Sharo (shah-row) – Another panther who assists his partner in crime, Dinnia, in training her student. Not a walking bag of assholes.

Kyra – Queen of the bears and good friend of Dinnia's. We like her.

Marin (mare-in) – We, uh… we don't talk about her. 10 out of 10 though. Kick ass dire bear.

Rowland – Blacksmith in Sunrise who decides he likes the travelers, especially the one with the tail—no bias.

Maebe (may-buh—soft buh—if she hears you talking shit, I'm not responsible, yeah?) – Unseelie Queen of Winter and Darkness who somehow gets thrown into the mix. Also Zeke's girlfriend. I know, right?

Thogan (ThO-gun) – Champion of the Unseelie Fae and a rather clingy Dwarf with a rough complexion.

Titania – Former Queen of the Seelie Fae, who has a predisposition of being a raging bitch to anyone and everyone she doesn't like. Like outsiders.

Craglim (Crag-limb) – Rowland's cousin. Racist piece of shit—but he's a good fighter.

Zhavron (Zah-vrun) – Orc Fighter with a sordid past. Muu's trainer in all things fighting. A little intense at times.

Pharazulla (Far-uh-zu-la) – A Bard of some renown, though a bit of a stuck-up asshole.

Vrawn – A lovely Orcish woman with a soft spot for our local Druid. She's built like a busty, brick shit house.

Sam – Mayor of Sunrise village. A fair man whose Bear-kin wife and Half-Bear-kin children believe in him wholeheartedly. Prefers to hunt for the village rather than govern.

The villagers of Sunrise – Great people who recently went through a lot of bullshit. Go easy on 'em, yeah?

Set – A decent little Fae-Orc kid, duped into hunting a belgar.

Ampharia (Am-far-ee-uh) – An elder green Dragon friend of Mother Nature's who comes to give Muu her blessing and teach him how to fight Dragons.

Natholdi and Granite(Nath-ol-dee) – A good, humble Dwarven family that both Muu and Zeke love dearly. Newest additions to the Light Hand Clan.

Fainnir (Fae-near) – Son of Natholdi and Granite and the very first Dwarven Mage! His specialty is earth magic, and his assistant Pebble thinks highly of him.

Farnik Mugfist (Far-nick) – Leader of the Mugfist clan and good friend to the party. Loves a good cup of mead and song.

Shellica Light Hand (Shell-ih-cuh) – Leader of the Light Hand clan and a grandmaster Enchanter. Crazy as shit with a diabolical wit. Zeke's trainer, unfortunately.

Silvannas (Sill-vahn-us) – Queen of the High elves on the Prime plane of existence. Sort of a role model to Maebe.

Questis (Quest-ihs) – A High Elf Druid enchanter who has a soft spot for kitties and bait. Pretty awesome guy. Seriously loves cats though.

Fern (Like the plant) – A saber-tooth cat that has a *serious* god complex. Loves to be fed and worshipped. Gives his Druid Questis hell all the time.

Telfino (Tell-fee-no) – Son of Queen Silvannas and inheritor of the throne. He's a good kid with a seriously strong class.

# THE BAD

War – Galactic conquerer who probably suffers from only child syndrome. Probably needs a hug, or he will keep trying to take over the universe.

Minions of War – Not the lovable minions everyone loves. You know, not the yellow ones, or that fish from that one Will Ferrell animated move. These guys seek to undermine the strength of the gods by eroding the world around them slowly, and they serve the other assholes in this list.

The Generals – A number of War's better warriors capable of taking out the strongest people upon the planet—and together they did. Dick move.

Rowan – I'm not gonna say much about this guy—read the book then you'll know what a dickbag he is. Haha, was—sonofabitch is dead now.

Pastella (Pahs-tell-uh) – Crazy Elven woman with a taste for torture and violence.

Tarron Dillingsley (Tair-run Dill-night-slee) – Gnomish enchanter who—let's face it, shall we?—sucks as a teacher for various reasons and, lest we forget, the asshole in charge of the Children of Brindolla.

Children of Brindolla – A group of misguided citizens who believe they are the only ones who can truly save their world. They found themselves on the receiving end of an ass kicking—but was that all of them?

Decay – A Greater Fiend who held his own against the party and Maebe. Fell due to a brilliant plan and a little bit of finesse.

Okay, the plan was half-cocked, and the finesse resulted in some bullshit—happy now?

Spiders – Just a bunch of overgrown pests that needed an ass kicking. Nightmare fuel FOREVER.

Lothir (Low-theer) – Big ol' wanna-be snake goddess who has a village of elves, Orcs, and Fae-Orcs under her command and demands sacrifices to restore and keep her beauty. All of that means that she's coo coo for Cocoa Puffs.

Melvaren (Mel-vah-ren) – General who took claim over Balmur and tortured him in the Hells for his entire tenure there. We killed the shit out of him. But not before he whipped our asses. Still dead though.

Archemillian (Ark-em-illion) – The demon who Yohsuke summoned and gets his warlock powers from. Has a huge hard on for souls, but he helped us this once. Didn't mean he was a fucking good guy, though.

Riktolth (Rick-talth) – The great black Dragon who killed a mother red in a bid to die in combat. Yeah, you guessed it. We kicked his ass.

## AND THE UGLY

Insane Wolves – Think crazy wolves, but you know, crazier and angrier for some reason. Due to proximity to a minion of War, the minds of these animals have eroded to nothing but the drive to kill and eat anything that is not them or another wolf.

Undead creatures – As you can imagine, due to proximity to a minion of War, these poor bastards rose from the dead in order to protect their alien masters. Even the stronger versions are worthy of a small bit of sympathy—they sure as hell didn't get any, but they are worthy of it.

Bone Dragon – I mean, pretty self-explanatory, right? It's a Bone Dragon! No skin, no muscle—all bleached bones and hate for the living.

General of War (Blight) – The asshole who did some truly terrible things, sent us on a supposedly one-way trip to the Fae realm, and got his ASS kicked. Yeah. That guy.

Ursolon – Think of a giant, striped bear with an anger management issue the size of North Dakota. Yeah. Now go fight one.

Werewolves – The heroes in some tales—but not this one. Oh no. These guys suck, big time! Hairy, needy pieces of crap.

Alpha Werewolf – The jerk in charge of the other jerks above. Bigger, badder, stronger, and usually *way* more cunning and ruthless.

The Wild Hunt – A flock of assholes (read Demons) who patrol the realm of the Fae and take out anything they believe doesn't belong there.

Order of the Prime – A bunch of human wizards bent on controlling the elements and restoring mankind to their rightful place as rulers. Some real xenophobic asshats, these ones.

Spiders – Oh, I mentioned these already? Because there were a lot of them. With fangs. And all the feet. Seriously, I need to book an appointment for therapy now.

Belgar – A rhino-like Fae creature with a surprising sense of honor and code that it lives by. Big as shit and it will run anyone in its way through.

Dofilnarr (Dough-fill-nar) – A Fae creature thought to have been hunted to extinction that takes the forms and abilities of creatures it touches while in its base state. Highly vulnerable to Fae Iron.

And other random jerks too unimportant for now to mention—they know who they are. Bunch of assholes.

www.ingramcontent.com/pod-product-compliance
Lightning Source LLC
Chambersburg PA
CBHW020628020726
47494CB00001B/94